Pra

THE EVIL INCLINATION

"*The Evil Inclination* tells the story of Lev Livitski, an Orthodox Jewish boy from Brooklyn's Flatbush neighborhood, who embarks on a secret, passionate and lust-filled affair with Angela Pizatto, a sharp-tongued Italian beauty from Bensonhurst. The novel is gripping from the start and grows more compelling as Lev and Angela struggle to understand the profoundly different universes they originate from. Don't be fooled by first impressions—Angela is not what she seems, and as Lev learns who she truly is, he discovers with some shock who he is, as well. *The Evil Inclination* tells an exhilarating, spellbinding tale, and if you are at all like me, the unanticipated but well-crafted ending will surprise, astonish and move you deeply. This might well be the most compelling novel I have read in the past decade, and with *The Evil Inclination*, an extraordinary talent has entered the world of fiction."

> —**Joseph Telushkin**, best selling author of seventeen books, including *Words that Hurt, Words that Heal* and *Jewish Literacy*

"Daniel Victor's novel *The Evil Inclination* is a captivating love story pitting passion against faith. Set in Brooklyn in the early years of the twenty-first century, the novel tells the story of Lev Livitski, who, testing the limits of his Orthodox Jewish upbringing, meets Angela Pizatto, a capricious Catholic beauty. Their affair threatens to derail their lives even as it challenges their assumptions—and ours. Daniel Victor's novel is an irresistible read, as well as, along the way, a tender tribute to the vanishing ethnic enclaves of Brooklyn."

> —**Judith Shulevitz**, journalist and culture critic; author of the bestselling book, *The Sabbath World*; columnist for *Slate, The New York Times Book Review, The New Republic* and *The Atlantic*

"*The Evil Inclination* is a wondrous and welcome literary debut by a writer of uncommon gifts. Daniel Victor treats us to everything from sacred texts to sordid sex. Remarkably, it all beautifully blends together into a riveting—and surprising—book about family, faith, lust, heresy, temptation, wisdom and God. I loved this book! Like all good ones, it took me to places I've never been."

> —**Ari Goldman**, Professor of Journalism at the Columbia School of Journalism; best-selling author of *The Search for God at Harvard*; regulator contributor to *The New York Times, The Washington Post, Salon, The New York Jewish Week,* and *The Forward*

THE EVIL INCLINATION

A NOVEL

DANIEL VICTOR

atmosphere press

Published by Atmosphere Press

Cover design by Kevin Stone

First Edition

Library of Congress Cataloging-in-Publication Data has been applied for.

ISBN
ISBN (E-book)

Atmospherepress.com

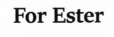

For Ester

I

Rebbe Yehudah expounded: In the future time, the Holy One, Blessed Be He, will take the Evil Inclination and slaughter it in the presence of the righteous and in the presence of the wicked.

To the righteous, the Evil Inclination will appear as a high mountain, and to the wicked it will appear as a strand of hair. The righteous will weep and the wicked will weep.

The righteous will weep and say: 'How were we capable of overcoming such a high mountain?'

And the wicked will weep and say: 'How were we incapable of overcoming this strand of hair?'

And so too the Holy One, Blessed Be He, will wonder with them . . .

- Babylonian Talmud, Tractate Succah 52A -

1.

Lev Livitski held his breath as Rabbi Berkowitz leaned forward, one hand clutching the edge of the prayer lectern, the other hand stroking his reddish-brown beard. The foot of the lectern was right at the edge of the dais—if it skidded just another inch or two, the rabbi would topple onto the students sitting in the first row of the assembly hall, a catastrophe that Lev had longed for since his first day of third grade. Lev narrowed his eyebrows and squinted his eyes as he focused his mind on Rabbi Berkowitz, muttering an incantation: "Come to me, Rabbi—you're almost there. Come to me."

But the Rabbi did not come to him. Instead, he continued lecturing Lev and his classmates about the Evil Inclination and about the Good Inclination—how these forces struggled one against the other for dominion over them every minute of their lives. Berkowitz was animated: the subject apparently excited him, the opportunity to make a difference in molding the character of his third-graders, setting them on the path to righteousness and steering them away from sin even before they really had a clear idea of what sin was. Because of the unusual intensity of the presentation, Lev Livitski stopped imagining Rabbi Berkowitz tumbling onto the first row and began listening to him; notwithstanding that Lev and his pals had already learned never to believe anything the Rabbi told them; notwithstanding that they routinely referred to Rabbi Berkowitz among themselves as Rabbi *Beserkowitz*. The Rabbi paused for a moment and dramatically raised his fist in the air in front of his face, and for an instant Lev was distracted by that fist, the way it looked clenching the air, like the fist of God containing lightning or the wind, assuming that God in fact possessed a fist, which, theologically, of course, He didn't.

Even at eight years old, Lev thought he had a pretty clear notion of what Evil was. Evil was doing what was prohibited. And he thought that he understood what Good was—doing what was permitted, and also, of course, what was expected. When Lev did something that was forbidden, it was usually because he was inattentive or distracted, like carelessly flicking a light switch on the Sabbath. When he did something that was good, it was usually because someone—a rabbi, a parent—was urging him to do it.

But what Lev didn't know, and what Rabbi Berkowitz never bothered to explain to him or to anyone else, was what an *inclination* was. What did it mean to have an inclination to do the forbidden—an urge, a compulsion, an irresistible craving?

One night Lev was sitting at the dining room table in his parents' apartment in Flatbush doing Bible homework when he saw his mother motion to his father to join her at the kitchen sink. Lev knew that she wanted to whisper a secret. Her gesture made it obvious—a sharp, short, beckoning movement with her hand, her thumb touching the tips of her fingers.

Lev's younger brother, Elya Meir, seven years old, was playing with toy trucks in the corner of the dining room. Shmuel, the youngest brother, who was three years old and called Shmu, was lying under the table, licking crumbs off the carpet, a habit for which he was already infamous.

Lev's parents stood side by side at the kitchen sink. His mother whispered to his father: "Shloime Strudler—he's off the *derech*. Golda told me."

Lev's father didn't say anything, but he raised his hand to his black velvet skullcap and moved it around on the top of his head as if he were using it to wipe something wet and sticky off his cranium. He peered up at the sputtering florescent light like he was searching for God Himself.

"It was only a matter of time," Lev's mother continued. "The cigarette. You remember the cigarette, don't you?"

Lev's father nodded. His parents' eyes met and they both turned and gave Lev a grave, anxious look. Lev continued to pretend that he was studying.

Lev knew what it meant to be "off the derech." *Derech* in Hebrew meant *path*, and to be off it was to begin to drift away from Jewish observance—the 248 affirmative religious obligations and the 365 prohibitions that comprised the basic core of *halacha*, Jewish law. So he understood in some rudimentary way that when you were off the derech, you were no longer observing halacha.

And Lev also knew about Shloime Strudler and the cigarette. It had happened the previous year on the holiday of *Simchas Torah*, which marks the end of the annual cycle of weekly Torah readings and the beginning of the next cycle. On Jewish holidays like Simchas Torah, Jewish law permits a Jew to light a gas burner, a candle, or even a cigarette from a flame that has been lit before the onset of the festival. But one can't actively extinguish that flame during the holiday. So when a cigarette has burned down, although a Jew can let it go out on its own, he or she is prohibited from stubbing it out.

It was reported that Shloime Strudler was smoking a cigarette and when it had burned down to the filter, instead of letting it go out by itself, he threw it on the ground, put his shoe on it, and moved his foot back and forth to grind it out.

Some people said Shloime was drunk because it's customary to drink a lot of schnapps on Simchas Torah. But those who were there said he hadn't been drinking.

Some speculated that maybe Shloime had forgotten and just did it by accident, without thinking. But those who were there said he had a determined look on his face. Some said he had a defiant look on his face. No one said it was an accident.

When Lev heard about it, he thought: That's wrong. To stomp on a lit cigarette on Simchas Torah instead of letting it go out on its own accord—that's just plain wrong. How could anyone who knew better do such a thing on purpose, something that was so wrong?

And now he had learned that Shloime Strudler was off the derech.

What Lev didn't understand was how Shloime had actually gotten off it. Did he go to sleep one night while on it and in the morning wake up off it? Was he surrounded by rabbis wearing black coats and carrying sticks who forced him off? Or did he fall off?

The falling image was the most plausible. Lev visualized the derech as a narrow bridge without railings, one that spanned a chasm. The bridge was so high that its terminus was obscured by swirling clouds; and the chasm was so deep that its floor could not be perceived. A solitary figure steadfastly made his way against a headwind that suddenly increased in velocity, turning into a howling tempest with torrents of rain and fiery barrages of lightning. Finally, after much struggle, the exhausted traveler toppled off the bridge and into the chasm.

That's the way Lev imagined it. But it was not the way it happened to him.

2.

Twelve years after Shloime Strudler fell off the derech, Lev was a sophomore at Brooklyn College. The year was 2002. Like most of his friends from the Orthodox Jewish world, even though Lev was in college, he was still living with his parents, sharing a bedroom with his younger brothers, who numbered four by then. Their Flatbush neighborhood had grown increasingly religious and was now characterized as *Black Hat*, which alluded to the broad-brimmed fedoras that their neighbors adopted to demarcate the seriousness of their Orthodoxy. Lev's family did not wear black hats; moreover, Lev and his brothers didn't parade around in the other fashion accoutrements that defined the more extreme religious fervor of their neighbors: large velvet skullcaps, black suits, white shirts and ritual fringes dangling to their knees. The Livitski boys wore jeans and sneakers and denim jackets, and their skullcaps were compact and colorful, crocheted by their mother. The family described themselves as Modern Orthodox because Lev's parents valued such profane things as a secular university education. But the truth was that his family wasn't really that modern and they were plenty Orthodox.

One Shabbos morning, Lev got out of his upper bunk bed while his brothers still slept. Rather than get dressed right away and head to synagogue to join his father, who always went earlier to hear a daily Talmud class, Lev went into the living room in his pajamas and sat on the sofa. He sat staring off into space, contemplating nothing.

In the Livitski apartment, no one ever sat in the living room. It was used maybe two or three hours a year, usually for gatherings like fundraising events for local Jewish charities or for an annual family Chanukah party. The living room was not intended to be used by Lev and his immediate family. Perhaps that was why his parents had selected such an uncomfortable sofa, Lev conjectured as he squirmed against the sticky plastic slipcovers—as thick as they were, he could

7

still feel the buttons from the back of the tufted sofa digging into his spine.

From his perch, Lev faced an olive-wood bas relief of the Wailing Wall in Jerusalem that hung on the wall beside a bookcase containing his father's nineteen-volume set of the Vilna Talmud. The Wailing Wall was depicted as a parquet of different shades of olive-wood. In front of the Wall were silhouettes of stooped Hasidic Jews holding holy books. Lev's father once showed Lev a yellowing label pasted on the back of the frame that read: "Palestine 1936." His father had nodded knowingly and Lev had understood that this artifact was from *before*—before the singularity that defined Lev's world: the Holocaust followed only a few years later by the establishment of the State of Israel.

Lev became aware of how quiet it was in the living room, at least as compared to the rest of the apartment. It was a pleasant sensation, this silence. He recalled that he had once overheard his father's wistful remark to a friend in synagogue: "The only time I'm ever alone," his father had confided, "is when I'm on the subway." Lev had long been perplexed by this statement until he began taking the subway each day to yeshiva high school and then to Brooklyn College. Standing in the crowded subway car, Lev thought he finally understood what his father had meant. There was so much tumult in Lev's life that it was soothing to just *be*: to stand anonymous in a tightly packed train with no one talking to him or expecting anything from him. And how much more so to just sit in the silence of the living room away from his four younger brothers and his parents.

His mother came out of the kitchen, wiping her hands on a dish towel. "What are you doing in the living room?" she called to Lev from the hallway.

"Nothing much," he replied.

"Well, if you're doing nothing much, get your *tuches* into gear and go to synagogue."

But Lev wasn't quite ready to surrender this sweet feeling of tranquility. He suspected it would be good for him if he had a little more time to reflect on . . . on . . . well, not so much time to reflect on anything in particular, but just time not to be bouncing off and reacting to one of his brothers or someone in synagogue. It wasn't as if there was something that had been bothering him for some time, something that he needed to work out. It was more that he hadn't really had much of a chance to even determine if something was bothering him at all. He recalled an axiom from a course he had taken freshman year, Political Philosophy 101: "An unexamined life is not worth living." Socrates had said that. Lev felt guilty thinking of something Socrates had said. Most of the rabbis of antiquity whom Lev had been taught to revere considered Socrates a pagan light-weight—at least that was what Lev had learned in the yeshivas in which he had studied. Lev turned to his mother standing in the hallway. "You know," he said, "I just don't feel like going to *shul* today. I think I'll sit this one out."

"What?" his mother shouted. "You don't feel like going? You don't *feel* like going? Since when has being Jewish anything to do with how you feel? Since when? Now get up and go meet your father!"

The conversation was over. Lev got to his feet, plodded to his room and began getting dressed while his brothers began to stir.

But his mother had asked a question that triggered a torrent of other questions, none of which had satisfactory answers. Since when did being Jewish—or more accurately, Lev's Jewish observance—have anything to do with what he was feeling? His mother was right. Judaism was not interested in how he felt about it. And because it was not interested in *him*, Lev had never asked himself what he felt about *it*, at least not until that moment when he sat slack-mouthed on the world's most uncomfortable sofa in the world's most unused living room.

And the sad truth was that he didn't feel anything about it at all. For his entire life, Lev had walked in its ways, but he'd never asked himself whether that was, in fact, what he wanted to do. It hadn't occurred to him that he might even form an opinion about observing halacha. He'd behaved like an automaton, performing the repetitive tasks expected of him without question until that moment when he just didn't feel like it.

Lev disliked the lingering sensation—a muffled indifference to the myriad of activities required each day, each hour, by Jewish practice. It might be enough for other Jews to merely tolerate the bustle of being Jewish, but that couldn't ever work for someone like Lev: the product of two decades of intensive Jewish education—*cheder*, day school, yeshiva high school, a post-high-school year in an Israeli yeshiva—the whole works. He was fluent in Hebrew and Aramaic, well-versed in Torah and Talmud and had excelled in the kind of intensive, comprehensive education in all things Jewish that is supposed to turn out serious young men devoted to performance of the 613 Commandments. And in addition, one had to consider his family's *yichus*, or pedigree, mostly from his mother's side (his father was a mongrel, Jewishly speaking). "Seventeen generations of rabbis!" his mother would proclaim when Lev or one of his brothers underperformed in religious studies. As she admonished her sons, she would raise her eyes to the framed tintype photograph of her grandparents—her grandfather, Rabbi Levi, and her grandmother, Rebbetzin Henya—which hung on the wall of the dining room. Lev and his brothers imagined that their great-grandparents supervised them from the photo as the boys did their homework at the dining room table. Lev had examined the photograph many times, mystified by how indistinguishable his great-grandfather was from his great-grandmother. If Rabbi Levi had not been wearing a hat, Lev wouldn't have been able to tell them apart at all.

So to be neutral about Judaism, or worse, not to know how he felt about it, was not an achievement. It was an enormous failure.

Lev was twenty years old and for the first time in his life, he began to question what he was getting out of this all-consuming Jewish enterprise in which he had been raised. He didn't think he was off the derech—at least not like Shloime Strudler—but Lev knew something had happened in that mild encounter with his mother that had bumped him over to the narrow shoulder of the wobbly bridge across the chasm. He suspected that he was veering toward the edge and that if he didn't do something to right his course, he might plummet into the abyss that had no bottom.

Is this a crisis of faith, Lev wondered? He didn't know because he didn't have in his experience any sense of what a crisis of faith felt like, what it did to you. But he did know that the history of the Jews was rife with crises of faith, of people being knocked to the edge of the derech, or in his case, being nudged toward it. So having a crisis was not the issue. The only question was how you dealt with it. How did you come out of it if you came out of it at all?

3.

Even the Talmud, which featured hundreds of anecdotes about the Sages and the remarkable tenacity of their faith, also contained stories of faith under assault. Lev recalled learning about one in particular in the second chapter of the Talmudic Tractate *Kiddushin*. There, Rebbe Yaakov was confronted with a conundrum. It is written in the Torah that one should honor one's mother and father *in order that your days will be lengthened and in order that it would be good for you*. And in another place, the Torah declares that before taking fledgling birds from a nest, it is an obligation that you chase away the mother bird so she does not witness your taking her young; again, *in order that it will be good for you and your days will be lengthened*. In Tractate Kiddushin, the Talmud reports:

> *A father once sent his son on an errand, saying to him, 'Go up to the tower and bring me chicks.' And the son, in furtherance of the commandment to honor his father, ascended the tower; there, in furtherance of the commandment to chase away a mother bird before taking its young, the son chased away the mother bird and took the fledgling birds. But as he returned to his father, he fell from the height and died. And Rebbe Yaakov asked: 'Where is the promised "lengthening" of the son's days? Where is the "good" promised for the son?'*

The quandary that Rebbe Yaakov confronted was so profound that the esteemed Elisha ben Abuya, when he learned of it, could not reconcile the contradictions. How could it be that a heartfelt effort to obey God's commandments results in an early death? And particularly so when the commandment itself promises a good life and many years? What kind of a God demands obedience, promises a reward and then annihilates you? Elisha ben Abuya could not answer these questions

11

and so, the Talmud discloses, *he went out and sinned*. He abandoned his faith and embraced alien ideologies, and thus he became known as *Aher*: the Other.

And what about Rebbe Yaakov, who had actually witnessed the tragic event? He doubled down on his faith. He concluded that there is, in fact, no reward in *this* world for the observance of God's will. The only reward is after death. Rebbe Yaakov declared: *Of all those commandments that are written in the Torah along with their reward, not one of them will yield its reward until the Resurrection of the Dead.*

So, Lev reflected, the same crisis of faith pushed one great rabbi away from God, and at the same time, drew another closer.

The rabbis say that one is permitted to drink a bottle of kosher wine if the cork has not previously been removed. But if the cork has been pulled and you don't know who pulled it or when, the wine is then forbidden to be drunk by a Jew because the wine could have been used for libations to false gods or in ceremonies devoted to idol worship—indeed, for the most depraved purposes. It must be true, Lev concluded, because once his mother asked her question, "Since when has being Jewish anything to do with how you feel?" the seal was broken and the cork was drawn.

4.

The next Monday at Brooklyn College, Lev took a seat in a lecture hall. The class was Econ 101. Three seats to his left and one row in front of him, Lev noticed a girl who looked familiar, someone he might have seen before but hardly noticed. For the first time he observed how beautiful she was. Or more precisely, he observed how beautiful she *might* be, because he could only see her from the back and at an angle.

Her shock of black hair was skewered by two ebony chopsticks that held it aloft and he could glimpse the pale flesh of her neck highlighted by stray wisps of her hair. From his vantage, Lev could discern only an oblique profile, just the tip of her nose, a prominent chin and the fluttering of her long eyelashes. A number of times during the lecture, she checked her makeup with a compact mirror. Lev could make out in the tiny circle of glass a flash of features: large, dark-brown eyes; high cheekbones; a small, pouting mouth.

At one point, the mirror paused. The reflection of one of her eyes met his gaze. His heart lurched. He almost looked away but steeled himself and continued his study of her, peering at the mirror image of her oval brown eye. She gazed back, unabashed. The examined had become the examiner; the observer, the observed, until she clicked the compact shut.

It was already the third week of class and Lev couldn't figure out why he had never noticed her before. Where had she been hiding? Or had it been Lev who had been hiding? He couldn't take his eyes off her for the rest of the lecture.

And there was a lot to see. She was never at rest, her hands repeatedly rooting around in her purse then flitting to her cell phone, which she flipped open every few minutes; to a nail file, which she used to touch up her manicured, red nails, and then back to her purse for some item or another; a perpetual cycle of movement that seemed powered by an inexhaustible reserve of energy. She looked up when the professor said something that caught her attention, but as busy as her hands were, they did not pick up a pen or pencil to jot down notes.

The lecture ended and the students roused themselves. She stood, and turning toward the back of the lecture hall, she bent over her purse in search of something. Lev edged two seats closer to her. He smothered his anxiety and said, "Excuse me . . ."

She swept her eyes up and Lev caught his breath. The whole of her face was more stunning than its parts. Isolated from one another, her features had seemed chiseled and sharp, but combined, they were tender, approachable.

And she had a nose! A substantial nose, not a kewpie-doll type of nose, not the kind of nose that looks as if someone had forgotten to put it on your face except as an afterthought. No, her nose began where it should, right between her enormous eyes, and ran right toward you for a few millimeters and then plummeted gracefully. Not a ski-jump kind of nose, but one that culminated in a slender tip, pointing straight at you, dignified, unapologetic.

And Lev thought: this nose could actually pass for a Jewish nose, if it weren't so damn perfect and if she wasn't so otherwise, in every conceivable way, a gentile, a *shiksa*.

"What did you think of today's lecture?" he stammered.

She studied him for a few seconds and then answered. "Boring. He talks to us like we're idiots."

Lev didn't think the professor talked to the class like they were idiots—in fact, he found the economics course pretty challenging, but he said, "Yeah, what's with that?"

She frowned and shrugged.

"My name is Lev Livitski," he said. "Have we ever met?"

"How do you spell it?" she asked.

"L-i-v-i-t—"

"The first name."

"L-e-v."

"What kind of name is that?"

"It's a Jewish name."

She trained her eyes up at the skullcap perched on the top of his head, held onto his curly hair by a bobby-pin, and said, "Well, *duh*. It mean something?"

"It means *heart* in Hebrew."

"Your parents named you Heart?"

"It's a boy's name."

"Yeah, well, so is Francis or Leslie, but I wouldn't go naming my son Francis or Leslie."

Lev thought: this is some sort of test to see if I can be rattled, an initiation. So I'm not going to take the bait.

"Well, what's your name?"

"Angela Pizatto."

"What kind of name is that?"

"It's an Italian name."

Lev slowly looked her up and down, taking in her tight-fitting satin blouse, short leather skirt and her black high-heeled boots, and said: "Well, *duh*."

Although she tried to hide it, a smile glimmered on her face for a moment.

"Well, Angela Pizatto, nice to meet you." Lev extended his hand to shake hers. She seemed momentarily confused by his interest, and as she glanced down at his hand, Lev saw in her face a flurry of indecision—who was this Jewish guy with the weird name who suddenly was so interested in her? Was this a step she should be taking? Would it lead to different, perhaps better things? Or was this just the loose stair at the top of a very steep and rickety staircase?

But she gave a weak smile and raised her hand to meet his.

Her hand was warm and thin, so fragile that Lev imagined he was holding a baby bird delicately in his palm and he felt that he had to concentrate all his effort on holding it just right, firm enough to keep it from flying away and yet not so tight that he would crush it.

"Can I buy you a cup of coffee?" he asked.

"Yeah, okay."

They went to the cafeteria, sat at a table and exchanged basic biographical information. They seemed to have a lot in common. Angela was from Bensonhurst, Brooklyn, and like Lev, she lived with four siblings: two older brothers and two younger sisters. She shared a room with one of her sisters. Angela was majoring in business administration and wanted to be an accountant.

While they chatted, Angela kept looking around the cafeteria. Lev couldn't tell whether she was looking for someone in particular or whether she was concerned that someone she knew might see her sitting with him. Lev shared the same concern and hoped that none of his friends would see him with Angela. What would he say? How could he explain having a cup of coffee with a girl like Angela Pizatto, someone who clearly inhabited a planet many light-years from his own? He could pretend they were talking about Econ 101, but he knew nobody from his crowd would buy that. Unlike Angela, however, Lev didn't sweep the cafeteria looking for his friends simply because he couldn't take his eyes off Angela. Instead, he struggled to make interesting conversation, to keep her engaged, but as she craned her neck yet again and focused her eyes beyond him, scanning the back of the cavernous room, Lev simply stopped talking in mid-sentence and looked at her in silence.

A minute passed and she suddenly became aware of the fact that the conversation had died.

"Sorry," she said. "This is a little strange for me. I never talked with one of you before."

"Oh, I'm sure you have, but you maybe just didn't know it."

"No, I mean one of you wearing the funny little beanie."

"It's called a *kippah*."

"Yeah, well, I never even talked one word with even one of you."

"And I've never talked with one of you, either."

"One of me?" she asked in dismay. "What exactly do you think I am? You think I'm some kind of category?"

Lev sat up a little straighter, wondering if she was angry or joking. "Well, if I can be in a category, why can't you?"

"Because you wear the beanie. When you wear the beanie, you make a choice to say to everyone: 'Look at me; I'm in the Jew category.' And I don't mean that in an anti-Semite sort of way," she added.

"Oh," Lev said with a snort of laughter, "and you don't think you're telegraphing to everyone that you're an Italian from Bensonhurst? Look at the way you're dressed. Everything about you says that's who you are. It's just like my wearing my beanie, as you put it."

"That's ridiculous!"

"Really? Let's take a look around the room and see if we can't pick out some of your pals from the neighborhood." Lev turned and began to scour the groups of students congregating around the tables, drinking coffee.

"Let's not," she said.

"Well, you get my point, right?"

She didn't answer his question. Instead, she said, "So you did us Italians a big favor. You never talked to one of us in your whole life, but today you decided that you would. So why all of a sudden?"

"Because you're so beautiful," Lev said, flushing.

She didn't react. Maybe she expected his compliment. Or perhaps she was tired of hearing how beautiful she was and the proposition had lost its meaning.

"I looked the same last week. I looked the same last year, too. But you didn't offer to buy me a coffee back then."

"Something has changed," Lev admitted.

She raised her eyebrows. "*I* haven't changed."

Lev didn't reply immediately. He looked across the table into her face and she gazed back at him insistently. Finally, he said, "Something changed, but I'm not ready to talk to you about it yet."

She continued her scrutiny and then grinned. "Right answer." Before he could reply, she said, "Yeah, because if you had an answer all set and ready to go, then it probably wouldn't mean anything—probably wouldn't be a true answer. Because yeah, if you were telling the truth, you wouldn't be ready to share your thing . . . your deep secret with me, with someone you just met. So, yeah, that was the right answer."

"You're a very suspicious person."

"Not suspicious. Cautious."

"Why?"

"Because men will say anything to get into my pants. Men are beasts."

"I'm not," he muttered. "I'm not a beast."

"You are, but from what I can tell so far, you just don't know it yet."

"No," Lev protested. He raised his hands, palms facing Angela, and wagged them back and forth. "You're mistaken. I'm not like that."

"No? You already told me that you think I'm beautiful. You just want to be pals? You just want to pal around with an Italian *Catholic* chick"—she emphasized the word as though she were spitting it out on the floor—"because we're so damn interesting to talk to? We can just be pals if that's what you want."

Lev was stunned by the accuracy of her diagnosis. He hadn't consciously admitted to himself that his interest in this Italian woman was sexual. It was true that he didn't want to just pal around with her—whatever that meant—or talk to her about issues of public importance. Lev smothered an impulse to stand up and flee from the cafeteria. "No, that's not exactly what I want," he managed to reply. He took a deep, sharp breath. "And yes, I'm attracted to you, but not in a . . . in a *beasty* sort of way."

She laughed. "Well, maybe I will have to be the judge of that."

Lev didn't know what to say next, so he didn't say anything.

Angela studied the room beyond him again, but this time, her face lit up and she half rose from her seat to give a little wave. She sat down and said, "Here comes one of those people from that category you described—Italians from Bensonhurst." She turned to a young woman approaching their table. "Hi, Marie," she said brightly.

"Hi, Angela," Marie said. Marie was dressed in a uniform similar to Angela's: knee-high black felt boots with heels, short skirt, tight silky blouse. But while Angela was fashionably thin—in fact skinny would be a better adjective—Marie was short and squat. Physically, Marie seemed much more formidable, like she could pick up a table and fling it across the room. She glanced at Lev for an instant, her eyebrows raised in a question.

"You gonna introduce me to your friend?"

"Yeah, sure," Angela said quickly. "Marie, this is Lev Levinski from my Econ class. Yeah, I know—the names kind of rhyme, but not really."

"Livitski."

"Whatever." She turned to Lev and asked, "Sorry, what did you say your name means?"

"I didn't," he replied.

"Don't matter," said Angela. She picked up her purse and joined Marie, but before she left, she looked back at him and said, "See you around."

Lev didn't reply. He stared at the back of her legs as she disappeared around a corner.

5.

That night as Lev lay above his sleeping younger brothers in his bunk bed, he could not get Angela Pizatto out of his mind. He replayed the scene of their encounter over and over, dissecting every word. She had rebuffed him, there was no doubt about that, but he couldn't help but ask himself what it had meant when she had said, "Well, maybe I will have to be the judge of that"—of whether he was a beast or not. She hadn't said, "I *would* have to be the judge . . ." She had said *will*. And she had said, "See you around." Maybe it meant they would reconnect with each other again?

Lev realized this close reading was an absurd exercise in Talmudic textual exegesis and that nothing about the casual nature of their conversation could justify such a precise deconstruction. Nevertheless, he resolved to try one more time.

The next day, he stood in the back of the economics lecture hall and searched the rows. Angela was nowhere in the crowd and finally, he was forced to take a seat near the back. Just as the professor began his lecture, she appeared and slid into the empty seat next to him. "Sorry I'm late," she whispered and gave him an arch smile, as if she knew full well that he had been looking for her.

During the lecture, Lev kept stealing glances at Angela. After a while, the effort of shifting his eyes to the side gave him a headache. He changed his tactics and merely studied her hands as they darted among her paraphernalia, just as they had the previous day. Her wrists were so thin that they looked like a child's. Her fingers seemed to undulate like willow tendrils in a current. Lev inhaled deeply through his nose so he could catch hints of her scent. She smelled like a pound cake baked for the Sabbath by his mother.

He didn't hear one word of the lecture.

After the professor concluded, Lev began to rise from his seat, but Angela put her hand on his arm for a second and said quietly, "Just sit for a few minutes while they all go." He sat back down. She shifted one space away from him to a now-empty seat, took out her cell phone and began furiously texting. Lev took the hint. He pretended to study his economics textbook. The last of the students filed out of the lecture hall and finally, they were alone.

She moved back to the seat beside him. "I don't want to sit in the cafeteria," she said. "Makes me nervous. I live in a fishbowl. I just don't got the energy to go around explaining why I'm having coffee with a . . . with a Jewish guy. It's not anti-Semitism, believe me."

Lev had briefly entertained the thought that it might be anti-Semitism that made her so reluctant to be seen with him, but as soon as Angela declared it wasn't, he concluded that it most certainly was. He leaned away and turned to study her. He wasn't surprised that a Catholic girl from Bensonhurst might be uncomfortable hanging around with a Jew, just perplexed that Angela didn't seem to be embarrassed in the least about admitting it. Lev certainly wouldn't admit that he felt the same way about Angela as she did about him.

Angela didn't notice his reaction or at least pretended that she didn't. "I know a place where we won't have to keep looking over our shoulder," she whispered even though they were alone in the room. She took from her purse a slip of paper on which she had written the name and address of a diner.

"It's in DUMBO," she explained. "Tonight? 6:30?"

"Okay," Lev said.

"What's your subway stop?"

"Kings Highway on the Q."

She got out of her seat and as she hoisted her purse onto her shoulder, she gave her instructions. "Take the Q to DeKalb; switch to the M or R going back down toward Coney and get off at 4th Ave-9th Street. Catch the F toward Manhattan to York Street. The diner is near the entrance ramp of the Manhattan Bridge." Then she left him sitting by himself in the back of the empty lecture hall.

6.

That evening, Lev arrived at the York Street station five minutes before 6:00. DUMBO was untrodden ground for him and he figured he should give himself some extra time to find the diner. As he exited the station onto a narrow sliver of York Street, he raised his eyes to the elevated roadway of the Brooklyn-Queens Expressway, and above that, to the entrance/exit ramp to the Manhattan Bridge. The ground shook as the traffic careened overhead and Lev felt his teeth rattling. He finally understood the weird redundancy of the acronym DUMBO: *Down Under* the Manhattan Bridge Overpass. The growl of the vehicles pounding the expressways overhead and the dimness of the streets shut away from the sky made the neighborhood not only *Under*, but *Down*, as well.

Since he was beneath the ramp leading to the bridge, he followed it toward the diner as Angela had suggested. But he soon got confused and ended up trudging alongside the BQE instead. By the time he realized he was lost, he found himself on a roadway empty of pedestrians and there was no one on the streets of whom he could ask directions. He wandered a bit further along side the façade of an enormous public housing project. At the end of the block, he came across a church by the name of The Church of the Open Door. It looked to Lev less like a church than a supermarket, with bars on its windows and crosses strewn all over its façade. Lev wondered whether the church's door, if it was open at all, would be open to someone like him. He decided to find out.

He charged up the steps and pushed his way into the lobby—apparently, the Church of the Open Door delivered what it promised. A security guard was dozing at a table inside. Mercifully, he knew exactly where the diner was and sent Lev off in the right direction. Lev had to reverse his trek, so to avoid being late, he jogged most of the way, slowing down as he neared the restaurant in a vain attempt

21

to cool down and stop sweating.

The last few blocks took him past warehouses squatting in the gathering darkness. He saw a hazy brightness in the distance, which he assumed was the diner. As he proceeded down the block, he came across a store-front church. At the entrance was an enclosure surrounded by chicken wire containing a grimy nativity scene basking in the light of a low-wattage bulb. Under the layers of dirt, Lev could make out the usual suspects: Mary, infant Jesus, bearded men in exotic turbans, barnyard animals.

These might be idols, Lev thought. I might be walking down a street past a shrine created by idol worshippers.

But that was unfair, Lev concluded. These weren't idols—physical depictions of God. The weight of rabbinical authority made it perfectly clear that Christians were not idolators.

Italian Catholic girls from Bensonhurst, in particular, were not idolaters.

As he approached the diner, he saw through one of its windows that Angela was already seated in a booth. She seemed to be seized by a fit of gesticulation, her arms and hands whirling about her: purse to cosmetic case to phone to hairbrush to purse to phone. When Lev entered, she gave a little wave to catch his attention.

As he slid into his side of the booth, Lev noticed Angela glance again to the top of his head where his kippah sat. He quickly reached up, swiped it off his head and put it in his coat pocket.

She seemed surprised. "You don't have to do that for me."

"Okay," he said. "I did it for me."

"I didn't think they came off so easily. I thought maybe you stapled them on." Angela cackled at her joke. "Why do you wear those things anyhow?"

"It's a sign of respect to God. It's supposed to remind us that we're always in His presence."

Angela swiveled her head around and then up and down as if she were searching for something floating in the air. "Think God is here right now, having dinner with us?"

"Not likely," Lev admitted. To himself, he muttered: Let's hope not.

Angela began talking nonstop. This place is a dive, but it's off the beaten track so they probably won't be disturbed; not that it matters; she really doesn't care what people think, but it's just such a bother to have to explain everything all the time because sometimes it seems that your friends are really only interested in prying—and for what purpose? Just to gossip. Why do people enjoy gossiping so much anyhow? They only gossip about negative things. Fall down on the street and everyone knows. But win a prize or pass a test and no one hears anything about it. Brooklyn College is even worse than the neighborhood. Does anyone ever study, or is it that all they do is watch everyone else? Maybe because Brooklyn dumbass College is so easy and no one has to work hard so they have all this time on their hands to make trouble, to stir things up. Or at least it's easy for her, the subjects she takes: math, accounting, economics, business planning. All that stuff just comes natural to her. She could do math in her head since she was a little girl. Not just adding and subtracting, but complicated equations. It's just something she was born with. But don't go thinking that it's heredity, because none of her brothers can do math at all, even with a calculator. She makes money by doing people's taxes. It's easy for her. She always gets people refunds. Sometimes she earns extra cash working as a lighting assistant to a video guy who films weddings. She hates that job because it feels like she's crashing a wedding of strangers—

"Hey, how about a couple of menus over here!" Angela suddenly demanded so loudly that Lev was startled.

The waitress brought menus. Lev had never eaten in a non-kosher restaurant, so he ordered a tuna sandwich and a coffee. Even though Angela was rail-thin, she ordered pea soup, meatloaf with gravy and mashed potatoes, an egg-cream and a hot-fudge sundae with whipped cream. Lev felt the urge to take out his wallet to determine whether he had enough cash to pay for Angela's big dinner. He tried to visualize just how much money was nestled in the folds of the wallet, but he couldn't recall.

Angela picked up from where she had left off. That economics course—what a waste of time! Let's hear that know-it-all say one thing we don't already know. Why even go to class except to get out of the house for a little while? The hardest course she ever took was Modern Poetry. She had to work so hard in reading and understanding the poems, harder than on any other subject, but it was so worth it. She loved the girl poets: Emily Dickinson (did you know she died an old maid—unbelievable, someone with so much talent!); Sylvia Plath (oh my, such a sad person! She killed herself—and she had a husband and two children, but she killed herself anyway! Can you believe that?). Not just girl poets, some of the guy poets are okay, but they seem to try to make it as difficult as possible to understand them, which, if you think about it, is a totally predictable guy-thing to do. But not Sylvia Plath, who hated her father. She thought he was like a Nazi. Not saying he was a Nazi . . . like a real Nazi . . . just telling you what Sylvia Plath said about him. It's not my personal opinion that he was a Nazi; I'm just saying. Anyway, you don't get to know much about Sylvia Plath's mother though.

Angela's mother disapproves of Angela and everything she does and the way that she dresses. But Angela doesn't take it personal because every girl she knows fights with her mother. It's just something that must have gone on throughout history, mothers and daughters resenting each other and fighting about ridiculous things, like how much you paid for a purse, or how many showers you took, or whether you cleaned the hair off the brush after you used it. They were probably fighting about stuff like that back in ancient Rome.

"But enough about my mother, what about your mother?"

Before Lev could answer, the Mexican busboy brought them two glasses of tap water. Angela demanded a separate cup filled with ice cubes; then she asked for a slice of lemon; then she called for a small plate of lemon slices so she wouldn't have to worry about running out of lemons. The busboy brought a basket of bread, but she deemed it "unfit for human beings," and delivered a lecture about how bread was the most important element in a meal. She sent it back. The poor busboy brought a fresh basket of bread, but it still did not meet her standards, so she demanded that he take it back again and warm it in the oven. When he brought the warm bread back to the table, she didn't even touch it.

Angela received her cup of pea soup with skepticism. Lev peered at it too, a watery concoction in which floated some horrifying bits of pink meat. This wasn't her chief complaint, though: evidently it wasn't hot enough, so she ordered it taken back to the kitchen to be reheated. Then she demanded additional soup croutons. The spoon was dirty—get her another one.

The busboy scurried over to clear away the empty soup bowl and spoon, immediately followed by the waitress, a middle-aged woman with a bouffant and heavy makeup. She placed the plates down on the table with a peremptory thud and shuffled away. The meatloaf was declared to be just what Angela had always dreamed of, but to Lev it was frightening—it had a greenish border and crimson bits, like blood. The slab of chopped meat floated in a lake of dark brown gravy. Beside the meatloaf crouched a mound of white mashed potatoes with a cube of butter melting and flowing down the sides in yellow rivulets like an erupting volcano. Steamed green beans were scattered next to the potatoes like uprooted trees.

The green pea soup with bits of ham floating in it; the meatloaf swimming in gravy while sharing a plate with mashed potatoes oozing melted butter; all of these sights and smells combined to nauseate Lev.

Lev's tuna fish sandwich looked conventional enough and he ordered his stomach to relax and accept the first exploratory bite.

But Angela did not like the look of it. She reached across the table and pushed on the bread with her index and middle finger, once, twice, three times, watching to see how the bread reacted. The imprint of her two fingers remained on the slice of bread.

"Not fresh bread," she concluded. "Send it back."

"It's fine," he said. "Let it be."

"You don't understand," she said. "Stale bread is an insult to God."

"Maybe to your God," Lev said, "but not to mine."

She shook her head with a frown and muttered, "No standards." Then her hand shot out and picked up the pickle next to his sandwich. She held it up to the light and waved it back and forth. It flopped around like a dead fish.

"Soggy," she declared with glee. "Maybe your God feels more stronger about pickles than about bread?"

He scowled at her. "May I have my pickle back, please?"

"Suit yourself," she said.

Angela loved the meatloaf and the gravy. "Try this!" she would exclaim as she extended a forkful of meat dripping with grease and gravy across the table toward his mouth. Each time, he politely declined and she would shrug and remark, again, "Okay, suit yourself." The food was not kosher, but Angela did not seem tuned in to that

25

subtlety. In a similar manner, Lev was offered mashed potatoes. He finally surrendered and tasted the egg-cream. It had a gritty feel to it, like someone had poured antacid into the glass.

When they had finished the main course, the cowering busboy cleared the plates and the waitress brought Angela her hot-fudge sundae, placed it before her and walked away. Angela took one look at it and her arm shot up. She started waving her hand back and forth to attract the waitress's attention, all the time peering intently at the sundae. When the waitress did not respond instantaneously, Angela began to snap her fingers. Lev looked across the table at her outstretched arm. It was so thin that he could see the faint blue lines of the veins crisscrossing her flesh. The skin of her inner forearm flashed white as ivory and the tiny bump of her sinew flexed up and down as she continued to snap her fingers.

The waitress slunk over. "What is it this time?"

"This is supposed to be a hot-fudge sundae," Angela said, looking contemptuously up at the waitress. "Well, the fudge isn't hot."

"The fudge was hot," the waitress said wearily. "We put it on the ice cream. The ice cream was cold. The fudge got cold." She crossed her arms over her ample chest and frowned at Angela. Angela did not look at the waitress as she spun out her explanation—instead, Angela stared straight ahead, her eyes trained on some distant spot across the diner. Then she directed her gaze to Lev, pretending to address him alone: "Do you think anyone has ever told her that the customer is always right? Could it possibly be that she doesn't know that the customer is always, always right?" Angela turned and squinted at the waitress. "Take it back. Put the hot fudge on the cold ice cream and then run it over to me right away before it gets cold."

The waitress said nothing and took the sundae away.

"What's wrong with you?" Lev whispered fiercely. "Why are you acting like this?"

"Like what?"

"So rude, almost like you're going out of your way to boss everyone around."

She waved the remark away. "In a joint like this you have to show them who's boss from the first minute you walk in, or they treat you like a peasant."

"That's crazy talk. That's just paranoid." Lev halted as the waitress

26

returned with a fresh hot-fudge sundae, which she plopped down in front of Angela, who didn't even acknowledge its presence.

"Thank you," Lev said to the waitress. She stalked away without a word.

"You didn't have to thank her," Angela said. "It wasn't your sundae."

"I've sat here all night and watched you go out of your way to humiliate everyone who works in this restaurant, so a simple 'thank you' is the least I could do."

"Why? What difference does it make to you? Why are you so worked up about it?"

"Because we're supposed to remember that we were once slaves in Egypt." As those words tumbled out of his mouth, Lev grimaced because he realized that Angela didn't have to remember that at all. In fact, Angela wasn't even remotely part of the *we* that formed the subject of his sentence.

Angela didn't miss the disconnect—she seemed to revel in it. "Forgot you were out with an Italian Catholic chick, huh? Thought for a second you were out with one of those Jewish girls!" She grinned, took a spoonful of her sundae, held it perpendicular to the table and with great concentration, licked it like an ice cream cone with her pink tongue. "The whole thing is ridiculous because you weren't any more a slave in Egypt than I was, so you can't possibly remember it."

"That's not the way it works for us. So maybe you don't know what you're talking about. Maybe there's more to it than just having no standards about whether the bread is fresh enough or not."

"Oh, so sorry," Angela said as she continued eating her sundae. "So sorry that you're embarrassed to be with me. So sorry—I didn't know I was out on a date with Mother Theresa."

Before he could answer, Angela reached across the table with a big spoonful of ice cream enfolded in hot fudge and whipped cream and said: "I know we're having a fight but this is so good, you have to try it right now while the hot fudge is still hot."

Lev was angry and upset, but Angela had such a look of delight on her face and she seemed so intent on his sharing what had made her so happy that he hesitated for a moment. Then Angela tilted her head down slightly and unleashed her eyes on him, slowly widening them and raising her face toward Lev, beckoning him to cooperate, to submit. Lev wondered: Was this something that she did naturally or was it a weapon in her arsenal?

He opened his mouth and she stuck the spoon in. She turned it over while it was still in his mouth so that the hot fudge on the concave side of the spoon would rub onto his tongue. Then she slowly pulled out the spoon and watched for his reaction.

Lev didn't want to acknowledge how delicious it was. He kept his face blank.

"See," she said as she continued to eat the sundae with great satisfaction. "The hot fudge has to be hot. It's not worth it otherwise."

This statement got Lev going again. "Angela, you can get what you want without being cruel to people who wait on you. You could try being nice."

She laughed. "Try being nice? You're joking! Let me tell you, in high school, I was a waitress in a joint like this and no one ever, ever treated me nice. In fact, they said the most disgusting things to me and they put their hands all over me and ordered me around like a slave. So no, you don't get what you want by being nice."

Lev was distracted for a moment by the image of Angela in a white waitress uniform and apron waiting on customers in the diner, customers who put their hands all over her. He softened his tone and leaned toward her. "But you hated being treated like that, didn't you?"

"Of course I hated it."

"Well, if you hated it, then why do you treat others that way?"

"I don't do it all the time, only when I'm the customer."

"Where I come from, we have a saying: 'What is hateful to you, do not do to others.'"

"Thanks for the sermon, Mother Theresa. Yeah, well Jesus once said, 'Love your neighbor like yourself.' Ever hear of it?"

Lev had an urge to correct her, to point out that Jesus hadn't made that up: that the Torah had said it first and that if Jesus had said it at all, it was only because he was quoting the Torah; that as an observant Jew, Jesus had known the sacred texts. But Lev held his tongue because he thought: now it's really going to get ugly. It was pretty clear to him that Angela was not a big fan of the Jews. The wisecracks that she had already made suggested that she had her issues; not to mention that when your Catholic date knows you're an Orthodox Jew and she starts quoting Jesus, you know it's going to get ugly. "Yes, I've heard of it."

"Well," she said, "I like Jesus' saying better than yours. It's more positive, loving someone like the way you love yourself."

"Yes, except if you don't love yourself, if you don't respect yourself, what Jesus said doesn't work, does it?"

Angela's eyes narrowed as she glared at him. She shifted her lips to the side, distorting her mouth. Lev expected her to begin to curse him, to excoriate him. But she didn't reply. As the silence lengthened, Lev wondered whether it could be that she didn't understand how he'd insulted her. Perhaps in addition to being callous and incapable of empathy, she was also stupid?

Angela studied what was left of her sundae, her spoon poised in the air, about to dip down again into the morass of melting ice cream and solidifying fudge. Then she looked across the table at Lev and she didn't appear hostile or angry anymore. She just looked tired.

"I've had enough, Levinski—"

"Livitski!"

"Whatever. I've had enough." She dropped her spoon into what was left of the sundae and it slowly sank into the sludge. "Let's get out of here," she said.

Lev shrugged. At this point, he really didn't care. He knew with certainty that his venture into this new, unexplored world was not going to work. He may have been skidding toward the edge of the derech, but if this was what falling might feel like, he was glad to have caught himself.

7.

The sullen waitress returned, slapped the check on the table and marched away. Angela placed the index finger of each hand on the check and ceremoniously slid it over to Lev's side of the table. "Thank you," she said unenthusiastically.

Lev extracted his wallet from his back pocket and peeked into it. As he suspected, he didn't have enough cash to pay for the entire meal and he didn't own a credit card. He searched the creases for additional cash, then finally looked up from his wallet at Angela.

"Don't tell me," she said. She looked away, her lips set in a line.

"Did you think I was rich?" Lev asked her. "Why? I certainly don't look rich, do I? Is it because you think all Jews must be rich?"

"Don't be silly. I mean I might have hoped you were, but I didn't really think so."

"Well, I'm not," he said. "I even bring my lunch in a paper bag to school so I don't have to pay for a sandwich." As he said these words, Lev painfully acknowledged to himself the other reason he brought his lunch every day—because he didn't eat food prepared in the non-kosher kitchen of the cafeteria. At least he hadn't until taking his seat across from Angela earlier that evening.

They sat in silence, staring at the table. "How much?" she finally asked.

"It's $30 and I have only $20.

She fished a twenty out of her purse. "Here. But I want change."

"I'm leaving everything."

"That's a tip of twenty-five percent!" she protested.

"Well, you are indeed good at math. I'm leaving all of it and believe me, it's not enough for what you put everyone through."

Lev and Angela headed to the subway in silence, walking near but not next to each other. They entered the desolate artificial cavern created by the elevated expressways towering over them. The traffic

30

thundered to and from Manhattan and to distant parts of Brooklyn and Queens. They could see the York Street subway station looming in the darkness a few hundred yards away. Beneath the overpass, several homeless men were gathered, warming their hands over a fire smoldering from an abandoned oil drum, their few belongings scattered about them on the ground.

Angela stopped abruptly. Lev continued a few steps before noticing that she had halted. He turned around to see what had happened. Angela swiveled her head around and then pivoted to look behind her as if searching for an escape route. She pointed to a street they had already passed half a block back and said brightly, "I know a short-cut to the subway!"

"That's not a shortcut," Lev replied. He pointed in the direction in which they had been headed. "The entrance is a couple of hundred yards over there."

"I don't want to go that way," she murmured.

"Why not?" he asked.

She lifted her hand a few inches toward the subway entrance. "Hobos!"

Lev laughed at her.

"Shhhh!" she hissed. "They'll hear us!"

"They're just homeless people and they're harmless. There haven't been hobos around since the Great Depression. And they were harmless, too."

Angela stood transfixed. "Lev, I don't like hobos. Please," she pleaded, "let's find another way home."

Lev sighed. "All right, I'll take care of this. Just come over on this side of me." He retraced his steps and stood between her and the homeless encampment. "Now take my arm and we'll cross over to the other side of the street and they won't even know you are there."

They walked briskly past the men. Angela clasped Lev's arm and didn't take her eyes off the ground in front of her until they were at the subway entrance. As soon as the entry door swung shut, she disengaged and dropped his arm as if it were some distasteful burden.

Lev examined the subway map mounted on the wall next to the turnstile as he fished in his pocket for a subway token.

"You don't know how to get home, do you?" Angela had recovered from her hobophobia immediately. She was back on the offensive, perhaps to let Lev know that even if she did fear one thing in this world, she didn't fear anything or anyone else.

"I can figure it out," he said. "Just give me a minute."

She rolled her eyes and without looking at the map, she said with authority, "We take the F down to 4th Ave-9th Street; I catch the M to Bensonhurst; you go back up to DeKalb on the M or R, and then get your Q to Flatbush."

They got on the train and stood next to each other without speaking. What a disaster the evening had been. He had imagined it going a hundred other ways, being out with a woman different from every other woman he had ever met—not just different, but *forbidden*. And yet from the first moment in the restaurant, he had realized that it had all been a mistake. Lev began to think of something very scary—what if when you fell off the derech, you ended up nowhere? What if you were unable to find another place where you could exist? What if you just had to live on a subsistence level, under or near the derech, a shadow existence where you could not really thrive or move on, where you simply had to wait out the weeks or months or years until you were able to climb back onto the derech? He thought of the homeless people living under the overpasses leading to the Manhattan Bridge, warming their hands around smoking oil drums. What if that was what existence would be like for people like him if he were to topple off the derech?

Beside him, Angela clung to the metal pole in the middle of the subway car. She was staring straight ahead, perhaps at her blurred image reflected in the dark train window. She looked a bit dazed and seemed lost in thought. Lev watched the small muscle at the hinge of her jaw throb as she clenched and unclenched her teeth.

The subway approached the 4th Ave-9th Street stop. As the train began to decelerate at the entrance to the station, Lev said, "Here's where we get off."

Angela shook herself from her reverie and turned to him, snatching his arm. "Stay on with me for a few stops, will you? I want to talk to you."

Lev didn't want to. He couldn't imagine there was anything they could say to one another that could rehabilitate the last couple of hours. He was exhausted with disappointment and wanted to go home. Angela sensed his hesitation, but she held tightly to his arm and pulled him closer to her. "Please," she said. "Just a couple of stops." The train lurched to a stop at the station and people began to get off. Angela pushed him toward a couple of now-vacant seats. They sat down as the door closed and the train gathered momentum.

Angela shifted closer to Lev and continued to grip his arm. "I didn't mean to . . ." She gave a slight shake of her head. She brought her face closer to his and spoke in a low voice as if she didn't want to be overheard. "I didn't want to . . . I mean . . . it wasn't supposed to . . ." She looked out the subway window as if gazing at the scenery, but outside the train car was only blackness. Only a half-hour earlier Angela seemed capable of talking without breathing, but now she was unable to complete a short sentence. Maybe this is what happens to her when she actually tries to think about what she wants to say before she starts saying it, Lev speculated.

But Angela didn't seem to be able to spit out what she needed to say and as the subway plowed deeper into Brooklyn, Lev began to feel a compulsion to jump from his seat and escape at the next stop. He felt like he was imprisoned in the train as it streaked deeper into enemy territory.

Angela clutched his arm even tighter. Finally, she found her voice and once she did, her confession gushed out of her in one long exhalation. "I know I behaved terribly tonight. I know you must think I'm an awful person, a cruel person . . . a psycho type of person. But the truth is that I said all those nasty things because I wanted to show you that I was tough . . . that I was a tough person who couldn't be pushed around. Because my girlfriend Marie went out with a Jewish guy and she told me that you're real snobs and that you judge everyone and look down on everyone. And this Jewish guy made her feel ashamed for her family and for who she was and the way she talked and the way she behaved. So I wanted to show you that I'm the one in charge, that I don't take shit from anyone. But I realize that I chose a really stupid way to show you that. And even while I was doing it I could see that you were disgusted by the way I behaved. And I kind of respected that you were disgusted, that you didn't like what I was doing. And even though I knew what I was doing was wrong and stupid, I couldn't figure out a way to stop doing it. And then when you told me that I didn't love myself or have any self-respect, well then I realized that there was no point anymore."

She relaxed her grip on his arm for a moment and then seized it again. "And I also want you to know I usually don't eat that much, but I was very nervous to go out with you so I pigged out . . . and I feel like I'm probably going to throw up when I get off the train." And then as an afterthought, she added, "But don't go thinking I have an eating disorder because believe me, I don't."

Lev wanted to say: That's all very well and good that you had a motive when you were abusing the busboy and the waitress, and it's great that you now realize how ludicrous that strategy was to make your point, but the real question is, what kind of person is willing to abuse others in the service of some twisted agenda?

But he didn't say anything.

They traveled sitting next to each other in silence for another stop. Finally, she said, "We need to get back on the right trains, so next stop, we need to get off and cross over inside the station so we don't have to pay another fare."

They exited the train and took an overpass to the uptown tracks. An F heading to Manhattan came almost immediately and they sat down again as they retraced their route. Lev glanced over at her as they sped down the tracks. She had a somber look on her face and she stared at her hands lying in her lap, palms up, fingers curled upwards as if they had been broken. For the first time that evening, in fact since Lev had first noticed her in the lecture hall, Angela's hands were still. She realized he was looking at her and she glanced up for a moment, gave an anemic smile, then looked back down at her hands with a slight shake of her head.

"I'm really embarrassed," she muttered, shaking her head again. "Please forgive me."

"You didn't wrong me," Lev said. "It's not up to me to forgive you."

"That waitress," she continued, half to herself, "that waitress reminds me of so many of my cousins and my aunts, women I love, who are so tired of serving really crummy people, rude people, mean people . . . and I was showing off to you by insulting her!" She turned to look at Lev. "How could I be so stupid? What was I thinking?"

She seemed genuinely distressed, so much so that Lev began to consider that maybe the whole thing was just a big mistake. But she had played her role of tormentor so well, with such relish, that he just wasn't convinced.

She saw his confusion and she bent her head and again regarded her open hands. Lev thought of a Yiddish expression he had heard his father utter once: *A human being is born with fists clenched, but dies with hands open.* The train began to slow down as it entered the next station.

"This is it, 4th Ave-9th Street," she said softly. "You know how to take it from here?"

"Yes," he said as he stood up.

She didn't reply, but she raised her hands and covered her face with them, her gleaming red nails facing outward where her eyes should be. She remained in her seat.

"Angela, aren't you supposed to get off here too?" Lev asked her.

"Just go," she said, keeping her hands over her eyes, her face. "Go. I can't be seen anymore. I can't be seen. Please, just go."

So Lev went, leaving her with her face covered by her hands on the F Train as it headed away from Angela's home in Bensonhurst toward the East River and onwards to Manhattan.

II

Rabbi Assi said regarding the Evil Inclination: 'Initially it is as thin as a filament from a spider's web, but ultimately, it grows as strong as a rope thick enough to pull a cart . . .'

- Babylonian Talmud, Tractate Succah 52A -

8.

An hour after he left Angela on the train, Lev climbed into his upper bunk, lay on his back and stared at the ceiling suspended only three feet above him in the darkened room. What a complete disaster! He couldn't think of one instant during the entire evening when he hadn't been staggered by Angela, by what she was saying, how she was acting. That crack about being Mother Theresa—how is someone supposed to react to that? Or that taunt about what Jesus had said. Who would make such a comment to a Jewish guy, one who wore a kippah?

And the way she had misbehaved, lecturing the poor busboy, speaking so harshly to the waitress! He pictured her arm extended straight up, the way her pale skin had rippled as she imperiously snapped her fingers. He recalled the way her eyes had waxed large and luminous as she beckoned him to taste the spoonful of ice cream and hot fudge. Why had he let her shove that spoon into his mouth in the first place? That ice cream was obtained through Angela's abuse of the waitress. It shouldn't have tasted so good. It shouldn't have tasted good at all. And then when she twisted the spoon and dragged it across his tongue as she pulled it out of his mouth! What did she know about his tongue, about his mouth, that she should do such a thing?

But Angela hovered before his eyes until late into the night, the line of her jaw that crowned her throat, the way her tongue fluttered about her lips when she thought that something he was saying was particularly disagreeable. Lev was finally beginning to understand what the Sages meant when they talked about the Evil Inclination. It was this after-image of Angela floating in his psychic cornea as if he had been staring too long into a light that was too bright. He admonished himself for obsessing about someone who was clearly a troubled person, a defective human being; someone whom he shouldn't want to know, whom he should try to forget.

Lev had always pictured the eternal struggle between the Evil

39

Inclination and the Good Inclination as trench warfare, where two armies are arrayed one against the other, dug into vast labyrinths of earthen works and trenches in the human heart, occasionally skirmishing and sniping at each other, but more or less in stalemate. Each was a force waiting and watching for a weakness in the other, a vulnerability that would prompt one side to storm out of its trenches in a frontal assault that would totally overwhelm the other side. Back and forth the Evil and Good Inclinations would battle over you—attack and counter-attack—with your deepest impulses serving as the pitted no-man's land between them.

But now Lev realized it wasn't like that. The battle between the Evil Inclination and the Good Inclination was not even a battle at all. It was like two people on the subway vying to sit down in a vacant seat. Each moves toward that seat and at the last instant, one of them manages by just a half-second to slip into that seat before the other, and the commuter who is robbed of the seat merely changes his trajectory by a few inches and stands, resigned, until he arrives at his station. There is no great conflict or battle, just a missed opportunity, one of countless other opportunities, some acquired, others flubbed.

If you are generally diligent and motivated, most times the Good Inclination will take the seat.

If you are slothful or negligent, or maybe distracted by questions that you should not be asking yourself, then sometimes the Evil Inclination will end up in the seat.

Lev's relationship with Angela Pizatto seemed to have reached its definitive conclusion, yet he could not shake the feeling that his Evil Inclination was still comfortably seated in the subway car while he stood before it wondering what had happened.

9.

Lev did his best to avoid looking for Angela the next day in class. When it ended, he was making his way out of the lecture hall when she emerged from nowhere and sidled up to him without a word. They began walking side by side in the hallway. Finally, she mumbled, "Let's go outside and find a place to talk. I brought you something."

Lev glanced sideways at her as they moved down the corridor. This is when you say, 'No, 1 don't think so,' he told himself, and you turn and leave her standing there. But he continued walking beside her.

They exited the campus at Avenue H and walked west. Neither of them spoke until they arrived at Coney Island Avenue. As they paused at the stoplight, Lev turned to her. "Where are we going?"

Angela looked at him as if it were completely obvious. "Ocean Parkway."

Lev didn't know why they were going to Ocean Parkway, but he didn't protest. He didn't ask himself why he was following Angela, why he was willing to follow her for block after block toward a vague destination and for an encounter he could not at that point imagine. But Angela was in charge—that was clear. Angela, the most tempestuous, most erratic person Lev had ever met, was clearly in charge.

When they reached Ocean Parkway, Lev followed Angela across the service road toward a row of benches on the median strip. He glanced at her in the late autumn sunlight. Her large, round eyes were sunken and her face was pale with fatigue.

She noticed his scrutiny and said, "I don't look very good, do I? I didn't sleep well."

He shrugged. "So what's up?"

She reached into her coat pocket and thrust a handful of cash toward him, the dollar bills clumped in an unruly tangle. "Here's your twenty dollars," she mumbled. "Under the circumstances, I think you

41

should get a refund."

"Is that what you think? You think this is about twenty dollars?"

"I don't think that," she said quietly. "I'm just trying to make this right. I need to."

"You want to make it right by insulting me? 'I'll give the Jew his money and he'll be happy?' Is that what you're thinking?"

"No, that's not it at all." She stuffed the bills back into her coat pocket. She looked down, shook her head and muttered: "I don't know. I just can't seem to stop screwing this up." She looked up at him. "I was trying to show you how sorry I am. Can't you forgive me?"

"I told you already: it's not up to me to forgive you."

"That's not enough."

"What would make it enough?"

"Go out with me again. I want to show you that I'm a normal person. That I'm not a wicked person."

"You don't have to prove yourself to me. Or to anyone. Why does it matter so much what I think?"

"I don't know!" she shouted, stamping her foot and spinning away from Lev. "I don't know why it matters!" Then she turned back to him and said in a low voice, but almost bitterly, "But it does." She glared at him, brow furrowed, breath quick. Angela was more resolute about this than Lev was about anything.

"I don't trust you, Angela. I don't want to go through another date like last night."

"I know you must think I'm a crazy bitch and I don't blame you. But I'm not. I can show you I'm not. So let's do a dress rehearsal. You told me you bring your lunch every day. Let's eat lunch right here, right now. I'll show you it can be a normal experience." She seized his arm and dragged him toward one of the benches just as she had done on the F Train the previous evening. She sat down heavily and tugged him down next to her onto the bench.

"Yes, so here we are," Angela said formally, "sitting down on a bench about to have lunch, just like normal people."

Lev stared straight ahead at the traffic as it sped by on the parkway. Resist! he told himself. Resist!

But the Evil Inclination stretched out its legs in the subway car and opened a newspaper.

Angela looked around at her surroundings as if she had never been on Ocean Parkway before and nodded in approval. "What do you want to talk about?"

Lev glanced at her. "What do *I* want to talk about? *You* were the one that called this meeting."

"Fair point," she conceded. "Okay, let's talk about something meaningful, the way normal people would talk." She paused. "Okay, maybe I shouldn't bring it up, but I'm wondering about something you said last night. Like when you told me you're from Egypt . . . what you said was that you were once a slave in Egypt. I mean like I never met anyone like that . . . from Egypt."

"I don't literally believe that I came from Egypt."

"From ancient Egypt, with the pyramids and stuff and like, mummies?"

"That's not what I meant."

"Okay, so explain it to me now."

"You mean I should pretend that you're interested?"

She looked so deflated by his comment that Lev almost regretted making it. She sat stock still and stared silently at him. The only reason that Lev knew she was still alive was that he could see her jugular throbbing beneath her translucent flesh. A minute passed. Lev began to feel that if he didn't say anything, they would be doomed to sit in awkward silence forever.

So he began to tell her about Egypt. "The Bible states in five different places," he explained, "that Jews should remember that we were slaves in Egypt. And another thing: it also says over and over that we need to remember that we were liberated from slavery in Egypt. In fact, we are required to remember that we were freed from slavery at least twice each day, every day, once in the morning and once in the evening. So it means remembering that you were once *enslaved* in Egypt can't mean the same thing as remembering that you were *liberated* from slavery in Egypt. It must mean something else."

Lev stopped. Let's see if she has a brain in her head, he told himself.

Angela sat in silence thinking about what Lev had told her. Then she said: "If you remember that you were a slave, you don't treat anyone else like a slave. In other words," she said, "what's hateful to you, do not do to others. But sometimes we forget what is hateful to us so

43

we need to remind ourselves of it, and once we remember it, we can avoid doing it to other people."

Lev was surprised. He hadn't thought of the precise connection between the two statements: remembering the enslavement in Egypt and not doing to others what was hateful to you.

"Now I'm thinking," Angela said, "that where I come from, sometimes our problem is that we can't even for one minute, even for one second, forget about the things we hate, the people we hate."

"Well, we have the opposite problem. There are so many people that we should hate, that we can't bear it. We try to forget as much as possible. But the rabbis don't want us to forget. That's why we have so many fast days—they want to remind us of all the horrible things that have been done to us."

"I'm one of those people, aren't I? The people you should remind yourself to hate."

His inclination was to deny it immediately, to avoid more unpleasantness and say, *Of course I don't hate you!* But Lev remained silent. He wondered: is my inclination to remain silent an Evil one or a Good one? And he thought, I *should* hate her. She's not a nice person. She's an angry, spiteful, self-centered person. The only reason she's here right now is probably because I'm the only guy who ever went out with her who doesn't want to go out with her again. And she can't stand rejection.

Angela sat impassively, emotionless, like a defendant awaiting the jury's verdict. She didn't smile; she wasn't trying to charm him into letting her off the hook. She was waiting for an answer to the question of whether he hated her or not. And even though Lev did despise the way she had behaved, something in him just couldn't stop. He needed to go down this road just a little further. He needed to make his way just a little more on this path, so profoundly different from the derech. Just until he got around the next bend and could see what was up ahead. Then he would get off; then he would find a more appropriate road.

That's what Lev told himself.

So he wondered: Who is Lev Livitski to judge Angela Pizatto? And hasn't Rambam—the incomparable Maimonides—declared that everyone is open to complete repentance? An individual can achieve atonement if he or she does three things: verbally confesses their sin; asks for forgiveness from the person wronged; and feels heartfelt regret. Angela had already confessed her transgressions on the subway ride the previous night; she had asked for forgiveness; but has she experienced genuine regret? Rambam was very clear that regret can be demonstrated in only one way: if the transgressor is presented with the same set of circumstances as when the sin was first committed, and refrains from sinning again, then the regret is indeed genuine.

So if I were to follow Rambam's teachings, Lev reasoned, I should give Angela the opportunity to demonstrate her sincere contrition by going out with her again. If she could act decently under similar circumstances, then she would have achieved complete repentance.

But maybe she didn't deserve the opportunity to repent. I'm not God, Lev thought; I don't have an obligation to offer her this opportunity. But Rambam also said that if a transgressor asks forgiveness three times from another person, and that person refuses to grant it, then the sin moves from the sinner's side of the ledger to the injured party's side. How many times had Angela asked for forgiveness? Lev recalled only two times.

At that moment, he heard Angela ask again: "Lev, please, won't you forgive me?"

So the matter was settled.

"So if we were to go, where would we go?"

Her face erupted in a smile.

"I didn't say I would go," Lev advised her, "I just asked where we would go *if* I agreed that we would go."

Angela brushed off his comment. As far as she was concerned, it was a done deal. "Let's eat Chinese tomorrow night. You like Chinese? I know the best Chinese place in Brooklyn. And it's real cheap." She reconsidered her choice of words. "It's affordable for people like us who don't got much money."

Lev had never eaten real Chinese food. In fact, he was afraid of it, more afraid of it than of the meatloaf from the prior evening. Its ingredients were all mushed up and you couldn't see what was in it. You couldn't tell what was permitted and what was forbidden. He might be teetering on the edge of the derech—indeed, he might have already fallen off for all he knew—but if he were to accidentally eat pork, he would die of revulsion. How could he explain this? He just sat there with a furtive look on his face, saying nothing.

Angela looked at him quizzically and then broke into a broad grin. "You've never had Chinese, have you?" She shook her head, still radiating good humor. "It's the pork thing, right? Well, don't worry, we'll get vegetarian stuff."

Lev was dubious. "Look," he said, "I had a near-death experience with your meatloaf last night. Can't we go out someplace just for coffee?"

"Fine," she said. "I know the perfect place." She rummaged through her purse, took out a small pad of paper and wrote down the name and address of a café in Brooklyn Heights. She also scribbled directions of how to get there by subway. Lev watched her as she bent over the pad and wrote out the directions with a child's concentration, the tip of her tongue peeking out of the side of her mouth. When she finished, she tore the page off the notepad, straightened up and handed him the paper with a flourish.

He carefully folded it and put it in his shirt pocket. They sat for a while, not saying anything, watching the cars as they sped north on Ocean Parkway toward Manhattan.

"Well," Lev said, "we might as well eat our lunches." He took out of his backpack a brown paper bag containing a sandwich that his mother had made that morning.

"Whatcha got?" Angela asked.

"I don't know. Probably PB&J. That's more or less what I have every day."

"My mother would never send me to school with a PB&J. It would be an insult to her cooking."

"Well my mother has to make six sandwiches every morning for my dad, me and my four brothers."

"My mother doesn't make sandwiches for any of us. It's every man for himself."

"So, whatcha got?" Lev asked.

"I don't have anything. I never eat lunch."

"Why not?"

"Because I'm too embarrassed to brown-bag it." Angela seemed surprised for a moment that she had admitted this to him.

"Why would you be embarrassed? Just because you don't have any

46

money doesn't make you . . . poor, you know. Not that there is any shame in being poor."

"But it's no great honor either," she said with a laugh.

Lev raised his eyebrows in surprise.

"Everyone knows *Fiddler on the Roof*," Angela said. "Even an Italian chick like me."

Lev's mother never bothered to cut the sandwiches in half, so he tore it as carefully as he could and handed her a half.

"It doesn't have any jelly," Angela observed.

"It's PB&J without the J. My mother says she doesn't have time to put the jelly on six sandwiches, but she still calls it PB&J. Maybe she thinks we won't notice."

Angela nodded, took a big bite out of her half and chewed mightily. The bread was marked with a perfect imprint of her mouth, the teeth marks notching the perimeter of the crescent left by her bite. Lev thought even Angela's teeth marks were delicate, sexy. They watched each other with a half-smile on their faces as they engaged in the belabored chewing required to consume peanut butter sandwiches without jelly.

When they finished eating, Lev fished around in the bag for the paper towel his mother always put in there, tore it in half and handed a piece to Angela. She wiped her hands and then quickly reached up with the paper towel and brushed a crumb off his cheek. She flicked another one off the front of his coat, sat back and nodded.

"Are you sure you don't want your twenty dollars back?" she asked.

"Angela!"

"Just kidding!" She stood up, laughing. "Fun's over. Time to head back to Brooklyn dumbass College."

47

10.

Lev returned home late the next afternoon after his last class to prepare for his date. His three youngest brothers were home with his
mother. Elya was still at school at Baruch College in Manhattan and
his father was at work. Shmu, the carpet-crumb licker who was now
fifteen, was seated at the dining room table doing his homework. Next
to him, also digging into his homework, sat Yehuda, two years junior
to Shmu. He was called Hudi. The baby, Mordechai, age six, whom
everyone called Moti, was sprawled on the floor, studying his baseball
cards.

Lev greeted his brothers and circled the table in order to touch
each of them: a squeeze to Shmu's shoulder; the palm of his hand
resting for a moment on the back of Hudi's neck. He stooped down
and buried his hand in Moti's bushy black hair. Each of them, in turn,
made contact with Lev as he passed, a pat on the hand, the arm, or in
Moti's case, a pinch to Lev's leg.

"At last you're home," sighed Shmu. "I got a tough one here. It's
for a halacha exam."

Lev pulled up a chair between Shmu and Hudi. He glanced over
at Hudi who was studying the Torah portion scheduled to be read
that week. He wore a baseball cap backwards over his kippah, street-
style. He drummed the fingers of both hands on the table, providing
the rhythm for a song he was humming under his breath. As if in
counterpoint, Moti was singing to himself a reedy meandering melody while he examined his baseball cards. Among random notes, Lev
heard a line from *HaTikvah*, Israel's national anthem, followed by a
chorus from a wedding song, followed by a line in Hebrew from a
nineteenth-century Hasidic melody.

Their mother bustled about the kitchen, preparing dinner. It
seemed to Lev that she was intentionally clanging pots against each
other as if to overpower the competing performances. Lev shook his

head to clear it and tried to listen to Shmu.

"So we know you can't open the fridge door on Shabbos if you know the light will go on. The forbidden category of work is *hav'arah*, lighting a fire. But my rabbi says there's something else going on here, but I can't figure out what it is."

"Okay," Lev said, "there's another rule at work, yes, but it's not another category of prohibited work. It's something about how the rabbis viewed causation, you know, when someone sets in motion something that ends up causing a result later on. Because one could say, 'Sure, I opened the fridge door, but I didn't turn on the light. The light went on as a result of the mechanism in the door; and even if you say that I did an act that set that mechanism in motion, in fact, I didn't even want the light to go on. I just wanted to open the door and get something out of the fridge.' It's a lot different than actually reaching out and flicking on the light switch."

"I know!" said Hudi, who momentarily ceased his drumming. "The rule of *kocho c'gufo dami*: your strength is like your body. Whatever you set in motion, it's like you yourself did it."

"Could be, Hudi," Lev said. "What do you think, Shmu?"

"I don't think that's it because that applies to damages. If I run in the street and my shoes kick up stones that break a pot, then I've got to pay for the pot. So it doesn't work here."

"What do you think, Hudi?"

"I think that just because Shmu says it, doesn't automatically make it wrong."

Shmu reached around Lev and punched Hudi's shoulder. "Hey!" Hudi shouted, and the horseplay began.

While the usual chaos unfolded, Lev looked down at the pile of holy books that Shmu had assembled on the table. Shmu had pulled Tractate *Shabbos* from his father's Talmud volumes in the bookcase in the living room. Suddenly, Lev remembered where the answer could be found.

"Shmu, look at page thirty-four or thirty-five of Tractate *Shabbos*, I think on the second side of the page. Somewhere around there you should find a discussion of the principle of *'psik reishe v'lo yamus,'* which literally means, 'Can you cut off the head of chicken and expect that it won't die?' You see the difference between that example and the other ones?"

"Maybe . . ."

"Okay, I'm in a hurry so I don't have time to pull it out of you. Psik reishe applies when you set in motion something that will inevitably result in another thing occurring. I pull open the fridge door and I know as the door opens that the light will turn on. In that case, I'm responsible for turning the light on. Get it? Can I cut off the head of a chicken and expect it won't die? No, there's no doubt it will die—it's inevitable. I've set in motion a chain of events that will result in the transgression. But if there's doubt about the outcome, then I'm not responsible."

"So the key is that it has to be inevitable?" asked Shmu.

"That's right. Even if you hope that the transgression won't happen, nevertheless, when the transgression is unavoidable, it doesn't matter what you intended. And the inevitable result doesn't have to happen right away. It can happen sometime in the future and you're still responsible."

"I think I've got it," Shmu said.

His mother appeared from the kitchen. "Hi, Imma," Lev said. "I'm going to take a shower."

"You're supposed to shower last," she said. "It's Moti's time for a shower."

"I've got a meeting at school tonight and I may not be back until pretty late, so I would like to shower now. Okay?"

"I don't mind," Moti piped.

"What kind of meeting?" she asked.

"About Israel. You know, how we can make arguments that would convince people not to hate Israel."

"People hate Israel?" Moti asked from the floor.

"Only stupid people hate Israel." His mother turned to Lev: "Since when are you interested in making arguments in support of Israel?"

"Imma!" Lev said, "how can you say that? I lived in Israel for a full year! I love Israel!"

"All right," she said, raising her hands in surrender, "don't get all out of joint about it. Take a shower out of order if it means so much to you."

"I don't mind," Moti said again.

"Of course you don't mind," his mother said. "If it were up to you, you would take a shower only once a year."

Moti stood up, his face serious as he peeked over the top of the dining room table. "That's right," he said, "once a year."

Lev was going to get up from the table, but before he could, Moti came over and climbed onto his lap, still clutching his baseball cards. He began to turn them over on the table in front of him one by one. Lev pulled him close. "What's up, monkey breath?"

"Nothing," Moti said. "Mets playing Pirates tonight." He arranged the Mets lineup on the table. When he had finished the starting roster, he put the rest of the cards on the table and reached behind his head with both hands, grabbing the back of Lev's head and pulling it down toward his. Moti turned his face and whispered directly into Lev's ear so only he could hear: "Do people really hate Israel?" he asked. "Why?"

"It's just like Imma said. Only stupid people. They're jealous. Don't worry about it."

"I don't like it," Moti said softly. He paused, but he didn't let go of Lev's neck. "Why do you and Shmu want to cut a chicken's head off?"

"We don't want to cut a chicken's head off," Lev whispered back. "We're just talking about the Talmud, about Torah. We would never, ever cut a chicken's head off. Okay?"

"Okay," Moti said, and he let go and turned back to his cards.

Lev kissed the top of his brother's head and deposited him between Shmu and Hudi so he could continue laying out his baseball cards on the table while they studied Torah. Because Moti was so small, he pulled his legs up and knelt on the chair. As Lev watched him, he noticed Moti's pants—dungarees repaired with thick brown patches. Indeed, there were patches sewn onto patches. Lev recognized those pants: they had been his when he was six years old and they had served each of his brothers in turn since. Lev saw Moti's tiny ritual fringes peeking out the back of his shirt. The garment had been laundered innumerable times and the fringes attached to its four corners had degenerated into fluffy balls of fraying yarn. On the corner of the *tzitzis*, Lev could make out a faint "LL" drawn by his mother with a black marking pen when he had been Moti's age. Those tzitzis had belonged to Lev at one time and had been passed down from brother to brother. Lev asked himself: Do we really have so little money or is it just that everything has to be a reenactment of the chain of tradition with us, even hand-me-downs? As Moti sat between his two older brothers flipping over his baseball cards, Shmu draped his arm over his slender shoulders.

Lev had observed scenes like this countless times before, but this time before turning away, he focused on the details. He was trying to preserve them in his memory the way an ancient voyager might, looking back at his homestead as he crested a hill, taking in his last view of the smoke rising from his family's hearth and disappearing into the wind.

Lev took his shower and then got dressed as quickly as he could. He wanted to wear one of his Shabbos shirts, the good shirts that the boys were only supposed to wear to synagogue on the Sabbath. The boys' bedroom had a closet, but the crowded beds blocked its door, so all of their "hang-up clothes" were stored in a small room off his parents' bedroom that his mother used for laundry and to store the Passover dishes and utensils. That room was supposed to have been for his baby sister, but Moti turned out to be a boy, and that was that. Lev chose the best of his Shabbos shirts, a pale blue Oxford, and stole back into the bedroom to finish dressing. He didn't want his mother to see him wearing a Shabbos shirt on a weekday evening, so Lev put on his outer coat, buttoned it up and went directly to the front door. "Shalom, everyone," he shouted.

His mother intercepted him just as Lev was about to escape. "Aren't you going to eat dinner?"

"They're going to serve pizza," he lied.

"Kosher pizza?"

"C'mon, Imma," he whined, "it's a Zionist group. Of course the pizza will be kosher."

"Haven't you ever heard of Socialist Zionists? Labor Zionists? Those guys would rather die than eat a slice of kosher pizza."

"Give me some credit, please."

"Okay," she said. But before she turned away and let the door close, she gave Lev a searching look, like she suspected the whole Zionist meeting thing was a hoax, like he was pulling a fast one on her.

As the door slammed shut, Lev couldn't help but ask himself whether he had just cut the head off a chicken.

11.

The café that Angela had selected was on the ground floor of a brownstone in Brooklyn Heights. When Lev arrived, he found her seated at a table in the corner near a window that faced the street. Logs were burning in the fireplace. As he entered, he pulled off his kippah.

It was already dark outside and the flickering light from the fireplace swirled around Angela. She was wearing a black woolen skirt and a red sweater that hung off her left shoulder. From time to time, she shifted its neckline from one shoulder to the other, as if she needed to let each one in turn have access to the air. He could see her prominent collarbones as they peeked out from the neckline, first on one side and then on the other. Her hair sat elegantly on the top of her head, crowned by two teak wooden chopsticks topped with carved orange coral coronets.

They each ordered cappuccinos and Angela ordered a slice of cheesecake. Angela warned Lev that she probably would be disappointed by the cheesecake. She liked the Italian kind, which was light and lemony, and this cheesecake was probably Jewish cheesecake, which was too sweet and dense. She hoped she didn't offend him by telling the truth.

No, she didn't offend him, Lev told her. Frankly, he didn't really care whether she had problems with Jewish cheesecake or not. She told him that she was happy he had that attitude because she had very strong opinions about food. She was convinced that no food on earth came close to Italian food, and she was not about to stop expressing her views. But she was glad that he understood that if she criticized Jewish cheesecake, it wasn't anti-Semitism. Lev told her that this was probably the third time in their brief acquaintance that she had said something about the Jews and had to add a proviso that she wasn't an anti-Semite. That wasn't a good average.

"Well," she said, "in point of fact, a sample of three is not enough to draw any statistical inferences, if you want to be technical about it."

He told her that, actually—in point of fact—he didn't want to be technical about it.

"Oh, I'm so glad you understand. So, Levinski—"

"Livitski!"

"Whatever. I talked the whole way through our last dinner. Tell me about yourself."

Lev froze, trying to figure out whether Angela was teasing him. No one ever asked him about himself. The question on its face seemed preposterous. Talk about yourself as just yourself? Not about where you came from and how you fit in? But Angela couldn't be asking him about how he fit in because relative to her, Lev didn't fit in at all. Wherever he fit in, it was in a realm other than where Angela fit in.

Angela leaned toward him across the table, fixed him with her large brown eyes and slowly raised her head, encouraging him to confide in her. In the face of his continued silence, she said, "You know, Lev, I can tell when I make you nervous because you put your front teeth over your lower lip and kind of chew on it."

Lev immediately pulled his lower lip from under his teeth and smiled with his lips closed tight. Angela sighed and said, "For example, what's going on right now in your apartment while you're here with me?"

So she wasn't teasing him; apparently she really wanted to know something about him. The floodgates opened. Lev began to tell Angela things he generally never talked about with anybody, even his friends from Brooklyn College. They weren't deep dark secrets; they were just things he never felt anyone was particularly interested in. He described how he shared a small bedroom with his four brothers. There were two sets of bunk beds set against opposite walls and one folding cot in between, which the boys opened only when it was time for Moti to go to sleep. When the cot was open, there was no room to walk between the lower bunks and the cot, and there was almost no floor space in front of the door. Each of his brothers had to climb into bed almost directly from the hallway. His younger brothers grabbed onto the foot-boards of the lower bunks and vaulted into bed. Elya and he reached up to the top bed posts and pulled themselves into the upper tiers. To get out of bed, they simply reversed the process.

Lev had never appreciated how strange this arrangement was until a friend from Israel had come to visit and had remarked, in passing, "I never knew that American Jews could be poor."

Angela laughed. She had a similar arrangement with her younger sister, Estelle. They shared a small room with a trundle bed. Every night when they opened it, there was no way to walk in the room without scrambling onto the bed.

Lev confessed that even though his setup was odd, the fact was that he really didn't mind it too much. He liked his brothers, they were a lot of fun, they were his best . . . He was going to say *friends*, but he thought that sounded pathetic—so he said they were his best *buddies*.

Angela laughed. "Buddies? *Buddies*? No one says *buddies* anymore. You're just embarrassed to call them your best friends, aren't you?"

"Yes. But I do have friends. I mean friends that I'm not related to."

"Well, you shouldn't be embarrassed—at least in front of me. Because I'll tell you something: my sister Estelle is my best friend. No—more than my best friend. She's my *only* friend."

"What about Marie?"

"Marie is my best buddy," she said, "but she's not my best friend. I think you know what I mean."

"What about your other siblings?" he asked her.

"Well," she said, "I have two older brothers and one other younger sister besides Estelle. Where I come from, when you're a girl and you have brothers, well that means that me and my sisters aren't expected to really amount to anything. That's up to my brothers. They're wonderful guys—they always stand up for me and they always try to be nice, even though they aren't that good at being nice, if you want to know the truth. And unfortunately, they really are pretty dim. I mean, they weren't even able to make it through Brooklyn dumbass College. But anyway, because there are two boys in the family, my parents don't have any expectations of us girls. The only thing they expect from us is that we don't get pregnant."

"You mean that you don't have sex?" Lev cringed that such an indecent thought had escaped his lips.

Angela snorted at his prudishness. "No, they've given up on that a long time ago. The only thing that really matters to them is that we don't get pregnant. Because that's a shame that can't be hidden."

At her prompting, Lev told Angela about his parents. His father was a mid-level bureaucrat in New York City government who worked for the Office of Management and Budget.

"Oh, he does budgets!" she exclaimed. "I love budgets. You can learn so much from budgets. You can learn what people care about. You can learn what they're afraid of. You can see how they try to plan for the future. You can even see the things that they wish would just go away. I love budgets!"

Lev's father also did the *New York Times* crossword puzzle every day—in ink because he never made a mistake. Lev told Angela this with pride, and also about how every evening at dinner, his father gave the boys a new word to memorize so they could *enhance their word-power*. "That's exactly how he says it, too."

"What word did he give you last night?" Angela asked.

"*Enigmatic.*"

"What's it mean?"

"Difficult to understand, mysterious, puzzling."

"Use it in a sentence."

"Angela Pizatto is very enigmatic."

She clapped her hands together. "Oh, I like that word!" she said. "Your father sounds cool. Maybe someday I'll meet your father and we can talk about budgets!"

"Maybe someday," Lev said, thinking *never*. "What does your father do?"

"He's an insurance adjuster. He travels around and looks at accidents and fires and disasters and tells people how much they can expect to get out of their little tragedy. You might think that would be a depressing job, but he likes it. He's a pretty upbeat guy. Unlike my mother."

Lev started to laugh as if she were making a joke, but abruptly stopped when he saw her expression darken. Angela continued with a frown, "I don't really like my mother. Not a nice person."

Lev was shocked. He didn't know that you even had an option not to like your mother.

"What about you?" she asked. "Do you like your mother?"

Now she was asking whether he liked his mother! Normally, he would have just said, *Sure, I like her.* But for some reason, he didn't feel like lying to anyone else that evening.

"I'm kind of afraid of my mother," he confessed.

"How about your father?"

"No. He's a sweet soul."

"I see: so you don't like your mother either."

"I didn't say that."

"Oh, you did say that," she said with a giggle. "You did. Yes, you did."

Graciously, Angela changed the subject. "Do you have any hobbies?" she asked.

"Any what?"

"Hobbies. You know, like stamp collecting or birdwatching."

"No—do you?"

"Of course not!" she exclaimed. "It was a trick question! But seriously, what do you do in your spare time?"

"I don't think I have any spare time. What do you do in your spare time?"

All of Angela's time is spare time, she divulged, since she doesn't work regularly, and since she doesn't do any homework because she doesn't have to, and she spends as much time out of the house as she can so she can avoid her mother and doing household chores. In tax season, she spends some of her time doing people's returns and makes enough spending money to last the rest of the year, but she generally spends it on clothes, which is why she never has enough to really do fun things. But the rest of the time, she just hangs around with her buddies. They just shoot the shit and mess around—it's so boring, boring, boring, boring, boring, and she rolled her eyes—she repeated the word over and over like she was driving a big nail into a thick piece of wood; until finally Lev interrupted her.

"Okay, I get the point."

"I'm just saying that I thought that once I got to college, I wouldn't be bored, but it isn't working out that way."

"Well," he said, "you have too much spare time and I have none, but I'm just as bored as you are. I get up at 6 a.m. every morning and I go to synagogue and pray the morning prayers. And then for the whole day, we have a lot of religious rules to observe—you know, there are at least 613 of them. And when I'm not following all those commandments, I go to Brooklyn dumbass College, but unlike you, it's not easy for me because I take all these political theory and history courses and then I have to do homework and then I come home and do more homework and then I help my brothers with their home-work, which is my major chore, and then we all *shlep* ourselves to evening prayers with my father; and then when I have a few minutes I have a Talmud study session a few times a week with a friend of mine and then the weekend comes and there's the Sabbath to observe and then everything starts all over again. So a lot of the time it's so boring, boring, boring, boring, boring." He rolled his eyes at her.

She laughed. "What's this Talmud study session thingy?"

He explained that Jews study the Babylonian Talmud, a discussion of the Torah and its laws that began to be compiled by the rabbis around two thousand years ago.

"Babylonia!" she shouted. "Get out of town!"

"Yes, Babylonia," he explained to her. "The Talmud is written in Aramaic and Hebrew."

"What's Aramaic?" she asked.

"It's a dialect of Hebrew. It's what most people in the Middle East spoke to each other back around a couple of thousand years ago. It's what Jesus spoke."

"No it isn't," she said authoritatively.

"Yes it is. Why? Do you think Jesus spoke English?"

Angela paused for just an instant. Her comebacks were usually so quick that Lev knew immediately she had thought exactly that. But instead she said: "No—Italian."

They both burst out laughing.

"Yeah, so more," Angela said.

"More what?"

"More stuff about the Talmud," she demanded.

Lev was through talking about the Talmud. When it came to An-gela, studying the Talmud seemed the least relevant thing about him. Lev reprimanded himself for his irresistible urge to scratch his Jewish itch in front of her. Why had he brought the whole thing up in the first place?

But he couldn't just leave it there.

So he explained that he had been studying the Talmud for almost fifteen years and he had barely just grazed the surface. There were so many pages that if you studied one folio page each day, which is really two pages, one on each side of the folio, it would take seven years and five months to finish if you didn't miss even one day.

"That's about 5,400 pages," Angela blurted. "And some change."

"There's that math thing again," he observed, "the one that's not hereditary."

"Yes!" she said proudly. "You remembered!"

"Anyway," Lev continued, "my father actually did it—he studied a folio page every day for seven years and five months, and then he went to a big party at Madison Square Garden with twenty-thousand other Jews who had done the same thing." What Lev didn't tell Angela was that he, too, had been studying every day and he had a little more than three years to go before he could join his father, who was repeating his study of the entire Talmud, at the celebration at Madison Square Garden. At least, that was what he had always planned.

"But it's very hard and most people forget what they learn faster than they learn new stuff."

"Most people," she repeated. "What about you?"

Lev deliberated how to answer. It was complicated and he wasn't enthusiastic about prolonging this discussion. That part of his world seemed off-limits when he was flirting so enthusiastically with a Catholic girl. A basic tenet of being Jewish was to avoid mixing the sacred with the profane, and it seemed that Talmudic study, on the one hand, and Angela, on the other, was an exemplar of just that forbidden compound. Not that Angela was profane in an indecent, vulgar way. Just profane in an irreligious way. Maybe the word he was searching for was *ordinary*. She was profane in an ordinary way. Not that she was ordinary, either—she was actually exceptional in so many ways. But ordinary in the way that Monday is ordinary and the Sabbath is holy. In that way.

Lev decided to get through it as quickly as possible, so he told Angela that he forgot each page of the Talmud as soon as he learned the next one, as if there were only a finite number of pages he could fit into his brain and he had to discard one page to make room for the next.

Angela was skeptical. "That don't make sense," she shot back at him. "You don't seem stupid enough to forget every page you learn and still keep on learning new pages."

"Yeah, well sometimes I can remember a page—you know, it might pop into my mind and I can remember it. But only that page."

"Wow," Angela said, shaking her head, "Lev, I can see your front teeth again. You're the worst liar I've ever met!"

"I'm not lying!" Lev protested.

"But you're not telling the truth either."

"It's hard to explain."

"Give it a try."

Lev gave it a try. He explained that each printed page of the Talmud had a unique topography, the Aramaic text arranged in blocks of print in the center of each page, surrounded by medieval Hebrew commentaries that were printed in a smaller exotic font on the margins of each page. Because the commentaries printed in the margins varied in length, the Talmudic text in the middle and the commentaries on the side changed shape on each page.

"It's like the text in the middle of each page is a country surrounded by an ocean," Lev explained. "For some reason, when I learn a page of the Talmud, I can recall the shape of the country on each page and where each item of information is stored, like cities that are spread across each country. The pages become like maps for me."

"You mean you have a photographic memory?"

"Not really. If you ask me where the Talmud discusses something specific, I won't be able to recall it. But the next day it might pop into my mind. Or sometimes even a few minutes later. Or sometimes, someone says something and a page pops into my mind and I can see the discussion about that thing. But I can't do it whenever I want to. Just happens."

Angela looked at him curiously and he felt he had to explain himself further. "Did you ever meet someone who when you're talking to them all of a sudden they say, 'That reminds me of a joke,' and then they tell you a joke that's kind of related to what you're talking about, or maybe not so much; and then a few minutes later the same thing will happen: 'Hey, that reminds me of another joke,' and they'll tell you another one?"

"Oh, yeah," Angela said, nodding. "I have an uncle just like that. He's loony."

Lev flinched. "Yeah," he muttered, "well it's kind of like that . . . only hopefully, not as obnoxious."

"You know, I kind of got the same problem," Angela confessed. "But for the subway. When I was a little girl, my family once went from Bensonhurst all the way to the Bronx and I was sitting on a seat with one of the subway maps stuck on the wall behind me. I got up on my knees on the seat and I began looking at the map, you know with all the colored subway lines. I just thought it was the coolest thing in the world. By the time we got to the Bronx, I had looked at the entire map and it's like I had traveled every subway line and stopped at every station. After that, I could tell you how to get to any place in New York without looking. And if I ever travel through a station, I can tell you where the entrance and exits are—where you should stand on the platform to get to the right exit or to make the quickest transfer and how to cross over without paying another fare. I think it's really interesting. So I'm always talking about it, you know, telling people how to go here or there, what lines to take, where to stand on the platform." Angela stopped suddenly and looked down at the table for an instant and then back at Lev. "Yeah, but I can tell a lot of people just aren't interested," she admitted. "I can tell they just don't want to hear it, but I tell them anyhow."

"I just thought it was because you were bossy."

"Well," she said, "it's also because I'm bossy."

"Can you do that trick with other things?"

"Nope, just the subway. You?"

"Just the Talmud. Once it crawls into my head, I can see the page where it lives, like a photographic memory. But not exactly, because it only works with the Talmud. I can't do that trick with anything else."

"Yeah, me too," Angela said with a tone of resignation. Then she perked up. "You know, if we had babies together, then you know, our genes could combine and those kids might just be fucking geniuses!"

Lev gaped at Angela. How completely outrageous her speculation had been! If we had babies together! What could she be thinking? He quickly checked his lower lip and sure enough, it was cowering beneath his front teeth.

Angela snickered. "Don't panic, Lev. It was just a hypo."

"Of course," he muttered. "I knew that."

"Yes, I'm sure you did. Still," she said, "your life sounds a lot more interesting than mine. It doesn't sound so boring to spend time in Babylonia."

"Maybe not," he said, "but it is."

"Was it always boring?"

Lev thought about that for a few moments. "Yes, always boring but I just didn't appreciate how boring it was."

"Why not?"

"Because I've been sleepwalking through my life."

"Oh," she said, nodding her head, "I know all about that. Oh yes, I know all about sleepwalking through life."

Angela paused and gave a little shake of her head, as if clearing it. "Well," she continued, "I can't remember ever having such a wholesome conversation."

"Wholesome?" he asked. "Wholesome, like it had one food from every food group? That kind of wholesome?"

"Yes, kind of. In a good way. You listened to me and I listened to you and we took each other seriously. I mean, I don't get that very often."

"Why not?"

"I'm not quite sure. I just talk trash with people, just stupid stuff. Trying to put each other down, trying to hide when our friends, our buddies, say things that hurt us. Everything is just put-downs. Where I come from, being smart and thinking about things only lets other people make fun of you. They don't give a rat's ass about being smart. Or maybe it's just like I told you when we first met, that people—or I should say, guys—are more interested in fucking me than talking to me."

Lev clamped his lips shut in an attempt to hide his front teeth from Angela. He pursed his lower lip to further deflect her from the effect her last statement had on him.

"But this was . . . yes . . . a wholesome conversation," she repeated.

"If you were to spend some time where I come from, wholesome conversations would get old pretty fast. All we Jews do is talk and argue and shout in one another's faces about the same things, year after year."

"That kind of sounds like fun."

"Until it isn't anymore."

"Ah," she said with a knowing smile. "Something changed. Care to talk about it?"

"I'm still not ready to talk to you about it."

"And I guess that's still the right answer."

They were silent for a while. Angela seemed lost in thought, gazing at the little candle on the café table, her eyes adorned by the glimmering light. He couldn't believe this was the same woman as the one who only two nights earlier had terrorized him and the diner staff.

Finally, Angela smiled. "I think we should do this. I think if we do, we won't be so bored with things. Maybe we'll wake up a little, sleepwalk a little less. And this could be fun—no one having the slightest idea." She grinned. "No one suspecting a thing. Like secret agents."

He feared she could hear his heart thumping in his chest. He looked out the window and saw that it had begun to rain. He thought: if we were standing naked together in the rain out there, the water would be running down her slender neck and gathering in little pools in the shallow indentations on the top of each of her collar bones. And I could put my mouth on them and I could take sips from those little pools.

"Hey, Levinski," she said.

"Livitski!"

"Whatever . . . I think I lost you there for a moment. Care to share your thoughts?"

"No . . . Anyhow, what thing should everyone not be suspecting?"

She shrugged her shoulders. "We'll have to see, won't we?"

"Yes," he said. "Like secret agents."

She leaned forward and folded her hands on the edge of the table as she spoke in a low voice. "Here are the rules. No talking with each other on campus. We pretend we don't know each other, or just enough to say hello. We meet in Brooklyn far away from Brooklyn dumbass College and our neighborhoods. Deal?"

"You just described how we avoid each other. What about when we are together?"

Her lips settled into a line. "How should I know?"

Then he said something that came out of a part of his brain that he had never used before, that he didn't even know existed until that moment. "Well, what do I get out of this deal?"

She looked at him impassively. Then she slowly shook her head back and forth as if to say: why is he asking me this stupid question? "You get *me*, is what you get," she said in a low voice. She said it with unembellished self-assurance as if she were entirely confident of her desirability. "The real question is, what do *I* get?"

"You get me," he shot back, but without much conviction. It came out of his mouth like a question, with a slight inflection at the end.

She narrowed her eyes and frowned. "Well, we'll have to see whether this is a square deal or not, won't we?"

Lev was stung and she must have seen his hurt, because she flashed him a bright smile. "Oh! You're so easy to tease! I love it."

Lev didn't respond. He was a novice at this flirtation game, the subtle intimation that said almost nothing but conveyed everything.

"Stop frowning," she said. "Is it a deal?"

"Deal."

She slid her two hands to the middle of the table, stood up and leaned over. "It's time to seal the deal," she said.

He looked up at her from his seat and the ceiling lamp above them framed her face in light. Wisps of her black hair glittered like a corona around her expectant face. The coral crowns of the chopsticks peaked over the top of her head.

"Lev, are you on Earth or what?"

"What do you mean?"

"We need to seal our deal." And she bent all the way forward and brought her face close to his, tilted her head and closed her eyes. "What are you waiting for?" she murmured. "The Second Coming?"

"The First," he replied. And then they kissed each other's lips very lightly and slowly, and she stuck her tongue just inside his mouth, and it was so cool and sweet, her pink tongue, like she had just finished licking that spoon of hot fudge, whipped cream and vanilla ice cream at the diner.

III

The prohibition forbidding a Jewish man from having sexual relations with the daughter of an idolater comes from a law transmitted to Moses himself at Mount Sinai. For the Master has said: 'If a Jew has sexual relations with an Aramean woman, zealots are permitted to kill him.'

But the Rabbis have added: This law given to Moses on Mount Sinai applies only to sexual acts between a Jewish man and the daughter of an idolater that are committed in public, but it does not apply to sexual intercourse committed privately, in secret.

- Babylonian Talmud, Tractate Avodah Zarah 36B -

12.

Their kiss changed everything. While it was inevitable that Lev and Angela would have shared a kiss eventually, Angela was impatient to begin, so she engineered that first deal-makers' kiss so they could put it behind them once and for all.

With that kiss, Lev realized a number of things. The first was that no matter what happened, Angela and he were not just going to be friends. As Angela had made clear at their first meeting, spinning out of the tight orbits that delineated their lives and colliding with one another wasn't just so they could be pals. No, she had been correct that he wanted more than just a series of conversations with, as she had described herself, an Italian *Catholic* chick.

Lev's second realization was that he was certainly no longer on the derech. Before that kiss, he wasn't sure exactly where he was. He suspected that he might have fallen off, but his first attempts with Angela to understand how that felt had been so disastrous that he wondered whether he hadn't, subconsciously at least, crawled back onto the path. But now he was convinced that he was off the derech. Because you couldn't kiss a girl like Angela—not just a Catholic girl, but a girl so entirely alluring and at the same time so unquestionably forbidden—and still entertain the delusion that somehow you were walking in the ways of your forefathers.

When he got home later that night, Lev climbed into his bunk bed and lay there thinking about Angela and where they might be headed. So much had changed; but so much hadn't. Come morning, Lev would be in synagogue with his father and Elya mumbling the morning prayers, kippah on his head and tzitzis under his shirt. As he lay there in the darkness, his eyes open to the hazy ceiling floating above him, Lev began to ponder the meaning of the preliminary morning blessings that he would be saying in a few short hours.

It had been years since he had thought about what they really meant. The first one was open to profoundly different interpretations. Its more literal interpretation was: *Blessed are you God who gave the rooster understanding to distinguish between day and night.* This made sense, for in ancient times, without the rooster to announce sunrise, Jews would have slept through the dawn, the proper time to rise and pray to God. But the Hebrew word for rooster had an alternative, more poetic meaning—*heart*—which would transform the blessing into *Blessed are you God who gave the heart understanding to distinguish between day and night.*

For the first time, Lev was convinced that the poetic interpretation had to be the right one. Because he knew that he was able to distinguish between day and night. Angela was night—scary, unknown, seductive, mysterious night—and his life on the derech was day. He knew the difference, but suddenly this blessing, which he had repeated each morning for years and years, meant something different to him. God had wanted human beings to be able to discern between the day and the night, between the sacred and the profane. He had endowed them with that capacity. The rabbis wanted their followers always to choose the day; but what the rabbis wanted was not necessarily what God wanted. God wouldn't have given humans the ability to differentiate between the day and the night, between the holy and the profane—and the Jews would not be required to bless Him for it—if they weren't expected to exercise that ability.

But God surely didn't expect that everyone would always get it right, did He? Otherwise, why grant the capacity to make choices in the first place? And had not the Sages of Blessed Memory, when musing on whether humans had free will or not, declared that *Everything is from Heaven, except the fear of Heaven?*

On the other hand, maybe the blessing was really just about a rooster. Maybe Lev was just a rooster.

13.

When Lev woke the next morning, he found a text message from Angela on his phone: *tonite 7:00 icarus diner fort greene corner dekalb
@ clinton G train to clinton-wash. ave your bud A*

He texted back to Angela: *ok your bud lev*

She immediately texted back: *no names use letters*

Lev thought that Angela was overdoing the secrecy thing a bit, but
he didn't protest. He texted back: *o & k - good enough?*

No reply.

That evening, as he made his way from the DeKalb Avenue subway stop to the Icarus Diner in Fort Greene, Lev passed the massive
nursing home where his grandmother had been living for the past few
years. He gazed up at the windows thinking he might see her, but the
windows were tinted and he could discern no signs of life in any of the
rooms that lined the street, only rectangles of black glass as though
the building had been abandoned.

Before entering the Icarus Diner, Lev paused and quickly glanced
behind him to see if anyone was watching before snatching his kippah
from his head and stuffing it into his pocket.

Lev wandered through the dining area until he finally located
Angela, who had again arrived earlier than he. She had chosen a secluded booth in the far corner of the main dining room and was seated
facing the wall, her back to the crowd, perusing the menu. When he
approached, she slid across the banquette and he sat next to her instead of across from her.

She gave him a kiss on the cheek and said: "Should we order a
hot-fudge sundae?" When she saw the hitch in his expression, she
laughed. "Trust me, I won't make a scene this time."

"Promise?"

She nodded. "But first things first. Give me one of your father's
words-of-the-day."

Earlier in the week, it had been *bovine*, but Lev wasn't going to squander the opportunity on a word like that.

"*Infatuated*," he told her.

"I know what that means, but use it in a sentence anyhow."

"Lev Livitski is infatuated with Angela Pizatto."

She grinned and wriggled her shoulders with pleasure. The waitress approached and Angela ordered the hot-fudge sundae.

"Okay, since I already knew that word, give me another," Angela said.

The only word that Lev could come up with was the one his father had taught them on Sunday night earlier in the week. "*Cudgel*," he said.

Angela laughed. Then she turned to Lev, her forehead crinkled in puzzlement. "Is that a Jewish word?"

"It's a big stick, a club, like the kind that ogres beat each other with in fairytales. Not a Jewish word."

"Use it in a sentence."

"The little ogre beat the big ogre over the head with a cudgel."

"*Cudgel!*" she said, giggling, and she lay her head back on the top edge of the banquette and gazed at the ceiling. "*Cudgel*," she repeated with relish. "I like the way that word tastes!"

Then Angela sat up straight and got down to business. She had been thinking about how to conceal their relationship from the rest of the world. She had developed a plan for how they could see each other and still keep everything secret. The theory had to do with the geography of Brooklyn. Not the geography so much as the *anatomy* of the borough.

"You see," she explained, "Brooklyn doesn't really exist by itself. It only exists as a part of Manhattan. I mean, if New York City was a person, Manhattan would be the person's head and body and Brooklyn would be . . . you know . . . its shoe. Not even a leg. Not even a foot. Just the shoe."

"Just the shoe?" Lev asked, a little dispirited.

"Yeah," she repeated, deep in thought. "Just the shoe. So people who live in Brooklyn only travel between where they live and where they want to go in Manhattan." Angela raised her eyes to the wall they faced as if visualizing a subway map hovering in the air before her eyes. "People will go up," she pointed toward the ceiling, "but they almost never go down," she pointed toward the floor. "And they never go left or right from where they live. I mean, a person might go left or right if they have to pick up their grandparents or some special cheese or something, or maybe in the summer they could go down to Coney and the beach. But the rest of the time, they only travel up-down between their apartment and Manhattan. You know what that means, don't you?"

Lev was lost in the up-down and left-right.

"It means that if we don't want anyone to see us hanging out to-gether, we just have to stay below or left or right of Flatbush and Bensonhurst!" She smiled proudly.

"But there's nothing below Bensonhurst. Just water."

"Okay, you have a point, but there's plenty of stuff to the left of it."

She began ticking off all the places they could go without being detected, but instead of listing neighborhoods, she began reciting a catalog of subway stops: "Gravesend; Neptune Avenue; Sheepshead Bay; Utica Ave; Knickerbocker Ave; New Lots; Kingston-Throop Ave; Canarsie-Rockaway Parkway, Fort Hamilton Parkway." Lev wasn't re-ally paying attention. Instead, he was captivated by her face, how ani-mated it was as she mentally scanned the territory demarcated by the arteries and veins of the New York City subway system that circulated its human cells throughout Brooklyn. Angela's features were as much in movement as her hands usually were. She clenched her eyes shut as she flung out the various subway stations; then she twisted her mouth into a frown as her mind headed further east to less familiar areas; she would suddenly widen her eyes with excitement as she recalled more obscure stops on the various lines; and finally, she cracked open her lips and stuck out her tongue with delight as she finished her list.

"Okay," she concluded, "got it?"

He hadn't been paying attention to what she said. "Angela, those are subway stops. Can you use the other names?"

"What other names?" she asked.

"The neighborhood names."

"Oh, sure. There's Dyker Heights, Gravesend, Sheepshead Bay, Ma-rine Park, Fort Greene, Bed-Stuy, Coney Island, Canarsie. After that, if you're not careful, you could end up in Queens." She said *Queens* with distaste.

Although he had lived in Brooklyn his entire life, Lev couldn't re-call visiting any of those neighborhoods except for Coney Island and Fort Greene to see his grandmother.

"I don't know those neighborhoods," he confessed.

"But I'm thinking," she continued, "that our best bet is someplace off the G line because that line totally misses Flatbush and Benson-hurst, which is why I picked this place."

The waitress brought Angela her hot-fudge sundae. Lev held his breath as she took a taste.

"The fudge isn't hot," she said sadly. "Fact is—it's almost never really hot. I've learned to live with it." Angela focused on devouring her sundae, from time to time offering Lev a bite and observing with delight as he sucked the ice cream and fudge from the spoon. Every time Angela lifted the spoon toward his lips, Lev experienced a tiny jolt. It seemed a bit risqué to him to exchange saliva, maybe even DNA, with Angela.

When Angela finished, she leaned back and turned to Lev with a contented smile. He looked down at her and the sight of her creamy throat stunned him. He stopped talking.

"What?" she asked.

"I'm afraid I was thinking unclean thoughts."

"It's funny," Angela said, "but you say 'unclean' and I say 'dirty.' It's the same thing, isn't it?"

"I suppose it is."

"I don't mind if you think dirty thoughts about me." She lowered her head as she laughed and he could see the gentle slope of her shoul-ders, with dark wisps of her hair hovering over her silky skin. Lev suddenly knew he needed to kiss Angela. Despite his lack of sexual experience, he needed to put his mouth on Angela's flesh. He placed his lips on the nape of her neck for a moment and moved them across her skin, audibly sucking air into his mouth as he breathed in her bouquet. She squirmed with pleasure, turned her head as she raised it, her eyes shut, and pushed her fragrant hair up against his lips as she nuzzled the side of his face. She slid her body even closer to him and ground her hip against his.

Lev put his arm around her waist as Angela shifted closer to him. She took his hand from her waist, placed it on her stomach and slowly moved it up her rib cage to caress her breast. At the same time, she dropped her other hand under the table and dangled her fingers lightly on his crotch.

Angela had moved his hand and hers just a few inches, but for Lev, it was as if she had plucked him from a world of gray abstraction to one of lurid physicality. His hand on her breast; her fingers lightly floating over his crotch—this was a cocktail of sensations that he had only fantasized about. But here it was, not an imagined sexual encounter, but a real, tactile experience with a woman who was so utterly desirable that he could not have conjured her out of his deepest longings.

Angela sensed that these caresses, which were merely routine for her, were an ecstatic experience for Lev. She turned toward him and flashed him a wry, knowing smile. She stuck out her tongue, leaned into him and licked the lobe of his ear. "Easy there, Mr. Levinski," she murmured.

He didn't correct her.

While Lev and Angela carried on with one another, the waitress approached their booth from behind and stood by their table, just out of their line of sight. They didn't notice her. Finally, she cleared her throat and asked: "Will there be anything else?"

Startled, Angela looked up at her. "No thank you. We're only having dessert tonight," she said with excessive formality and then she burst out laughing. "Check, please!"

The waitress let herself grin. "Look at this one—he's blushing! How sweet!"

"He *is* sweet," Angela said, looking into Lev's face. "Imagine going out with a guy who blushes! Who woulda' thought?"

But Angela didn't blush. She didn't seem embarrassed in the least.

The prior week, Lev's father had enhanced the family's vocabulary by teaching them the word *brazen* and Lev knew its definition. But he hadn't really known how to use it in a sentence until that very moment.

Later that night as he lay in his narrow bunk bed, Lev pictured Angela lying next to her younger sister, Estelle, in the trundle bed that filled their bedroom. They were surely whispering together. Angela would be saying something like, "And then he blushed in front of the waitress. He turned red as spaghetti sauce!" Estelle, a faceless

73

but younger version of Angela in Lev's imagination, said, "Get out of town! Blushed!" And Angela would reply, "Yes. He was embarrassed." And her sister would say, "I would like to meet a guy who could be embarrassed about sex. That would be special." And Angela would say, "Yeah, you're so right. It *is* special... it is."

Or maybe not, Lev reflected. Maybe the conversation went like this: Angela would say: "And then he blushed in front of the waitress. He turned red as spaghetti sauce!" Estelle: "Get out of town! Blushed!" Angela: "Yes. He was embarrassed. Can you believe these Jews? Embarrassed that he had a hard-on, like there's something unnatural about that, like what did he expect if he was going to go out with *me*?" And Estelle would snort and say, "This guy sounds like a loser to me." And after a thoughtful pause, Angela would agree. "Yeah, you're so right. He *is* a loser . . . he is."

14.

Because Angela was so familiar with the subway system, she considered it a magical portal that could instantaneously transport them to anywhere within the Five Boroughs. In the early weeks of their relationship, she led Lev on a number of adventures in Brooklyn and Manhattan neighborhoods that Lev had rarely, if ever, visited. Given her acumen, Angela not only knew how to get to any destination touched by the underground system, but how to do it the fastest and most convenient way. Lev, on the other hand, had always been content to stay close to home, comfortable in the self-regulated ghetto of Flatbush where he lived. Before Angela, he was always a bit nervous when he was on the trains, compulsively checking the subway map on the wall of the cars, counting down the stations as he approached his destination. Traveling underground with Angela was a liberating experience.

It was also fun. Angela did not so much enter a subway car as commandeer it. As soon as the doors closed behind her, she would survey the train and set about fixing what she regarded as imperfect. If a passenger dropped trash on the floor of the car, Angela would announce, "Excuse me, you dropped something," and she would point to the crumpled trash on the floor. If the litterer tried to ignore her, Angela would repeat her message, only louder. She spoke with such authority that no one ignored her a second time. If Angela saw an old person standing in the car, she would push her way through the crowd to stand before any young man or woman who Angela believed should yield their seat. She showed no inhibition whatsoever. Angela would tap the seated person on the shoulder and tilt her head toward the swaying elder. There was no room for misinterpretation. Again, Lev never saw anyone refuse, but he wondered with just a hint of trepidation how Angela would react if they did.

As self-assured as Angela was in ushering Lev to their destination, she was otherwise incompetent in sorting out the details of what they were supposed to do when they got there. She dragged him to Coney Island in late October because she heard that you could see the aurora borealis there, which was not remotely true, in October or at any other time of year. They also traveled to the Brooklyn Aquarium late one night and stood outside in the cold in order to see the birth of a baby seal that Angela claimed was imminent. (It finally did happen—three weeks later.) They subwayed to Central Park to participate in a candlelight vigil mourning the death of John Lennon, but Angela had bungled the dates and they were two months early. They traveled to the Natural History Museum on a Monday, the only day of the week when it was closed.

But it didn't really matter to Lev whether these excursions met their stated objectives or not. He was content to embark on the most pointless adventures just to spend time with Angela. She was exuberant about everything she encountered and that exuberance animated Lev as well. When they walked in Brooklyn together, Angela's dark eyes would roam the streets and sidewalks, feasting on every sight. Everything for her was a superlative. "This is the windiest block in Brooklyn!" she would proclaim. "This is the most beautiful tree in Prospect Park!" "This bench right here has the best view of Manhattan!" "There is no better cannoli than this one anywhere in the world!"

There was one foolproof plan they came to prefer and many evenings after classes ended, they hopped the 2 Train to Clark Street, walked a couple of blocks to the Promenade in Brooklyn Heights, appropriated a park bench and gazed at the brilliant Manhattan skyline. Angela's favorite bench was where she had sat just a month before they started seeing each other. She'd gone there to view the searchlights beaming into the night skies as a memorial to the Twin Towers. Every time they visited that bench now, Angela peered across the harbor as if she expected the lights to be switched back on. She and Lev would spend a few hours there, talking, kissing and fondling each other until they became too chilled to sit still. Then they would make their way back to the Clark Street station and grab different trains that returned them to their different worlds.

15.

If Jewish denominations could be applied to Italians, Angela would have been deemed Modern Orthodox. Like Lev, she lived in an insular ethnic environment, where every person she routinely saw was the same as she was. And Lev was as forbidden to Angela as she was to him.

Consequently, Lev and Angela continued to take elaborate precautions to keep their relationship clandestine. Neither of them wanted to risk the fallout from families and friends. They continued to meet at obscure diners in outlying neighborhoods in Brooklyn. The Icarus Diner in Fort Greene was their favorite. The waitresses there indulged them: "Let us know when it's safe to come over, sweetie," they would whisper to Angela when the two were seated in their secluded booth.

Lev continued to remove his kippah. Without the skullcap, he thought they looked like a couple of Italian kids out on a date.

He made that observation to Angela one night a couple of weeks after they began seeing each other and she scoffed. They were walking on Atlantic Avenue on the northern edge of Cobble Hill and the street-lights were on. She stopped in front of an unlit window of a shop. "Look at us," she instructed as they turned and gazed at their murky reflections in the window.

"Yes," he observed, "just like I said: a couple of Italian kids."

"Let me tell you why you're full of crap," Angela said. She pointed to the reflection. "Your coat is two sizes too big for you and it's an old man's coat. Hand-me-down from your father, right?"

"Yes," he said defensively, "but it's camel hair."

"No Italian guy would be caught dead in that coat. Take a look at your pants: black Levis, right?"

"Yes, what's wrong with that?"

"Nothing, but Italian guys wear woolen pleated pants, slight flair at the bottom, no cuffs. And your shoes: you don't ever wear shoes, just sneakers."

"Very comfortable!"

"No doubt, but Italian guys only wear stylish shoes. They're not interested in comfort. Soles have to be leather too. And your shirt: button down, oxford blue or white. World's most boring shirt."

"Sorry."

"Don't apologize. Oh, and your hair—who cuts your hair?"

Lev didn't answer.

"You don't have to tell me. Your mother cuts your hair. She probably lines up you and your brothers, I bet even your father, once a month over some newspapers and uses that weird clipper they advertise on television late at night."

Lev wondered to himself: Who told her? Which of my brothers told her?

"Well, Italian guys spend as much money on getting their hair cut as you spend on your entire wardrobe." Finally, she said: "Look at your body. It's not an Italian's body."

"Not an Italian's body! In what way isn't it an Italian's body?"

"You're as skinny as I am!" she said, laughing. "What, you're just over six feet tall and you probably weigh around 175 pounds, am I right?

He weighed 170 pounds. "I'm not skinny; I'm wiry."

She burst out laughing. "Call it what you like; you're much skinnier than any Italian man I've ever seen. I can feel your ribs through your shirt! Italian men with your body would be in the gym all day bulking up so their necks would be thicker than your waist."

"Wow, I didn't know I was such a disappointment to you," he said morosely.

She took his arm in hers and pulled him along with her. She was laughing. "Don't change a thing! I like everything about you. I like the big overcoat, the black Levis; the comfy sneakers; even the Oxford button-down shirts with the fraying collars. And I especially like your *wiry* body."

"Yeah, but none of that stuff is up to your regular standards, is it?"

"That's right. But the truth is, Lev, I never really had any standards. I don't give a rat's ass about that shit. Boring, boring, boring: I just can't stand it anymore. Like leather soles matter; like anyone cares that your pleats sit flat against your dick and your cuffs break across the instep of your shoe."

"It doesn't matter to me," he said.

"It doesn't matter to you because you don't even know what I'm talking about." She stopped walking suddenly and held up her index finger as if she had suddenly remembered something. "That's one of the things I like about you. That you don't give a rat's ass about fashion."

They began walking again, arms linked. "Angela, speaking of fashion, let me ask you something. What's with the chopsticks you wear all the time to keep your hair up? Where'd that come from?"

"They're hair sticks, not chopsticks. I saw them on the shopping channel a couple of years ago and I knew that I wanted them. Some actress from a daytime soap showed how to use them and I knew they would look great on me."

"How did you know?"

"Because I've got a sexy neck. Many people have told me that."

"Yes, you do have a sexy neck. You must have a lot of those sticks. They look different every day."

"Oh yeah, maybe twenty or twenty-five pairs. They're my trademark, you know."

"Trademark?"

"Yeah, you're not going to see another chick that knows me ever wearing them while I'm still around. Everyone knows that they're my trademark."

Lev stopped and turned to Angela. "So even though you don't care about the fashion stuff for me, apparently you still care about that stuff when it comes to the way you dress."

She shook her head as if what he had suggested was so obvious that it was stupid to even mention it. "Yes, but I'm a woman," she declared as if the explanation answered all questions. They continued on in silence for a few minutes. "But I wonder: if you were wearing your kippah and we went to a delicatessen or something, I bet you all the Jews would think we were just another couple of Jewish kids out on a date, right?"

Before he answered, he thought, Now let's see how she takes it. Let's stop in front of a dark shop window and peer into it and let me point out her leather boots with the high heels; her stockings with the ornate fishnet pattern; her hyper-short skirt; her sleeveless silk blouse with the three upper buttons open to show off her décolletage, enhanced by her push-up bra; her perfect hair suspended in the heavens by her trademark chopsticks; her made-up face with the bright red lipstick; her garish red nails; and then let me point out to her the way she sashays when she walks, swinging her ass back and forth to tantalize anyone by her departure who wasn't otherwise entranced by her approach; yes, let's see how that comparison goes.

That's what he thought, but instead, he said: "Absolutely, that's what they would think. Just a couple of Jewish kids out on a date."

And Angela showed him a proud, self-satisfied smile.

16.

But they weren't just another couple of Italian or Jewish kids out on a date. From the moment of their first handshake, that conventional, businesslike physical contact, Lev was completely intoxicated by Angela. He had never felt such a consuming desire for anyone in his life. When he was with her, everything she said, every motion she made, seemed erotically charged. Brushing up against her or smelling her perfume would trigger a sexual response in him, not just in the place where lust generally resides, but in that more mysterious place beyond mere desire, not in the groin but slightly above it, in the unprotected soft somewhere between the navel and the spine where overwhelming longing lurks, waiting to be unleashed.

Angela knew that he was a sexual novice, but Lev didn't think that she understood just how chaste he was. And he also suspected that she had no idea how innocent was his clique of Orthodox friends at Brooklyn College, including two of his oldest and closest friends whom he had known since first grade. Their names were Tuvia and Pincus. Tuvi and Pinky and a dozen other observant Jewish young men and women from various neighborhoods throughout Brooklyn constituted their college social group, their *chevra*.

All of the Orthodox Jewish boys in Lev's circle were preoccupied with sex, but they had no outlet for their desire and for them to indulge in it was demeaning. They struggled to project indifference to the girls they hung around with. It was unthinkable that any of the guys would be brash enough to proposition the opposite sex; even innuendoes were inappropriate. To conspicuously come on to a woman—even to touch her casually without her permission—would have been not only scandalous but a humiliating display of one's weak willpower. Yet the sexual tension that sputtered among the Jewish crowd as they hung out together at college or at synagogue was unmistakable if one was attuned to its signs.

81

The Orthodox crowd had many strategies for stealing at least the semblance of sexual contact with one another. Young men and women crowded tightly together at the cafeteria tables with chairs pushed against one another, the outer surfaces of thighs, shoulders and arms of one sex grazing those of the other. Whispering secrets was another ersatz sexual contact. Either gender could cozy up close to the other and lean body against body, their lips mere millimeters from ears, able to breathe in the fragrance of the other, feeling the rush of breath in the erogenous zone of the ear as the secret was imparted. As the Jewish kids sat and flirted in their abstinent way, even taking a sip of soda from someone else's cup conveyed intimacy.

But the borders of acceptable behavior were brightly demarcated and when they were trespassed—if ever—nobody in Lev's constricted social universe ever heard about it. The idea that you would have meaningful erotic contact with a member of the opposite sex and then boast about it to others was out of the question. For example, over the fifteen years or so that Lev had been friends with Tuvi and Pinky, he had never heard either of them mention their exploits and he was uncertain whether they ever had any or whether they were merely being discreet.

While everyone knew where the borders were, the unstated rule was that if one of the guys succumbed to his urges and recklessly trespassed over the line, it was ultimately the responsibility of the girl to put a stop to what was transpiring. The rules required that the male take the initiative, to the extent that there was any initiative to take, and it was the responsibility of the female to politely refuse. On very rare occasions, one might be lucky enough to go out with an Orthodox woman who actually was willing to wander over the border. Invariably, however, she would make out for a while, just until it seemed that things might be getting interesting, then pull back and push the guy's hands away with a prim shake of her head and an indulgent smile.

These rules of conduct contributed to a misconception that Lev and his Orthodox male friends shared about women generally; namely, that women were not interested in sex at all. They believed that the most one could expect from a girl was that she would *permit* you to have sex with her, but certainly not that she herself would ever *want* it to happen. Lev and his friends believed women only put up with sex in order to become wives and mothers, but not that they, too, might seek sexual pleasure.

But Angela wasted no time in demonstrating to Lev that sex was, in fact, a two-way street. She corrected his ignorance with that first caress in the remote corner booth of the Icarus Diner. From the beginning, Angela was as interested in sex with Lev as he was with her.

It was only after Angela set him straight about the reciprocity of desire that Lev realized the evidence had been in front of his eyes all along. For years he had been hanging around with a girl from his neighborhood named Faigie Gruenstein. They weren't "in a relationship"—in fact, if asked, Lev would say they weren't even dating—but Lev and Faigie tended to gravitate toward one another whenever their circle gathered. One Friday afternoon in high school, he bumped into Faigie on the street. He had been sent by his mother to pick up an order of challah loaves for Shabbos and stopped to talk with Faigie on the corner of Coney Island Avenue and Quentin Road. It was spring and the cottonwood trees had shed their seeds in dense waves, the fluffy spores drifting through the afternoon air like snow. As Faigie and Lev chatted with one another, a cottonwood seed lodged in Faigie's curly auburn hair. Lev casually put out his hand and touched her hair to remove the seed. But the seed had become entangled and he couldn't just grab it with his two fingers and pull it out. He had to lean forward and use his other hand to brush away the cascade of hair adjacent to the trapped seed. The back of Lev's hand brushed against the side of Faigie's face and that casual touch aroused him. When he looked into Faigie Gruenstein's face, he could tell she also had been aroused. She stared into his eyes for a brief moment and then lowered her gaze modestly, a blush rising from her neck to her face.

But nothing came of that encounter. And when he looked back at what he had witnessed—a faint glimmer of Faigie's desire—he began to doubt the accuracy of his observation. It just didn't fit in with Lev's conception of the way women were wired.

Even Angela had been deceived into thinking lust was a man's prerogative. In her world, men were so overtly aggressive in seeking sexual favors that women almost always had to play defense; and when you're playing defense, it doesn't give you much of an opportunity to wonder how you might feel about the whole undertaking. Because

Angela never had to initiate sex, only beat it back within reasonable bounds, she rarely had a chance to ask herself what she really wanted.

Unlike Lev, however, she was familiar with the power of desire, at least when she was the object of it. As she had told him the first time they met, men were more interested in fucking her than talking to her. So Angela capitalized on her desirability to control the men who wanted her so badly. She imposed her will on them; made clear to her suitors and her boyfriends that in return for her occasionally giving it up, they would otherwise have to submit to her.

But early on, Angela understood that Lev's inexperience and tentativeness about sex would not make him an implacable pursuer; that if she rebuffed him in his amateur efforts at intimacy, he would stay rebuffed. That had been one of the motivations for her premeditated tantrum at the diner on their first date: she was looking for a leverage point. She had more or less admitted it to Lev when she confessed on the subsequent train ride toward Bensonhurst that she had misbehaved so badly because she wanted to show him that she was the one in charge, "that I don't take shit from anyone."

Lev's sexual reticence required Angela to take the initiative for the first time. And apparently, she learned that she liked sex a lot more when she set it in motion herself.

Even though Lev and Angela came to one another with vastly different levels of prior sexual experience—one having a lot of it and one having none at all—each of them, in their own way, was famished. Accordingly, Angela and Lev found themselves making out everywhere and anywhere they could. They embraced and groped each other feverishly, usually at night on the subway platforms because they didn't have any other place to do it. It was a frenzy of lips, tongues, teeth and hands in each other's shirts and pants and underwear. Angela never pushed Lev away—instead, they would tear themselves from each other, panting with desire and frustration, just as the subway train hurtled into the station, its iron wheels screeching. They would look wildly at each other and Lev could see in Angela's face the same question that was apparent in his: "What is this? What? Where is this coming from?"

17.

Because he had never hidden from Angela who he was—indeed, he had worn his kippah when he first approached her and even discussed with her the challenges of being Jewish—Lev made the mistake of thinking that Angela had at least a passing familiarity with the bundle of obligations he hauled around with him at all times. But he soon discovered that she understood very little about what it meant to be an observant Jew.

For the first few weeks of dating each other, Lev and Angela had gone out only on weeknights but never on Friday or Saturday nights. Lev assumed Angela understood that he was unavailable on the Sabbath. But in the fifth week of their relationship, she proposed visiting a dance club in Marine Park on a Friday evening, and Lev realized that she only had a cursory understanding of what Jewish life demanded.

He didn't really want to get into the details, so he demurred. "Yeah, well, I don't really know how to dance."

"I'll teach you."

"It's not a priority for me. To learn to dance."

"What's that supposed to mean?"

"C'mon, Angela, you know I can't go out on Friday night. You've got to know that Friday night to Saturday night is the Jewish Sabbath. It's called Shabbos."

"I know *that*, but I don't know why I *gotta* know it."

"Well, you live only a couple of blocks from Boro Park, so you must have noticed that neighborhood more or less shuts down every Friday night and all day Saturday."

"Yeah, of course I noticed that. All of us know that Boro Park doesn't budge on Friday nights and Saturdays. But anyhow, that's what *they* do. You don't do all the stuff that they do, do you?"

"Well, more or less."

"Get out of town! You mean you do what all the ones who dress in costumes do, the ones in the big black hats and the black bathrobes and the beards and the ear curls? They're called Hasidim, right?"

"Right."

"You know when I was little, I was scared of them. I thought they were witches or something. I used to think they were called 'I-see-dem' because when we saw a bunch of them, someone would always point and say 'I-see-dem.' But they were really saying 'Hasidim.'"

"Well, I'm not really like them. I'm modern. I mean in outlook and stuff."

"But you do a lot of the things that they do, right?"

"Yes, but I also do a lot of things that they would never do."

"Like, for example?"

"I go to college. I talk to people who aren't exactly just like me."

"Oh, you mean *me*, right?"

"Well, yes, I suppose so."

"They would never be caught dead talking to a chick like me, would they? I mean a Catholic chick."

"Or even a Jewish one."

"Who do they talk to?"

"Each other."

"They wouldn't be sticking their tongue into a Catholic chick's mouth, would they?"

"Into anyone's mouth."

Angela placed the heels of each hand on the slope of her hips, her fingers pointing down. Her elbows jutted out as she waggled her fingers against the side of her thighs in building irritation. "I don't get it. I thought you were over all that stuff."

"All what stuff?"

"All that Sabbath stuff."

"What made you think that?"

"Me."

"You?"

"Yeah, you're with me now. I thought you can't be a member of two clubs. You know, the Jewish club and the Catholic-girlfriend club."

"Well, I don't know why you thought that. *You're* a member of two clubs, aren't you?"

"No, I'm not. And by the way, we had this argument the first time we met, remember?"

"You have to admit that you're a member of the Jewish-boyfriend club and the Italian-Catholic-girl-from-Bensonhurst club," he said.

"That's not a real club, the Italian-Catholic-girl-from-Bensonhurst club. We don't have serious members in that club. You can go to church once a year and eat pizza or pasta now and then and still be a member. But your club is a lot more serious. So it's just not the same."

Lev looked away, closed his eyes for an instant and took a deep breath. Then he turned back to Angela. "Okay, but I'm still a member of both clubs. I haven't resigned from any clubs, okay?"

"What are you saying—we aren't ever going to go out on a Friday or Saturday?"

"More or less. I mean, for those twenty-four hours—or actually twenty-five hours—I don't go out or anything."

"You don't leave the house?"

"No, I leave the house to go to synagogue and visit friends and stuff, but I don't take the subway."

Angela did a double take and opened her mouth in dismay. "What do you have against the subway?"

"It's not that. We don't cook or travel in cars or buses or subways. We don't use electricity or turn lights on or off, stuff like that."

"You're shitting me."

"This will be really hard for you to believe, but I don't use the cell phone either."

"But you text, right?"

"Not even text."

"So that's why you don't answer my texts on Saturday," she muttered, covering her mouth with both her hands. She removed her hands, peered intently at Lev and asked, "What do you do for twenty-five hours each week?"

"On Friday night, I have dinner with my family. On Saturday, we go to synagogue and then I read books or hang out with my family or go to see friends."

"Hang out with chicks?"

"Sometimes, but not usually." Lev shook his head. "And not in the way you mean."

"And you're not watching TV or banging video games?"

"Nope."

"You're just talking to each other that whole time?"

"Sometimes we sing songs on Friday night."

She again covered her mouth. "Oh my God. They sing songs to each other," she whispered beneath her hands.

"Sometimes the whole family will play Monopoly. We like Scrabble, but we're not allowed to write down the scores, so that's kind of hard."

She summarized what he said in a whisper: "They play Monopoly. And they don't write anything down . . . so it's hard to play Scrabble . . . Scrabble! Lev! How can you stand it?"

"I don't mind it. I look forward to it every week. My whole family does. All the Jews look forward to it, at least the ones who bother about it like we do."

She shook her head in disbelief. "So you're saying that I'm on my own from Friday night to Saturday night, every week?"

"Saturday nights are fine, particularly in the winter when the sun sets early."

"Wait a minute—is there some sort of vampire thing going on here?"

Lev explained how the Jews demarcated the boundaries of the Sabbath from sundown on a Friday night to sunset on a Saturday.

"Well," Angela said, "Friday night is a big date night in my world. I'm not used to just hanging out with my family on Friday nights, you know. I'll have to find something to do to keep me busy if you're not around."

"Are you telling me you'll go out with other guys on Friday nights?"

Angela took a step toward him, straightened her back and pushed her chin out defiantly. "Yeah, that's what I'm telling you."

Lev stared at her. She returned a matter-of-fact smile that said, "What did you expect, that I would sit around waiting for the sun to set every week?" They had never discussed whether they were going to date each other exclusively, but it was clear from her threat that was precisely what she had expected, because otherwise, she wouldn't have brought it up at all. And exclusivity was what Lev had expected as well, judging by the sinking feeling in his heart. Angela was threatening Lev with infidelity if he refused to give up Shabbos.

Sure, he was off the derech; he was falling away from Jewish observance, but only because he wanted it to happen—or perhaps because he couldn't prevent it from happening—and not because anyone manipulated him into doing it. As smitten as he was with Angela, he wouldn't walk further away from the derech just to become somebody's lackey. He still believed that when you drifted away from the path, it had to be because you were confronted with irresolvable questions. There had to be a certain nobility to it, a questing after truth . . . or after something. As it was said about Aher, Elisha ben Abuya, he didn't just walk away. He left only after he heard the story of the son who fell to his death while performing commandments that guaranteed him a long and good life. But you don't breach the Covenant merely because your shiksa girlfriend threatens to date other guys on Shabbos. There had to be some standards, even when you were betraying your tradition.

"If you want to hang out with your girlfriends at some club and now and then dance with some of those guys who wear those nice clothes and shoes that you claim you don't care about, go ahead. But if I find out you're seeing other guys, then it's over between us."

For a second, Angela unwittingly registered her surprise that Lev had stood up to her, but she recovered quickly. "You're being pretty damn selfish with this Shabbos thing and not very sensitive to my needs."

"Angela, this is who I am. This is where I come from. I come from a place with a lot of obligations, a lot of debts I have to pay every day. You want to go out with me, then this is who I am. If you want me to be someone else, then you should go out with someone else. But don't expect me to be someone else for you. I'm not going to ask you to be someone else for me."

Angela went silent, shaking her head, her mouth set in a grim line. Minutes passed.

"You stubborn bastard," she said, but not angrily, almost in a tone of wonder. "Stubborn, stubborn bastard. All right, have it your way. Don't worry about old Angela. She'll be okay. She'll just sit in the dark with her ass on her hands on Friday nights so you can play Monopoly and sing songs to each other. But let me tell you something, mister," she said, wagging her finger in his face, "the rest of the time we hang out together had better be worth it. I'm putting you on notice that it better be worth it."

Lev liked this new feeling, this sensation of playing and not always being played; of being desired and not always being the only one desiring. He thought for an instant: Maybe this is what Angela experiences most of the time, why she makes herself so enticing and flirts so relentlessly. It felt like he had power and authority, and that felt good.

"Yeah," he said, "well, I'm not worried about that. And neither should you."

She shook her head and smiled. "Stubborn bastard."

18.

They had been seeing each other for nearly two months when early one evening, Angela said, "It's time for you to have the best slice of pizza in the entire world."

"Are we going to Italy?"

"Almost," she said. "We're going to Bensonhurst."

"Isn't that a little too close to home?"

"Don't worry about it. If anyone comes over to talk to me, don't say anything. Let me do all the talking."

They caught the 2 at the Brooklyn College/Flatbush Avenue station to Atlantic Avenue and walked through the underground tunnel to Pacific Street, where they picked up the M Train heading south toward Gravesend. They got off at the 18th Avenue stop and Angela led them down one of the main shopping thoroughfares in that part of Bensonhurst that was still dominated by Italians. Angela walked fast, her head down. Lev swept his eyes along the storefronts they passed. He was a bit surprised at how similar they seemed to the shops that lined King's Highway where his family did most of its shopping. He had expected Bensonhurst to be as different from Flatbush as Angela was different from anyone he had ever known. But from what he could see, the major differences were about food. In Bensonhurst, cheese and pasta shops stood in for Flatbush's delicatessens and appetizer establishments. That, plus the fact that there were many more pizzerias in Bensonhurst—more pizzerias per block than Lev could have imagined, and almost all of them named after Italian men: "Uncle Benno's Pizza," "Paulio's," "Pappa Renzo's," "Cousin Vincent and Son Pizza," and of course, "Tony's".

After a few short blocks, Angela turned east down a narrow street. A quarter of the way down the block, she stopped abruptly in front of a dim storefront. She turned to Lev and with a flourish of her hand, gestured toward the door. "Here it is," she announced, "the best pizza joint in Bensonhurst—maybe in the whole world!"

Above the door a worn tin sign announced the name of the establishment, "Nino's." Beneath the sign were other announcements, namely that this was "The Original Nino's—not to be confused with cheap imitators." Lev peeked through the dirty front window at a spare interior empty of customers. If he hadn't been with Angela, he would have assumed the pizzeria was closed.

He followed Angela as she pushed inside. Nino was there, an obese, hairy man in a soiled white apron, sitting by the cash register reading the *NY Post*. He was almost totally bald, but he had combed a furtive fringe of hair over his pate. He gave a warm greeting to Angela.

"Two of your best," she told Nino. "One pepperoni and one plain."

"Who don't like pepperoni?" Nino asked.

"This guy," Angela said, pointing to Lev with her thumb.

"Who's this fella?" Nino asked.

"Just a school buddy," Angela said casually. "I told him about your pizza and he made me drag him down here."

"Smart fella," Nino said.

Nino slid off the stool by the register, opened the grubby pizza oven and shoveled two slices of pizza into its depths, one with and one without pepperoni. As the pizza heated up, Nino and Angela gossiped about people and events that were entirely foreign to Lev. At one point, he heard Angela say: "Whaddya think he meant? Go figger that one out—it don't make no sense." Lev suddenly realized that Angela had two distinct ways of speaking—maybe even more than two. The one he had just overheard was the southern Brooklyn agglomeration of syllables, the stereotypical street accent that treated words like blunt instruments to be swung at one another. The other way that Angela talked was the way she talked with Lev—fluent, free-flowing, articulate. Does she lapse into Brooklyn-speak because she is most comfortable in her own environment, Lev wondered? Or was she just trying to fit in, like a chameleon? Was it habit or camouflage? Which was Angela's real voice—the one he had just overheard or the one she murmured to him when they caressed each other in the darkness of subway stations?

The gossip session tailed off and Angela and Lev took their seats at one of the small white Formica tables. Angela swung her head around as if inspecting the drab interior. "I spent a lot of time hanging out in here during high school," she confided to Lev.

"Good time or not-so-good time?" he asked.

She closed her eyes for a few moments as if reviewing a mental record of the hours she had clocked at Nino's. "Not so good; not so bad. Just wasted. Wasted time." She shook her head as if trying to erase the memory.

Nino rapped his knuckles on the counter to get Angela's attention. She skipped over to the counter and brought back the pizza slices on thin paper plates that immediately began to turn grey from the olive oil suffusing the crust. As they waited for the slices to cool, the door opened and a man carrying a motorcycle helmet entered. He was compact, with a bodybuilder's wedge-like shape and wearing green coveralls stained with what looked like motor oil but could have been blood. He had long black hair tied back into a ponytail. He looked around and when he saw Angela, he smiled.

"Angela, baby," he said, "what's happening?"

Angela made a face as if she smelled something foul. "Ricky," she said, glancing back at him over her shoulder, "I didn't come here to talk to you."

"We don't have to talk at all," he said with a smirk. "We can just get down to business."

"Fuck off." Angela turned her back on him.

He came over and stood beside the table, looking down at Lev and Angela. "Who's this guy? He your new boyfriend?"

"None of your business."

"He don't look like he belongs down here."

"You mean he don't look like no Wop-Dago like you?"

"That's what I'm asking."

"His name is Larry and he's Greek."

"Can Larry speak English? I don't hear him sayin' nothin'."

"What's up with you, Ricky?" Angela asked. "You tryin' to show us how big your dick is? Cuz you know somethin'? We're not impressed."

Lev's heart began to pound as Angela laid into Ricky, who in turn scowled at the two of them. Lev didn't understand why Angela was provoking Ricky. I'm going to be left cleaning up this mess, he thought.

"Yeah, well maybe Larry Souvlaki here wants to show me *his*—we can compare and then he can make up his own mind."

Lev looked across the table at the slice of Nino's pizza cooling on Angela's paper plate as she and Ricky exchanged barbs. The bubbling cheese was starting to congeal; the edges of the quarter-sized pepperoni slices were curling toward the ceiling. At that moment, everything about that slice of pizza was repulsive to Lev. Why was he down here in Bensonhurst where he was alien and unwanted? Was it only to kiss the lips of Angela Pizatto, lips that were accustomed to eating such a nauseating piece of *trayf*?

Ricky leaned over and placed his grimy hands palm down on the table as he turned his head, first to glare at Angela and then at Lev. Lev looked down at the backs of Ricky's hands and thought he could make out faint letters through his grease-stained flesh. On the left hand, *L-O-V-E* was tattooed on his knuckles; on the right was *H-A-T-E*. What a moron! Lev thought. What kind of a brain could possibly think that tattooing L-O-V-E and H-A-T-E on your knuckles meant something? How was that witty or insightful, anything but silly and ridiculous? Lev could barely contain a snicker.

Ricky turned and growled at him: "What's so funny Larry Souvlaki?"

"Nothing," Lev said, but he couldn't wipe the grin from his face. The next thing that will happen, Lev concluded, is that Ricky will clobber me. Or he'll grab Angela and I'll have to defend her. Or he'll say something really so offensive that I'll have to push my chair back and stand up and then Ricky will demolish me. Lev was resigned to this—it seemed to him the head of the chicken had already been cut off.

Lev was not afraid of being beaten up by Ricky. They were, after all, in a public place. He would not be killed. Cuts and bruises were just physical punishment and he wasn't afraid of that.

What Lev really feared was the aftermath. He imagined the call to his parents reporting that their son had been assaulted and was being treated in the emergency room. He imagined his parents rushing to the hospital and meeting Angela; their learning from her that he was out on a date with her at a pizza parlor in Bensonhurst when he was attacked. He visualized his parents' faces as they assimilated this information: the fact that their oldest son had been living a secret life. What would they find most revolting—that he was on a date with this Italian tart or that he had been eating in a trayf pizza joint?

Lev was angry at Angela for putting him in this position. Picking a fight with a guy in bloody coveralls and H-A-T-E tattooed on his right hand didn't seem like a very secret-agent type thing to do. But he didn't know how to extricate himself from the confrontation. Where is a cudgel when you need one, Lev asked himself?

Then he heard Nino say, "Ricky, pack it up."

"What?" Ricky said.

"You heard me. You bothering my clientele." Nino articulated the word *clientele* delicately, hitting every syllable. "Now get the fuck out of my establishment."

"I ain't doin' nothin'!" Ricky protested.

"Do I have to make a call, Ricky?" Nino reached for the phone. "Do you want me to have to make a call?"

"All right, Nino, don't have a hernia or nothin'." He turned to Angela. "You're just pissed off because we ain't together no more, Angela." Ricky observed the look of shock on Lev's face. "That's right, Larry Souvlaki, we were a hot item in high school. Right, Angela?"

"In your imagination, Ricky."

"No," he said, "I didn't imagine it." And he turned and stalked out of the pizza joint.

After Ricky left, Angela began to eat her slice of pizza as if nothing had happened. Lev had lost his appetite, but he didn't want to look rattled by the encounter, so he ate his slice as well. When they had finished, Angela went over to Nino to thank him while Lev stood silently beside her.

"I owe you one, Nino."

"Yeah, a big one," he said with a frown. "Cuz' that guy ain't named Larry and he ain't no Greek. What are you doin' getting under Ricky's skin like that?"

Angela just shrugged.

"This one—" Nino gestured toward Lev with his chin—"this one is a dead-end for you."

Angela shrugged again. "I'm bored."

"Find some excitement someplace else. This one is a dead-end."

Angela raised her hands, palms up. "C'mon, Nino. This whole place is a dead-end for me. I got nobody here. I got nothin' to lose."

"You think you're so tough that you can roll over everyone, but I know this one—" this time he gestured to Lev with a sharp tilt of his head—"I know the type. Stubborn. Won't bend. Would rather break than bend." He turned to Lev. "Hey, Larry, you don't like pepperoni? I've got some handmade from my special recipe. You wanna' try it? You'll change your mind."

"Mr. Nino," Lev said, "I like pepperoni fine, but I can't eat it. Got allergies."

"What are you allergic to?"

"Pepperoni."

"You see," Nino said, turning back to Angela. "Stubborn. A dead-end."

"You're sweet," Angela said, and extended her arm and cupped his abundant chin in her hand as she gazed at him. "Thanks for caring, Nino."

He frowned at her. "Scram," he said. "Leave me five bucks and then scram." Nino turned back to his newspaper.

Rather than retracing their steps to return to the subway, Angela struck out further east, which took them down the residential streets of Bensonhurst instead of the bustling commercial strip. Lev speculated that perhaps Angela was taking a less traveled route to avoid running into Ricky, who might be stalking them, plotting his revenge for the humiliation he suffered at Nino's. The streets were lined with stunted two-family row-houses, each family sharing a front porch and entrance. Most of the homes had tiny fenced-in front yards, some carpeted with manicured lawns, some with strewn white gravel and some just concrete. These postage-stamp-sized front yards were frequently decorated with centerpieces—a marble bird feeder or imitation Roman fountain. Sometimes the Virgin or a Saint made an appearance, like sentinels guarding each homestead.

Angela was striding forcefully ahead of Lev and he had to make an effort to catch up. When he did, he turned and asked: "You were with that guy Ricky in high school?"

"In his dreams."

"He seemed pretty sure of it."

"Do you really want to go down this road?"

He didn't. They walked another block in silence. He turned to her abruptly, seized her shoulders and pulled her toward him until his face was just inches from hers. "Why did you bring me down here?

What was so important that you had to bring me down here?"

She held her ground and said defiantly, "Because you need to know that you aren't the only one with a story to tell. I've got history too, you know. I've got traditions too. You're not the only one with debts that have to be paid. I've got debts that have to be paid every day, just like you. I've got stuff to give up, too, you know."

Lev dropped his hands, stepped back and looked around at the street, at the featureless houses fenced off from one another; at the monotonous statuary that masqueraded as decoration in the ridiculous pocket-size front yards. It was better to have no yard at all, he told himself, better to live in a crowded and noisy apartment than to delude yourself into thinking you weren't. Lev noticed that some of the houses still displayed the remnants of last year's Christmas lights, tangles of green wire drooping from the eaves like Spanish moss. Even the scrawny trees that lined the streets looked to Lev like imitations of real trees. He didn't see anything that looked like it was worth anything, no stuff that one would have to think one second about giving up.

They continued making their way toward the subway. "Are you really just going out with me because you're bored?" he asked.

She stopped and turned to him. "I'll answer that question if you answer mine: Is Nino right? Are you really just a dead-end?"

They stood glowering at each other and Lev struggled against all the impulses so ingrained in him to smooth things over, to say the comforting thing, to side-step the truth. He could say: No, Nino's wrong. We're just two human beings getting to know each other; there are no presumptions, no pre-conditions; this relationship can go anywhere. I'm free to go anywhere my heart will take me. But one of the things he had already learned from Angela was that if you wanted to *feel* alive, you needed to *be* alive; and to be alive was not to pretend everything was so pat and neatly packaged. It didn't require you to be brutally honest about everything, to say aloud what no one wanted to hear or no one could bear to hear, but at the very least, it did require you not to lie all the time about everything, to everyone around you and especially to yourself. So he didn't answer her question.

Instead, he took her hand and pulled her toward the subway.

"I don't like this place," Lev said. "I don't like Bensonhurst. I don't like the way everyone sticks their nose in everyone else's business. I don't like the way people here treat Greek people. I would feel sorry that we came down here . . . except that Nino's slice of pizza was worth it. Wasn't it just the best slice of pizza you ever had? Maybe even the best in the whole world?"

Angela stopped short and yanked his arm so that he spun toward her. She grabbed the lapels of his father's overcoat and peered up into his face. She was beaming at him, the way a teacher smiles at a student who wins the spelling bee or, from where Lev came from, the way your rabbi smiles at you when you win the "Quotations from the Torah Competition."

"You know, I'm not bored anymore, in case you were wondering," she said, and she pulled him toward her and gave him a light kiss on the lips, lingering there for just that brief extra moment that made all the difference. "Now, let's get out of this shit-hole."

19.

Their sexual frustration grew and grew. "I don't understand why there's an epidemic of unwed teenage mothers in the city," Lev complained bitterly. "Where are they having sex? How come they can find places and we can't?"

"Cars," Angela declared. "That's where the job gets done."

"But I thought they're all more or less poor, these teenage unwed mothers. They have cars?"

"Their boyfriends have cars," she explained patiently.

"You sound like you know. I mean know about the cars."

She smirked. "Since you asked, yes, I do know."

He shut up.

They were desperate and that engendered some ridiculous ideas. Lev hatched a plan to get his driver's license. He found a place where you could prepare for the written test in forty-eight hours. You could take the driver's education classes over three Sundays instead of over three months.

"Then I would have my driver's license!" he explained to Angela.

"That's great!" she said sarcastically. "And then we can make it in a car, just like the teenage unwed mothers!"

"Yes," he exclaimed, not immediately catching her tone. "We just need to get our hands on a car! Do you have a car?"

"I don't have a car," she said.

"I don't have a car, either," he said. "And my family doesn't have one."

"My father has a company car, but he's not about to let me get fucked in it."

So that idea was a bust.

Angela grew impatient. "Finding a place to screw your girlfriend is a guy thing, you know," she said. "It's a guy problem and the guy should be the one to find a solution."

"I'm new at this whole thing. I'm doing the best I can."

"Oh, I can see that like everything else, I'm going to have to take care of this too!"

In the meantime, they began to hang out more and more at subway stations at night, down at the ends of the platforms near the signal lights at the tunnel's mouth. It was as private a space as they could find because after dark, most passengers avoided the secluded, gloomy perimeters. But there were challenges. First, there was no place to sit, so they would have to stand as they frenetically pawed each other. The second challenge was that it was late October and it began to grow cold. Angela, with her short skirts and her stylish-but-not-very-warm jackets, would start to shiver after fifteen minutes. The third problem was that Angela was a bit freaked out by being so close to the murky tunnels. Periodically, Lev could feel her tense up and pull away from him to gaze down into the tunnel, her eyes narrowing in focus.

"Hobos," she would whisper. "They move around in the dark. They live down here in the subway in their cities. They have all these hobo cities and hobo towns underground."

Lev tried to dispel this bizarre delusion. "Angela, homeless people aren't some strange, evil gang. They're just like you and me, except that they've had some bad luck or they have mental problems or they lose their job. Or there's a fire or a flood and they lose their apartment or their home."

"Ha! You are so naïve. These hobos don't just have bad luck or are crazy in the head or something. I mean they're mostly drug addicts or juice-heads. But that's not all they are. These people have done something so bad, so terrible, that they have no one left. You have a fire in your building, someone in your family puts you up in their living room. You lose your job, you move back in with your parents. But these people who live on the street, they must have burned through all their family and all their friends. They must have done things so rotten that no one will have anything to do with them anymore." Her eyes widened and she nodded emphatically at the truth of what she was espousing. "Can you imagine?" she asked. "Can you imagine doing something so bad that nobody you ever knew or cared about will have anything to do with you anymore?"

She was so spooked by hanging out at the ends of the platforms that they stopped trying to grope each other down there.

They were miserable with frustration.

20.

A few weeks after their adventure in Bensonhurst, Lev followed Angela's texted travel instructions and rendezvoused with her at the J Street/Borough Hall station on the F Train platform. They felt distant enough from their respective home territories to sit next to each other as the F headed south into Brooklyn. "We're going to Red Hook," Angela told Lev as she handed him a canvas tote bag bulging with what appeared to be sheets and pillows.

Lev was used to letting Angela determine the itinerary, but the little he knew of Red Hook did not enthuse him. His image was of a destitute neighborhood of abandoned factories and warehouses set against a skyline of gasoline storage tanks.

"What's in Red Hook?"

"A surprise," Angela replied with a grin.

"Surprise in a good way or in a bad way?"

"I tell you what," Angela said, "when we get there, if you're not interested, then we don't have to stay."

They got off at the Smith-9th St. Station. The elevated platform straddled the Gowanus Canal. Lev and Angela paused on the rampart of the station and took in the panorama of Red Hook sprawled before them. The dominant features were the elevated expressways that slashed right through the midsection of the neighborhood: the BQE and the Gowanus Expressway. Everything in Red Hook seemed to be cowering beneath these monstrous roadways and the thunder of the distant traffic provided a constant undercurrent of sound droning around them. The oil storage tanks that Lev had envisaged earlier protruded below the subway platform. To the west loomed the Red Hook Houses public housing development. In the distance was the blue swath of New York Harbor. Governor's Island floated to the northwest and the tiny figurine of the Statue of Liberty seemed to wave to them from the waters beyond. They turned to the north and saw beneath them an indistinct blur of narrow streets and low-rise housing and shops, and beyond, the towering skyscrapers of Manhattan.

Lev's nose twitched. "What's that smell?" he asked. Angela gave a thumbs-down sign to him and they peered over the railing into the Gowanus Canal beneath them. The stagnant waters were grey, slick with a greasy sheen. Bubbles belched to the surface like the last gasps of something—or someone—drowning in the deep.

The Gowanus Canal was where the Mafia dumped its bodies, Lev reminded himself. "Not a great first impression," he remarked to Angela.

"Don't be a spoiled brat," Angela replied. "Red Hook will grow on you."

They descended from the station, emerging onto West 9th Street. They passed a decrepit luncheonette, a laundromat, a felafel stand and a handful of other shops. They turned north at Court Street and continued a few blocks past a cluster of storefronts—shoe repair shops, bakeries, auto driving schools, pizzerias. The shops were topped by double floors of efficiency apartments overlooking the street. At Nelson Street, they turned the corner and headed west. The street seemed depopulated—there was no one in sight. Angela paused at the corner and searched her purse until she found a scrap of paper with an address. Then she rummaged deeper and emerged with a chrome Playboy Bunny key ring to which was attached a half-dozen keys. They passed a cluster of single-car garages, followed by three-story row houses with main entrances accessible by stoops with five or six steps. On one side of each stoop was an entrance to a basement apartment, most of which was underground; half-height windows with security bars were at sidewalk level. The other side of each stoop was crowded with dented metal garbage cans. The cans were chained together and each lid was chained to its respective pail, suggesting that these garbage cans were the only precious items on the block and thus, most likely to be stolen.

"Almost there," Angela remarked. Lev couldn't imagine that Nelson Street harbored a destination that justified passing through this dreary scenery.

Angela examined each shabby stoop and entrance until she stopped at the end of the block, held up the piece of paper and nodded.

"This is it," she said.

"This is what?"

"Our apartment."

It was indistinguishable from the other buildings on the street. Lev glanced behind him at a vacant lot that occupied the corner. It was only later that he realized it was not a vacant lot at all, just a forgotten pocket-park neglected by the City.

Angela opened the entry door with one of the keys from the key ring. They thumped up the three flights of stairs, feeling their way as their eyes adjusted from the outside light to the murkiness of the interior. The wooden stairs were bowed in the middle as if worn down from millions of heavy footfalls inflicted by hundreds of exhausted tenants over many decades. It took Angela five tries to find the right key for the lock on the door to an apartment on the third floor. Finally, she opened the door and pulled Lev inside after her.

It was early evening by then and the apartment was dark. Angela stumbled about looking for the light switch. As Lev took another step deeper into the room, he felt something touch his forehead: a bell-shaped piece of tin at the end of a pull-string. He reached up and pulled.

Light from a 100-watt bare bulb flooded the apartment and they both flinched at its harshness. The studio apartment was dominated by a sagging queen-size bed that occupied almost all of the living space. Besides the bed, there was a shallow alcove containing a sink, a counter with one drawer, a hot plate and a mini-refrigerator. There was no closet, only a pipe strung on wire from the ceiling and bearing a handful of forlorn hangers.

"What is this place?" Lev asked.

"It's my cousin's apartment. He's upstate for another eighteen months but he arranged to get me the keys while he's away."

"What's he doing upstate?"

Angela looked at Lev and shook her head. "You really don't know anything, do you? Being 'upstate' means you're doing time. He beat up a guy who drives an ice cream truck."

Lev took note of this new tidbit of information—Angela had a cousin who was a convict. He didn't know whether he was surprised at this revelation or whether it was totally predictable.

Lev inspected the bed. He had never seen such a big mattress.

His parents slept in single beds that enabled them to separate during the times of the month when they were forbidden to each other. The sheer size of the Red Hook bed seemed lascivious. What things could happen in a bed of such size? It had no sheets and was splattered with reddish-brown stains.

Angela saw Lev scrutinizing the stains. "It's spilled coffee," she explained.

"Your cousin drinks coffee in bed?"

Angela swept her arms to encompass the tiny apartment. "Where else is he supposed to drink his coffee? On the sofa?"

The apartment was coated with dust. Angela ducked into the bathroom and then quickly emerged, shutting the door behind her.

"Let's not inspect the bathroom quite yet," she advised.

She hung their coats on the hangers dangling from the suspended iron pipe. Then she pulled a couple of thread-bare sheets, a blanket and pillowcases out of the canvas tote bag. "Help me with this," she ordered. They made the bed. She had even brought two pillows and as she stuffed them into pillowcases, she finally explained what was happening.

"Our troubles are over," she said. "This place is all ours while my cousin is upstate. And he's not even charging me. Once I saw a TV show about hotels in Japan where you rent a room for an hour or two to have sex. They call them 'love hotels.' This is just like that . . . but maybe not so clean. Anyhow, I didn't tell my cousin that I wanted it for sex because he's always hitting on me. I told him it was just a place to get away from my mother. He totally got it."

Angela was so caught up in her narrative that she didn't notice Lev's eyes widen in terror. To just spring it on him—it didn't seem very fair. So what if they had been scheming for weeks about how to find a secluded place to have sex—nevertheless, Lev felt he ought to get some time to think about this and to prepare, even though he didn't know how one was to prepare for a moment like this, or even if such a thing were possible.

Lev stepped back and leaned against one of the windowsills. Angela had brought a roll of paper towels and a spray cleanser, and she ricocheted around the apartment as she sprayed and then wiped up the accumulated dust. She turned to Lev. "Give me five minutes," she said, and then she took a deep breath and charged into the bathroom.

Lev heard the spraying of the cleanser and running water and the flushing of the toilet once, twice, three times. Finally, Angela emerged and reported, "It needs work, but it's good enough for now."

Angela went to the window where Lev was standing, sprayed the cleanser on the glass and vigorously scrubbed the pane. A circle of smudged glass gradually emerged in the center of each window, like a ship's portholes. Angela inspected the paper towel, which had turned black with grime.

"I'm not touching the windows anymore right now," she said. "There are no curtains anyhow, so it's not such a bad thing that we can't see out. Means that nobody can see in."

Lev stooped over and peered out the window. Parked cars lined the street and behind them the Gowanus Expressway dipped almost to street level; Lev could feel the vibrations of the expressway traffic in his gut. He watched the drivers as they clutched their steering wheels, lurching forward as the traffic slowed to a crawl. A chain link fence shut the expressway off from the street and piled against it were mounds of trash—plastic bags, bottles, cans, take-out food containers, even an occasional hubcap—detritus that could have blown across all of Brooklyn before being trapped against the metal grid.

Angela stepped back and regarded her handiwork. She was so pleased with what she had accomplished that she didn't notice that Lev had been standing mute for close to twenty minutes. She returned to the tote bag and pulled out a scented candle. She lit it with a lighter from her purse and placed it on top of the half-height refrigerator. Then she pulled on the drawstring to turn off the overhead bulb. She started undressing in the candle-lit room, carefully hanging each item of her clothing on the suspended iron pipe. She did this with great absorption, humming to herself. Whenever she turned to lift a hangar to the pipe, Lev could just make out the vertebrae in her back and the hazy outline of the flat wings of her pelvis just above her ass. When all that remained on her body was her bra and panties, she turned to Lev and smiled with surprise that he had not started taking off his clothes.

She took a step closer to him and began unbuttoning his shirt. She unhitched his belt, opened the waist button and unzipped his jeans. They fell around his ankles. Angela gave him a mild shove and to avoid falling, he was forced to step out of his jeans. "You can take off your own socks," Angela said as she picked his clothes off the floor and carefully hung them on the iron pipe.

Finally, Lev stood before her with just his underpants on, covering his groin with both hands.

"Well," she declared, "we're almost all the way there!"

Lev was paralyzed. He knew that Angela had a lot more sexual experience than he had. She hadn't gone into the details, but he knew she had slept with other guys, even with that thug, Ricky. As much as he wanted her, he could not shake off his apprehension about what was to follow.

"You . . . you go first," he stammered.

"Okay. Of course." Angela drew her arms behind her arched back, her elbows sticking out like wings, and unsnapped her bra. She swiftly drew her arms back and snagged the cups of the bra, hugging them to her chest. "I'll let you see a little bit and then you let me see a little bit," she suggested. She peeled back the cup and revealed one breast and nipple for a second and then covered them up again.

"Your turn," she said.

"That's not fair. All I have is . . . you know . . . the . . . all I have to show is home plate."

"Home plate? Don't you dare start talking about sports! That's the lamest way to talk about sex!"

Lev, who didn't talk about sex with anyone ever, groped for a more acceptable metaphor. "I'm just trying to explain that you have some local stops before we get to Times Square, but I'm on the express."

Angela tittered. "Better," she admitted.

"I'm just not used to this."

"Well this is my first time, too."

"Really? You're a virgin too?"

She shook her head. "I didn't say *that*. This is the first time I'm letting anyone see me without clothes on. Any guy, I mean."

"Really?"

"You know it's not so easy for me, either. So guess what—you're going to be the first ever. The first guy ever."

Lev felt a knot of tension begin to untangle. "Let me see a little more," he coaxed.

Angela placed her hands on both cups of her bra, dropped her arms for a moment and then quickly slapped the cups back on her breasts.

"That was great!" he blurted.

"Your turn," she declared.

It still seemed to him unfair. "But . . ."

"Just peel down the top of your jockeys so I can see *something*."

"I don't know. I think it would help if you took off all your clothes first."

Angela's gaze sharpened. He didn't get the feeling she was enjoying this game of who-goes-first, even though she was the one who had suggested it.

"Okay, here's what we're gonna do. I'm going to let you see all of it for just three seconds and then it will be your turn." Before he could reply, she let the bra drop to the floor, stripped off her panties and tossed them over her shoulder. She closed her eyes, held up her arms with her palms facing Lev and shouted: "One-Mississippi!"

Lev was astonished by how beautiful she was—her petite breasts with dark nipples framed by her delicate collarbone. The crescent of her hips as they swept into her waist. Her white, willowy legs were ornamented with red toenails that seemed to shimmer in the candle-light. His roving eyes repeatedly traveled to the dark triangle of her pubic hair.

Lev wanted to stop the clock and take her in, to study this marvel that had revealed herself to him. *Nakedness*—he had been off the derech for only a couple of months and already he was experiencing this extraordinary condition called *nakedness*. It wasn't anything that he had expected would happen to him. Seeing a beautiful woman naked had not been an objective he had set out to achieve when he fell off the derech. At least not an objective he would have considered achievable. He doubted very much that his parents had ever paraded in front of each other totally naked—where he came from, that wasn't considered appropriate even for couples sanctified by matrimony.

"Two Mississippi!"

On the other hand, didn't Rebbe Yitzchak say in Tractate *Berachos* that if a man saw a woman's flesh just four finger-breadths in size, it is as if he has seen her entire nakedness? And on the same page, didn't Rav Sheishess say that if a man gazes at even the little finger of a woman, it's as if he has gazed at her place of nakedness? But, really, what did Rav Sheishess know—he was blind, wasn't he? The Rabbis surely couldn't even imagine a woman standing in front of them with her arms spread out showing her entire nakedness, which is why they were getting so worked up about four finger-breadths of skin or a little finger. And besides, Lev had seen the little finger of many women over the years, hadn't he? And he had certainly seen Angela's little finger. He hadn't studied it, but he certainly had observed it on many occasions. He had even touched it from time to time. Maybe Rabbi Sheishess was right—maybe he had already seen and touched the place of Angela's nakedness. Maybe this whole thing wasn't such a big deal?

"Three Mississippi!"

Already three Mississippis!

Angela dropped her arms, turned to the candle and blew it out.

The room plunged into darkness. As Lev's eyes adjusted to the dimness, he could just detect Angela's form an arm's length away.

"Is that better?" she murmured.

"Yes."

"Your turn."

He hesitated.

"Lev, a deal is a deal. And I can hardly see you anyway."

He slowly brought his hands to the waistband of his briefs and stuck his thumbs inside the elastic. All he had to do was push his hands down and gravity would do the rest. But his arms wouldn't move, as if his wrists had been chained tightly to his waist like a defendant before the judge.

"The secret is to close your eyes," Angela whispered.

He shut his eyes, but his limbs still refused to obey. Angela placed her hands on the tops of his wrists and gently pushed them down until his briefs slid to the floor.

"That wasn't so bad, was it? Lev, you can open your eyes now."

He obeyed. Angela floated before him in the dusk of the room. She inched toward him. They weren't touching, but they were standing so close to each other that he could feel the heat radiating off her body.

His arms hung limply by his side. She seized his hands and guided them to each side of her waist, just above the gentle slope of her hips.

His thumb and forefinger cradled her waist and his palms rested on the flesh of her hips. If she had led them to caress her breasts, it would have just been for the purpose of enticing him, of arousing him. But by placing his palms on her hips, she was creating the illusion that he was in control of what was going on. When a man has his hands on a woman's hips, he might think he can steer that vessel wherever he wanted it to go. He might think he could twirl her around like a ballroom dancer or lift her up over his head like a figure skater, or he might imagine that he could push her down on the floor or onto the bed and do whatever he wanted to do with her.

But of course Lev wasn't in control of anything.

Angela stood on her tiptoes and began kissing him softly on the mouth, light, staccato kisses that just barely grazed his lips. He felt her nipples as they skimmed across his chest. He was so knotted with apprehension he barely responded.

Angela took a step back. Lev's eyes had adjusted to the dusky interior of the apartment and light from the expressway traffic penetrated through the murky porthole that Angela had cleansed in the window, flickering about her in the darkness. "Lev," she asked, "are you watching?"

He grunted. She stuck her right arm straight up and then lowered it with a slow flourish to the coral tips of the two bamboo sticks she wore to keep her hair piled on the top of her head. She hummed a little fanfare and wiggled her hips as she slowly pulled them straight up and out of her tangle of hair.

Her hair tumbled from her head and cascaded onto her shoulders. Lev gasped as he stared at her. She wasn't Angela anymore. Her hair was a portal through which the brassy, flirtatious Italian kid from Bensonhurst had suddenly been transformed into a . . . Lev groped for the word . . . into a *besulah*—that was the word the Talmud used. A *maiden*, just like the maidens of Jerusalem who danced in white frocks among the olive groves in the hills of Judea, so virginal, so perfect. Yes, probably virginal, but maybe not. With her luxuriant hair framing her face, Lev felt a shock of recognition as if this wasn't the first time he had encountered Angela; as if standing before each other at this moment was a reenactment of a seduction that had taken place many times over the millennia. This is the way that Jacob felt when he first beheld Rachel, Lev thought. Or Boaz when he saw Ruth gleaning in his fields. Or when Samson had first seen Delilah. No, not when Samson met Delilah. When David had spied on Batsheva in her tub on the roof. That was what this was like.

Lev gathered Angela's hair in his hands as he buried his face in her tresses and inhaled her bouquet. He nuzzled the side of her face and she flung her arms around his neck and pulled him tightly to her. This is supposed to be happening, Lev thought. I was meant to be here entwined in the arms of this woman, Angela Pizatto, a person who didn't even exist for me just a few months ago. My life has led me to this moment.

Lev wasn't deluding himself that Angela was the woman that God had selected for him, or even that she was Jewish. He knew Angela was not Jewish, neither in this incarnation or in some other one in centuries past. He wasn't even trying to justify to himself that what he was doing wasn't sinful. He knew it was sinful; he knew that if the Sages had spent another thousand years dreaming up hypotheticals of how the Evil Inclination can seduce a nice Jewish boy to sin, they couldn't have come up with a better example.

No, Lev knew he was sinning with Angela. But he also knew that it was worth it. Because to squander your virtue for someone unworthy or just to satisfy your urges—what a pathetic waste that is. What an embarrassment.

But for someone like Angela, it was worth it. Angela: the most unpredictable, headstrong, opinionated and fearless person he had ever met. And beautiful and sexy and all that other stuff, too. No, this upheaval Lev was feeling, this earthquake, was not an urge. It was so much beyond an urge that he didn't know what it was. He only knew it was worth it.

Lev moved his mouth to Angela's and they ground their lips into each other. Their teeth clicked as they explored each other with their tongues. Angela tightened her arms around Lev's neck and pulled him onto her as she lay back on the bed. She sprawled with one arm splayed across her eyes as Lev kissed her breasts. A sigh escaped from her, one that seemed to express the release of months of longing for this very moment. Lev could taste Angela's sigh; he could sing a duet of longing with that sigh.

Angela lolled on the mattress for a few more minutes while Lev ineptly floundered around on top of her. Then she took control of the operation again, slowing him down, drawing him out, bringing him in. At just the right time she murmured, "Don't worry—I'm on the pill," and Lev lifted his head from her body, his mouth open and eyes wide with the realization that he hadn't even considered that aspect of the whole encounter. She giggled at him, gently took his lower lip in her teeth and shook her head back and forth in mock disapproval.

"That was my job, wasn't it?" he panted.

"That's what I like about you," she replied. "You don't even know what you don't even know."

And Lev realized that from the first moment he had gazed at the back of Angela's neck and the oblique angle of her face in the lecture hall, everything he had thought and said and done—in fact everything both of them had thought and said and done—was leading them right to where they were at that instant. Of course, they'd had other thoughts, other distractions, but those had just been momentary digressions from the overpowering desire both had shared from the very beginning. It wasn't so much that Lev had fallen off the derech and had been blundering through shadows. No, he had immediately found a new path and this path led here.

And he thought: It's so clear to me why this is the most important thing I have ever done in my pathetic little life, even though I can't explain it. And he thought: What would I say to my brothers if they asked me why I was doing what I was doing?

And, as usual, as if it were preordained, a page of the Talmud presented itself in his mind. He could visualize the page, the unique geography of the borders of that distinct little country delineated by the medieval commentaries among the 5,400 other countries of the Talmud. And it described what the extraordinarily evil King Menashe had said to the Rabbis who had asked him why, even though he was so wise, he was also such a sinner, such an unabashed idol worshipper: *If you had been there with me at that time, you would have picked up the hem of your robes and sprinted after me . . .*

That's what Lev thought and then he gave himself some really smart advice: stop thinking already.

IV

Certain women who had been held captive and then redeemed were brought to the home of Rav Amram the Pious in Nehardea. They were placed in the second story of his house to seclude them and the ladder was removed from before them.

One of the redeemed women passed by a window and she was so beautiful that a light radiated from her face, lighting up the house. Rav Amram the Pious was so entranced by her beauty that he took a ladder so heavy that ten men could not lift it, and he lifted it himself and proceeded to ascend to proposition her.

When he reached the middle of the ladder, he spread his feet apart to steady himself and shouted: 'Fire in the house of Rav Amram!' The Rabbis came running and they said to him, 'You have put us to shame!' . . .

Rav Amram commanded the Evil Inclination to leave him and it issued from him in the form of a column of fire. Rav Amram said to the Evil Inclination: 'Observe—you are fire and I am mere flesh, yet I am stronger than you!'

- Babylonian Talmud, Tractate Kiddushin 81A -

21.

Lev, who was fed up with rituals, and Angela, who had none, soon devised a number of elaborate ones, all centered around their Red Hook love shack.

The first was the painstaking hanging of their clothes on the iron bar suspended by a wire from the ceiling. Angela did this meticulously. She cared about *her* clothes and by extension, she cared about *all* clothes. Lev, on the other hand, didn't care about clothes in the least. He didn't even have a closet at home. The five Livitski brothers kept their clothes in cardboard boxes stored under the two bunk beds. That was where their mother deposited them when she was finished laundering them and that was where the brothers expected them to be. Everything that required care was hung on hangers by their mother in that little side room set aside for Lev's baby sister, who had emerged as Moti. So the ritual of hanging clothes on the iron bar in Red Hook was exclusively Angela's.

Lev thought himself fortunate to observe her performing this ritual. She shed her clothing slowly and deliberately, item by item. It was like an elaborate striptease conducted with sober concentration. It was only when Angela reached her bra and panties that she wavered, as she had in their first encounter. She was otherwise so obsessed with her wardrobe that the experience of being totally unclothed in front of Lev was the first time she let her body speak for itself. As she hesitated for a moment before revealing herself to Lev, she would give a little shake of her head in frustration. Then a look of resolve would sweep over her face and she would remove her undergarments. She was determined to train Lev to shed his inhibitions as well, although Lev had the feeling that he was an afterthought.

Angela devised a process for desensitizing herself and Lev to the embarrassment of appearing naked in front of each other. Each succeeding time they met in the dank Red Hook apartment, Angela would increase the amount of time that they displayed their naked bodies to each other. At first she counted Mississippis, but after ten, she seemed to have made it across the mountains and no longer needed to count. A few sessions after that, she began to delay blowing out the candle. Finally, even Lev got used to standing in his skin in front of her. But he never was able to attain Angela's imperturbability at being naked. In a matter of weeks, she had cast off her self-consciousness and was comfortable padding around the constricted apartment without a stitch of clothing.

Sometimes as they gawked at each other's unclothed bodies, a verse from Genesis would come to Lev's mind: *And the two of them were naked, the human and his woman, and they were not ashamed.* But Adam and Eve were, at least at that time, innocents. Could it be that Angela sought that primordial innocence and that is why she was not ashamed?

Just then in his speculations, his Talmudist's mind whisked Lev to the second side of the sixty-third page of Tractate *Yevamos*, right in the middle of a river of text before it spreads into a valley of Aramaic. Right there, precisely in that location, the Rabbis, who were not inclined to spend a lot of time pondering the truths that might lie beneath the statement that the first man and woman could gaze at each other naked and not be ashamed—those same Rabbis instead made the following observation: *The men of Barbary and the men of Mauritania walk naked in the marketplace and you will not find a more abhorrent and repulsive thing before the Omnipresent than one who walks naked in the marketplace.*

The men of Barbary: some say they were the source for the word *barbarian*.

So which one was it? Was Angela innocent? Or was she simply a barbarian who didn't know any better?

Lev suspected that she was a little of both.

Whatever the answer, he didn't care. What was important to Lev was the lack of shame, not the reason for it. That's what Angela wanted; that's what Lev strove to achieve. And they did it, too, although Lev was unable to bring it off as completely as Angela did.

Lev knew that his lack of shame was not because he was an innocent. No, Lev had left his innocence on the derech like someone fleeing for his life who discards a garment that might inhibit his flight, leaving it crumpled and abandoned on the ground.

If not an innocent, then a barbarian.

The second ritual was that Angela, in commemoration of their first time together, concocted an elaborate ceremony for the removal of her hair sticks, so diverse in their appearance and design. Lev's excitement during their first sexual experience had not escaped her. She knew that Lev had somehow transcended his anxiety when he saw her hair spill onto her shoulders and she decided to incorporate the experience into their pre-coital dance, as if she were a bird that flashes its plumage to her mate prior to sexual intercourse. As soon as they were standing in front of each other completely naked, Angela would start humming a tune that Lev thought sounded like it originated in a burlesque show. She would raise her arm leisurely, letting it gyrate up, her fingers fluttering as if her hand and forearm were a lick of smoke spiraling skyward in a soft breeze. Then she would slowly drop her hand until it met the coral peaks—or faux-pearl, crystal, ceramic, or silver-plated tips—of the hair sticks. Often, she would spin around as she pulled the sticks slowly from her hair, swinging her ass back and forth as her hair crashed onto her shoulders and down her back.

After Lev and Angela made love, they would indulge in a third ritual—sharing a can of Diet Dr. Pepper. Lev was convinced that this was a ritual and not a habit, because Angela didn't seem capable of human speech until she had taken a few sips from the can of Dr. Pepper, which she religiously kept stocked in the mini-fridge. "Dr. P," she would croak after they made love. Lev didn't know the origins of that ritual. It certainly did not start with him. But he had learned it was never a good idea to ask Angela where certain practices came from. It was better if their origins remained obscure. He didn't want to know too much.

After, or sometimes during, the consuming of the Diet Dr. Pepper, the fourth ritual would unfold. Lev and Angela would lie on their sides, their heads propped on pillows, gazing at each other and talking. From time to time, Lev would place his index finger on the top of Angela's thigh and trace the curve of her hip, moving to the subtle arc of her bone, gliding briefly on the flat plane of her thigh, following her silken skin as it sloped down to her waist—that special junction where she had placed his hands their first time together—and then up the side of her ribcage to her breast. He would do this over and over again, and every time his finger tracked the undulations of her hip and waist in this fashion, Angela would fall into a brief trance, overwhelmed by the sensation: her eyes would roll back into their sockets, her breathing would quicken, and as Lev's finger emerged from the delicious incline of her hip as it plunged to her waistline, she would surrender to a slight shudder.

And there was one final ritual. They talked about a lot of things, but of course the elephant in the room was religion. Except, contrary to the cliché, the elephant in the room was always the one thing they compulsively returned to time and again.

Angela did not consider herself a serious Catholic, but she certainly seemed devout to Lev. "I don't know what it is," she explained to him, "but I just love Jesus. I love everything about him. Of course, I respect the sacrifice that he was willing to make for us, for all mankind. But what really got me to love Jesus was Baby Jesus. You know, when he's born and he's all wrapped up in blankets and resting in the manger with all the barnyard animals and the three Wise Men come—I just love that about him. And I've noticed that some babies are just so cute, so adorable, that it just makes sense that people would want to, you know, make up a whole religion around them."

"He was Jewish, you know."

"Of course! I know that! Everyone knows he was born Jewish."

"Yes, born Jewish, but also he was more or less an Orthodox Jew his whole life. He observed all those commandments I was telling you about."

"You don't have to lecture me about that," she said. "I took Comparative Religions 101 too when I was a freshman. I learned all about how the Jews invented everything. I learned about how the Jews discovered God and how everything else that ever came afterward was just a . . . a spinoff of Judaism—Christianity, the Muslims—everything just a spinoff, like the television show *Angel* was a spin-off of *Buffy the Vampire Slayer*. Frankly, I'm skeptical."

"Skeptical or not, that's the way it happened. I don't care whether you believe me."

"Then for the record, I don't."

"What if a Catholic priest who was a scholar told you the same thing? Would you believe it then?"

"I might. Depends on what kind of Catholic priest."

"How about a Jesuit?"

"Jesuit—sure, I would believe it then. But good luck finding a Jesuit who's going to admit that the Jews invented everything."

"I can bring you a book about it from Comparative Religions 101. Written by a Jesuit."

"Don't bring me any book. I don't give a rat's ass about some book. You promised me a Jesuit. Bring me a Jesuit or just shut up about it."

22.

Despite her reluctance to acknowledge Christianity's debt to Judaism, Angela bombarded Lev with endless questions about what it meant to be Jewish. When he told her that he was supposed to pray three times a day, she was amazed. "We only have to show up now and then and on special occasions."

"Yeah, well for us it's an obligation. I get pulled into it all the time."

"Is it, you know, spiritual for you?" she asked.

Lev didn't quite know what the word *spiritual* meant to Angela. In fact, he really didn't know what the term meant to him either. He knew from Comparative Religions 101 that *spiritual* was used in contradistinction to the *physical*, but that merely told him what *spiritual* wasn't, not what it was. He suspected that the term was far more relevant to Christianity than to Judaism because early Christianity had rejected the obligation of physically performing those hundreds of commandments that Jews observed every day. A more apt question about Jewish prayer was whether it was an *ecstatic* experience. He thought for a moment of how the ultra-Orthodox Hasidic sects worshipped, swaying extravagantly and shouting out their entreaties to God. That was *ecstatic*. Maybe even *spiritual*.

But daily prayer certainly had never been either for Lev.

"Spiritual?" he replied. "Not usually."

"Then why do you do it?"

Lev did it because he had always done it. The question of why he observed Jewish law fell into the category of questions about whether or not you liked your mother—until Lev had skidded off the derech, he hadn't even known that such questions could be asked. "Because . . . I'm supposed to," he answered. "It's my obligation to do it."

"In other words, you don't know why you do it."

In his defense, Lev told her that he wasn't the only one who struggled with finding spiritual satisfaction in praying three times each day. He told her about the time, a year or so after his bar mitzvah, when he talked with his father about it. His father had summoned Lev to join him to help make a *minyan* for a Jewish prayer service. It was a Sunday night and Lev was lying in his upper bunk bed. His younger brothers were already sleeping. He was listening to the Mets game on a transistor radio.

"C'mon, Abba," he protested, "do I really have to go?"

"Yes," he said calmly. "It's a *mitzvah*. They are expecting us. Let's get going."

They walked together to the *shteibel*, the little synagogue a block away from their apartment. They mumbled quickly through the evening prayers and then headed back home. His father noticed that Lev was sulking and he asked him why.

"I'm not into all this *davening*," Lev told him. "It's boring. Three times a day—I don't get anything out of it!"

"I understand," he said. "Just stick with it."

"Oh, great," Lev grumbled.

"Okay," his father said as they walked, "here's the way that I think about it. Every day when it's time to daven, I imagine I'm down on a subway platform waiting for a train to arrive. And every time I'm there, the train pulls into the station. The doors open for a few moments and I can either keep standing on the platform or I can walk through the doors and get on the train. The vast majority of times—in fact, to be honest, almost every time—I remain standing there on the platform and the doors close and the train moves on down the tracks without me. But now and then, not very often, but now and then, the doors open and I get on that train and it takes me to where I want to go, where I should go. And that makes all the difference. But I'll never get on the train if I'm not on that platform. Three times each day."

He stopped and looked at Lev. "Do you understand what I'm saying?"

"Yes, Abba."

"Does it help?"

"I don't know. Maybe. I'm not sure."

"Okay," he said as he put his arm on Lev's shoulder and they continued walking. "But don't tell your mother I said that, okay?"

The fact is, Lev told Angela, it did help. It calmed him down. Maybe it just sedated him a bit. At least for six years or so.

"Oh, I think I'm in love with your father!" Angela said. "He loves budgets and he obviously loves subways. Those are his two biggest passions—just like me! It made a lot of sense what he told you, but do you still buy it?"

"Not anymore."

She didn't reply right away. Then she turned to Lev, her head propped on her hand, her elbow on the bed. She put out her other hand and toyed with the hair on his chest. "I know what's bothering you," she said. "When you go to morning prayers, all you can think about are my tits, right?"

Lev didn't answer her.

"And when you go to afternoon prayers, all you can think about is my ass, right?"

He remained silent.

"And when you go to evening prayers, all you can think about is my—"

"Don't say it!" Lev shouted.

She looked at him with a smirk on her face. "You really are a prude, aren't you? That's really kind of strange, considering that you don't believe in God anymore."

"Don't say that either! I *do* believe in God. I do."

She gave him a knowing smile and said, "You may still believe in Him. But you aren't afraid of Him anymore, are you?"

23.

"What about you?" Lev asked. "Do you go to church a lot?"

"Like I said, only now and then." She was curled up against Lev, her head resting on his shoulder, her leg flung across his stomach.

"How many times a week?"

"What, are you nuts?"

"Well, how often then?"

"Once or twice a month. Some months—zero. . . . Maybe most months zero."

"Do you do the confession thing?"

"Not too often. I like to save stuff up to confess to and then get the whole thing over with. You know, it's like going to the dentist for a cleaning once a year instead of twice a year."

"Next time you go, are you going to confess to, you know . . . to *us*?"

"I haven't thought about it. I'll probably have to mention it."

Lev was silent as he imagined Angela in the confessional admitting to her priest that she was regularly copulating with a Jewish guy. "You don't mention names, do you?"

"Of course I mention names. I also give your address and cell phone number." Angela pushed herself arm's length away from Lev as she regarded him. "What are you worried about?" she asked. "No one is going to call your mother if that's what's on your mind."

"Okay, okay."

Angela returned to Lev's shoulder. Lev wasn't finished, though. "Do you do the communion thing in church?"

"Of course. What else is there to do?"

"What's it taste like?"

"What's what taste like?"

"The wafer."

"Saltines."

"The wine?"

"Mad Dog."

"What's Mad Dog?"

"You should know what Mad Dog is. It's the Jewish wine with the picture of Jews playing poker on the label."

"That's Mogen Dovid wine. They're not playing poker. They're having a Passover seder."

"Whatever."

Lev took a deep breath. He had to ask. "But at some point, you know, when the wafer and the wine are supposed to turn into something else—"

"Something else? The wafer and wine turn into something else?"

"You know what I mean. They're supposed to turn into the body and blood of Jesus. I mean, at some point. Anyway, at that point, when it's supposed to do that, what does it taste like? I mean, does it taste different to you?"

Lev felt Angela's body tense up. She stopped breathing and then he felt her quiver as if she were trying to repress her outrage at the audacity of his question—the Jew prying into the secrets of the Sacrament that he had learned about in Comparative Religions 101. But as she continued to twitch beside him, Lev realized that she wasn't outraged at all; she was just trying to suppress her laughter. After a few moments, it erupted from her belly.

"What's so funny?" he asked, turning his head to look at Angela.

Angela wiped her tearing eyes with the back of her wrist. "What's it taste like? What's . . . what's it *taste* like!" she wheezed. Finally, she calmed down. "What's it taste like?" she repeated. She turned her head and put her mouth on Lev's bare shoulder, nibbling lightly on his flesh with her front teeth, like a beaver. Then she raised her head, stuck out her tongue and slowly drew it over the flesh of his shoulder to his neck. She pulled back a few inches, smacked her lips and smiled into his face. "He tastes a lot like you," she murmured.

24.

Lev was twenty years old and had never done anything that required him to lie to his parents, except once he spilled a bowl of soup on the carpet and blamed it on Hudi, who was only three at the time. But in a little over two months, Lev had moved from nearly two decades without ever having done something that he really had to be deceitful about to screwing an Italian Catholic girl whenever he could.

Starting with his first date with Angela, Lev went from being a truth-teller to someone who lied about absolutely everything. Every day required not just one lie, but lies heaped upon other lies to keep his family from detecting Angela's existence in his life.

His father only saw the good in his family and in other people, their strengths, their positive attributes of character—what was called *midos*. Lev's mother, on the other hand, only saw the defects, the lesions. Lev's father always assumed that anything anyone ever said to him was the truth, so in one sense, Lev found it easy to lie to him, but more painful, much more of a betrayal. Lev's mother always assumed that everything that was said to her was false and a cover-up. To lie to her and get away with it was a lot harder, but it didn't hurt much at all.

The lies weren't just about ridiculous things like the subway was delayed—that's why I'm late; I forgot a book and had to go back—that's why I missed dinner. Unlike Angela, whom apparently no one ever expected to be home when she was supposed to be, it was anticipated that Lev would always be home except when he was supposed to be somewhere else—home for dinner; home to help his brothers with homework; home to read a bed-time story to Moti. So he had to invent a host of elaborate excuses for his now regular and extensive absences. And to do that, he had to lie about important things, things that nobody should subvert for their selfish interests.

Lev told his parents that he had become an ardent Zionist and that he was engaged with other Jewish students in combatting anti-Israel sentiment on campus; that this required his frequent attendance at planning meetings and demonstrations at Brooklyn College. His mother was dubious, but his father was proud of Lev—and that was agonizing. Lev also told them that he was becoming active in student government, which also required him to be absent from the apartment for late meetings. His mother gave him a look that said: *Really? Is there a point to that?* But again, his father seemed delighted with this development and encouraged Lev to take as much time as he needed.

And it wasn't just lying to his parents. There were multiple concentric circles of deceit spinning out from his forbidden relationship. At the epicenter were the lies to his parents, but gyrating out from there were lies to his brother Elya, with whom Lev had an especially close and intimate relationship. And he had to tell even more lies to his other brothers and to his Jewish friends at Brooklyn College.

To lie to Elya was the worst of all. He was thirteen months younger than Lev, but they had always thought of themselves as twins. The family lore was that when they brought Elya home from the hospital, Lev spent all his time crawling around the newborn's bassinet, watching him, guarding him. Lev couldn't bear to hear Elya cry. Whenever Elya began to cry, Lev would join in with him. When Elya was around six months old, he began to reciprocate—he would begin to wail whenever Lev was in tears. By that time, Lev had begun tottering around the apartment. If he ever started to walk away from Elya, the baby would begin to howl. So Lev began dragging him around the apartment behind him, holding Elya tightly by his foot.

Elya could not bear to be left out of any activity that his older brother was engaged in, so when Lev began to talk, Elya began to babble, imitating the cadence of real speech. Lev, in turn, would jabber nonsense back at him so that Elya wouldn't feel left out. Their parents came to believe that the boys had developed their own secret language.

Around the same time, the brothers began to insist that they sleep in the same crib, even though each had a crib side by side in what later became the bedroom for Lev and his four brothers. Each night, Lev and Elya would cry and shake their cribs until their parents succumbed and put them to bed together. And when they graduated to beds, they continued to insist on sleeping together until Lev turned six years old. By that time, he was being pushed out of bed so regularly by Elya's spasmodic slumber that even Lev had had enough.

They insisted on wearing the same clothes. For that reason, and also because they looked so similar when they were younger, people who didn't know the Livitski family well often mistook Lev and Elya for twins. In the neighborhood, they were often confused for one another, and it became second nature for one boy to answer when someone hailed him by the other's name.

Lev and Elya were so comfortable with their special relationship, so confident of each other, that they weren't exclusive about it. When each of their other brothers was born, Lev and Elya made room for them, welcomed them, loved them. The younger boys were not threats to their older brothers' bond. Lev and Elya treated them like brothers, but not like twin brothers. The three younger boys understood there was something that Lev and Elya shared that they could not attain. But they were not a covetous bunch, the Livitski boys.

Lev believed that his brothers were content with the love that Lev and Elya offered them only because of Elya's special nobility of character. Because when Elya loved you—and he loved many people—you were convinced that it was because you deserved to be loved. He possessed a rare talent: to shower affection on someone only because he perceived all the reasons that they deserved it. In that sense, Elya took after their father.

As much as he appreciated Elya's talent for loving what was best in his fellow humans, Lev also knew that he was nothing like his brother in that regard. At first, it bothered Lev that he could not attain that purity of spirit. And as Lev matured, it became clearer to him what he got out of this special relationship with Elya, but less clear what Elya got out of it. Because Lev came to regard himself as the raw material and Elya as the finished product. Lev was the lump of coal and Elya was the polished diamond.

Physically, Elya was beautiful. All of Lev's brothers were good-looking in different ways. They were, or ultimately became, at least six feet tall; they each had broad foreheads, almond-shaped brown eyes and thick eyebrows; profuse, bushy hair so black that it seemed to have a purplish aura to it and assertive chins with just a hint of a cleft. But

Elya's face was put together with a certain delicacy that eclipsed the good looks of his brothers. It was not a feminine delicacy, but merely a harmony of all his features that somehow improved the total in some exponential way.

Women adored Elya. Mothers of the boys' friends; their friends' sisters; the little girls in kindergarten; the girls at synagogue; the girls who attended their Orthodox youth groups; and finally, the young women Elya met when he began his studies at Baruch College in Manhattan. All of them pined for him. When the Livitski family attended weddings and Elya entered the hall, there was always a ripple of excitement among the young women.

But Elya seemed oblivious to all of this adulation and his lack of conceit and genuine modesty only enhanced his charisma.

Elya and Lev had always thought of themselves as part of the same sentence. Sometimes Lev was the noun and Elya was the direct object; sometimes Elya was the noun and Lev was the direct object. But it was always the same sentence. They never quarreled about which one would be the subject of the sentence and which one would be the direct object. Because it didn't matter to them: as long as they were both in the same sentence, they knew what the sentence meant.

This was Lev's brother, his twin, his best friend. This was the brother on whom Lev could always depend. And this was Elya, the source of Lev's deep shame. Elya, his brother into whose eyes Lev looked many times a day and lied to, over and over, day after day, for only one reason—so that Lev could take his pleasure with a Catholic girl in a creaky bed in Red Hook, Brooklyn.

25.

Lev was surprised that even though he was now regularly satisfying his desire for Angela, his obsession with her did not abate. Indeed, it didn't even level off. Instead, Lev found that the more he indulged his passion for Angela, the more fixated on her he became. And his obsession was accompanied by possessiveness, and with possessiveness came jealousy.

Lev had never relished playing the secret agent game with Angela, certainly not as much as she did. Since they had started sleeping together, the game was not merely irritating to Lev; it had become painful. He tried to avoid seeing her in public, but even catching a glimpse of her at Brooklyn College prompted a longing to be with her, to talk to her, to touch her. And it was excruciating when for some reason he found himself in the same public space with her in his full view, which occasionally happened in the cafeteria.

About two or three weeks after they started their liaisons in Red Hook, Lev was hanging out with Tuvi, Pinky and a few other members of the chevra in the cafeteria when he saw Angela enter with several of her pals and gather around a table on the other side of the room. She didn't notice Lev. The throng of Italians was standing around the table talking over one another. A tall, beefy guy hovered at Angela's shoulder and Lev saw his hand drop slowly and brush her behind. She turned and showed the guy a frown. A few moments later, his hand again fell to his side and then moved slowly until it was resting on her ass. Angela brushed it away, continuing the conversation. Minutes later, his hand again migrated to her butt and again she swatted it away, like one shoos a housefly.

Lev's eyes were burning and he became so worked up that he entertained a vision of violating all of their rules and going over to Angela and pulling her away from the creep. Instead, he took out his cell phone and texted her: *tell gorilla hands off*

Lev saw her flip open her phone. She texted back: *mind own bus*

He texted: *coming over*

She glanced at her phone again and then she looked over her shoulder, scanning the room until she saw Lev. She scowled at him through clenched teeth and gave a barely perceptible shake of her head. 'Don't you dare,' she was saying to him.

It only took an instant to convey this warning and she turned back to her friends. Again, the lunk's hand came to rest on her ass. But this time Angela let it stay there for what seemed like minutes and minutes, but was probably just a few extra moments. She was making sure that Lev remembered who was boss.

He couldn't bear it any longer, so he jumped from his seat and stalked out of the cafeteria.

The next night when Lev met Angela in Red Hook, she oozed sweetness and solicitude—she knew she had upset him.

"I was just teasing you," she said as she brushed up against him and began to unbutton his shirt.

Lev shouldered away. "When I see you with that bunch, it seems that everyone's got their hands all over you."

"Oh, it sounds like you're jealous."

"I'm not jealous. I just don't understand: if these people are just your friends, why are they always pawing you."

"Well, you know we Italians are touchy-feely."

"Touchy-feely is one thing; putting their hands on you is another."

"You're being insensitive to my culture. Just because you Jews can't stand to touch one another doesn't mean that's the way the rest of us should behave."

"Maybe so. But somewhere between refusing to shake hands and squeezing your ass, there must be a middle ground. Something appropriate."

"You don't get it. Guys like that put their hands on everybody's ass. And because they put their hands on everybody's ass, putting their hands on my ass doesn't mean a thing."

"Well, where I come from, we put our hands on nobody's ass, so when I see someone put their hands on your ass, it means everything."

"What you're describing is pretty interesting, don't you think? I mean a person could write an anthropology paper or something on what it means when one person comes from a tribe where stupid guys put their hands on your ass all the time and another person comes from a tribe where, you know, nobody ever puts their hands on your ass. Or anywhere else for that matter. It would make for an interesting paper don't you think?"

"It might. But I'm not the one who's going to write it, I can tell you that right now."

"Oh, I like when you get angry and you get jealous. It makes me think you're a lot more human than you make out to be."

"I'm plenty human. People throughout history have accused us of not being human and I don't like to hear it said by anyone. Particularly by you. And I'll tell you another thing. You know I'm right. We may not be behaving properly—screwing each other, hiding from everyone, living this secret fantasy for as long as we can—but that doesn't mean there are no rules, no boundaries. That doesn't mean we are totally depraved people who do whatever pops into our minds. Who let people feel us up and pinch our ass whenever they want. It doesn't mean that we shouldn't feel some obligation to each other to be . . . to be physical only with each other . . . to be . . . only with each other and with no one else."

Angela was shocked by what Lev said, as if he had said something so heretical and blasphemous that she wanted to block her ears from hearing it. Her mouth twisted into a grimace and Lev thought that the next words out of her mouth would be curses, terrible ranting accusations and recriminations.

But instead of curses, Angela muttered, a bit to Lev, but mostly to herself, "You don't really get it, but I'm not saying you're wrong. Shit, you might even be right. But it's not so easy. Easy for you, maybe, with all your rules, but not so easy where I come from."

Then she turned away from him and put her hands to her face, just like she had on the F Train when she didn't want to be seen anymore after their first disastrous experience at the diner.

26.

It was early November and Thanksgiving was only three weeks away. Lev overtook Angela on her way to the apartment at the corner of Court and Nelson Streets. She was lugging a canvas bag filled with an old frying pan and assorted cooking implements. Lev took the bag from her and carried it up the stairs to the apartment. The pots and pans were so old and beat up that they looked like they had come from Italy with her grandparents.

"My mother was throwing these out," she explained. "So I rescued them. Know why? I'm going to make dinner for you here." She pointed to the hot plate in the corner. "Just using that old piece of iron. It will be hard without a real stove and no oven, but I'm going to make you my specialty—veal parmigiana."

"Thanks, Angela, I appreciate the thought, but I don't eat veal parmigiana."

"Don't worry about it," she said, "I'll get kosher for you. All the stuff in the ingredients will be kosher."

"The problem is that I can't eat meat that's cooked with cheese."

"Since when?"

"Since the last three thousand years."

"Who says?"

"The Torah, the Old Testament . . ."

"Jesus, I know what the Torah is by this point!"

"Okay, it's the Torah who says."

"The Torah says you can't have veal parmigiana?"

"In so many words, yes, that's what it says."

"Do you know what you're saying? Do you know how delicious veal parmigiana is?"

"I'm sure it's very delicious."

"You know how sad a life without veal parmigiana would be?"

"I guess I do know. But *you* can eat all the veal parmigiana you want."

"But you won't."

"No."

"But you eat tuna fish in a non-kosher restaurant!"

"Veal parmigiana is different."

"How is it different?"

"Because the Torah says: *You shall not boil a kid in its mother's milk.*"

"Easy then, because there's no boiling in the recipe for veal parmigiana."

"It's the principle of the thing."

"It's a god-damn recipe, Lev. What principle are you talking about?"

"Angela, before you start arguing with me, just think about what it means to boil a kid in its mother's milk."

"I've never heard of such a thing. I can tell you right now, none of us boil a kid in its mother's milk."

"Well baking a calf in cheese is more or less the same thing."

"Spoken by a man who has never cooked anything."

"I'm saying it's still a repulsive idea."

Angela planted the heels of her hands on her hips, wiggling her fingers in agitation. This was her fighting stance. "Are you saying that veal parmigiana is repulsive? You've never even tasted it!"

"I'm sure it's delicious." Lev paused for a moment and took a deep breath. "Angela, apparently at one time, people did boil kids and calves in milk. Think about how horrible that is! The mother's milk gives life to the baby. To use the liquid that gives life to the baby to murder the baby in order to eat it—it's revolting! It's so disgusting that the question in my mind is why did the Torah have to tell us this at all? But apparently, it was a very common practice, so the Torah made it clear not to do it. It's telling us not to harden our hearts and boil baby cows and goats in their mothers' milk."

Angela didn't reply. She just glared at him. Then she dragged the canvas bag full of pots and pans to the door, opened it and tossed the bag into the hallway. She let the door slam.

"Have it your way. I'm not going to force you to eat my foods, the foods that make me and my family feel special. Before you met me, you wouldn't even eat a tuna fish sandwich in a diner, but you managed to come to terms with that."

"Angela, I'm telling you that this is different. It's just not something I can do."

"You could get used to it. You could do it for me, to make me feel good."

"I want you to feel good, but on this one, I can't do it."

"Why? Because God doesn't want you to?"

"Yes."

"Well, God doesn't want you to fuck me, a Catholic girl, but you manage to do it anyhow. Even though it must be repulsive to you, you manage to do it. In fact, you manage to do it as much as you possibly can!"

Lev didn't know what to say, so he said nothing. Finally, he muttered: "I guess I really don't know what God wants from me."

"Ha!" she exclaimed. "You know exactly what God wants from you. You just don't want to give it to Him anymore."

The next morning, while Lev was in his political science course, he got a text from Angela.

chicken parm? chicken = no tits (breasts tho) = no milk = permitted

He texted back:

nice try still no good don't hate me

Her reply:

yes hate you

27.

That fall semester, Lev was enrolled in a seminar entitled Introduction to Political Theory. Even though there were only twelve students in the class, the professor had assigned everyone seats in the crowded seminar room. Lev ended up sitting next to another student named Cecile Willis. Apart from being seated adjacent to one another, Cecile and Lev had little to do with each other. They nodded politely when they sat down at the beginning of the class and they nodded again when the class ended, but they hardly ever exchanged more than a handful of words.

Cecile appeared to be some kind of political ideologue. Her comments in class generally focused on Marxism and class struggle. The professor had assigned Marx's *The Eighteenth Brumaire of Louis Bonaparte*, a book which Lev regarded as the most boring text he had ever confronted, but which seemed to bring Cecile Willis to life. On the day scheduled to discuss the book, Cecile took her seat next to Lev and turned to him holding the book in her hand. She met his eyes and then elevated the book before her face and shook it like it was a holy object deserving of reverence. Cecile apparently was moved by the book, a book that Lev, in order to avoid falling asleep, had to read standing up at the dining room table while he did his homework.

To complement her interest in class struggle, Cecile adorned herself in working-class garb. She wore black leather work boots, a pale blue work shirt and threadbare denim jeans. Lev couldn't really make sense of Cecile Willis, nor was he inclined to spend much time trying to.

But a couple of weeks after Lev started having sex with Angela in Red Hook, he began to appreciate things about Cecile Willis that he hadn't previously. He began to notice, for example, the sheen of her chestnut brown hair, which she either wore in a long braid or which she coiled on the top of her head, held in place by a humble rubber-band. He observed her olive-shaped hazel eyes. He caught a glimpse of a number of strategically placed slits in her jeans, one slashed across her right knee, another on the inner thigh of her left leg, that showed off Cecile's pale flesh underneath. He noticed that she left the top two or three buttons of her work shirt open just enough that he could make out the upper panel of her lacey bra. It didn't seem to Lev to be a working-class type of bra.

Lev not only became aware of these new aspects of Cecile Willis, but he became aware of his new awareness as well. He asked himself why he hadn't perceived these features of Cecile earlier. He concluded that his initial indifference was because of the derech. He speculated that while you were on the derech, you were insulated somehow from the carnality of the rest of the world, immunized against the lure of sex and other vices. But once you were off the derech, you had no resistance. Once you began having sex with a woman like Angela Pizatto, you were helpless before these contagions. You became a petri dish in which all kinds of bacteria of illicit desire could multiply exponentially.

And Lev noticed something else. About the same time that he began to discreetly ogle Cecile Willis, she, in turn, began to return his attention. It started with a few casual remarks they exchanged, routine observations about the weather, about homework, about nothing at all. Their exchange of smiles shifted from perfunctory to earnest. Somehow, Cecile Willis must have perceived Lev's loss of virginity. Somehow, she sensed that he was screwing someone; that he had been corrupted and having been corrupted, he was now available for further corruption.

Some people, Lev mused, could see depravity as soon it fastened itself to you. Those people could take one look at you and know you were in freefall. They could smell it oozing from your pores. The people who could perceive that change were certainly not on the derech themselves. Either they had never been on it, or they had been on it and had fallen off. Because as far as Lev could tell, people who were still on the derech couldn't tell that he had fallen off. They couldn't see the degeneracy clinging to him.

Introduction to Political Theory was a hard course, so hard that many of the students in the seminar didn't understand it at all. In fact, it was so hard that some of the students who didn't understand it at all didn't even know that they didn't understand it. Many of the students said stupid things in class without knowing how laughable they were. Lev knew that these remarks were stupid and way off the mark, but he was not quite confident enough in his own learning to volunteer much in class. The fact that you knew what was stupid in class didn't guarantee that you knew what was smart.

Cecile Willis did not say stupid things in class, although she did say things that were digressions from the point being made by the professor. She generally tried to steer the discussion to what interested her the most, namely, dialectical materialism of Marx and Engels, which she believed was the lens through which all political matters were made clearer. Cecile was smart enough to appreciate when someone else in class was saying something stupid and wrong. She would glance at Lev when that happened and give a sly smile. Sometimes, if the comment was really off base, she would snigger so that only he could hear. Once or twice, she stuck her hand under the seminar table and squeezed his thigh, a gesture of disbelief at the dull-wittedness of someone's comment.

This mild flirtation continued to simmer until one day in mid-November, as they were gathering their things after the conclusion of the seminar, Cecile turned to Lev and said: "Let's get coffee." It was not a question or even an invitation. It was more of a summons.

They settled at an empty table in the cafeteria. "What did you think of today's lecture?" Lev asked.

"Boring."

"Yeah, what's with that?"

Cecile shrugged. "You know, the world is on fire and he's going on and on about fundamental principles of democracy."

Lev thought Cecile was making a joke and he gave a short bark of a laugh. Cecile stared at him gravely. Lev was disconcerted by her disapproval.

"Where did you pick up all this revolutionary fervor?" he asked.

Cecile lifted her arms and gestured to the pockets of students scattered around the cafeteria. "Isn't it obvious?" she asked. "Take a look around. It's all so phony and meaningless."

Lev protested. "My life isn't meaningless."

She glanced at the kippah pinned to the top of his head. "You hide the meaninglessness of your life with religious bullshit."

"Ah yes," Lev sighed, "the opiate of the masses. Not a very original thought. But Marx is long gone and we're still here."

Cecile appeared to want to back off from her blanket condemnation. "I'm not speaking about you personally when I say that," she explained. "I'm speaking of religious institutions, not religious beliefs that someone might have."

"The Jews don't really have religious institutions," Lev said.

"You don't?" Cecile asked skeptically.

"Well, not like you do. Not like the Vatican and stuff like that."

"I'm not a Catholic," Cecile replied. She didn't offer further elaboration, as if such distinctions were not meaningful enough to comment on.

Lev wanted to know what exactly she was, but he didn't ask. Instead, he changed the subject. "So tell me about the revolution. Besides wiping out religion, what else will you wipe out?" Lev asked.

"I'm not going to take that bait."

"Okay, seriously, what's it all about?"

Cecile smiled and leaned across the table. She spoke in a soft voice as if she were afraid of being overheard. "Take a look around," she said again, but instead of gesturing with her hands, she tossed her head toward the tumult behind them in the cafeteria. "Everything that's going on is just one big long negotiation. Every conversation is about buying something or selling something and not one true thing is being said by anyone. It's all about getting something in return for giving something else and everyone wants to get more than they have to give. Most of it is about sex, but some of it is just trying to get someone to do you a favor to make your life easier. In the meantime, people are being exploited until they can't stand it anymore. The black people, the brown people, the yellow people, women, children—they're all being exploited and they can't do anything about it. Aren't you sick of it? Don't you want to do something about it?"

Lev blinked and thought that he did want to do something about it. He wondered why he had never asked himself that question; why no one he knew had ever asked him that question. He thought of the Torah, of all the rules and prescriptions for creating an equitable society, for redistributing wealth and for protecting the nation's most vulnerable citizens; things like paying workers a just wage on time; permitting the poor to glean the fields during harvest; setting aside the corners of one's field for the impoverished. But most Torah-mandated mechanisms for ensuring a just society were based on an agrarian economy. If you didn't have a field or a vineyard, how were you to follow these aspirational mandates? He had never heard one rabbi suggest an answer to this question. They preferred to imagine what it would have been like two thousand years ago to adhere to all these obligations rather than suggest ways that the Jews could fulfill the spirit and letter of the law while living in urban Brooklyn.

Lev was about to reply to Cecile when a shadow fell across the table where they were sitting, and even before Lev lifted his eyes to see what cast it, he smelled Angela, her unique scent that he had become so intimate with. She stood at the corner of the table closest to Cecile, her hands on her hips, scowling down at them. It was a reprise of Ricky's visit to their greasy table in Nino's pizza joint in Bensonhurst, only in this scene, Angela had assumed the role of Ricky.

Cecile glanced up at Angela, slid her chair back a few inches and looked her up and down. "Angela, how delightful to see you," Cecile said in a monotone.

Angela didn't return the greeting. She slid into the empty chair next to Cecile and diagonally across from Lev and leaned across the table to stare at Lev. "Mind if I sit down, Cecile?" Angela asked once she was firmly enthroned in her seat.

Before Cecile could answer, Angela continued, "Now, who's this dude?"

Lev didn't interpret the question as being addressed to him, so he remained silent.

"He's an innocent bystander, that's all," Cecile responded.

Lev felt he needed to explain himself to Angela before she made a scene, so he began to introduce himself and explain that he and Cecile were classmates.

Cecile cut him off. "You don't owe her no explanations," she said to Lev. There was an uncomfortable silence. Then, Cecile rolled her eyes and said, "Lev, meet Angela; Angela meet Lev. Angela is going to be an accountant." Cecile's tone dripped poison. "That's why she dresses the way she does."

"And Cecile is going to be a communist, right Cecile? She's going to save the world. That's why she only spends a couple of hours making up her face and choosing her work boots and why she has her mother put holes in her blue jeans right next to her juicy parts."

"I'll let our faces speak for themselves," Cecile said, winking at Lev as if they were sharing a joke at Angela's expense.

Cecile didn't seem intimidated in the slightest by Angela, which made Lev even more nervous than he had become when Angela had broken all their rules and approached him publicly. He tried to tamp down the tension.

"So apparently you girls know each other?"

"Sure," Cecile said, "we go back a long way, don't we Angela?"

Angela abruptly stood up and said to Lev, "Nice meeting you, whatever-you-said-your-name-was." Then she stalked away.

Lev was momentarily speechless as he tried to decipher Angela's behavior. "What was that about?" he stammered.

Cecile laughed. "Pizatto just wants whatever anyone else has. She was checking you out, that's all."

"Checking me out for what?"

"To see whether she was going to go after you. Whether she was going to try to take you away from me."

"From you?"

"She doesn't know we're just . . . just, like, in the same class. She sees us sitting together and she figures we're poking each other or something, and she was just trying to see whether she wanted to mess that up or not."

"Why would she want to mess that up?"

"I told you," Cecile said in an exasperated tone, "her happiness depends on the unhappiness of others. Don't let that slut worry you. If she comes around again, I'll step on her like a cockroach."

Lev winced at hearing Cecile characterize his lover as a slut and cockroach, and Cecile looked at him curiously. "Anyway," she remarked, "let's not waste any more time talking about Angela Pizatto. Where were we?"

Lev's mind was so preoccupied with trying to unravel Cecile's antipathy for Angela that he had no idea where they had left off. He took a guess: "You were telling me about how everyone is buying and selling each other?"

"Right, they're just trying to exploit each other. There's no solidarity there. There's no understanding that we're all in this together. The consumer culture has made us despise each other. The consumer culture has trained us to look at each other as things, as objects, to be acquired and then consumed."

"I'm not following you."

"Okay, a good example is that chick, Pizatto. When she came over to this table, she was window shopping the same way she would be looking at a skirt or a pair of shoes. She was measuring up whether you were someone she wanted to buy, not because she needs one more guy to drool all over her; and not just because she and me hate each other and it would be an opportunity for her to humiliate me and hurt me, assuming I cared about you. No, she was sizing you up because she's just a tool of consumerism, of capitalism. I'm not saying Angela Pizatto is the *cause* of capitalism. I'm just saying she is the symbol of it . . . well, not the symbol, but she's . . . she's . . ." Cecile groped for the word. "She's *emblematic* of it. Of all what's wrong with capitalism."

"How's that?"

"The way she dresses. The way she talks to people, to men. It's all about consumption with Angela Pizatto. She sells herself as a commodity. Every time she talks to another human being, she's trying to sell something or trade something in return for something else. She thinks of human relations as one big market like the stock market, where everyone is competing to make the most off of everyone else."

"I don't see it," Lev said carefully. He wanted to defend Angela but not too zealously.

"Let me put it in terms that you might understand," Cecile said. "Angela Pizatto is a cunt." And then she giggled.

Lev recoiled. "That's a terrible thing to say about someone! To say about another woman."

Cecile seemed caught out by Lev's reaction. She hastened to explain herself. She spoke calmly but earnestly as if they were discussing a political concept from *The Eighteenth Brumaire of Louis Bonaparte*. "Oh, don't misunderstand me. I'm not insulting her, you know, the way some men or women will call other women 'bitches,' you know, when a woman is assertive and stands up for herself. So that's not what I'm doing when I call Angela Pizatto a 'cunt.' Because, you know, I'm a feminist and I would never use that term to insult another woman. I'm just using it to describe her. I'm using it as an adjective, not as an insult. Because that's exactly what she is. In fact, that's the sum total of what Angela Pizatto is. That's the way she thinks of herself. That's the way she wants men to think of her, too. When she sat down across from you and stuck her painted face in your face and asked who you were, she was trying to get you to see her for what she is—a cunt. Get it?"

Lev asked himself how it had happened: how had he, in only a couple of months with Angela, gotten himself in a situation where someone was saying these things to him, saying such abhorrent and disgusting things to him? Not only saying them, but laughing and expecting him to return her laugh? Is this the way it works? You leave the derech and suddenly you find yourself submerged in filth? Just by having sex with someone, is that what happens? He felt like he had picked up a venereal disease from Angela and the conversation with Cecile was just the first symptom.

The blood rushed out of Lev's head. He leaned forward and put his elbows on the table to try to staunch the vertigo sweeping over him. He looked down at the pitted surface of the table and pretended to be contemplating what Cecile had just said.

Cecile sat quietly watching Lev, waiting for his reaction. Lev's lightheadedness tailed off. He sat up straight.

"I don't care what your history is with Angela Pizatto, you shouldn't use the *c-word* about her. About anybody."

Cecile laughed at him. "You can't even bring yourself to say it, can you?"

"That's right. I can't even bring myself to say it."

She clicked her tongue in disapproval. "What a pussy," she commented.

"Now I understand how you see the world. Either someone is a pussy like me, or the c-word like Angela Pizatto."

"You don't understand me at all," Cecile said.

Lev was fed up. "Don't you know what I am, Cecile? Didn't you notice the beanie I wear on my head? Don't you know I'm an Orthodox Jew, and Orthodox Jews don't like to use the c-word? Or any type of word like that?"

"What do you think, I'm blind? I know what you are. But you're not like the others."

"I'm not?"

"No," she said, nodding, "you're not a pure little innocent anymore, are you? You've been taken down, haven't you?"

Lev sucked air into his lungs and held his breath. After a couple of beats, he asked in as casual a tone as he could muster, "What makes you say that?"

"The way you look at me. The way you look at other girls. Even the way you looked at cunt-head when she sat down at our table."

Lev's muscles tensed and he struggled to contain himself from bolting from his seat and fleeing for the exit. He looked at Cecile and he thought he saw her true self for the first time. She wasn't just some starry-eyed idealist infatuated with Karl Marx and affecting working-class chic. She was completely determined in her agenda. Whether it was class struggle or some ridiculous flirtation with an Orthodox Jewish classmate, Cecile was totally committed. What she wanted from him remained a mystery, but it was clear from her last comment that her invitation to coffee was not on a whim: it was premeditated, after she had analyzed him and come to certain conclusions about him. Conclusions that were terrifyingly accurate.

Lev had always regarded Angela, who could be so caustic when she wanted to be, as occupying the top of a kind of predator food chain, but he suddenly understood that Cecile was leagues ahead of Angela, and that Angela didn't even seem to know it. And Lev sensed that whatever history of insults and wrongs traded between Cecile and Angela, Cecile was far more capable of retaliating than Angela was.

Lev couldn't physically flee from Cecile, but he knew he was out of his depth. Run away, his heart told him; run away.

"I'm sorry if I gave you that impression," he muttered, "but I'm not interested."

Cecile shrugged. "Fine," she said. "I can see you're not ready anyhow."

"Right, I'm not ready."

She gave him a snarl. "You think I'll be waiting around until you're ready?"

"I don't think that. I don't think anything."

"I thought it might be fun hanging out with an innocent little virgin like you."

Despite his resolve to get out of there as soon as he could, Lev couldn't tolerate Cecile's insult, her suggestion that screwing someone made someone morally superior to anyone who hadn't. Lev put his hands over his stomach and doubled over as if he had been shot. "Ouch!" he said. "Oh, how you've hurt my feelings, calling me a virgin and everything! Oh, how will I ever get over it?"

Cecile seemed surprised that Lev had responded to her so forcefully. "Something tells me you're already well on your way to getting over it." She stood. "Let me give you a little advice. Stay away from Angela Pizatto. She'll tear your heart out."

"Thanks for watching out for me, but frankly, I don't give a rat's ass."

Cecile's eyebrows shot up with recognition. "A rat's ass, hmm? That's one of *her* expressions," she said. "That's one of Angela Pizatto's witty sayings. Do you know her? Have you been hanging with her?"

Lev's heart raced. Cecile didn't really know him, didn't have any history with him, didn't know any of Lev's friends; she had no leverage over him. But the implacability of her hatred of Angela and her apparent lack of any conventional inhibitions frightened him.

"I don't know her . . . I don't know what you're talking about," he mumbled.

Cecile stood for a few moments glowering at him and then she retreated, her clunky work boots echoing on the floor.

During the encounter, Lev had felt the cell phone stuffed into his pants pocket buzzing with a series of text messages. As soon as Cecile left him, Lev flipped it open. There were half a dozen peremptory texts from Angela, each one escalating over the prior one in frustration at his failure to respond:

how could you
my biggest enemy
total gangster
what you doing with her
coffee my ass
where r u

Lev texted back:

hi whats up

meet ocean pkwy later

Then Angela immediately texted a follow-up message:

!!!!!!!!!!!!!!

Lev and Angela would occasionally meet at the bench where Angela had led him the afternoon after their first date, the place where she had convinced him to give her another chance. It was still a place they could spend some time together in private if they were not going to see each other in Red Hook.

As Lev walked toward Ocean Parkway later that afternoon, he resolved that he would not tell Angela what Cecile had said about her. He didn't want the conflagration to burn any hotter.

When Lev turned from Avenue H, he saw Angela already pacing back and forth in front of a bench. He gave a little wave as he entered her line of sight. She didn't return the wave. As soon as he was in earshot, she tore into him.

"How could you?" she exclaimed. "We're total enemies!"

"I didn't do anything," Lev protested. "She came over and sat down with me and started talking about political theory."

"We have history; that's what we have!"

"How am I supposed to know?"

"Besides, she's the biggest whore at Brooklyn dumbass College and believe me, that's saying something! You can't stand being seen with me in public, but it's okay for you to sit and drink coffee with the biggest whore in town?"

Lev was astonished that suddenly it was Angela who claimed that the whole prohibition about being seen together in public was his idea. He just raised his hands, palms-up in exasperation. "How would I know anything about her? This was the first time we ever spoke one word to each other." He didn't mention that he and Cecile had been flirting for weeks. "What kind of history?"

"I stole her boyfriend in high school."

"Why did you do that?"

"Because I felt like it. Then she tried to steal one of my boyfriends, but all she got him to do was fuck her."

Lev flinched. His reaction seemed to give Angela a pang of shame and she looked away. Lev observed her stealing a return glance at him for an instant as if checking on whether he had figured something out. Angela almost never bothered to assess the impact of the verbal grenades she routinely lobbed at Lev and when he saw her do so, something clicked. Lev groaned. "Oh, no. Not Ricky! It wasn't Ricky, was it?"

"Yeah, it was Ricky."

"The one you stole from her, or the one she stole from you?"

"Both," Angela admitted, again looking away. But then she swung her head back and looked defiantly at Lev. "And by the way, she didn't get him back; she only got to fuck him again once."

Angela saw how appalled Lev was at the sordid backstory. She tried to put it in context for Lev. "At one time Ricky wasn't such an asshole. In high school he was considered very . . . *popular*. When you saw him at Nino's, he wasn't looking his best, for sure."

"Oh," Lev replied, "if he cleaned himself up, it would make it all okay."

"Don't you dare judge me!"

Lev knew that Angela was right: he shouldn't judge her, but he definitely would. He was as compelled by his upbringing to judge her as her upbringing compelled her to do things that deserved judgment. That was a great part of what it was all about, wasn't it? Neither of them wanted to continue spending their time with other people who either had done nothing worthy of being judged, or who didn't perceive their misconduct as anything unusual. Wasn't that part of the attraction, this incongruence in sinful behavior? Wasn't that part of the temptation—maybe even its essence?

Lev's silence unnerved Angela. She witnessed the distress on his face as he struggled to move past the love triangle she had just described to him. She pulled him over to a nearby bench and gave him a gentle shove to make him sit down. She took her seat next to him.

"What's done is done," she offered. "That's all ancient history."

"If it's ancient history, then why are you still so pissed off at Cecile?"

"You don't get it," Angela snapped. "There's no forgiving what she

146

did. It has nothing to do with Ricky."

"Then there's no forgiving what *you* did, stealing him away in the first place."

"I don't expect her to forgive me. I don't even give a rat's ass if she forgives me."

Lev wondered at Angela, at a soul who didn't want forgiveness for something she knew was wrong, for an offense she herself regarded as unforgivable. He couldn't begin to imagine that kind of license, that kind of permission to indulge your passions with so little consequence. It scared him that Angela's rules were so different from his own; that perhaps Angela didn't have any rules at all.

Angela slid closer to him on the bench and slouched against him. She picked up his arm and draped it around her shoulders. She turned her face to him and pushed her hair and forehead against the side of his face. "Hey," she murmured, "hey; don't let that whore upset you. We were just kids back then. It doesn't mean anything."

Lev realized that was the real problem—that Angela pretended that the whole thing didn't mean anything. He didn't quite know what it meant, but the one thing he did know was that it meant *something*, even if he couldn't say what it was.

"You loved Ricky, didn't you?"

"We were into each other, but I didn't love him," Angela admitted.

"How could you love someone who has *H-A-T-E* tattooed on his knuckles?"

"That came later."

"But he was in love with *you*, wasn't he? He probably still is."

"Yeah, probably still is," Angela conceded.

"If he loved you so much, then why did he sleep with Cecile?"

Angela drew back a little from Lev and peered at him for a moment as if checking to see whether Lev's question was in jest. "Because Ricky didn't think he had a choice. Ricky thought that if a chick offers herself to you, then you got to fuck her. If you don't fuck her, then everyone thinks you're a pussy; that's what Ricky thought." Angela withdrew her gaze and snuggled closer to him, folding herself against him.

"He probably still thinks that," Lev said.

"Oh, yeah, for sure. He was a fucking idiot then and he's a fucking idiot now." Angela tugged Lev's hand so that his arm tightened around her shoulders.

147

"That Cecile, she's really committed to revolution. She went on and on about how we're all using each other, exploiting each other; how that's what capitalism has done to us."

"Yeah, she believes it too. It's not an act. She had it tough as a kid. Her father's a drunk; her parents split up. They got no money, even less than we got."

"Now you sound like you feel sorry for her."

"I kind of do, I guess."

"Then you should forgive her."

Angela pushed herself away from under Lev's arm and turned to him. She looked into his face. "Okay, I forgive her," she said. "She won't ever forgive *me*, but I forgive *her*."

"You don't have to do that for me."

"I'm not doing it for you. I'm doing it for me."

She's not like Cecile at all, Lev told himself. He wanted to shout it out loud in exultation, but he was ashamed that even for one instant he had feared that Angela had shared the same dogged vindictiveness that he had felt pouring off Cecile. Angela would never use the c-word to describe another woman, even an enemy. Angela even had it within her heart to forgive someone she felt had committed the unforgivable. Angela could even pity someone like that. Lev felt within him a surge of tenderness for Angela.

Angela saw the disquiet in Lev's face disappearing. She turned her face up toward his, flung her arms around his neck and pulled him to her. "Doesn't mean one goddamn thing anymore," she whispered. She placed her open lips gently on his mouth and sighed deeply as if she were trying to exhale her spirit into him.

Lev and Angela sat on the bench entwined, their lips cleaving to one another, but so lightly that if one of them had moved a millimeter, the contact and the spell would be broken. Lev marveled at this new sensation. He hadn't felt this way before, something both wonderful and terrifying at the same time.

More terrifying than even the c-word.

Could it be the *l-word*?

V

Having captured the Evil Inclination that leads to idol worship and imprisoned it in a lead cauldron, the Rabbis of the Great Assembly said: 'Let us pray also concerning the Evil Inclination that leads to sexual immorality.' They prayed and the Evil Inclination for sexual immorality was delivered into their hands.

The Evil Inclination said to them: 'If you kill me, then the entire world will become desolate because without me there will be no procreation.'

The Rabbis imprisoned the Evil Inclination in the lead cauldron for three days and during this time they searched for a freshly laid egg throughout the land of Israel, and not one could be found. They said: 'If we kill the Evil Inclination, the world will become desolate. . . .'

Instead of killing the Evil Inclination, the Rabbis blinded it and then released it back into the world . . . .

- Babylonian Talmud, Tractate Yoma 69B -

28.

"Take a look at this!" Angela exclaimed as Lev entered the Red Hook apartment. "I bought this on the street for five bucks. What a bargain! You know this book, right?"

He examined the book, which was about seven or eight hundred pages thick. On its worn paper cover was the title: *How Strange the Jews! A Compendium of True Facts About God's Chosen People.* The title was superimposed on a blue Star of David, which in turn was depicted as dangling from the hook of a red question mark. To Lev, it was not only a book he did not know, but it seemed to be the type of book that was written for an audience that by definition would exclude anyone even remotely familiar with Jewish practice and belief. Its author was Rabbi Dr. Erwon Arkadi. What kind of name was that? Certainly not a Jewish name.

"What do you think?" Angela asked.

"I don't know it," he said.

"It's written by a rabbi *and* a doctor."

"I've never heard of him."

"You've got to be kidding! The guy on the street said every Jew knows him! He's definitely famous."

"Was 'the guy on the street' Jewish?"

"Probably not. A Jamaican guy."

"The prosecution rests. Think about it: why would we be reading books about how strange we are and how strange our customs and laws are? They're strange to everyone else. Not strange to us."

Angela grabbed her chin in thought like she were a rabbi stroking his beard as he puzzled over a difficult Talmudic passage. "Good point," she finally admitted. She flopped down on her stomach on the bed and opened the book. She began thumbing through it, intermittently smiling as she perused the passages. She bent her legs at the knee, crossing and uncrossing her ankles.

"Why did you buy that enormous, silly book?" Lev asked.

Without taking her eyes off the page, Angela answered, "I don't want any more veal parmigiana surprises, if you know what I mean."

"Actually, I don't know what you mean."

Angela ignored Lev and continued reading.

"How about this one?" she called out. "This section is called 'The Fetishization of the Torah.'" She continued reading aloud:

> In the late Middle Ages, the Jews began to regard the Torah not merely as a record of God's revelation to Israel, but also as a talismanic object that was imbued with magical properties. Thus began the ritual fetishization of the scroll itself.
>
> The Torah is stored in an Ark located in the front central space of the synagogue. Only males may approach and touch the Ark, the decorative curtain that covers the Ark's doors, and the Torah scroll itself. When the curtain is pulled open, inner doors are then opened, and the Torah scrolls are displayed standing erect as if waiting for this moment. They are dressed in velvet tunics elaborately embroidered with gold thread. The male who is honored to fetch the Torah tenderly removes her from the Ark and then proceeds to adorn her with a silver breastplate, two crowns placed on each wooden stave of the scroll, and a chain from which hangs a silver cylinder topped with a hand pointing with its index finger. The Ark is closed and the male cradles the scroll in his arms. The congregation sings songs to her as the Torah is marched around the male section of the synagogue. Each male either kisses the Torah scroll's tunic or touches it and then kisses his hand. The Torah is then brought to the central lectern, where her clothing and jewelry are removed. She is then opened and read. The reader uses the silver hand to point to each word as seven different males are called to the lectern to recite blessings over the Torah. When the weekly portion is completed, another male is called to the lectern to raise the scroll while she is open and display her to the congregation. A second male dresses the Torah scroll, puts her jewelry back on and the entire ritual is repeated in reverse.

"He makes it sound like some voodoo rite, but that's not what it is at all," Lev complained.

"You mean it's not like that?"

"It's like that, but it's not because we believe that the Torah scroll has magical powers."

Angela read further in the book. "Oh, oh, look at this. Now Rabbi Dr. Erwon Arkadi is saying that one of the songs you sing to her is, *She is a tree of life to those that hold tightly to her.* So obviously, if you hold onto her, you will be protected from death. It does sound pretty voodoo to me."

"Wrong again!" Lev protested. "It's speaking poetically. The rest of that verse is, *and all its paths are peace.* Hardly a superstitious statement about living longer! And by the way, the Torah is not a 'she.' I mean the word in Hebrew is feminine, but no one calls it a 'she.'"

"Rabbi Dr. Erwon Arkadi calls her a 'she.'"

"Take my word for it—he's full of it."

"You may not be seeing the whole thing clearly; you know you got a lot riding on seeing it different, on seeing it the way you were taught to see it."

"You choose to believe that guy with the weird name, a guy who has every incentive to distort Jewish practice in order to sell his stupid book! You prefer to believe him over me."

"He's not just a guy. He's a doctor *and* a rabbi."

"I don't even think he's Jewish."

"He wouldn't call himself a rabbi if he wasn't Jewish. You could probably be sent upstate for doing something like that."

Lev didn't reply. He just shook his head in disbelief.

"Stop sulking," Angela said as she closed the book and pushed it to the side. She had a pensive frown on her face. "For your information," she said, "I don't believe him over you. But I don't take everything you say on faith either. The truth is probably somewhere in between. I'm going to have to make up my own mind."

"Yeah, well good luck with that," Lev muttered.

29.

Rabbi Dr. Erwon Arkadi soon became a regular participant in their time together. For Angela, every entry in that compilation of "facts"— which Lev regarded as ridiculous— became the subject of extended discussion.

"Rabbi Dr. Erwon Arkadi reports that Jews say a prayer every time you go to the bathroom." They had just finished making love. Lev was lying on his back with Angela sprawled on top of him, her hands folded on his chest, her chin resting on her hands. This was her preferred posture for talking about the teachings of Rabbi Dr. Erwon Arkadi because she could look into Lev's face while she languidly engaged in her investigation of the strange rites of the Jewish people.

"Well," Lev said, "if he reports it, then it must be true."

"It can't be true! A prayer to God thanking him for taking a crap!"

"That's not what the prayer says. We don't say, 'Bless You God for letting us go to the bathroom.' We say, *Bless You, God . . . who created within man many tubes and orifices; it is obvious and known before Your Throne of Glory that if even one of them were to rupture or even one of them were to be blocked up, it would be impossible to survive and stand before you; blessed are You God who heals all flesh and acts wondrously.*"

"You say it, don't you? You actually say that blessing! You wouldn't know the words if you didn't say it."

"Occasionally, I say it, yes. When I think of it." The truth was that Lev always said it. He still said it, even since falling off the derech. It had been drummed into him by his parents and teachers along with scores of other blessings that observant Jews say every day. In fact, Lev suspected that one blessing or another was among the first words that he had ever uttered as a toddler.

"I don't understand why you would take such a blessing seriously."

"Listen, Angela, it's actually a beautiful prayer. It has a tone of

154

wonder to it, don't you think? We are created with all sorts of tubes and holes and it reminds us of how much we're at God's mercy; if just one of those tubes or holes busts or gets blocked up, it's all over for us. It reminds us that we shouldn't take life for granted."

Angela grew silent while she reflected on what he had said. She didn't indicate that she agreed but, uncharacteristically, she didn't attempt to rebut what he said either.

"Rabbi Dr. Erwon Arkadi says that you have blessings for different types of food, like one for melons and another one for oranges and another one for grapes and another one for cakes; even blessings for drinks and stuff."

"He's not wrong about that."

"You say those also, don't you? You say them to yourself. I notice you pause for just a second before you take a drink of water."

"I say them occasionally."

"Occasionally, as in all the time, right?"

"Most of the time."

"What blessing do you say when you drink water?"

"*Bless you God, through Whose word everything came to be.*"

"What blessing do you whisper to yourself when we drink our Diet Dr. Pepper?"

"Same one. It's the same blessing for all liquids except wine, which has a special blessing."

"Get out of town!" Angela shouted so loudly that Lev flinched. "You mean to say that you would say the same blessing for Diet Dr. Pepper as you would say for some disgusting soft drink that only a teenage boy would drink, like Mountain Dew or something? Like you should be as thankful for one as you are for the other? That's fucked up!"

"Maybe the explanation is that when the rabbis came up with the blessings, there was no such thing as Diet Dr. Pepper. I'm sure if there had been, they would have come up with a special blessing for it."

"Okay," she said, "that's just a little possible." She put her head down on his chest, her face turned to the side. He felt the tips of her long eyelashes brush his skin as she blinked. Lev knew Angela was not quite finished probing the secrets of the Jewish people, that she was thinking about what they had just discussed.

Indeed, after a few minutes, she picked up her head and again placed her chin on the backs of her folded hands. "Rabbi Dr. Erwon Arkadi says there are blessings for almost everything in Judaism. There's a blessing for when you see a rainbow; for when you hear thunder; for when you see lightning; for when you see the ocean. There's even a blessing for when you see a really beautiful woman."

"That's right."

"Did you say that blessing when you first met me?"

"No."

"Why not?"

Lev was about to answer her, but instead he found himself in Tractate *Avodah Zarah*, near the bottom of a page where the Aramaic text breaks out of its glen and begins to broaden into a plain:

> *When Rabbi Akiva first saw the beautiful wife of Turnus Rufus, the wicked Roman governor, Akiva spat, he laughed and he wept. He spat because she had been formed from a putrid drop of semen; he laughed because he knew that she would ultimately convert to Judaism and become his wife; and he wept to think that such beauty would one day rot in the earth.*

"Because I was too nervous to think of it," Lev answered.

"Lame excuse. You remembered to say the I-just-went-to-the-bathroom blessing, but you couldn't remember to say the she's-a-knock-out blessing when you first met me. I think something may be wrong with you."

"Guilty as charged."

"Rabbi Dr. Erwon Arkadi says there's a blessing you say when you experience something new, like when you taste a fruit you haven't tasted ever, or when you celebrate a special holiday. Did you say that blessing the first time we fucked?"

"No. That also didn't occur to me."

"Too nervous, huh?"

Lev could have answered that you don't say blessings before you commit a transgression. But all he said was, "Too nervous."

"That was a mistake," Angela said wistfully. "Now you'll never ever be able to say that blessing before making love . . . to me . . . to anyone."

30.

As soon as Lev entered the apartment in Red Hook, Angela rushed over and slipped her hand under his belt and into his pants. "Whoa!" he exclaimed, "at least give me a chance to catch my breath!"

"I'm looking for your fringes," she explained. "I just read Rabbi Dr. Erwon Arkadi's explanation for the fringes and I want to see yours. I've seen them hanging outside other Jewish guys' pants, for example like with some of the guys you hang out with in the cafeteria, but I want to see them up close."

"Sorry to disappoint you, but I don't wear them."

"Don't bullshit me," she said. "You may not wear them hanging out of your pants, but you wear them."

"Nope. Don't wear them. You've never seen them on me, have you?"

She took a step back and scrutinized his face. Lev stared back at her, his face open, not hiding anything.

"Lev, I know when you're fibbing and when you're not. You definitely wear them. You must take them off before you come here." She held out her palm. "C'mon, I want to see them."

He turned away from her and cursed himself for being unable to fool her. It seemed that he could lie to everyone and pull it off, but not to Angela, who was so intimate with deceit that she could not be fooled. The truth was that Lev did wear tzitzis, although he had always worn them with the fringes tucked into his pants where they could not be seen. In fact, all his brothers did the same. The little room off their parents' bedroom where his mother hung the boys' Shabbos shirts was where their tzitzis were hung to dry after his mother washed them by hand. The flock of white garments dangled from hangers in a row, drooping from a rod suspended near the ceiling—very much like the rod Angela hung their clothes on in the Love Hotel in Red Hook. The white, four-cornered garments were suspended in order of size, from the tiny ones for Moti to the largest ones for his father, like a brood of albino bats slumbering upside down from the roof of a cave. Whenever Lev needed a clean pair, he grabbed the tzitzis that looked most likely to fit and deposited the dirty pair in a plastic bucket sitting in a corner of the room for that purpose.

Lev wore them every day, but whenever he headed to Red Hook to see Angela, he slipped them off and stuffed them into a side pocket of his backpack.

There was no point in trying to fool her. "Yeah, sometimes I might wear them, but not here."

"So let me see them."

"Why?"

"Rabbi Dr. Erwon Arkadi says that the fringes are a special symbol. The fringes are a symbol of all those gazillion commandments you guys have to do. He says they are tied in knots in a special way to remind you of all those gazillion commandments. That's why I want to see them."

Lev froze, his stomach roiling. Even though he and Angela were regularly exploring each other's private parts, her request to examine his tzitzis seemed to him like an invasion of his person. His mind flashed to imagining his ushering Angela into his family's apartment when no one was home and letting her wander through it, touching everything, fondling his father's kiddush cup, stroking his mother's candle sticks. Unthinkable! Not in a million years!

"No. Off limits."

"You're not being shy, are you?" she asked. She came over to Lev and put her hand on his chest, just below his neck where his shirt opened. She stuck out her index finger and moved it gently back and forth on the indentation sitting just below his Adam's apple. "I see you in your underwear all the time. I see you naked all the time. What's the big deal?"

"This is different. This isn't just underwear."

Angela moved closer to him, pushing her body lightly against his. "I just want to look at the funny knots," she said.

"Not going to happen."

Then Angela dipped her head just slightly and slowly raised her face to him, unfurling her gaze in the way she did when she wanted to seduce him—or anyone—into getting her way. Lev knew the drill: first cajoling; then seduction; and if that didn't work, they were heading to a slugfest.

"Out of the question," he said and, turning abruptly away from her, went to sit on the edge of the bed.

Angela wasn't about to give up and Lev watched her review her tactical options.

"It's not like I'm asking to see some sacred object or something," she said as she sat next to him on the bed. To his surprise, she was trying reason. "Rabbi Dr. Erwon Arkadi says that the fringes are not sacred objects in themselves. They may become like sacred when you bless them and wear them, but they're not sacred in themselves the way the Torah is, or even the little black boxes with the leather straps that you wear on your head and stuff—what do you call them?"

"*Tefillin.*"

"Right. I'm not asking to see your tefillin, am I?" Angela smiled sweetly at him and tilted her head as if she were the most reasonable, innocent being in the universe.

Lev was surprised at how much and how quickly Angela had learned from that charlatan, Rabbi Dr. Erwon Arkadi.

"You can't see the tefillin either," he said.

"Right. But those are different. I just want to look at the fringes for a few seconds."

He shook his head.

"Why not?" Her tone was getting sharper.

"I don't know why not. I just don't want to."

"That's not a good enough reason."

"I just don't want to. I don't know why. I just have a bad feeling about it and I don't want to do it."

Angela's patience had run out and she prepared for battle by standing up in front of him, her hands on her hips, her elbows flaring. "I don't deny you nothing," she said bitterly. "You get to do to me anything you want to. And all I get in return is a stubborn *no* without any explanation!"

"Oh," he replied, sarcastically, "I didn't know that the things I do to you are only for my own pleasure and not for yours as well."

She turned away and reached for her coat. "You know what," she shouted at Lev, "you're disrespecting me—I'm leaving!"

She made as if she was heading to the door, but Lev reached out and snagged her arm. "Angela, don't leave." Lev saw just the slightest hint of a smile sneak across her face, reflecting her satisfaction at having predicted his reaction so accurately and at playing him so expertly. "Sit down," he said to her.

She sat down next to him. Lev got up from the bed and stood in front of her. "You don't have to walk out. This is your cousin's apartment. You shouldn't have to leave. I'll leave instead."

He grabbed his coat, scooped up his backpack and went to the door. He opened it, stepped into the hallway and turned to go down the stairs. Only then did Angela shout: "All right, I give up. I don't have to see your fucking fringes, you stubborn bastard!"

Lev paused at the top of the stairs. Now it was his turn to feel a little thrill of victory in this pathetic struggle with Angela over whether she could examine his tzitzis. The last battle Lev had won with Angela was over whether she could date other guys on Shabbos, but since then, he had never prevailed when she had set her mind on getting what she wanted. He had always succumbed to her relentless assault—a blend of bravado mixed with aggression and, always, peppered with seduction.

The curious thing was that Lev still didn't know why he had drawn the line at this particular issue, why letting her see and touch the tzitzis was unacceptable to him.

He came back into the apartment. Angela stood up and began undressing, carefully hanging her clothes on the iron bar suspended from the ceiling. "You know," she said almost as if she were thinking aloud, "someday when you're not looking I'm going to go through your things to figure out where you are hiding them and I'll get my hands on them anyhow."

"If you do, it will be last thing your hand ever touches that has anything to do with me."

She stopped fussing with her clothes and looked back at him. There was a strange look on her face, one that Lev hadn't seen in many weeks. He thought maybe it was a look of consternation that her dominance of him might be waning. Or maybe it was a look of respect.

She raised her hands in front of her in a gesture of capitulation. "Okay," she said, calmly, without recrimination, "I'm over the fringes thing. Already forgotten, I promise."

He nodded to her.

She continued undressing until she was stark naked. Lev remained standing by the door, watching her.

"Are you coming over here, or do I have to drag you by the balls?" she asked.

31.

Because Shloime Strudler had been his first exemplar of what it meant to be off the derech, Lev had always thought that falling off the derech was a zero-sum game. One minute you were observing almost all of the commandments; then you were publicly going out of your way to mock the mitzvos by, say, stomping on a lit cigarette on Simchas Torah. After that, you completely rejected all of the mitzvos until such time, if ever, you managed to find your way back onto the derech. Lev concluded that this was the case simply because after he had overheard his parents whispering about Shloime Strudler, Lev never saw him again. Shloime had been a fixture in their synagogue for as long as Lev could remember, along with a number of other teenage boys, but immediately after falling off the derech, Shloime disappeared entirely, never to reappear. Lev and his brothers heard rumors about Shloime from time to time: he had been seen eating a cheeseburger; he had enlisted in the Marine Corps; he was a drug addict; he was a professional gambler. So Lev had always thought that when you left the derech, the very thought of performing even one mitzvah became so detestable to you that you immediately stopped performing all of them.

But that was not the way it was for Lev. He was off the derech, yes, but he hadn't plunged totally into a world of non-observance, of indulging in acts of depravity and excess—except for his relationship with Angela. Apart from that one extravagant act of iniquity, he toed the line of Jewish observance. It was his attitude toward that observance, rather than the observance itself, that festered. It wasn't so much that he questioned everything that he continued to do. It was not an open rebellion—it was more a surrender to indifference. He attended prayer services, but the challenges of connecting to the Divine in his prayer seemed completely overwhelming. The requirements of halacha suddenly seemed burdensome. Before they had seemed either like habits or, occasionally, like small challenges he felt virtuous in overcoming. But now they were, all of them, mildly irritating.

Except for Shabbos. Those twenty-five hours of the Sabbath with his parents and his four brothers, even the time spent in synagogue, were still sweet. He still looked forward to it as the week ebbed.

Lev had expected that an entire day without Angela would have been a difficult challenge. It was true that during Shabbos, he often thought of Angela and longed to be with her. But for the most part, Shabbos was actually a time to divest himself of his obsession. It was only as Saturday afternoon began to recede into evening and then nightfall that Lev became impatient for Shabbos to end so he could meet Angela in Red Hook.

He recalled one of his yeshiva rabbis, a chain-smoker with a grey beard stained reddish brown by tobacco, describe how he experienced his tobacco addiction on Shabbos. "Holy people who are addicted to smoking don't feel the absence of it on Shabbos," he had said. "But when Shabbos is over, the craving returns immediately and they light up right after sunset and *havdala*. The rest of us start strong—we don't really miss it until Saturday afternoon. But then the hunger starts working on us and the rest of Shabbos is torture. For weak people, that's what being an addict is about."

Although Lev didn't really start to miss Angela until shortly before Shabbos ended, he realized it wasn't because he was a holy man. He suspected it was only because Angela was such an intense experience that each week he needed some time away from her to decompress.

But as soon as his father chanted the closing blessings of the Sabbath and the three-wick braided candle was extinguished with a hiss in a shallow saucer of wine, Lev couldn't wait to rush to Red Hook where he knew Angela would be waiting for him.

On one of those Saturday nights in early December, Lev sprinted up the stairs to the apartment in Red Hook, slammed the door behind him and leaned against it as if he was taking refuge from something horrible and hungry that had been pursuing him. Angela, who had been lounging on the bed reading *How Strange the Jews*, sat up abruptly. "What's the matter? What's going on?" she cried.

"They almost found out!" he panted. "We came this close to being found out!" Lev displayed to Angela his finger and thumb just an inch apart from one another.

"Found out what?"

"Found out about you. About you and me."

"All right, calm down. Don't get so worked up. Take off your coat and calm down and tell me what happened."

Lev shed his coat and threw it on the floor. Angela scowled at his slovenliness. He sat beside Angela on the bed. "It was during Big Time Wrestling," he began. "We were all in our room for Big Time Wrestling—"

Angela put her hand on his arm. "I don't know what you're talking about," she said, "so start at the beginning."

"So at the end of dinner before dessert, we have a wrestling match—"

"First I want to hear about the dinner."

"But it's not relevant."

"It could be."

"It's not."

"I want to hear about it anyhow. You never tell me anything about what you do all night and day on the Sabbath. So start at the beginning."

Lev rubbed the back of his fist against his forehead and clenched his eyes shut, but he started at the beginning. "After synagogue, we go home and we sit around the table. Then we start . . ."

"Where does everyone sit?"

Lev sighed in frustration. "Everyone has their special place. Abba at the head; I'm to his right, followed by each of my brothers, oldest to youngest, ending with Moti who sits on a Brooklyn Yellow Pages next to Imma and she sits in the seat to the left of Abba, which is closest to the kitchen. Then we drink some wine—"

"What about the angel song?"

Lev glanced at Angela. How did she know so much about the Friday night rituals? She smiled back at him indulgently and with her index finger, tapped the cover of *How Strange the Jews* lying beside her on the bed. The tome answered to Angela's tap with a baritone thud. The book at least *sounded* credible. Lev realized what Angela's interrogation was all about: she was comparing notes—how closely did the Livitski family's Sabbath rites conform to those described by Rabbi Dr. Erwon Arkadi. Lev surrendered to the realization that Angela would not be appeased until he described the entire choreography of the Livitski Shabbos evening. "Okay, first we sing a special hymn in Hebrew welcoming the angels that accompany and herald the onset of Shabbos. Then we sing a hymn of praise to our mom."

"What's it say?"

"It starts: *A woman of valor who can find, for her price is far above rubies?* And then it lists all the special stuff that she does for us."

"So hokey!"

"I guess it is, maybe . . . but it's our favorite part. Because, you know, my parents are not affectionate with one another, at least not in front of us boys. I can't remember ever seeing them hug each other or kiss each other in front of us. Ever. But when we sing *A Woman of Valor*, my dad holds my mom's hand and he looks at her with a big smile on his face. And my mom, who, believe me is never embarrassed about anything, she blushes and looks down at her plate like she's a bride. And when we reach the verse: *Her mouth is open in wisdom and the Torah of loving-kindness is on her tongue,* my dad very dramatically brings her hand to his lips and kisses it. All of us are watching them and then when he kisses her hand, we all clap our hands and laugh and my mother blushes even more and then she frowns at us, which only makes us laugh harder." Lev smiled at the recollection and Angela prodded him to continue.

"And then?"

"Then we all stand up and Abba raises his silver cup and chants the *Kiddush*, which sanctifies the Sabbath day. He takes a sip from the cup, offers a sip to Imma and then the cup is passed to me for a sip and so on down the line until it gets to Moti. Moti doesn't drink the wine, but he has a little cup of grape juice that he drinks from."

"And then?"

"After we clean up the spill, we—"

"Wait a second. What spill?"

"Moti spills his grape juice and then we have to sop it up and wipe down the plastic table cloth."

"He spills it every Shabbos?"

"Oh yes, every Shabbos. He tries so hard not to—I see him concentrating so hard to hold it steady and not to knock it over, but as soon as he lets down his guard for even a moment, his hand or his elbow flies out and over it goes."

"That Moti! He sounds like such a little . . ." She searched for the right word. "Such a little . . . *boy*."

"But all of us spilled our grape juice when we were young," Lev explained. "Sometimes as many as four glasses of grape juice would be spilled at one Shabbos meal. After a while, my parents just accepted it. They used the plastic tablecloth and put newspapers on the floor at every Shabbos meal."

"And then you wash your hands and eat the special bread, right?"

"We wash our hands, say a blessing and return to the table. We're not supposed to talk between the time we say the blessing after washing our hands and the time Abba recites the next blessing over the challah and until we have each eaten from the challah. But because we are such a disorganized bunch, it takes forever for each of us to wash our hands, make the blessing and return to the table. It's the only time in the whole evening when no one is talking, but my younger brothers like to grunt at one another while the rest of us wash. Then Abba blesses the bread, sprinkles it with salt and cuts slices for all of us to eat. After that, we eat dinner."

Angela stirred herself, sat up straight on the bed and turned toward Lev. "What's for dinner?"

"Well, it's more or less the same thing every week: roast chicken, green beans or peas, fried mushrooms and barley, fruit and chocolate babka for dessert."

"When do you sing songs and play Monopoly?"

"Maybe we sing some songs after clearing the table while we sit on each other's laps."

Angela's hand flew out and jabbed Lev on the shoulder. "Say again?"

Lev explained. The tradition of sitting on laps at the Shabbos table originated when Lev and Elya were babies. While their mother cleared the table and did the dishes, their father sat both of them on his lap and sang Sabbath songs to them. When Shmu was born, their father sat Elya and Lev on his lap for a brief period, and then they made way for Shmu to spend a lot more time on his father's lap than the older boys did. When Hudi came on the scene, both Elya and Lev were old enough to take turns holding Shmu on their laps. And finally, when Moti made his appearance, all the brothers were passing Hudi around from Lev to Elya and from Elya to Shmu. Now Moti, even though he was six years old, still took a turn on everyone's lap at the Shabbos table.

The older, bigger boys continued to sit on their father's lap, but only symbolically. At some point in the meal, their father would push back his chair and each of them would sit on his lap and he would put his arms around their midriffs from behind and give a tight hug. Because their father suffered from a slipped disc, Lev and Elya would sit for only a moment and they made sure they didn't put their full weight on their father's legs. But the family demanded that ritual each Shabbos.

"I can't imagine such a thing happening in my family," Angela said in wonder. "A grown-up son sitting on his father's lap; even a brother sitting on a brother's lap! It's completely impossible that such a thing would happen. If it did, everyone would make fun of both of them for years."

Lev shrugged. "Okay, so now we come to the point of this story." Lev set out to explain a Shabbos rite perhaps observed only by Lev's family: Big Time Wrestling. After they finished removing the main course from the table, Moti would rush ahead to the brothers' bedroom and pull his special red wrestling cape (a threadbare baby blanket) out of his particular cardboard box stored under one of the bunk beds. Hudi and Shmu would follow him and open the cot that filled the narrow space between the two beds. By the time Elya and Lev arrive, Moti would be standing on the cot draped in his cape, holding his arms at right angles to his frame, flexing his puny muscles like a body builder and roaring in his high bird-like voice: "Come and get punished!"

That Friday night, Elya and Lev lay face down horizontally across the cot as they usually did, their heads on one bunk bed and their feet on the other; their torsos supported by Moti's open cot in between. Shmu joined them. Hudi was already big enough to play the role of wrestling mat with his brothers, but he had to remain on the sidelines in order to provide a wrestling opponent for Moti, who was still small enough to cavort on his brothers' backs without hurting anyone.

Lev was the designated announcer at the weekly Big Time Wrestling events. "In this corner," he intoned in his most sonorous voice, "is Mad Dog Moti the Maccabee." On cue, Moti again bellowed his rage. "And in this corner is Horrible Hudi the Hassid."

Hudi, who knew that he was there primarily to keep Moti from falling off and breaking his arm or leg, gave a half-hearted howl of aggression.

"Let the match begin!" Lev announced.

At that signal, Moti began to wrestle, primarily with himself, rolling and tumbling back and forth on their backs; occasionally engaging Hudi in mild grappling. For the three brothers who served as his wrestling mat, Moti's leaping across their backs was like a vigorous massage. As Moti tired, he turned to each of them and grabbed their heads or necks and threatened to tear their heads off unless they cried uncle. As they lay there impassively, each brother gave Moti auditory hints of their struggle against his prowess. "Never!" Elya cried, but moments later, he pleaded: "I give up, Moti! Have mercy!"

Their father came and stood in the doorway to observe. Finally, Moti, worn out by his frenzied brawling, lay down on Lev's back, grabbed his neck and pulled on it with all his might. "I give up!" Lev cried. "I surrender!"

Moti lay on Lev's back panting, his face buried in the hair on the back of Lev's head. After a few moments, Moti lifted his head and said: "Someone smells like a girl."

"Yeah," said Hudi, "I smelled it too. One of you guys smells like a girl."

Shmu chimed in, as well. "I thought I was imagining it, but I smelled it too."

Moti stuck his face into Lev's hair again and declared authoritatively, "It's Lev. Lev smells like a girl."

Lev froze. He turned his head and looked at Elya who was lying face down beside him. Elya turned to regard him. Lev thought Elya was smirking.

Moti wouldn't leave it alone. "How come Lev smells like a girl?"

His father interrupted. "No one smells like a girl," he declared. "It's your imagination. Now come back to the table for dessert and some Shabbos songs."

As they filed back to the kitchen, Lev ducked into the bathroom. He knew what had set Moti off: Lev had slept with Angela on Friday afternoon and he had arrived home too close to the beginning of

Shabbat to shower. He knew that Angela's fragrance had lingered on him. He washed his face and hands to try to rid himself of Angela's scent. He pulled out his shirt tails and smelled them. He sniffed his armpits. Lev couldn't detect any odor of Angela, or her perfume or her body. Maybe he had grown so accustomed to it that he could not discern it. But he was certain that had his father not been there to cut Moti's investigation short, they would have discovered his secret.

And Lev wondered about his father, whether he also suspected. For the fleeting moment Lev had symbolically sat on his lap earlier that evening when his father had hugged him tightly, his arms across Lev's stomach, he too might have caught a whiff.

Lev returned to the table and the evening proceeded like nothing had happened. Apparently, his father's declaration had persuaded everyone that the smell of Angela on Lev's body had been some sort of hallucination.

Lev clutched Angela's shoulder. "If they had continued to ask me about it, what could I have said?" he asked.

"When that happens," she counseled him, "you need to come up with as small a lie as you can; you know, avoid starting with a really big lie. For example, one way to get them off the trail is to immediately agree with them. You could have said: 'I *do* smell like a girl, don't I? My friends at school were teasing me about it all day. I can't understand where it came from. Maybe I picked it up in the subway?' Or another approach is to tell a lie that is really close to the truth. Like, 'I was sitting next to an Italian girl in econ class and she took out perfume and sprayed herself and it went all over me.' When there is a little hint of truth in a lie, your conscience somehow knows it and it comes out of your mouth much more believably. Take it from me—I know."

Lev marveled at his girlfriend, the Queen of Lies. "Well, Elya knew. Later on he said something to me."

"You told him?"

"We're very close, Elya and me. So, yeah, I let him know."

Angela searched Lev's face. "You let him know what?"

"That I was seeing someone. That I was, you know, involved."

"But you didn't tell him you were fucking a Catholic chick, did you?"

"No."

"I see. So you don't trust him."

"I do trust him. I just don't want him to know so much that he has to lie to our parents to protect me."

"Well, you don't trust him the way I trust my sister, Estelle. I've told her everything."

"Everything?" Lev paused for a moment as he contemplated the meaning of the word *everything*. "What did she say?"

"She's happy for me. She just wants me to be happy."

"Will she tell anyone?"

"She would die first."

"She sounds pretty cool. How old is she again?"

"She'll be seventeen in August."

"Will she go to Brooklyn dumbass College?"

"Estelle? Of course not!"

"Why not?"

"She's got Down syndrome. She hasn't been in school for years. She works at a sheltered workshop making plastic flower arrangements in little pots. Did you forget?"

Lev was speechless. He was certain Angela had never told him her sister—the sister she shared a bedroom and a bed with—had Down syndrome. Was that because Angela was ashamed? Lev didn't think so. She hadn't hesitated to remind him of it. Did Lev forget or had Angela failed to ever mention it?

And then Lev began to wonder about an even more important question: What did it mean that Angela's best friend—no, *only friend*, to use Angela's own words—was her younger sister who had Down syndrome? Was Angela really that much alone, so alone that her only confidante was a kid sister who couldn't fully understand? Lev recalled what Angela had said to Nino back in October when they had made their foray into Bensonhurst: *This whole place is a dead-end for me. I got nobody here. I got nothin' to lose.*

Angela watched him deliberate with himself. Part of him felt sorry for her, that she could be so solitary, so forsaken by everyone. To mistrust everyone so profoundly. To be so alone. Part of him was frightened of her—that she could live in such isolation without people she could trust, friends that she could confide in; and yet Angela could be so confident of everything, so headstrong and zealous about her passions and her obsessions.

And then Lev asked himself, for the second time: who is Lev Livits-ki to judge Angela Pizatto? Because he realized that he was in exactly the same circumstances as Angela. He had no friends that he could confide in about what he was up to with Angela. He could not even bring himself to confide in his beloved brother, truly his best friend in the world. Elya would never betray him, would never criticize Lev; but Lev suspected that in Elya's heart, maybe so deep that even Elya would not be conscious of it, he would condemn Lev for the sins he was committing with Angela. So Lev was just as alone and forsaken as Angela. Maybe even more alone.

Finally, he said, "You're lucky to have someone like Estelle, some-one who loves you without judging you."

Her face softened and she gave a wan smile. She reached out and caressed the side of his face with her fingers. "Someday, maybe," she said, "we won't have to worry about all that kind of shit."

What Lev didn't share with Angela in his account of what transpired that Friday night was his subsequent conversation with Elya. After ev-eryone else had gone to bed, Lev furtively took a shower, even though his family had always regarded showering on Shabbos as prohibited. Then he slipped quietly into the darkened room he shared with his brothers and gingerly climbed up to his bunk bed. He looked across the room at the upper bunk opposite his own, where he had assumed Elya was already sleeping. A sliver of light from the streetlamp outside the window fell across Elya's face and reflected in his eyes, and Lev could see he was still awake.

"That little bandit, Moti," Lev whispered. "He really had you guys going tonight."

"Do you think he's the first to notice?" Elya whispered back. His voice was bitter. "I've smelled it for weeks. Abba suspects. That's why he covered for you."

Lev felt like he was falling backward from a rooftop, hurtling to-ward the pavement. Finally, he was able to whisper: "Has Abba said anything to you?"

"No," Elya replied, "but I can tell. Whenever you come in late—'Oh,

I had a meeting with the Young Democrats,' or, 'We were rehearsing debates about the West Bank'—he puts his hand on his kippah and moves it around on the top of his head like he's trying to clean up an oil spill or something."

Lev didn't know what to say, so he didn't say anything.

Elya continued: "You're not fooling anyone, not even Shmu and Hudi. Moti only knows what he can smell. We all suspect something. All except Imma, I don't think. At least not more than she usually suspects about each of us. That's pretty mystifying."

As close as the two brothers were, Lev had never had such a candid conversation with Elya about their mother, or even their father. Those little things that Lev had observed all these years—his father's nervous tic with his skullcap; his mother's innate suspicions—were private thoughts. Lev had worried that perhaps it was just he who noticed these things, something defective in his character that caused him to see his parents in less than idealized terms. But even Elya, perfect Elya, noticed them too.

The two lay in silence in their cramped bunk beds. As a car passed in the street outside, a slender band of light moved up Elya's reclining frame from his feet to his head and then zipped sharply around the corner of the room and disappeared.

"Why are you keeping secrets from me?" Elya asked. His voice was strained as if he was close to tears.

Lev thought: If you lie to Elya and he finds out that you lied, then it's over, this special bond we have; it'll be shattered and it will never be the same. And you'll no longer have a twin brother, a brother better than you are, who can at least try to keep you honest. And if you tell him the truth—tell him you have fallen for a shiksa, a Catholic girl, and you are sleeping with her—he'll be appalled and shocked and disappointed, but he'll eventually come to understand and he'll never reject you. And he'll wait for you to straighten out and return to the derech. And when that happens, when you return to the derech, you'll be twin brothers again and you'll still have each other in that special way.

But Lev couldn't tell Elya about Angela because he was too ashamed. And Lev couldn't lie to him either. So instead, he told Elya something that was true, but not the truth.

"I'm seeing someone, yes, it's true. Anyhow, this girl has made me swear not to tell anyone about us. And I agreed. But I should never have agreed—I should have said, 'I won't tell anyone but Elya,' but I didn't say it."

"Go back to her and tell her you need to tell me."

"I've thought of that, but it's not a good idea."

"Why not?"

"Because, Elya, I'm lying to Imma and Abba and everyone all the time now about what I'm doing and where I am, and sooner or later they'll figure it out. And then you know the first thing they'll do is ask *you* what's going on. And you need to be able to say to them that you don't know what's going on. And you need to be able to say that truthfully. I can't drag you into lying for me."

"I'm willing to lie for you," he said simply.

"I know you are, but I'm not willing to have you do it for me."

Elya thought about this for a few moments. Lev could see his illuminated eyes blinking. Then Elya asked: "What's so terrible about this girl?" he asked. "Why such a secret?"

"Nothing too terrible. We're just a little too carried away with each other right now. And her family would not be too excited about a guy like me."

Elya's eyes grew larger in wonder. "Oh no," he asked, "she's not a Reform Jew, is she?"

"No," Lev said, suppressing a smile. "Not a Reform Jew."

"Well, thank goodness," he replied. "That would be a tough road."

"Yes," Lev said, "a tough road."

"Is she nice, this girl?"

"Oh, yeah."

"Pretty?"

"Very."

They were silent for a while.

"Elya, right now we're just spending a lot of time together. But I promise you, if something changes, either way, I'll tell you. I'll tell you right away. Okay? I don't like to keep secrets from you. But please don't worry about me."

"Okay, brother," he said. He stuck out his hand across the space that separated the two beds. Underneath them, Moti slumbered on the cot in his little-boy, frenetic way. Lev stuck out his hand and touched Elya's fingertips as they had done so many nights before, all the nights of their lives together, from the time they shared a crib to the time when they first slept each in their own little beds, even before their spindly arms had grown long enough to reach from bed to bed. And then Elya turned to the wall and began to recite the *Shema*, to acknowledge the oneness of God, and to remind himself that it is their duty to love Him with all their heart, all their soul and all their might, as they had been commanded.

And Lev turned to the other wall and did the same.

32.

A week later, Lev was greeted in Red Hook by Angela siting demurely on the edge of the bed, her legs crossed, her hands folded in her lap. He immediately knew something was wrong. She didn't welcome him; her face was locked into studied impassivity. She watched him coldly as he hung up his coat.

"I saw you today," she reported. "You didn't see me, but I watched you have lunch with that chick with the frizzy red hair."

"Auburn hair," Lev said. "That's Faigie Gruenstein. I sometimes have lunch with her."

"What kind of name is Faigie?"

"It's a Jewish name."

"Double *duh*."

"What's your point, Angela?"

"You seemed to be having a jolly good time with Faggy Gruntstein."

"Faigie Gruenstein."

"Whatever. You spent almost an hour with her, chatting, having a jolly old time."

"She's a good kid. Easy to talk to. We've known each other for years. She's majoring in poli-sci, so we take some of the same courses."

"Isn't that convenient," Angela said. "You get to spend a few hours in class with each other and then you get to have lunch with each other. What else do you do together—hang out in your synagogue in the choir loft?"

"Wow," Lev said, starting to enjoy the situation. "For your information, synagogues don't have choir lofts. You have a suspicious mind, don't you? What do you think? That I spend time with Faigie in another apartment a few blocks away when I'm not with you?"

She frowned, crossed her arms and turned away from him, bouncing her foot on the floor in anger. Lev sat next to her and reached over to stroke her shoulder. "Angela," he murmured, "you're the only one."

She relaxed and turned back to him. Lev lay down on the bed and Angela nestled next to him, her head in the crook of his arm.

"She's pretty," she said.

"She's pretty, but not beautiful the way you are."

"What's the difference between pretty and beautiful?"

"Pretty means attractive. Beautiful means . . . you know . . . irresistible."

"That's not good enough. Give me more."

"If my mother were here, she would call Faigie 'chayn.' That's a word we use to describe pretty—chayn. It means attractive but in a warm or graceful way. Like the inner person is of good character and that somehow makes it into the way they look. Like they are nice people and therefore they look kind of nice."

"And that's something good, right?"

"Yes."

"It's not like a booby prize or something?"

"No."

"It's not like a weakness or something?"

"No."

"She's definitely chayn."

"Yes."

"I'm definitely not chayn."

Lev laughed. "I suppose that's true too."

"If you weren't with me, you would be with her."

"We're just friends. We've never even gone out on a date."

"No, you would be with her. She's infatuated with you. I can tell."

"She's not infatuated with me. We just enjoy talking with each other."

Angela abruptly sat up and swung her leg over his torso, straddling his waist. She was still dressed—she even had her boots on, which surprised Lev because Angela felt very strongly about no shoes on the bed. But now she was focused on something far more important to her. She swung her head down toward him and peered into his eyes.

"Let me tell you something about this JAP—"

Lev cut her off. "Say what you're going to say, but don't be calling her or anyone else a JAP. That's just a way Jew-hater can call a Jewish girl a kike and think that we won't notice."

Angela paused in mid-sentence and her eyes grew wide with surprise. She raised her head and considered what Lev said for the briefest moment and then she lowered her face to his and continued as if he hadn't interrupted her. "Let me tell you something about this *tramp*," she said. "This tramp is in love with you; she's after you and she won't give up. I watched her—everything she did, every move she made, was to get you with that boring chayn thing you just described. The idiot smile that never left her face; the way she looked down at the table and pretended to be shy; the way she patted her mouth with her napkin; how she laughed at everything you said—everything she did was planned out ahead of time in order to grab you. There wasn't one thing she did—and I bet not one thing she said—that was real. That's the way chicks behave when they're chasing after someone, when they are zeroing in on their target. And you won't know what really hit you until your wedding night."

"Angela," Lev said, grinning, "now you're the one who's jealous."

"You're damn straight I'm jealous," she said fiercely. "Unlike you, where I come from, being jealous isn't something we're ashamed of. Being jealous means you care about what you want, what you desire. Where I come from, the only people who aren't jealous are dead people."

Lev stared into Angela's face suspended just a few inches from his.

"You can spend as much time as you like with her," Angela continued. "You can lead her on; go ahead and flirt with her, as far as I'm concerned. Make her think she has a chance with you. Go right ahead. In fact, go ahead and tell her that she can have you after I'm done with you. But not one minute *before* I'm done with you." And then, with emphasis on each word, she said: "Except by that time, you'll be *all . . . used . . . up*."

And then she thumped her open hands on Lev's chest, bent over and kissed him hard on the mouth, grinding her teeth into his lips until it hurt. Her chest was heaving in and out as if she had just sprinted up the three flights of stairs to the apartment.

"Now fuck me, Levinski," she commanded. "Fuck me now!"

33.

It was a Sunday, their favorite day. Lev arrived early to the apartment in Red Hook to do homework. Angela, coming from her family's Sunday lunch, arrived late in the afternoon, just as the sun had begun to set. As she took off her coat, she turned to Lev. With a mischievous grin, she bugged out her enormous eyes.

"Guess where I went yesterday?" She paused for dramatic effect. "To a synagogue!"

Lev stopped breathing. His first thought was: did they escort her out? Did they have to call the police?

"Which one?" he managed to say.

"Don't worry, not any place near you. It was in Park Slope."

"Was it Orthodox?"

"How should I know?"

"Were men and women seated together or separately?"

"Separately."

"It was Orthodox."

"Whatever. Want to know how I did it? I wore my youngest sister's skirt, which is way too long for me, so I looked very modest and a bit ugly so I would fit in. And I wore long sleeves. And I just followed what everyone else did. I stood up and sat down whenever they did. It was easy. No one suspected a thing!"

Lev recalled their conversation months earlier when Angela imagined that she could pass for a Jewish girl and he thought to himself that not one person there could possibly have been misled about who she was and what she wasn't.

"Did people there talk to you?"

"You bet they did. A lot of the women came over and introduced themselves and asked me about myself."

"What did you say?"

"I told them I was from Coney Island and that I went to Queens College."

"You think they believed you?"

"Sure. I had it all worked out. The only thing I hadn't thought about before was what my name was. I mean, like, I couldn't give them my real name."

"What name did you give them?"

"Well I borrowed a name from someone. I told them that I was Faigie—"

"No! You didn't tell them you were Faigie Gruenstein, did you?"

"Do you think I'm an idiot? No, I borrowed a last name, too, but not hers. I told them I was Faigie Levinski. They definitely bought it!"

Angela flounced down on the bed where Lev had been reading and regaled him with her impressions. "The first thing is that the whole thing went on forever! It went on for over two and a half hours! If Catholic Mass was two and a half hours, the religion would be finished. I liked the singing, but there wasn't very much of it. But the really amazing thing was the Torah reading."

"Okay," Lev challenged her, "who was right about that? Rabbi Dr. Erwon Arkadi or me?"

"You were both full of shit," she declared. "I'm not taking anything either of you say about being Jewish as gospel anymore. None of you even hinted at the fact that the Torah service is all about sex. That's so clearly what it is, that there's no excuse for not being honest about it."

"About sex? What are you talking about?"

"Okay, I know you won't like it, but I'll tell you the way I saw it. The high point of the service is reached. Everyone gets real excited and stands up and begins singing to the Torah. The Torah lives in this little palace in the synagogue with the other Torahs. The men go to get her and they select the female they prefer. She's dressed in her sexy little dress and they take her out and they dress her with all the best jewelry, all this bling. Then they hug her and touch her; they sing to her and all the men get to kiss her as they show her off. Then they bring her to that big table that looks like a bed because it's covered with a velvet bed sheet. And they strip off her jewelry and her little dress and then they take hold of her little legs and they spread her wide open so everyone can see. Then they read from her—okay, that's not so weird—but when they are finished, they dress her back up and they put her bling back on; then they parade her around and kiss her and touch her again until they finally put her back in her little house with the other females until the next week." Angela stared at the ceiling, lost in thought. "So powerful," she murmured, "I have to admit—the whole thing was really powerful!"

Lev sat there unable to utter a word. Everything she said was so totally wrong, so totally distorted; he couldn't bear it.

"You don't know what you're talking about! That's just a sick, twisted way of looking at a beautiful thing. Not everything is about sex, you know—you might believe that it is, but not everything is!"

"What are you shouting at me for?" she yelled back at him. "I didn't make up that weird ceremony. You Jews made it up. I don't sit every Saturday morning with my guy pals for a few hours and get my kicks from it—you do! Why is it my fault?"

"I don't know why you just can't let it be. Let things be what they are! They don't need your warped interpretation. Just let them go on for another two thousand years without interfering!"

"I'm not interfering," she replied. She had stopped shouting. "I'm just trying to understand, that's all. I want to understand what it's all about."

"Why do you need to understand what it's all about? It has nothing to do with you. You have your own religion to figure out—why don't you focus on that? You don't need to understand."

She gave Lev a dark look. He couldn't tell if it was a look of anger or hurt. Then Angela grabbed her coat and yanked open the front door of the apartment. "Lev, you think you're so smart just because you know every country and state and city in those 5,400 pages of the Talmud, but you don't know anything about what's important. You don't know anything about caring about other people. You don't know anything about *love*." Angela said the word so emphatically, it was almost as if she had tattooed it on the knuckles of her hand and then punched him in the face. Then she stomped out of the apartment and slammed the door. Lev sat there stunned, listening to her bootheels clatter down the stairs. The outer door banged shut after her.

He leapt off the bed, pulled on his sneakers and ran down the stairs. Nelson Street was empty. How had she gotten to the corner and turned down Court Street so quickly? He rushed to Court Street. "Angela!" he shouted. The few pedestrians there were startled; they looked curiously at each other as if asking, "Are *you* Angela?" He ran to the next corner. "Angela!" Lev hollered. No Angela. Lev figured she was headed to the subway, so he sprinted the remaining four blocks to the station. People in the street saw him barreling toward them and skipped out of his way—he must have looked deranged as he charged at top speed down the sidewalk. He burst through the station doors and searched his pockets for a subway token. But he had left his tokens in his coat, so he vaulted over the turnstile and rushed up the stairs onto the platform. Except for a lone figure who clearly wasn't Angela, both sides of the platform were empty.

Lev couldn't figure out where she had gone. There was another subway stop in Red Hook, but it was almost ten blocks away and Lev couldn't imagine Angela pursuing that option.

It was bitter cold and he hadn't taken his overcoat. He was left with no choice but to return to the apartment and try to reach her with his cell phone, which he had left behind. He was beginning to shiver in the freezing late afternoon air, so he jogged back in the gathering darkness, his hands in his pockets.

When Lev opened the door to the apartment, the lights were out and the candle perched on top of the refrigerator was lit. In the half-light, he saw Angela lying in bed, the covers pulled up to her chin. Only her head stuck out of the blanket as if she were a little girl who had been tucked in for the night.

"How did you do that?" Lev panted.

"I pretended to rush out and slam the street door, but instead I hid under the stair-well on the first floor waiting for you to come running after me. When you left, I came up here and made myself comfortable."

"How did you know I would run after you?"

"Because, like I told you, you don't know anything about it and I know everything about it."

"Angela, I just want to say—"

She cut him off. "We don't have to talk about it anymore."

"But I want to. I want to tell you how I feel."

"Lev, I know how you feel. I'm not saying it's not important for you to say how you feel, but it's too late now. It wouldn't mean anything now. When people talk about how they feel about each other, it's kind of like they're doing some kind of deal—one of them says this and the other one says that because they think they have to. I've been down that road and I'm not interested. Someday, it will be said in a way that means something or it won't be said at all. But I'm not interested in swapping these kind of feelings with you. Understand?"

Lev did understand, and it seemed to be so true that all he could do was marvel at the riddle of Angela, a woman snarled with such profound contradictions—someone who at one moment could pollute a central ceremony of Judaism with the most carnal interpretation and at the next instant understand what love was supposed to be.

"Yes," he said to her, "I get it."

"Besides," she said, "I didn't say anything about how I feel about you. I just pointed out that you don't know what you're talking about."

Lev didn't know how to respond, so he didn't say anything.

Her smile turned impish.

"But you should be punished for not being sensitive. Right? I'm right, aren't I?"

Lev shrugged.

"Okay, your punishment is to do all my chores for the rest of the day. First, you have to hang your clothes up. Not sloppy, but neat, the way I do it."

Lev looked at the iron rod and saw that Angela had already hung her clothes there.

"Anything else?"

"Yes," she continued, "when you're done with your first chore, grab a Diet Dr. Pepper out of the fridge and pop it open on your way over here."

34.

Lev found himself frequently cursing Rabbi Dr. Erwon Arkadi and his odious book. What kind of a man—allegedly a rabbi—devotes his life to gathering in one place all of the hundred upon hundreds of embarrassing, illogical and bizarre practices of the Jewish faith? He certainly didn't do it for the edification of the Jews. And he certainly couldn't have written it to endear Jews to gentiles.

Angela couldn't get enough of *How Strange the Jews!* The hours that Lev spent doing his homework in the apartment in Red Hook, Angela spent reading the tome. She would lie on her stomach with the book open before her on the bed, usually in just her bra and panties, and read it page by page. "Get this!" she would exclaim. "Did you know that the priests in the Temple would grow the nail on their thumb really long so that when they had to offer some poor little bird as a sacrifice, they could cut its head off with their thumbnail while holding it in one hand? Did you know that?"

"Yes."

"I can't believe you never told me that!"

"Why should I tell you that?"

"Because it's so weird! To cut off a little bird's head while you're holding it in your hand . . . You *do* think it's weird, don't you?"

"I thought you already knew all about it."

"Me? How should I know?"

"It's in the Old Testament. In the book you would call Leviticus."

"What would you call that book?"

"*Vayikra.*"

"Sounds like you're saying *eureka*."

"Well I'm not."

"Why didn't you tell me about it?"

"Never came up."

"Of course it didn't *come* up. It's the kind of thing you have to *bring* up."

How Strange the Jews! was so voluminous that it was too heavy for
Angela to carry around, and the only time she could read it was when
they were in Red Hook. But after a while, Lev noticed that she was
covering a lot of ground pretty fast. One day she would be asking him
whether he knew about the purification rites of the red heifer and the
next day, she would be cross-examining him about how houses could
contract leprosy merely because their tenants were rumor-mongers.
Lev had thumbed through the book and knew that Rabbi Dr. Erwon
Arkadi's chapter about family purity—the minutiae of how the rabbis would examine the secretions of women to determine when they
could have sex with their husbands—came relatively late in the book.
Lev dreaded the day when Angela finally hit that chapter.

Lev couldn't figure out how she was moving so fast through the
eight-hundred-page opus until one day, as they were getting ready to
leave the apartment, he saw her take a paring knife from the kitchen
drawer and run the blade down the inside margin of the book. Rough-
ly twenty pages dropped out. She neatly folded the pages and stuck
them in her purse.

Lev was appalled. "Angela, did you just cut pages out of that book?"
he asked.

"Sure did. I'm not going to lug that monster around."

"Angela, you can't cut up a book. It's not right to cut up a book."

"I thought you hated that book. Anyhow, the book doesn't mind.
Rabbi Dr. Erwon Arkadi doesn't mind."

"Well, I mind. You can't cut up a book, even one that I don't like.
It's . . . it's uncivilized."

"Says you."

"The Nazis burned books. That's why it's uncivilized. And the
Church burned Talmuds. It's not right."

"Are you calling me a Nazi?"

"Of course not! All I'm saying is that certain things have to be
treated with respect. Life is a slippery slope. If you start cutting up
books, who knows where it could lead?"

"That's totally ridiculous! I'm not cutting it up to use as toilet paper or to toast marshmallows. I'm cutting it up so I can read it and
learn about you and your weird religion. Cutting up a book doesn't
lead to committing war crimes if that's what you're getting at!"

"It doesn't matter *why* you are doing it. It just matters that you *are* doing it."

She looked startled. "Well, there it is! That's exactly what Rabbi Dr. Erwon Arkadi says is the difference between Christians and Jews. Christians care about *why* they are doing things, about their motives, a lot more than they care about what they are actually doing, but you Jews care more about the things you are doing than why you are doing them. And here we are having an argument exactly about the same thing!" She seemed proud to be acting out the discordance to which Rabbi Dr. Erwon Arkadi had alerted the world in his ponderous work.

"Well, I finally agree with something Rabbi Dr. Erwon Arkadi says. It's true that Christians care more about why they do things than what they actually do. That's why they find it so easy to burn people at the stake in order to save their souls."

Angela's face soured. Lev braced himself for one of her over-wrought reactions. But to his surprise, she merely set her eyes on him, her mouth closed in a neutral line, and studied him, her forehead wrinkled in puzzlement. She scrutinized Lev in silence. Finally, she said with a shrug: "I have no answer to your question."

"It wasn't a question."

"Yes, it was," she stated.

"Are you going to knock off cutting up the book?"

"Why should I? I don't ask you to do Christian things, so don't ask me to do Jewish things."

"I'm not asking you to do Jewish things. I'm asking you to stop doing something that upsets me."

"It upsets you because you're Jewish."

"That's right. That's what I am. It's about time you came to terms with that."

Finally, the fuse had been lit. "How dare you! I'm the one who bought this book and I read it as much as I can—not so I can under-stand Jews, but only so I can understand *you*! So don't lecture me about coming to terms with you're being Jewish. I don't see you read-ing books about Christianity!"

Lev watched Angela as she berated him, holding the paring knife in her hand, gripping it so hard that her knuckles looked like little knobs of bleached bone against her skin, and waving it around as she elaborated all the reasons why she was right and he was wrong.

And Lev realized: Angela is excited. She gets excited arguing with me about things like this, things that matter. She's not upset about what I accused Christianity of—she's enjoying herself! She's been so bored with arguing about where to have a slice of pizza or which TV show to watch, but now she's eager to argue about ideas, about theories and beliefs. She knew she irritated him with what he regarded as pointless disputes. But Angela needed them.

Was it because no one ever argued with her about things that mattered before, Lev wondered, or because nothing *had* ever mattered to her before?

35.

Winter descended upon them early and it was one of those emphatic winters when the temperature loitered in the teens and twenties and snow dusted the streets with three or four inches every week or so. Throughout Brooklyn, these light snowfalls clothed the close streets and apartment buildings in white purity for at least a few hours until the vehicular traffic and pedestrian footfalls transformed the pristine whiteness into a grey sludge. Red Hook, however, was so dreary to begin with that it seemed to Lev that the snow always fell pre-sullied, so that by the time each flake settled on the ground, it was already befouled. But Lev and Angela hardly paid attention to anything that existed in Red Hook as they hurried through the cold from the Smith–9th St. subway stop to their shabby apartment. They continued to meet there several times a week, usually in the late afternoon after classes ended. After they engaged in the same preliminary rituals, they would stand naked beside the bed and ogle each other for a while until, at some point that each of them somehow always reached simultaneously, they would hurl themselves at each other with such ardor that Lev imagined he could actually hear the sound of their bony bodies colliding, like two pieces of wood clacked one against the other.

They abandoned the practice of kissing each other while they made love; of his moving his lips over Angela's in a caress; of Angela flicking her tongue into his mouth. Instead, each of them planted their open mouths one on the other during their lovemaking and inhaled each other's saliva and spittle, breathing each other's air mouth-to-mouth almost as if one was resuscitating the other.

This was something Lev had never imagined: the urge to pour their bodies, their fluids, their breath one into the other until neither of them existed as separate beings. Or maybe it was more of a yearning to devour each other, to consume each other and annihilate the boundaries in that way. Was it really sinful to want to merge with another human being, for one person to enter into another and possess her while being absorbed by her? It seemed a return to that primal state described by the Sages when male and female were one creature before being torn asunder. When Adam and Eve were one living organism in the Garden, were they lonely? Perhaps bored, but surely not lonely.

And when they finished with each other, Lev would roll off Angela, or she off him, and they would lie on their backs gazing up at the tin ceiling, holding hands and catching their breath. And Lev would think: This is it. Absolutely, categorically, it. I will never experience lovemaking like this, better than this, more intense or passionate than this. And then he would think: After this, if we never made love again, I wouldn't care. Because my passion is satisfied. At last, it has been quenched. My urge has finally left me in a column of fire.

But two or three days later, they would be back in that room, circling each other, leering at each other, ravenous, until that moment when they would fling themselves on one another and do the whole thing over again.

And Lev would think: This is love; this has got to be what love is. What else could it be? Because if it isn't love—if love is something more than this, more intense than this—then love is too much. If love is more than this, then it is too terrifying to even contemplate.

And so that overheated dump in Red Hook—with the peeling wallpaper, the clanging radiator, the drafty bathroom with the toilet that always ran and the sink stained red from rust, the hot plate that sparked when they tried to brew tea, the half-height refrigerator that was barely large enough to hold a sandwich and a can of Diet Dr. Pepper, and that queen-size bed with the musty odor and the sagging middle which occupied almost the entire floor space—that dump in Red Hook became the world that Angela Pizatto and Lev Livitski inhabited together, to the exclusion of the other world, the world that most people, except for Angela and Lev, regarded as the real world.

They stopped meeting each other in diners in far-away neighborhoods. They stopped traveling to aquariums to see baby seals born. They did away with making out on benches on the Promenade in Brooklyn Heights while gazing at the Manhattan skyline, lit up, they had told themselves, to inspire only them.

Instead, their world shrunk to a mattress and box-spring in a third-floor walk-up in Red Hook, Brooklyn.

VI

Rabbi Shimon ben Elazar. . . said: if one tears his garments in his anger; or breaks utensils in his anger; or scatters his money in his anger—he should be in your eyes as if he is worshipping idols. For so is the craft of the Evil Inclination: today it tells him: 'Do this!' Tomorrow it tells him: 'Do this!' Until it tells him: 'Perform idolatry!'

And he goes and performs it.

- Babylonian Talmud, Tractate Shabbos 105B -

36.

Then began the fundamental clash of civilizations, the endless dispute between Christians and Jews as to whether Christmas was a celebration superior to Chanukah, or whether Chanukah was the preferred opportunity to indulge.

Angela came to the disputation with her mind totally made up: Christmas was so obviously better than Chanukah that pity was the only appropriate emotion to show to those excluded from its joys. A few weeks before Christmas, Angela began to express sympathy for Lev's unhappy situation. Sympathy was so uncharacteristic of her that Lev found himself irritated by it.

"Let's go to Rockefeller Center for the Christmas tree lighting," she suggested. "You should at least get a chance to celebrate a little bit." She smiled and squeezed his arm.

"Not interested."

"You poor thing," she said, patting his hand. "Really, let's go."

"Really," he said, "I don't care about Christmas trees."

She shook her head and clucked.

And the truth was that Lev, in fact, didn't care about Christmas or Christmas trees at all. The whole thing seemed absurd to him, particularly Santa Claus. Lev believed that the Jews had all the advantages: eight days of celebration; special foods like doughnuts and potato latkes; parties virtually every night; gifts of all types. Instead of schlepping Christmas trees into the apartment and decorating them with breakable ornaments and lights, the Jews had the distraction of fiddling over a variety of menorahs that they filled with olive oil and wicks or with multicolored candles.

But Angela couldn't conceive of indifference to the Christmas rites. She construed Lev's protests to the contrary as obstinacy, an inability to acknowledge the depths of his disappointment. To make the point, she often reflected on Moti and her sadness at his imagined

193

wretchedness at being shut out of Christmas festivities.

"Poor Moti," she kept saying, "is he in a funk? I wouldn't blame him if he was."

"No, he's fine," Lev reported. "He's excited about Chanukah. He already has a list of things he is going to buy with his Chanukah money."

"Oh, you mean Chanukah *jelt*," she said.

"*Gelt*. Who told you about Chanukah gelt?"

"Rabbi Dr. Erwon Arkadi has a whole section about it. I think it's kind of strange that you give each other jelt instead of gifts."

"*Gelt*." Why she persisted in calling it jelt was a mystery to Lev. Perhaps she assumed that all Yiddish words must be pronounced differently from the way they were spelled in English.

"Whatever," she responded. "Anyhow, I'm not judging you."

"Angela, if you were to decide to judge us, what would you be saying?"

"Well," she replied carefully, "don't you think giving money instead of gifts kind of plays into people's prejudices about Jews? Not *my* prejudices . . . I mean I don't have any prejudices about Jews, at least not anymore since I got to know one, I mean got to know *you*." As Angela demonstrated her enlightened attitudes about the Jewish people, she presented Lev with a reassuring smile.

"Yes, well you might be surprised to learn that we don't really care what people think. We're used to everyone blaming us for everything. So we're quite happy giving each other money on Chanukah."

"Really, Lev," she said in exasperation, "after all these months together, do you think you're telling me something that I don't already know? I've never met someone as stubborn as you! Nino was right about you. You don't bend. You would rather break than bend."

She nodded her head as she made this definitive declaration and while she did so, Lev thought: Angela, I'm the weakest member of the Tribe; you have no idea how irresolute I am, particularly when it comes to you.

Fortunately, Christmas and Chanukah overlapped that year, so neither Angela nor Lev had to sit on the sidelines doing nothing while the other celebrated. Christmas was on a Thursday, the seventh day of Chanukah, so Lev and Angela decided they would exchange gifts the preceding Sunday.

Buying Angela a Christmas gift was a double challenge. Lev had never bought a gift for a girlfriend (never having had one) and he had never bought anyone a Christmas gift. Lev had saved as much as he could of his weekly allowance and the money he had picked up from odd jobs around the neighborhood, amassing a hundred and fifty dollars in cash. He couldn't spend it all on Angela. Lev had obligations to get Chanukah gifts for his brothers, and the five brothers would pool their money to buy something for their mother. After doing a careful calculation of what he had to spend to get through the Chanukah season, Lev concluded that he had exactly seventy dollars to spend on a gift for Angela.

That seemed like an extraordinary amount and he resolved to get something very special. Some sort of ring? No, too fraught with symbolism about the future. Lev had been to the Diamond District in Midtown a few times, so he figured: why not get her a diamond necklace?

One day in mid-December, he took the subway to 47th Street and began wandering among the little jewelry stalls situated in the Diamond Exchange there. The array was overwhelming. Lev bounced from one counter to another, studying the display cases. Whenever one of the proprietors asked him what he was looking for, he would mutter, "Just looking," and retreat. Finally, after an hour of knocking around the narrow corridors, Lev found himself in front of a small counter overseen by a matronly Orthodox woman wearing an elaborate head-covering that looked like a turban. The proprietress looked at him and smiled.

"Something special for your girl?" she asked.

Worn down by the quest, Lev threw himself on her mercy. "Yes, for my girlfriend. A nice Chanukah present."

"*Oy,*" she said, "this is a lucky *maidele*. What do you have in mind?"

"A diamond necklace."

Her eyebrows rose in surprise.

"Not too fancy," he added. "Something affordable."

"This is some lucky maidele," she repeated. She reached down and pulled out a felt-lined tray with dozens of small diamond pendants lined up in each row. "Take a good look," she said. "Tell me if you see something."

Lev scanned the rows of pendants. "Can you recommend something?"

She took a closer look at Lev, at his father's oversized overcoat, at the cuffs of his shirts that were worn to threads. She reached down and took out another tray, this one with smaller pendants. "Look at this one," she suggested. She pulled out a triangular pendant with a little glint of light in the center. It could have been a diamond, or more likely, a shard of one.

Lev picked it up and held it close to his face. He liked it and he thought maybe he could even afford to buy it.

"Nice!" he said. "How much would this cost?"

"Two hundred and twenty and I would throw in the chain," she said, nodding magnanimously.

Lev's face betrayed him. She looked at him with concern. "*Boychik*," she asked, "how much do you have to spend?"

"Seventy dollars," Lev confessed.

"Why didn't you say?" She pulled the trays off the counter and put them back. She reached behind her and pulled out another tray of jewelry. "A diamond pendant is not for you," she confided. "But a *Mogen Dovid* is right up your alley. Your maidele will love one of these." She shoved the tray filled with rows of Jewish stars in front of his face and bid him to examine them closely. "I can sell you one of these plus a silver chain, and you'll still have enough change to buy a knish," she added.

Lev pretended to survey the assortment of Jewish stars arrayed in rows like soldiers in a phalanx, but his heart cringed at the hopelessness of his situation. This should have been an adventure for him, buying a special gift for his first girlfriend, but instead it had turned into a farce of deceit. He even went through the motions of pulling one or two of the Jewish stars out of their black felt slots and placing them in the palm of his hand as he examined them. "Nice," the sheitel-wearing lady remarked. "She'll love that one. Very modern, not run-of-the mill."

Finally, after spending what Lev thought was a respectable amount of time in pursuit of the perfect Mogen Dovid, he raised his eyes to her and told another lie. "I think I need to think about it a little more. She seems to have a few of these already. I think I'll ask her best friend what she might want."

"Whatever you say, boychik," she said. "But you know, the price of silver isn't coming down."

"Thanks," he said. "I'll keep that in mind. I'll be back," he lied.

Lev pushed his way through the narrow aisles of the exchange and finally broke out into the open of 47th Street. The sidewalks were clogged with throngs of Jews from the diamond line, shouting into their phones and jostling one another as they navigated back and forth from the jewelry exchanges to diamond-cutting shops in the upper stories of the buildings lining the street. He felt that everyone was looking at him and knowing that he had been shopping for a diamond necklace for his shiksa girlfriend.

Lev made his way down 5th Avenue, gradually heading east to Grand Central, where he would catch a train back to Flatbush. He was dejected at his failure and anxious about having only seventy dollars to spend. He entered Grand Central and moved with the crowd down the ramp toward the subway entrance when he saw a small store window on the flanks of the corridor leading to the Great Hall. The sign on the window read: *MTA Museum Gift Shop*.

Lev stopped and peered into the window display. Draped on a blue velvet backing under the lights was a silver necklace with a subway token mounted as a pendant. The subway token was somewhat of an antique from the early 1950s. It was the smaller variant of the current token, with a Y cutout design from a bygone era, highly polished so that its brass patina glowed in the intense display lighting. It was the perfect size for Angela's dainty neck. The token was mounted in a sterling silver subway track edging, with a silver chain.

The price tag was $69.99.

37.

On the Sunday before Christmas, Angela and Lev met in Red Hook to exchange gifts. They sat next to each other on the side of the bed, their feet on the floor. Lev went first. He handed Angela the gift box for which he had paid an additional $2 to have wrapped in festive Christmas paper.

"Wrapped!" Angela exclaimed with delight. She quickly tore off the paper and threw it on the floor as if she were a little girl. When she saw that the gift was in a velvet-lined jewelry box, her eyes grew wide.

"Oh," she whispered, "this looks . . . wow."

Lev held his breath. Perhaps the gift box was setting Angela's expectations too high and the gift wasn't quite wow enough. She held the box up to her face before her eyes and slowly, ceremoniously opened the hinged lid. She peeked inside for an instant and then immediately snapped it shut. The lid made a sharp click.

"What's wrong?" he asked her. "I thought you would—"

She quickly put her hand up and pressed her index finger against his lips to silence him. Then she opened the box again, took out the necklace and held it up before her eyes, studying it as she turned it over in her hand. She draped it around her neck and then turned her back so Lev could fasten the clasp. Angela rose and went into the bathroom to look at her reflection in the faded mirror. She left the door open and Lev could see her as she gazed at herself, turning slightly to the left and then the right to view the necklace on her neck. Then she returned and sat on the bed.

"Do you like it?" he asked her.

Angela opened her mouth to say something, but nothing came out. She clamped her mouth shut and looked down, shaking her head. She was unable to utter a word.

Angela, speechless!

Instead, she squeezed closer to Lev and put her arm around his neck. Her other hand kept flitting to the subway token pendant, stroking it. "Lev," she finally whispered, "no one has ever given me a gift that was just for me, for Angela and not for some person . . . that they thought I was, or . . . that they thought I should be. Something just for me . . . something that I really would love, not something that they thought I *should* love."

She pulled him to her and kissed him gently on the lips.

"My gift isn't like this," she confessed. "My gift is not as good as this gift."

Tentatively she reached into her purse and withdrew a small box. It was wrapped in blue Chanukah wrapping paper decorated with Mogen Dovids. When Lev saw the paper, he laughed. He followed Angela's example and tore off the paper and threw it on the floor. Inside was a small velvet box, just like the one that had contained Angela's necklace. Like Angela, he ceremoniously opened the box.

Inside was a silver dollar. Lev looked at it and his face must have displayed his surprise because Angela immediately launched into a long explanation.

"It's Chanukah jelt," she explained. "But Lev, it's not just a silver dollar. It's a special silver dollar that was minted in 1904. I mean this silver dollar is a collector's item. Lev, don't go thinking that this silver dollar cost . . . you know, cost a dollar. It's a collector's item. It cost a lot more than a dollar. But I wanted to get you something that was, you know . . . not Christmassy. Something that was, you know . . . Chanukah-y. You know, some jelt."

Lev put his index finger on her lips. He turned the box over and the silver dollar fell into the palm of his open hand. He continued to imitate everything Angela had done when she had received the subway token necklace. He held the silver dollar up to his face and examined it.

"That's Lady Liberty and she's wearing a crown or something, or a tiara, yeah, maybe a tiara," Angela told him. "And the tiara says 'Liberty' on it. Look at the little stars around the edge. There's thirteen of them for the original States. I know you like that July 4th–type of stuff." A little breathlessly, she added, "Did you notice the stars are little Jewish stars? Not Christmas stars—Jewish stars!"

Lev nodded his head and turned the coin over, scrutinizing every detail. A bald eagle in profile perched proudly on the back, wings unfurled, clutching a bundle of arrows and an olive branch in its talons. Inscribed above the eagle was "In God We Trust."

While Angela perched on the edge of the bed, Lev went to the window to finish his examination in the dim light that filtered through the porthole that Angela had scoured into the grimy windowpane. Then he came back and sat on the bed next to Angela. When he thought enough time had passed to register his admiration, Lev turned to her and whispered: "This is the most wonderful Chanukah gift ever, Angela."

Angela nodded her head in agreement. She rose and lit the candle on top of the refrigerator and flipped off the light.

38.

Wednesday night was Christmas Eve, so Lev's family deemed it the perfect time to have the family Chanukah Party.

Lev's paternal grandparents had both died young and although Elya and Lev were often told how they had spent a lot of time with them in Crown Heights when they were infants, neither had any memory of them. Lev's mother's parents, however, had been a presence in the boys' lives for years. His grandfather, Mordechai, had died shortly after Lev's Bar Mitzvah and Moti had been named in his memory. Bubbie Malke, as his maternal grandmother was called, continued to be a frequent guest in the Livitski apartment.

Lev's father's four siblings had all made aliyah to Israel, but his mother's two brothers lived nearby: one in Staten Island, the other in Monsey. Lev's mother was the eldest and for that reason, and because she was the only daughter, it fell on her shoulders to look after Bubbie Malke. For a number of years after Lev's grandfather's death, Bubbie Malke spent almost every Shabbos with Lev's family. They would set up a folding cot for her in the little room adjacent to his parents' bedroom. The rest of the week she lived by herself in Williamsburg in the apartment where Lev's mother and her brothers had grown up.

Bubbie Malke continued to live independently for a few years, but then she began to fall. The turning point came when she slipped in the bathtub and couldn't get out. For a day and a half, she didn't answer the phone. Bubbie Malke had almost died from exposure by the time Lev's mother found her. At that point, the family met and decided she would live with Uncle Mende, his mother's next-eldest sibling. Mende made a lot of money as a stockbroker and he had a big house in Monsey with a spare room and bathroom. Bubbie Malke resisted leaving Brooklyn but a few weeks before she was due to leave for Monsey, she was diagnosed with dementia and her doctors recommended that she would get better care in a nursing home. The family found a decent one in Fort Greene and Bubbie Malke lived there uneventfully for the past three years. That was the fortress-like nursing home across the street from the Icarus Diner.

Despite his uncle's big home in Monsey, the family Chanukah Party traditionally took place at the Livitski apartment. Uncle Berish, the Staten Island uncle, was charged with picking up Bubbie Malke from the nursing home in Fort Greene and schlepping her to Flatbush.

Each year before the Chanukah party, Lev's mother was seized by a spasm of cleaning and home improvement, a vain attempt to convince her brothers—more accurately, her sisters-in-law, because her brothers couldn't have cared less—that the Livitskis were more well-off than they actually were. All of the boys, even Moti, were made to scrub the apartment for a week. The under-utilized living room was the particular focus of the cleaning frenzy, especially the plastic slip covers of the world's most uncomfortable couch, which seemed to increase in stickiness the more they were sponged with hot soapy water. The boys often wondered whether it was worth it. Their cousins were so Orthodox, sporting their expensive, broad-brimmed black hats with arrogance, that the brothers didn't really like them very much. The boys knew that they were just as learned and as observant as their cousins were, but the fact that the Livitskis rejected the Orthodox regalia diminished them in the eyes of their relatives.

Uncle Berish was the first to arrive that Wednesday night. Elya and Lev went down to the street to help extract Bubbie Malke from the back seat of Berish's minivan. They flanked her as she shuffled her way to the elevator with the assistance of an aluminum walker. It took another ten minutes to get her from the elevator into the apartment. While they were occupied with Bubbie Malke, Uncle Berish and the rest of his family scoured the streets for a parking space.

Everyone was instructed to smile brightly at Bubbie Malke at every opportunity. She didn't really remember who they were, but if they all smiled at her, she responded in good humor. If the group stopped smiling, Bubbie Malke would grow anxious and start screeching that she had been kidnapped and that someone should call the police.

After Lev and Elya managed to get Bubbie Malke ensconced in the easy chair adjacent to the couch in the living room, the rest of the family arrived. Lev's mother was busy frying latkes in the kitchen, filling the air with the redolent odor of bubbling oil. It would suffuse everyone's clothing by the end of the evening. Later, Lev's mother would order the boys to pile all the clothes in front of the washing machine so she could launder the oily reek away.

The entire family clustered together to light the multiple menorahs set up on a sheet of aluminum foil on the sideboard in the dining room. Then the festivities began in earnest. Moti and his little cousin Chayim intently played *dreidel*. They were using pistachio nuts for chips. Moti was killing him and his pile of nuts continued to grow.

Lev's mother made a plate of latkes with sour cream and applesauce for Bubbie Malke and told Lev to bring it to her in the living room. When he handed her the plate, she looked up at him and for a moment, it seemed as if the clouds had dissipated from her mind.

"You're Levi," she declared in a loud and clear voice. "How's that cute little girlfriend of yours that I've seen you with?"

Lev didn't panic because Bubbie Malke, even before she had lost most of her mind, always thought that she saw one of the brothers carrying on with a girl.

"I don't have a girlfriend, Bubbie," Lev replied. He spoke up because Bubbie Malke was not only a bit loony, but a bit deaf as well.

"You know the one I'm talking about," she said with authority. "The one with the short skirts."

This time Lev was rattled, and he stood there not knowing how to respond. But Elya, who was seated at the end of the couch as he chatted with Uncle Mende, leaned over and shouted to Bubbie Malke, "You're confused, Bubbie. Lev doesn't have a girlfriend."

Bubbie Malke didn't answer. Instead she began eating her latke, slathering it with sour cream as she picked it up with her fingers. Occasionally, she would lift the plate up to her mouth and lick a bit of the apple sauce. Lev turned to go back to the kitchen when suddenly she said, "It was Levi and she was a shiksa. She looked like an Italian. An Italian shiksa."

Elya burst out laughing and Uncle Mende joined in. Lev couldn't figure out what had gotten into the old lady, but he forced himself to laugh, as well. Moti scrambled into the living room pursued by Chayim. Bubbie Malke had taken another lick of applesauce from her plate, but the sour cream had gotten in the way and when she put down her plate, she had a little goatee of white sour cream on her chin. Moti and Chayim saw it and started rolling on the floor, shrieking with laughter. Other family members came to look in on the commotion and when they saw Bubbie Malke with her creamy white beard, they too joined in. Bubbie Malke looked at everyone and blinked in puzzlement, but she soon responded to the merriment and began to wheeze with laughter as well. Finally, Lev's mother came in with a wet paper towel and cleaned off her mother's face The family settled down to serious eating.

The party ended and they all fussed around Bubbie Malke, pulling her to her feet and tugging on her coat. Elya and Lev were charged with slowly escorting her to the elevator and supporting her while she tottered with her walker to the street to await Uncle Berish and his minivan, which was parked several blocks away. When they got to the curb, Elya, who was just in shirt-sleeves, said his goodbyes and went back upstairs to help clean up. Lev waited with his grandmother.

It was cold so he turned to her, pulled her coat tighter around her chest and buttoned the top button. She looked into his face and she said: "Get rid of the Italian girl, Lev. I saw you two a couple of times. Get rid of her." She said this so calmly and matter-of-factly that Lev didn't react with his usual alarm. Nor could he lie to the old woman. He didn't know how much more time Bubbie Malke had left in this world, and he didn't want to end what they had shared all these years with a lie.

"Where did you see us?" he asked.

"What do you think I do all day? I sit by my window in Fort Greene and watch people go about their business. Do you love the shiksa, Lev?"

"It's nothing, Bubbie. We're just friends."

"I saw you holding hands."

"Holding hands is nothing, Bubbie. Means nothing."

Bubbie Malke smiled sadly and shook her head. "I saw you holding hands. I saw you put her hand up to your lips and kiss it."

Lev shrugged and didn't answer.

"Don't bring her home, Lev," Bubbie Malke said. "Your mother will murder you. She'll murder all of us."

"Bubbie, I would never bring a shiksa home."

"I mean a convert. Don't bring home a convert either." Bubbie Malka nodded her head to emphasize how serious she was. Suddenly, she glared at him. "How come you never visit me?" she asked. "You can walk around Fort Greene holding a shiksa's hand—that you have time for—but not to stop and visit me?"

"Bubbie, maybe the Italian girl and I could drop by the home and we could visit you?"

"I don't want to know from her," she said.

Lev wanted to protest, but he knew it was pointless. He just looked into her eyes, searching for some hope. But she gazed back without any encouragement.

Finally, Lev said: "Bubbie, you're not really senile, are you?"

"How should I know? When you're senile, you're not supposed to know anything."

"I don't really think you are."

"They were going to send me to Monsey. It's better to be senile in Brooklyn than to be just an old lady in Monsey."

"Why don't you move in with us?" Lev suggested.

"You may not know this," she said, "but with the five of you boys around all the time, your place is like Bellevue."

"Well, I don't think you're senile."

"A senile person like me doesn't even know how to argue with you."

"I'm going to tell Imma," and Lev smiled to let her know he was joking.

She suddenly looked confused. "Tell Imma what?"

"That you're not senile."

"I'm not?" Bubbie asked. As Berish's minivan glided up to the curb, Lev thought he witnessed Bubbie Malke beckoning the fog of dementia back into her face, but he really couldn't tell. She grunted and moaned as Lev worked to slide her into the back seat of the van. Once he had her installed in her seat, he leaned in, reached over her and began fumbling with her seatbelt.

He whispered in her ear, "Thanks for the nice talk, Bubbie."

She turned to Lev and shouted: "What talk? What nice talk? Elya, stop making tricks on Moti!"

Lev thought for a moment that she was merely playing up her

charade, but when he looked into her eyes, the light had left them. There was only a dull glimmer reflecting the tedium of her confusion. And he wondered whether in fact their conversation was merely one brief instant of lucidity out of the long seasons of Bubbie Malke's befuddlement. Or possibly it was a stopover that Bubbie Malke had made from the world of dementia, which after all is a bit like sleep, like having part of yourself drift into sleep; or maybe a visit from the world of sleep itself, which the Talmud declares is a sixtieth part of death; in any case, a brief expedition from those other worlds to this world, Lev's world, that Bubbie Malke made as her true self, to talk to him, to give him her warning.

39.

Angela and Lev had not seen each other since exchanging holiday gifts, and Lev didn't expect her to be able to get away from the Christmas festivities at her apartment until late afternoon on Christmas Day. But he went over to the Red Hook apartment around noon, committed to catching up on some of his reading for school. Late in the afternoon as it was beginning to get dark, Lev heard Angela treading slowly up the stairs. She came into the room, closed the door and leaned her back against it. She was pasty and haggard. She looked like she was about to collapse.

"What's wrong? Did something happen?" Lev asked her.

"Yes, something happened," she said wearily. "You bet something happened. I'll tell you what happened. You ruined Christmas for me."

"Me? How did I ruin Christmas for you?"

And this is what she told Lev, in one long soliloquy, which spilled out of her as she stood in her winter coat, her back up against the front door.

"Everything was fine on Christmas Eve. We had dinner and went to Midnight Mass. Everyone was getting along—even the usual wise-cracks and picking on one another didn't matter so much. We went to sleep and woke up early the next morning to exchange presents under the tree. It was almost the best Christmas we ever had. For some reason, this year, even when someone in the family got a present that they didn't like or need—well, in fact, the family has a talent for buying presents that not only you don't like or need, but that you actually hate, presents that are disgusting to you—but in any event, this year, even the disgusting gifts got a pass.

"The relatives began to show up for Christmas dinner and most of them seemed to be in a cheery mood. My father's brother Vito, the used-car salesman, and his wife, Aunt Edna, were both feeling good. Their son Franco—the one who rents this apartment—is still upstate,

207

so there was no opportunity for them to fight. It was a lot more pleasant with Franco not sitting near me and hitting on me so much that my father would shout, 'Back off, Franco, back off!' That got rid of a lot of the usual tension. My mother's sister, Aunt Octavia, was there with Uncle Nicky—by the way, they've been married thirty-five years and no one has ever heard Uncle Nicky say a word other than, 'Pass the salt,' or, 'More wine,' and the funny thing is that he's my favorite uncle! So they are all there with my brothers and sisters and then the food starts coming out. And I'm sitting there feeling pretty good about things and I'm thinking this could be the best Christmas in a long time.

"Oh my God!—you wouldn't believe the food! Uncle Nicky brought some prosciutto from some place in New Jersey where it took him three hours in traffic. And Aunt Edna's calamari was just the best ever—you know Edna's calamari can be too tough, but if she overcooks it, there's this aftertaste—but this year, it was perfect! And then Aunt Octavia brought out her stuffed Clams Casino—outstanding! We were eating and drinking and having just the best time.

"And then it was time for the main course—the dish that everyone looks forward to all year, the most divine dish that you can imagine (although I know you can't imagine it, for which I was prepared to forgive you, until tonight)—my mother's veal parmigiana.

"Just so you understand, my mother's veal parmigiana is a legend not only in our family, but in all of Bensonhurst. In fact, some people have been heard to say that the only reason my father married my mother was for this dish, which might explain why she only makes it once a year in order to punish him. And by the way, the only nice thing my mother ever did for me in her whole life was to teach me to make the family recipe of veal parmigiana—that's right, my birthright, that you reject because you're a stiff-necked person—I'm using the phrase used in *How Strange the Jews!* so don't go blaming me!

"Anyway, we all look forward to that moment each Christmas when my mother brings in this huge platter of veal parmigiana just out of the oven, the sauce and cheese still bubbling over the meat and the aromas filling the house and our heads. For us, it's the symbol of everything that is wonderful and special about Christmas.

"The platter is passed around and I help myself to a big plateful, and I take my fork and knife in my hand and I'm about to dig in and I look down into my plate, and what do I see? I see an ocean of boiling milk and devils driving baby cows in a herd over a cliff and I watch them as they are pushed over the cliff and they fall tumbling all over themselves and then they fall into the boiling milk and they start screaming in baby cow voices as they are boiled alive in the sea of their mothers' milk. Thanks to you, that's what I see when I look into my plate of veal parmigiana.

"I push my chair back and run to the bathroom and I close the door and lock it and then I puke my guts out into the toilet: the prosciutto, the calamari, the Clams Casino. Can you imagine what that's like? No, you're probably the one person I know who can't imagine what that's like. And I puked and puked—I know how the sound carries in our apartment and even as I have my head in the toilet, I know that everyone at the dining room table is hearing my performance and the cheese from the veal parmigiana is dripping from their forks as they hold them frozen in the air between their plates and their mouths, and they just can't bring themselves to go through with it.

"After around fifteen minutes, I'm done puking and I clean myself up and open the bathroom door. My mother is outside waiting for me. She has in her eyes a new kind of hate like I've never seen before. She shakes her fist at me and she whispers—her whisper is equal to someone hollering at the top of their lungs—she whispers: 'Don't think I don't know that you're carrying on with someone, you whore! I know everything.'

"So I say, 'What are you talking about? I don't feel well. Something didn't agree with me.'

"'Don't bullshit me,' she says. 'You're pregnant; that's the only explanation.'

"I shout, 'I'm not pregnant!'—actually, we were both shouting now because no one in my house can whisper for more than five or six words. 'You're crazy,' I say.

"'Crazy am I? Where are you spending all your time these days? You're not in the library and you're certainly not helping me here in the house. Who's the father? That Greek guy you been seeing? You think you're so smart, but I know everything.' At that point, she's really getting into it, but I can tell she's also pleased with herself. She begins bragging: 'I know all about him,' she hollers, 'even his name.

His name is Larry! Larry Souvlaki! That's right, I even know his last name!'

"I almost start laughing at that point, she's being so ridiculous. But that would totally break the rules of our arguments, so I don't dare. So I say, 'I can't talk to you when you go nutty on me. Go tend to our guests and leave me alone.'

"Then she makes a motion with her head where she opens her mouth and snaps her teeth together like she wants to bite me, bite my neck, and then she hisses at me: 'If you're pregnant, you whore, I swear I will shave your head and send you to a convent!' And then she stomps away and I shout after her that there aren't even any convents anymore and even if there were, nuns don't shave their heads."

"And then you came here?" Lev asked. "You poor thing!"

"No, I didn't come here. I went back to the table. I smiled at everyone and they smiled at me—that's the only way we can stand each other, to put up with these outbursts. When they're over, you just return to where you were and everyone just goes on as if they never happened. It's kind of like getting the hiccups—everyone is relieved when they are over. But there's no criticism, no finger-pointing. Hiccups just happen to you. In our family, outbursts in which the most hateful things are said, just . . . explode. And then they're over and then we just go on as if they didn't happen.

"And then they finished the meal—I just sat there trying not to be nauseous. We said our goodbyes, and I came here."

She stopped talking and her eyes filled with tears. She struggled to contain them, not to accompany them with sobs, but the sobs overtook her and she put her hands to her face and began weeping. Lev jumped up and went to her—she was still leaning against the front door. He hugged her, helped her out of her coat and led her to the bed. She lay down with her head on the pillow. Lev sat beside her.

"Angela," he said to her, "people say terrible things when they're angry or disappointed, things they don't mean. I'm sure your mother didn't mean what she said."

"No," Angela said, sniffling, "my mother knew exactly what she was saying. She would say it again right now if you called her and asked her how she felt. I'm not upset that she said those things. She's been calling me a whore since I was eleven or twelve years old. I'm used to it."

"So then why are you crying?"

"I cry when I think things have ended, ended for good, and there's nothing I can ever do to get them back. I don't cry when something hurts or something is sad. I only cry when I realize that things are over for me. Christmas is finished for me. I know you can't understand that. Veal parmigiana served by my mother was Christmas for me, not just for me, but for all of us. You think it's just food, but you don't get it. You made it into a big issue about whether it's moral or something. You made it into a question of whether we're human beings or not. Are we human enough? Are we sensitive enough? Are we kind enough to really understand what veal parmigiana is? Are our souls big enough to know that veal parmigiana is really boiling baby cows in their mothers' milk?"

"I didn't say that. I certainly didn't mean to say that."

"It doesn't matter what you meant to say. That's how you made me feel." She stopped crying. She stared at the ceiling, thinking out loud. "I'm not really angry at you. I know you didn't mean to spoil Christmas for me. But you did it anyway, just by thinking about things too much, just by being so stubborn about what you think about. You guys do that a lot. Maybe that's why so many people hate you Jews." She turned to Lev and added: "Go right ahead—go right ahead and feel free to add that statement to your Angela Pizatto Database of Anti-Semitic Remarks!"

40.

One afternoon in mid-January after the disruptions of the holiday season had receded, Lev started down the stairs to the crowded train platform at the Brooklyn College/Flatbush Avenue station to board either the 2 or 5 Train—whatever would arrive first. He was headed to Atlantic Avenue, the first of the three trains he needed to get to Red Hook for an assignation with Angela, who would join him as soon as she finished her last class. Lev was smiling, thinking of the things they would soon be doing with each other. His cell phone buzzed and he pulled it from his pocket and flipped it open. There was a message from Angela:

she follow u

who he texted back

platform in back

Lev was in the middle of the station platform, so he turned and peered to the rear, but he didn't recognize anyone.

where r u he texted.

upstair take train to Manh lose her at chambers turn around see u in red h

Lev stared at the little screen as a feeling of foreboding washed over him. Someone was on to them. Someone had gotten wind of what was going on and was stalking him to see where they rendez-voused. And the someone who was doing this was a person Angela did not want to tangle with, someone Angela wanted him to flee from and lose in the labyrinth of the subway. His stomach constricted with fear.

Surely it was Cecile. It could only be Cecile, the one person not in-timidated by Angela. He had not spoken with Cecile since their fright-ening conversation in the student cafeteria, but he had seen her glar-ing at him as they took their seats in the seminar or when they passed in the hallways at Brooklyn College. What could have reawakened her interest in whether Lev was somehow involved with her archenemy? Could Cecile have joined forces with her former lover, Ricky? Could they have hatched a plan to wreak vengeance on Angela and Lev? But why now? Maybe something had happened in Bensonhurst that Angela hadn't shared with Lev, another run-in with Ricky?

The 5 Train pulled into the northbound platform as Lev quickly made his way to the front end. He resisted the urge to twist his head around to see if he could discover Cecile lurking behind him in the pack of milling passengers. He ducked into the car as soon as the doors opened. He stole a quick glance around the car as it accelerated, but he did not see Cecile.

Lev found himself standing in front of the framed map of the subway system, the map that served as Angela's sacred text. As he stared at it, he felt Angela's acumen flood into his brain and he began to decipher the map's mysteries. Angela's text message had told him to get off at Chambers Street, lose Cecile in the station and reverse direction to head back down into Brooklyn to Red Hook. But Angela hadn't known he was boarding a 5 Train that would take him across the East River away from Chambers Street to the east side of Manhattan, not the west. The map seemed to ask him a question: why cross the river into Manhattan at all? That would only take him further away from Red Hook. It would be a lot more efficient if he exited at the Atlantic Avenue station and lost Cecile in the warren of pedestrian tunnels and platforms that fed into a number of other train lines, including the 2 and 3 Trains, the LIRR, or the M, N, R and W lines that were accessible through the underground connection to Pacific Street. Cecile would probably stay on the 5 Train anyhow, thought Lev, but even if she chose to get off the train at Atlantic Avenue, her pursuit would be overwhelmed by the options.

When the train came to a stop at Atlantic Avenue, he exited and walked swiftly to the underground passageway that would connect him to the Pacific Street station and the four alphabet lines that swerved through Manhattan on their way to Queens. The corridor led him into the bowels of the Atlantic Avenue hub crowded with people. He passed a series of small alcoves leading to locked MTA utility closets and storerooms and ducked into one alcove as the throng of passengers surged by. He figured that if Cecile paused at the entrance to the tunnel and peered down it to see if he were there, she would not be able to see him; and even if she got lucky and entered the tunnel, there was a good chance she would walk right by him without noticing.

He resolved to wait ten minutes while his pursuer either continued onward aboard the 5 Train or grabbed another line into Manhattan. Then he would resume his trek through the pedestrian tunnel to Pacific Street, hop on one of the trains heading south, transfer to the F and end up at Smith–9th St. in Red Hook.

Lev turned to the wall of the alcove so that his face was partially hidden from passers-by. He whipped out his phone and pretended to be furiously texting, even though he was too deep underground for a signal. He studied the digits of the clock on the screen of his tiny phone, ticking off the minutes.

Ten minutes passed and he finally raised his eyes. He relaxed. He had avoided discovery. Cecile was probably fuming on the 5 as it rumbled under the East River to Manhattan, suspecting that somehow he had evaded her.

Lev emerged from the alcove and continued down the underground pedestrian tunnel toward Pacific Street. He took a wrong turn, realized he was on the uptown platform, and paused to search for a sign leading him to the downtown connection.

He felt a tap on his shoulder.

She had found him.

He slowly turned to confront Cecile, but instead, Faigie Gruenstein stood before him in a bulky ski-jacket. Lev couldn't hide his surprise—and his relief. "Faigie," he said, "how nice to see you!"

"Nice to see me?" she asked. "Am I interrupting you, Lev? Are you on your way someplace special?"

"No, I'm just on my way to see a friend . . . some friends."

"Anyone I would know?" Faigie peered at Lev, searching his face for something, as if her question, instead of small-talk, was in fact the most important question she had ever asked him.

Lev understood that the *she* following him, the woman to be feared, had been Faigie all along. "I don't think you know these people, no," Lev stammered.

"On your way to see your shiksa girlfriend, Lev?" Faigie snarled.

His face convulsed in such a look of horror that Faigie immediately regretted saying what she had said. She placed her hand on his forearm. "I'm sorry I said that, Lev. I know you wouldn't do that. I know

you wouldn't go out with a shiksa. It's just that I'm so upset . . . hurt
. . . upset at the way you've treated me!"

Lev struggled to regain control of himself, to slow his racing pulse.
"Faigie, what do you mean, the way I've treated you?"

"Oh, Lev! You know exactly what I'm talking about."

"No, Faigie, I don't."

"If you were going to dump me, you should at least have had the
courage to talk to me about it. You should have at least had the courage to tell me what was happening and why."

"Faigie, I didn't dump you. I don't know what you're referring to."

Her eyes began to tear up, but she managed to retain her compo-
sure. "One day we were seeing each other, spending time with each
other, enjoying each other's company—at least I was, but I don't know
anymore what you were feeling. And the next day you cut me off. No
more lunches, no more hanging out. Just cold shoulder all the way."

"Oh I see, I see, but I've just been very busy, that's all. I've been
running around with all sorts of stuff to do. I'm sorry I neglected you.
But we can have lunch this week. Let's have lunch this week."

"Lev," she said sadly, "you're just making it worse."

Lev didn't know what to make of it at all, how to respond to her
accusations. So he started playing for time—a few moments that
would give him a chance to try to figure out what was happening.

"Faigie, help me here. Help me understand what you're saying."

"I shouldn't have to spell this out for you," she said. "We were, you
know . . . we were *involved*, Lev!"

Lev's first thought was how full of crap Faigie was. *Involved*—what
did that mean? He had touched Faigie's hair, her face; maybe he had
sat next to her, maybe even brushed up against her, but that's not
being involved. Being involved was licking, sucking, fingering, penetrating each other, coming all over each other. He tried to remember
what it had been like to think about love the way Faigie apparently
thought about it, but he couldn't recall. He looked at her blankly.

"You're denying we were involved, Lev?"

"No, I'm not denying it. I'm not denying anything."

"But you're not admitting it either, are you?"

Suddenly, Lev felt as if Angela had snuck into his mind, like a *dybbuk*, and he said forcefully: "Damn it, Faigie, speak your mind already."

She drew back for an instant, startled by his assertiveness. "Okay," she said, "I'll speak my mind. We were involved! You seem to deny that now, or you're pretending that you didn't think that we were. But we've spent a lot of time together, Lev, since high school. We've been flirting with each other for years now. And then there was that kiss. You aren't going to deny that kiss, are you?"

Lev didn't know what she was talking about. "What kiss, Faigie?"

"Oh my God!" she exclaimed, and she swayed as if she was going to faint—faint and tumble onto the subway tracks where she would be dismembered or electrocuted or both. Lev grabbed her shoulder and steadied her. When she seemed to have recovered, he asked her again: "What kiss, Faigie?"

"Lev! How could you? We were coming back from the Israel rally in Washington, DC when we were seniors in high school and we were sitting next to each other on the bus, and the lights were turned down low and everyone was tired and we were leaning on each other and then you kissed me. You don't remember that?"

Lev did remember that trip, the excitement of marching together; the manic foolishness on the bus; then finally, the fatigue slamming everyone as they hit traffic on the New Jersey Turnpike; and sitting next to Faigie as she leaned against him, dozing. But he didn't re-member a kiss. The former Lev Livitski—the one who existed before becoming a lover of Angela Pizatto—would have said, *Of course I re-member. It was unforgettable!* But instead, he told her the truth.

"Faigie, I remember that trip; I remember sitting next to you on the bus; but I didn't kiss you. I would remember if I had, so I didn't."

She jerked her head back as if he had spit in her face. Her eyes grew wide and a wildness snuck into them as if she were witnessing some horrible, violent crime. She opened her mouth as if to scream, but no sound came out. And then Lev watched her face as the import of what he said penetrated her. Her face transformed from initial outrage and denial to hesitation, then to uncertainty, to doubt. Then sorrow. Faigie started to totter, and he again feared she might topple backwards onto the subway tracks.

Lev seized her arm to steady her.

"No kiss?" she muttered.

And the Angela dybbuk who had seized his soul whispered: *Finish*

216

it. Just remind her again that she dreamed the whole thing up. Stop bothering me and find someone who might fancy you. But there was still some part of Lev that could resist that dybbuk, that could summon enough independence to rebel against being so ruthless. And Lev Livitski pushed the dybbuk out of his consciousness and suddenly he was back in that bus heading to Brooklyn on the New Jersey Turnpike, sitting as close to Faigie as two human beings can get without screwing each other, her head leaning on his shoulder. And he thought that she was sleeping and leaned over and nestled closer to her, his face in her hair, inhaling her scent.

Lev pulled her to him. "Faigie," he murmured, "no kiss, but you're right; it was just like a kiss. It might as well have been a kiss."

She clung to him, struggling to collect herself. Finally, her breathing slowed. She wiped her eyes on her sleeve, disengaged herself from Lev and looked into his face.

"You're right," he said. "I haven't done the right thing by you."

"You're seeing someone else, aren't you? Who is she? Do I know her?"

"You don't know her. I've promised not to tell anyone. Her family is against it."

Faigie frowned and looked down for a moment. Then she said: "I can guess. A rich girl. Someone who lives in Manhattan. On the Upper East Side. One of those girls who go to Jewish prep schools."

He didn't respond.

"Are you going to marry this girl, Lev?"

Lev didn't know what to say, so he answered a different question. One that Faigie had wanted to ask, but hadn't asked. "Don't wait for me, Faigie. If that's your question, then the answer is don't wait for me."

She flashed him a bitter look. "I can't afford to wait for you, Lev. Maybe your rich girlfriend from the Upper East Side can wait, but not someone like me. We may call ourselves Modern Orthodox and parrot all that stuff about getting a college education and a career, but you know as well as I do that I can't wait for anyone. I need to get a husband before I graduate. That's the only reason my parents let me go to college at all. So if I don't, then I may never get one, and then I'll be a nothing. So, no, I'm not going to wait for you, Lev."

"Good, because I'm not worth waiting for."

"Are you saying that because you believe it, or only to hear me say, 'Oh no, Lev, you are definitively worth it; you are so worth waiting for?' Because I'm not going to say it."

Faigie took a half step closer to him and scrutinized his face. "You look different, Lev," she muttered. "Like you've done something wrong. Or like you don't believe in anything anymore."

Lev shrugged.

"Goodbye, Lev. Next time, do right by someone you're involved with. Just don't wander off without saying anything."

As Faigie trudged down the subway platform toward the Q Train to Flatbush, he thought: It's not true what I had told Angela—I had thought of Faigie as more than a friend. He had imagined her, or someone like her, as a wife, someone to journey with on the derech, someone to shoulder that burden, someone who could understand that particular challenge. But that fantasy was now a distant memory for Lev. And he thought of Angela, how she had intimidated him, bullied him into severing his connections with Faigie just by being so intense, so ready to be extreme about it, to be dire about Lev's tepid relationship with Faigie. Lev resented that Angela had made him burn his bridges; that by being so immoderate about everything, she called all the shots. Lev wondered—was Angela genuinely like that or was it just a strategy for her to control him, to always get her way?

And then he started to wonder whether it was Angela at all, or whether it was just him, just a defective person too self-centered to realize that someone else was in love with him, too cut off from other people to sense feelings other than his own. Maybe that's why he was with Angela after all, because she was such a zealot about everything that even someone as deadened to empathy as he was could still feel something. Wasn't that what really happened? Faigie was in love with him and he hadn't the slightest notion. Angela had seen it immediately. Angela, for all her mercurial behavior, was not insulated from the emotional turmoil of other people, even people she identified as her enemies. Lev had abandoned Faigie without hesitation, maybe because he wasn't human enough to appreciate who she was and what she was feeling. He was human enough to imagine the agony of baby cows boiled in their mothers' milk, but not the heartache of a girl he had known since childhood, a girl he had led on for years and years with the illusion that they had a shared future together.

So he couldn't really blame Angela. It was his fault, his transgression.

Did I become like this only after I fell off the derech? Lev wondered. Was this a symptom of leaving the path? Or was I always like this—just a self-absorbed jerk?

Lev felt a deep sadness and he wanted to talk to Angela about it. He wanted to examine what had happened and perhaps hear her say, "No, it wasn't your fault; it was just one of those things." But Lev knew if he shared what had happened on that subway platform, Angela's reaction would have been just one big victory dance, crowing about her vindication at being right about Faigie's feelings for him and her triumph in the competition for his affections. It had been a war, and someone had to take casualties—that would be Angela's perspective. In a war, you don't mourn your enemy's dead; you mourn your own. She would regard his sadness as weakness, an indulgence, something to get over immediately. No, he decided, it just wouldn't work to share his thoughts with his lover. Angela wouldn't give him the time of day on this one.

Lev did hate her just a little for that.

41.

A distant cousin of Lev's was getting married and the entire family was invited to the wedding at a huge catering hall deep in Queens. The bride was wealthy and it promised to be an extravaganza. Lev explained to Angela that he would not be able to keep their Thursday night rendezvous in Red Hook.

"Maybe we can see each other afterward?" she suggested.

"I doubt it," Lev explained. "It's at that big catering hall in Flushing. By the time I get home to Brooklyn with my family, it will be too late."

"Oh, yeah," she nodded. "I know that place. I've worked with the video guy there. We call it the Wedding Factory." Angela seemed disappointed.

"Believe me, these weddings go on forever," he explained. "Nothing happening. Boring. Just an obligation." After a few minutes of sulking, Angela seemed to make her peace with it.

Some people attend weddings for the romance of it all; some go for the food; some for the liquor; some to socialize and to gossip. But the Livitski boys went to weddings for only one reason: to dance. None of the brothers could remember when that started or why. But the five brothers, even Moti, went to weddings so they could dance.

That Thursday evening, his entire family took the subway to Flushing and walked the five blocks to the catering hall. When they arrived, the festivities were in full swing.

First came the elaborate smorgasbord. Then Lev and his father and brothers paid their respects to the groom at the *Choson's tisch*, where the required marriage contract was examined, witnessed and signed. With that formality out of the way, the male guests danced in a mob around the groom as he made his way to the bride, who sat ensconced on a throne-like chair in the main hall, surrounded by her mother, grand-mother, mother-in-law, sisters, future sisters-in-law and various female cousins and aunts. The groom strutted to where his bride sat, raised her veil to verify that she was indeed his intended and then lowered it over her eager face.

The crowd was herded into the large hall where the wedding ceremony was to take place. Men sat separately from women and as Lev took his seat beside his father and brothers, he waved to Tuvi and Pinky a few rows away. The ceremony began with an elaborate processional of immediate family members of the bride and groom, each of whom had so many siblings that it seemed to go on forever. Finally, each of the Seven Blessings were chanted by one eminent rabbi after another. After the breaking of the glass that marked the end of the ceremony, the multitude was funneled back into the large catering hall where people loitered, waiting for the bride and groom to emerge from the room where they were secluded by themselves, giving them sufficient time, theoretically, to consummate the marriage.

The band started playing. Moti's specialty was Jewish line-dancing: the synchronized, choreographed dance to Jewish and Hasidic melodies. He made it his business to memorize all the intricate steps of the various dances. As soon as he heard the music, he made his way to the center of the floor. It didn't matter to him that no one else had begun to dance—that there was no "line" of others moving along with him. This is what he had come to the wedding for and this was what he was going to do.

Lev's mother had dressed Moti in a new pair of pants, a double-breasted blazer (Hudi's hand-me-down), a white shirt and clip-on tie. He looked uncharacteristically tidy. But within three minutes of starting to dance, his jacket was unbuttoned, his shirttails and tzitzis were flapping outside his pants, and his clip-on tie was askew and dangling from his collar.

Moti was so focused on the dance that he didn't notice the indulgent smiles of the people milling around him, watching this six-year-old gamboling to the music. Shmu and Hudi stood to the side laughing at Moti's earnestness, but then they began to dance as well. Moti's face broke into a broad grin when he realized his brothers had joined in. Touched by the contagious enthusiasm, other men put down their glasses and lined up behind the dancers. Lev's father, Elya and Lev had already enlisted. Soon there were scores of men dancing along with Moti. On the other side of the *mechitzah*, the short curtain that ran down the middle of the dance floor to separate men from women, the women, inspired by Moti's example, also began to line-dance.

As the band changed from tune to tune, Moti's choreography changed as well. Lev noticed that he was improvising, adding flourishes, little capers and half-steps, flaps of his scrawny arms and thrusts of his hips. He was just like the other Livitski brothers, but because of his small stature compared to the rest of them, he seemed to embody a concentrated elixir of Livitski ingredients, possessing all of his brothers' characteristics in a more condensed, potent compound.

After four or five line dances, the bride and groom burst into the catering hall with great fanfare and the band really let loose. The line dancing ended and scores of additional guests streamed out to the floor. The bride and groom, separated by the mechitzah, danced frenetically with their families, their friends and their rabbis while the horde surged around them like a huge school of fish cavorting in the currents of the dance that coursed through the room and washed over the crowd.

The tempo of the dance increased until the bride was escorted to the men's side of the room, and both bride and groom were induced to sit on two chairs pulled from the closest dinner table. A group of the younger men raised the chairs on their shoulders, carrying the couple around as the music blared. The bride and groom clutched the opposite ends of a table napkin as they sat atop the two elevated chairs—it would have been immodest for them to hold hands as they were paraded around on their litters, even though they were already officially married.

The band continued playing, one song transitioning seamlessly into another. The music grew increasingly manic. The bride and groom, still enthroned, were deposited onto the dance floor next to each other. The next phase of the celebration began. This was the cue for Elya and Lev. It was time to dance before the bride and groom.

When they lunged into the space set aside before the newlyweds, the crowd roared. People had been waiting for them, for their performance. Lev and Elya began their repertoire. They didn't know where they picked up all the moves. Some seemed vaguely Slavic, as if they were imitating the way Cossacks danced; others were more conventional, inspired by pop culture. They stooped to their knees and thrust out their legs, arms crossed to their chests; they flipped their legs up across their bodies, striking their heels with their hands. With arms linked to one another's shoulders, Lev and Elya kicked their feet high into the air, like members of a chorus line; they imitated a bullfight, Elya acting like a charging bull that Lev deflected with the favorite prop of the evening, another table napkin.

Their dancing escalated as the band upped the tempo. The brothers increased their acrobatics. They jumped straight up from a crouch, thrusting both their legs out to each side and touching their toes with outstretched hands. Elya dropped to the floor, executing breakdancing moves that ended with him spinning in a tight circle on his back. Lev did a handstand and walked on his palms before the seated couple, lifting one hand and then the other as if stepping to the music.

Suddenly, Hudi barged into the circle with Moti standing straight up on his shoulders waving another napkin as if it were a flag. Behind them danced Shmu, who was spotting Moti in case he tumbled off Hudi's shoulders. Lev was astonished when he saw Hudi holding his little brother on his shoulders. Hudi was twelve years old, but it was as if Lev was seeing him for the first time. He had grown thick and strong without Lev's noticing. Hudi looked solid, like timber, as he moved back and forth under the weight of his brother.

Hudi raised his hands and Moti grabbed them. At some predetermined cue that Lev could not perceive, Moti threw his legs up, somersaulted in the air and tumbled backwards from Hudi's shoulders. The crowd gasped as Lev started toward Moti to try to break his fall, but there was Shmu waiting to catch him. When Moti fell into Shmu's waiting arms, the crowd howled its approval.

The frenzy continued, but Lev stood for a few moments wondering about what he had just witnessed. Clearly, his younger brothers had been rehearsing this sequence for some time. Why hadn't he known about it? Then Lev remembered: he didn't know about it because he had checked out. He had checked out in order to spend all his free time with Angela in Red Hook.

His brothers moved in a circle before the seated bride and groom and they grabbed Lev as they spun. The younger ones dropped back and left Elya and Lev to more acrobatics. The finale came when they faced each other, crossed their wrists and grabbed onto one another's hands. With their heads thrown back, Lev and Elya whirled in a circle faster and faster like Dervishes in an ecstatic trance. The crowd cheered.

When the performance was over, hundreds of onlookers surged into a flow of humanity around the bride and groom, who rose from their seats and returned to their respective sides of the hall to finish the dance. The euphoric dancing continued for another ten minutes and finally ended with one last spasm of acrobatics by others.

After the dancing stopped, Lev staggered to the table reserved for his family. He gulped down a glass of water. Sweat was dripping off of his forehead and running down his face. His shirt was saturated with it. Pinky came over, also flushed from his exertions.

"Awesome!" he exclaimed. "Hey, Lev, I just ran into someone who wants to talk to you. Says she knows you. Says her name is Andrea or something."

"Andrea who?" Lev asked.

"I don't know. I never met her before." Pinky pointed across the crowded banquet hall. "Look," he said, "there she is holding the big light for the video guy. She's working for the video guy."

"The video guy?" Lev knew only one person who occasionally worked for a "video guy," and he immediately suspected the worst: that Angela had taken a job assisting the video photographer so she could crash the wedding of Lev's cousin. He squinted in the direction Pinky was pointing and in the distance, he made out a figure in blue holding a brilliant spotlight on an aluminum pole. He couldn't be sure that it was Angela or not, but he was nevertheless seized by a feeling of profound dread, as if he was about to be arrested for some terrible crime, hand-cuffed and dragged out to a patrol car in front of his entire family and everyone he had ever known.

"I don't recognize her," Lev said, "but, okay, I'll go over and talk to her."

Lev started across the room toward the girl holding the spotlight. As he got closer, Lev confirmed that it was in fact Angela, but dressed in a way he could never have imagined. She looked the way a gas station attendant looks when depicted in a television commercial: blue pants, sneakers, blue shirt and a wide blue polyester tie. Her hair was tied back in a ponytail and on her head was a blue cap reading "Highlights Video."

"What are you doing here?" Lev asked when he finally stood before her.

"I'm working. What are you doing here? Are you having a good time?" She scowled.

"It's my cousin's wedding! Why are you pissed off? I'm the one who should be pissed off that you showed up here without telling me. Talk about breaking the rules!"

"You lied to me. You said that these weddings are boring. You told me you don't know how to dance! So don't talk to me about breaking the rules!"

Before he could respond, Angela started moving away to keep pace with the video-camera, which was roaming through the room filming the festivities. Lev trailed after her.

"The video guy says that in a few minutes you're all going to sit down and have dinner and I can have twenty minutes off. Meet me at the beat-up white van in the back of the parking lot."

"I can't just walk out of here and leave everyone wondering where I've gone."

She gave Lev a grave look. "When the Jews sit down to eat, you better meet me at that van, mister!" Then she turned, trailing after the video camera as it drank in images of the revelers.

The band took a break and people began to take their seats for the meal. Lev headed toward the men's room and unobtrusively peeled off to a back exit that led to the parking lot. He squinted into the darkness until he located a dirty white van parked in the rear of the lot. It had a faded stencil on the back and side that read "Highlights Video." He strode to the van, glancing around to see whether he was being observed. He peered into the filthy rear window and knocked. Lev felt a push as the door swung open and Angela beckoned him inside.

Lev pulled the door shut behind him. The van was strewn with video equipment and assorted other detritus. A wooden framed couch was jammed across the van's midsection, facing the rear door. It was drooping in the middle, reeking of mildew. Angela pulled him down next to her onto the couch. Lev thought she was going to continue to rebuke him, but instead, her face lit up in rapture.

"It looked like so much fun!" she exclaimed. "It must be so much fun to go crazy like that. I can't believe you told me it was boring! I can't believe you never told me about this! I can't believe you told me that you don't know how to dance!"

"I don't know how to do your dances, you know, dances with one girl and one guy holding each other."

"My dances are nothing. Don't even think about my dances. I want to do these dances, the Jew dances, with you in Red Hook!"

"It can't be done with two people whenever you want. It has to be done at a time of joy, at a celebration, like a wedding."

"Don't I make you feel joy?"

"You make me feel happy. Joy and happy are two different things."

"You'll have to do better than that. Anyway, you looked so sexy—you and those guys jumping all around. Who was that gorgeous guy that you kept throwing around?"

"That's Elya, my brother, the next oldest."

"You looked so sexy—you looked so strong and sexy. You were dancing around like a wild man! The girls were screaming—they were having orgasms, I'm telling you, when you and your brother started dancing in front of the bride and groom, the girls were screaming and having orgasms."

"You're totally out of your mind!"

"I know when a chick is having an orgasm and I'm telling you, they were!"

"Look, I don't know how to dance with women. We're not supposed to dance with women! So I really don't know how to dance."

"Of course you're not supposed to dance with each other. Your dances are so hot that if you touched one another you would be fucking each other on the floor. That's why you don't dare touch each other while you're dancing."

"Angela, you're talking nonsense! What do you want me to say?"

"You don't have to say anything. But you have to fuck me, right now. Right here. You got me all hot and bothered."

Angela reached down, pulled off one of her sneakers and with her socked foot, she pushed off the other one. She stood up from the couch half-crouching in the back of the van, quickly unbuttoned her blue pants and pulled them off. Then she pulled off her panties. Except for her white socks, she was naked below the blue shirt and the polyester tie, which was still neatly tied and pulled up to her neck.

"C'mon Angela . . . I can't do this now."

She swung her leg over his lap and sat with her knees on the couch facing him. She put her hands around his neck and pulled him close. She placed her mouth on his and gave him a long, probing kiss. Lev could hear her breathing and thought he could feel the thump of her quickening heart.

"It's my cousin's wedding."

"Lame excuse," she whispered in his ear. "You owe me. Pay up."

"I can't. It's impossible."

"Pretend I'm an unwed mother. There was a time when you would have fucked me in a car if you had even ten seconds to do it. Now you can live your fantasy."

"I'm all sweaty and smelly. You won't like it."

"I want that sweat. That's what I want right now. I want the sweat of the wild man."

"I'm not going to do it—"

She slid one of her hands down his chest and grabbed his crotch. "That's what you're saying, but your friend down here is saying something else," she murmured.

"I can't do it. I can't concentrate."

"Really? Can't concentrate? Try harder, Lev. I know you can do it. Try harder!" She was rolling her head back and forth against his face and his neck, and she began kissing him on the mouth again with her tongue and her teeth. She leaned back for a moment, reaching down to unzip his fly. Then she raised her body and gently guided him into her. She began moving up and down on his lap, slowly, while continuing to kiss him passionately.

And while this was happening, he was angry, so angry: at himself for succumbing once again to his Evil Inclination; at Angela for insisting so emphatically on getting what she wanted. And Lev was disgusted with himself. Disgusted that he had no discipline. Disgusted that he was so weak. Disgusted that he was so hungry for Angela that he couldn't resist her even at his cousin's wedding.

But Lev didn't stop. He didn't say anything. He didn't say: "Stop— this is wrong; it's wrong to do this at a wedding, at a moment when we are supposed to be sanctifying love."

Lev said nothing.

As they continued with one another, their movements became more and more frenzied and the ancient shock absorbers in the decrepit van began to squeak as the chassis moved up and down. Angela began shouting as she approached climax; then Lev was hollering too.

When it was over, they were sprawled on that fetid couch, slumped on one another. Lev suddenly realized it was cold. He could see Angela's breath steaming from her mouth as she panted from her efforts. He put his hands around her buttocks as she leaned into him, her face pressed against his shoulder and neck. Her flesh felt chilled like she had been sitting on a block of ice.

She turned her face to him and murmured into his ear: "I knew you were a wild man when I first caught you spying on me and you didn't look away. You couldn't look away. That's when I knew." She kissed Lev, extending her tongue deep into his mouth and letting it writhe against his teeth, his palate, his own tongue. Finally, she pulled back and looked into his eyes. "Now I don't care anymore that all those Jewish girls in there are having orgasms when they see you dance. I have the real thing. They're just kidding themselves. *I'm* the one that has the real thing. *I'm* the one who has the wild man."

"We shouldn't have done this. I feel lousy that we did this."

"You'll get over it. I guarantee that you'll get over it. I guarantee that when I see you Saturday night in Red Hook, you'll have gotten over it."

She disengaged from him and slid off of his lap. She reached under the couch searching for her panties. She found them, pulled them on and then her pants. As she tied her sneakers, she chatted amiably as if nothing had happened.

"That little kid who was leading the line-dancing in the beginning—was that Moti?"

"Yes."

"What a little gangster!" she said in admiration. "And the two other guys who look like little clones of you—were they the other two? What are their funny names again?"

"Shmu and Hudi."

"Moti, Shmu and Hudi," Angela repeated, relishing the foreignness of their names. Lev cringed inwardly as his brothers' names spilled out of her mouth. Those were names of people who expected more from him; who were at that very moment waiting for him to join them at the wedding feast; the names of people he had just betrayed. "Yeah," Angela continued, "those boys are going to be hot-shots with the ladies, too. Wild men, all of you. All of you are wild men." She flung her arms expansively in the air. "I don't get it," she marveled, "these are the same guys who sit on each other's laps, sing songs and play Monopoly on Friday nights, right?"

Lev didn't answer her. He hung his head and looked blankly at the floor of the van.

"I missed dinner because of this, you know. It didn't look half bad either. Maybe you can get me a plate of something?"

Lev lifted his eyes and just stared at her.

"Okay, never mind. Don't put yourself out or anything." She turned the handle of the rear door of the van and kicked it open with her foot. As the door swung open, Lev was seized with a terrifying vision that hundreds of wedding guests had massed outside the van as it shook on its chassis, waiting to see who the perpetrator of this desecration might be.

"Check to see whether anyone is watching before we get out, okay?" he asked her.

"No one is watching us! What do you think—we're the center of the world? No one gives a damn."

Lev let Angela go in first. He waited three or four minutes before he followed. He stopped in the men's room to wash his hands and splash water on his face before making his way past the tables packed with people attacking their plates of chicken. He saw his family sitting at their table, almost finished with their main course. Moti was happily holding a chicken drumstick in his hand and licking it like a popsicle. His plate was surrounded by a pile of cloth napkins soaked with what looked to be orange soda—evidently, Moti had already spilled not one, but several glasses of whatever he was drinking. His mother was seated next to him and one of his legs was splayed across her lap. She had dipped a cloth napkin in a glass of water and was rubbing at a stain on his knee while berating him. "How can someone," she asked him, "get grass stains on his new pants at a wedding? A nighttime wedding in Queens!"

Elya was sitting sideways on his chair chatting with two blushing girls who had come to talk to him. They were apparently classmates from Baruch College. They ogled him with admiration they could barely contain and he, true to his character, wasn't noticing a thing. Hudi and Shmu were mixing salt and pepper and other condiments into their glasses of ginger ale and daring each other to try a taste. Lev's father was sitting back contentedly, gazing at his sons and smiling in his gentle, unqualified happiness at observing what had issued from his loins. When he saw Lev, his face brightened in welcome.

Lev loved them all so much. They were, each one of them, even his mother, so pure, so true to whom they were and where they came from. They were content to enjoy the life that had been granted to them, to dance with joy at someone else's wedding, to celebrate with the bride and groom. It was one of the greatest and most important mitzvos commanded of them. They seemed sanctified to him; *kedoshim*—holy. These are the types of beings that reside in the Heavens, Lev thought. These are the celestial creatures that the liturgy celebrates, the ones who dwell with God, who look human but are incapable of sin.

They were incapable of sin—they didn't need to pollute themselves by screwing in the back of a van in a parking lot—and even worse, screwing the daughter of an idolater. He thought: we're not wild men. Angela wants us to be wild men. She thinks that's a good thing, a desirable thing to be, but we know it's not a good thing. We know that being a wild man is a repudiation of everything we've been taught, a rejection of everything we should aspire to be. No, his brothers were not wild men. And Lev? He just wanted to be whatever Angela wanted him to be. He was that far gone. He was that lost.

Lev's mother looked up and asked sharply. "Where have you been? You haven't eaten anything."

"I was so overheated that I went out to cool down in the parking lot."

"You don't look like you've cooled down very much. The sweat is still pouring off you."

Lev sat down in the empty seat next to Moti. He guzzled the glass of water set in front of his plate. He looked at Moti and raised his eyebrows. Moti nodded, so Lev drank down Moti's glass of water too. Lev looked at the chicken squatting in some iridescent crimson sauce and he felt like he was going to vomit. He pushed the plate away.

His mother looked at him quizzically. "Just not hungry," Lev muttered.

She shook her head and scowled.

The music started again and people began to make their way to the dance floor. Lev stood up and grabbed Elya, pulling him into the middle of the crowd to dance once more before the bride and groom. As they whirled around each other, the throng screamed. Lev imagined that he could sense the orgasmic quivering of the wombs of all the girls, just as Angela had observed. But he wasn't dancing for them.

Everyone's face blended into an indistinct tracer of colors as the brothers gyrated in a wide arc. For Lev, there was only one discrete source of light in the entire room as they spun each other in orbit around the bride and groom—a pale, luminescent face in a baseball cap holding a bright light on a big stick. It was as if the moon were holding up the sun, a beacon beckoning to him across the surging room. It was for her that Lev danced. It was for Angela. It was for Angela Pizatto, the Catholic girl from Bensonhurst that he flung himself into the air while clasping the hands of his holy brother, Elya.

For Angela, and for no one else.

VII

Rav Yehudah said in the name of Rav: There was an incident in which a certain man set his eyes on a certain woman and his heart became so obsessed with her that he became ill. They came and asked the doctors and the doctors replied: 'There is no cure for him unless they have relations.'

The Sages declared: 'Let him die—the man and woman should not have relations.'

The doctors proposed: 'Then let her stand naked before him.'

The Sages answered: 'Let him die—she should not stand naked before him.'

The doctors suggested: 'Then permit her to converse with the man while she stands behind a curtain.'

The Sages ruled: 'Let him die—she should not converse with him from behind a curtain . . .'

The Gemara asks: But if she were unmarried, couldn't the man have simply married her and satisfied his obsession in a permissible manner?

The Gemara answers: His obsession would not have been satisfied by marriage . . . for as Rebbe Yitzchak said: 'Since the day the Holy Temple was destroyed, the delight of sexual intimacy was taken from married people and given to sinners, as it is written in Proverbs: "Stolen waters are sweet, and the bread of secrecy is pleasant."'

- Babylonian Talmud, Tractate Sanhedrin 75A -

42.

Valentine's Day for Lev and Angela was not so much a massacre as a melee, occasioned by Lev's failure to even acknowledge the special day. Lev explained to Angela that observant Jews did not pay attention to Valentine's Day since it was purportedly established to commemorate a Saint. Angela didn't accept his version of the facts and immediately consulted *How Strange the Jews!* for corroboration of Lev's flimsy excuse. But Rabbi Dr. Erwon Arkadi had written a book that cataloged the strange things that Jews did, not the strange things they omitted to do. Lev speculated that perhaps an exhaustive list of the omissions of the Jews might comprise the second volume of the series. It took days of apologies and pleading to finally placate Angela—that, and a vow never to forget Valentine's Day again.

A couple of weeks later after Lev and Angela finished their last classes for the day, they followed their routine and headed to Red Hook from campus. Angela stood near the stairs leading to the subway platform, texting back and forth to her friends. Lev was positioned thirty feet from her, reading a book about the American Revolution. Occasionally, they would glance at each other. Each time, Angela managed to look past him—or perhaps through him—with such utter indifference that he felt like he didn't exist. Angela was utilizing what she called her Subway Face, the look she affected to discourage unwanted attention when she rode the trains.

It was a bit exciting, this play-acting at indifference, both of them knowing that in a short while they would be performing their favorite rituals in Red Hook.

The subway was delayed. The weather had turned unexpectedly bitter. After an earlier light rain had stopped, the temperature had plummeted to single digits. The tracks lower down in Brooklyn had iced over and the delay grew from five minutes to fifteen, then to thirty. Angela was underdressed for the sudden freeze, wearing mesh pantyhose, short boots, a waist-length woolen coat and thin black gloves. As Lev watched her out of the corner of his eye, he saw that she was growing colder by the minute. She began shifting from one foot to the other and moving her arms back and forth, clasping and unclasping herself. Lev, too, was growing chilled, dressed only in his father's overcoat with no scarf or hat. If they had been anywhere but on the Brooklyn College platform, he would have gone to Angela and folded her into his oversized coat with him for warmth as they had done before on more remote subway platforms.

Finally, the 2 Train arrived and they quickly traveled the eleven stops to Atlantic Avenue. They rushed through the underground transverse to Pacific Street and waited for the M to 4th Avenue–9th Street. From there, they hopped the F one stop to Smith–9th Streets.

As the doors opened to the elevated platform, they were met by a blast of glacial air sweeping across Red Hook from the bay in the distance. Lev glanced down at the Gowanus Canal. The surface of the gunmetal waters was already covered by a patina of ice. "So cold," Angela said, taking his arm. "I need to warm up before we walk to the apartment." They descended the station steps to West 9th Street and entered a small luncheonette dominated by a magazine rack and a narrow counter. They sat at the counter nestling cups of coffee in their hands.

"So," Angela asked, "what's the Livitski family up to this Shabbos? Anything special?"

"Not that I know of. I imagine Big Time Wrestling is on the agenda."

"You and the brothers going to practice any dance moves?"

"Could be."

"Going to sit on each other's laps?"

Lev nodded. Angela took a sip of her coffee. "You like hanging out with them, don't you? I couldn't do three hours of time with my family, never mind twenty-five hours."

"If my family was as messed up as yours, I couldn't either."

"What's that supposed to mean?"

"Sorry, just that, you know, you have kind of a dysfunctional family."

"Where did you get the idea that my family is dysfunctional?"

"Where? From you is where."

She put down her coffee and raised her eyebrows in indignation. "I never said that."

"Maybe you never used that word, but the way you talk about them—"

"I would never use that word to describe my family!"

"Okay, but the way you describe them is pretty sad. Fighting all the time, screeching at each other."

"'Screeching?' That's a terrible, awful word! I would never describe my family as screeching."

"Okay, yelling."

"Yelling doesn't mean anything. I don't know where you get the impression that my family is dysfunctional, whatever the fuck that's supposed to mean." Angela started to raise her voice. She was sitting on the counter stool ramrod straight, her mouth pursed with irritation.

"Let me translate it for you. It means screwed up, messed up, not working right."

"That's just your prejudice talking."

He leaned over to her and said in a low voice, "Look, we can fight about this in private, in the apartment. Let's get out of here." He threw a couple of bucks on the counter and pushed the door open.

A gust of freezing air almost sucked the breath out of their lungs. It felt like the temperature had dropped another twenty degrees. The contrast was so dramatic that it was unsettling, as if the Earth had begun to drift from its orbit around the sun, moving deeper into the frigid void of deep space. They hurried down the sidewalk as the wind battered them. The wet pavement had iced over and they clutched each other as they skidded back and forth.

Angela couldn't wait until they reached the apartment to resume the argument. "You got a lot of nerve," she said as they stumbled along, "judging my family—actually giving your diagnosis or something that we're dysfunctional! Like you're some sort of shrink or social worker or something!"

Lev stopped walking and turned to face her. "Look, Angela," he said, "I've never met anyone in your family except you and you've told me a ton of stories about how your family shouts in each other's faces; how your brothers are dimwits; how your cousin hits on you all the time; how ridiculous your aunts and uncles are; how your mother abuses you, criticizing you all the time—she even calls you a whore! These are the stories *you* have told me. I didn't make them up. So don't go accusing me of being prejudiced when I come to the conclusion that your family is messed up."

Angela looked horrified as if she were hearing Lev utter the most unbelievable, outrageous falsehoods.

"Yes," she said, "I've told you those stories, but you've totally twisted them!"

They were shouting by this time because they were angry, but also because it was the only way for them to hear one another over the wind that was pummeling them.

"I haven't twisted anything! You've told me any number of times that you don't like your mother, that she's a nasty person. You deny that?"

"That's right—I don't like her and she doesn't like me. But I love her. And she loves me! She doesn't always know how to show it and she's got a lot of baggage about her life that she's dragging around, but I know she loves me and that's what counts. You don't like your mother, but you love her, don't you?"

"Yes, of course I do."

"Then why is it different for you than for me?"

"Because we don't sit around hurling insults at one another."

"No, you just keep them inside of you where they can't get out. They sit there and build up. You know why? Because you're afraid of them! You're afraid of letting them out, of seeing them for what they are. That's why you have all those rules and laws to follow—to keep you in line, to keep you from feeling what is really going on inside of you. But not us; we aren't afraid. We aren't afraid to say what's on our mind even if it sounds like an insult; even if it sounds like disrespect. Because we know how to love, we know what love means. We know that we can say anything to one another and it doesn't mean that we don't love each other. But you don't know that."

"We certainly do know that! But we also know that when you indulge yourself and speak what you might call *your mind* and you say nasty things to people, those words are hurtful. The rabbis say nasty words are as painful as blows with a stick. Yes, the people you love can recover from it, but it's hurtful anyhow. So don't go boasting how great it is to beat each other up all the time with your deepest resentments and hostilities."

Angela didn't say anything immediately. They started down the sidewalk again, holding on to each other despite their anger, trying not to slip and tumble onto the icy concrete. Then she stopped abruptly and hollered through the wind: "You know, Marie was right—you're such a judgmental, snobbish bunch, you Jews. You think you're so superior!"

"How predictable!" Lev bellowed back. "Whenever I stand up to you about anything, you blame it on the Jews! I'm not the one who claims to be superior—you are! You're the one who's always telling me that I don't know anything about how to love someone and that you're the big expert. I tried to tell you I loved you weeks ago, but you said, 'No, it wouldn't mean anything; you have to tell me at the right time; I'll let you know when it's the right time!' And like an idiot, I've been waiting for you to give me the green light to tell you I love you. But you don't really want to hear it. And the only reason is because you're the one who is frightened of it, of love! So don't accuse me of not feeling anything or of acting like I'm superior. You're the one who puts on airs—you're not such an expert about it, so why not stop being so high and mighty!"

Angela looked at him wildly, her eyes popping out of her skull. The wind roared around the buildings and assaulted them—she was swaying as it ripped around her. Lev suddenly noticed that she was shivering; her whole body was quaking. He realized that he was shivering, as well, and he felt icy blasts penetrate his father's coat straight through to his skin. Lev tried to say something, but his mouth had become numb and the words couldn't come out. More squalls of wind buffeted them; for a second, Lev thought that Angela was going to be blown to the ground. He grabbed her and began tugging her toward the apartment. The pavement was coated with black ice and they had to inch their way along the sidewalk. Whenever Lev let go of Angela, she simply stopped moving, standing immobile and trembling in the wind, her eyes tightly shut.

They reached a narrow band of grass that bordered the sidewalk adjacent to the street. The turf gave Lev enough traction to finally make some progress. They took halting steps, crunching against the blades of grass encrusted in glistening sheaths of ice. Clinging to one another, they slowly made their way the remaining two blocks, staggering against the polar wind, until they finally reached their building.

Lev pulled himself up the railing that abutted the six stairs to the doorway, but Angela hung back and he realized she couldn't take the last steps by herself. He made his way down again, stretched his hand out to her, beckoning her to extend her arm so he could help her up, but she couldn't manage to move her arm—in fact, she seemed paralyzed as if in some dark fairytale she had become totally encased in ice. Lev took another step and finally gripped her hand tightly, hauling her up the stoop to the doorway. His hands were frozen and he had trouble finding the key and fitting it in the lock. When he finally got the door open, he tugged her into the hallway.

Angela's lips were blue and she could barely stand up. Lev lifted her in his arms the way husbands in movies carry their new brides across the threshold. He lurched up the three flights to the apartment. He put her feet on the floor as she clung to him, her arms around his neck, until he managed to get the door open. Then he dragged her inside, pulled off her flimsy jacket, threw her on the bed and immediately covered her with a blanket.

Angela's teeth were knocking against each other and she was making a low moaning sound from the depths of her chest. She sounded like a malfunctioning air conditioner vibrating in a window. Lev tore off his coat, slipped under the blankets and clutched Angela's body close to his to try to warm her up.

They were trembling together and it seemed as if the bed itself was quaking. After a while, their bodies together generated enough heat that feeling began to return to their limbs. Lev stopped shivering, but he could still feel Angela's waif-like body quivering. She was breathing irregularly, sucking in her breath in short gasps as if she were weeping. She pressed her blue lips against the side of his neck where his pulse throbbed.

Lev finally was able to whisper, "Angela, are you okay?"

She grunted her assent. He lay quietly beside her and felt their shared body heat building. Finally, after many minutes, Angela said in a low voice, her speech still a little slurred from her numb mouth: "I wanted to hear you say that you loved me for so long, in a way that I knew you would mean it and I wanted to make it happen so that I knew it would be true, but it never seemed the right time. But now you've said it and it was so perfect, the way it happened. So much more perfect than I could imagine. You were so angry at me and we were beginning to freeze to death and I was treating you so badly, but you said it anyway!" She threw her arms around Lev and he felt her cold hands on his neck as she began kissing him passionately on the mouth. Her lips were strangely cold, like he was receiving kisses from a corpse.

At that moment, Angela didn't tell Lev that she loved him back. It would have been, in Lev's opinion, a good time, an appropriate time for her to do so. He told himself that Angela, apparently, still believed that declarations of love should never be reciprocal—one should never be made in exchange for the other. And he marveled once again at how unpredictable Angela was. Most women would like to hear a declaration of love on a moonlit night, with soft music playing and the scent of roses wafting up from the garden. Not Angela. That was so much claptrap to her. She preferred to hear her lover howl his love into an artic gale while heaping abuse on her for her unreasonableness as their lips turned blue and their extremities began to succumb to frostbite. That scene was, for Angela, "so much more perfect than she could imagine."

But that night she did let him know how she felt in her typical Angela way, when the blade goes in and out of you so fast that you don't know what happened to you until later, when you look down and wonder at the trickle of blood that oozes, usually painlessly, from the wound, and you examine it curiously, almost in wonder. She made her feelings known to him that night when, for the first time since he had known her, Angela referred to their having sex together as "making love," instead of fucking. And from then on, *making love* was what she always called it.

But still, Lev couldn't help but ask himself: what had it meant to her before, when she had regarded it merely as fucking?

43.

They fell asleep. When Lev awoke, it was already 7:30 at night. Outside, the wind gusted, rattling the windows and heavy snow was falling. He woke Angela and told her they had to go back out and make their way home. He could see that the thought of going out again into the cold truly frightened Angela. To see fear in Angela's face—Angela, who was always so intrepid—disconcerted him. The only time he had ever seen her afraid was the night of their first date, when she had tried to avoid the gathering of homeless men.

"Let's not go home tonight!" she exclaimed. "Let's stay the whole night together! We've never slept together the whole night!"

"Angela, if I don't go home, then they'll know. They'll figure it out and then it will be all over for me."

"Lev, I can't go out again. I won't make it. I just can't do it."

"Can you get someone to cover for you?"

"Yes, I'll get Marie to cover for me. She'll do it."

Angela called Marie and they cooked up a story about being stranded at her house. Then Angela called her mother. Her mother wasn't buying it, but Marie was ready to corroborate. Angela also arranged for Marie to get her some winter clothes. Lev would meet Marie the next morning at Brooklyn College to pick them up, and he would then bring them to Angela so she could get out of Red Hook the next day without freezing to death.

Angela remained in bed huddling under the blanket, half dozing. Lev got up and went to the window. The snow was blowing horizontally in the tempest. The traffic on the Gowanus Expressway outside their window had slowed to a crawl as the snow began to drift against the guardrails. He went into the bathroom, closed the door and sat on the side of the rust-stained bathtub. He took out his phone and dialed his home number. Maybe he could pull it off—maybe he could convince his parents that he had a good enough reason not to come home that evening. His father answered and Lev felt a rush of relief. His father would be reasonable, certainly more reasonable than his mother.

"Abba," he said, "I'm way down in Brooklyn at a friend's and I'm trapped by this storm. I think I'll stay the night and come home tomorrow morning when things blow over."

"That sounds sensible," he said. "We were worried about you."

Then Lev heard his mother say sharply to his father: "Give me the phone."

His mother came on the line in her most authoritarian voice. "Where have you been? We've been worried sick."

Lev looked down at his phone and saw that he had missed a number of calls over the last few hours. He had inadvertently turned off the ringer. "The phone ran out of juice and I had to charge it," he lied.

"When are you getting home?"

"I was telling Abba that I'm going to stay overnight at a friend's down in Brighton Beach."

"Brighton Beach? There's no one in Brighton Beach except Russians."

"Not exactly Brighton Beach, more like Avenue U." Lev thought of Angela's advice that when you lie, you should try to say something that is as true as you can make it, so you can sound credible even to the suspicious. "My friend Andy from my big econ class lives there. You don't know him."

"Avenue U? That's Syrian territory. Are you hanging out with Syrian Jewish kids? You know how they look down on us, don't you?"

"Andy's not like that. He's a good guy."

"I bet he calls you 'J-Dub' behind your back. That's what the Syrian Jews call us Ashkenazim."

"No, Andy's a good person."

"Well, I hate to disappoint Andy," his mother said, not even trying to conceal her skepticism, "but you will have to have a sleepover some other time. I need you home tonight."

"Imma," Lev protested, "have you looked outside? It's a blizzard! I don't have boots, a hat, a scarf, nothing!"

"It's my grandfather Levi's *yahrzeit* tonight, peace be upon him. The rabbi you were named after. On the anniversary of his death, I want you to be here."

"Imma, I would be happy to join the family on Grandpa Levi's yahrzeit, but I'm telling you it's dangerous out there!"

"Grandpa Levi will want you to be there for him."

"Imma, it says in the Talmud, in Berachos, that the dead don't care any longer what happens in the other world, in our world. They don't care what happens among the living."

This statement incensed his mother. "Don't you ever quote Talmud to me again! You're not my rabbi. You're not *anyone's* rabbi!"

She abruptly stopped and Lev heard an indistinct conversation on the other end of the phone line between his father and mother. After a few moments, his mother was back on the line. "Fine," she said, a tone of resignation in her voice. "Fine, Lev, you're old enough to make up your own mind as to whether it's too awful out for you to get home." And then she really kicked him in the face. "Do what you think is right." She clicked off.

Lev sat for a few minutes, furious at his mother's last manipulative comment, which had transformed a dispute about bad weather into a test of whether he had the moral fortitude to trudge through the snow so he could gaze for a few moments at his grandfather's memorial candle. Had she barked at him the way she usually did, he would have felt free to decide on his own whether to stay the night with Angela. But Grandpa Levi—Lev's namesake—had been a man who was renowned in the family for his learning and piety, who was also celebrated for his abject poverty, the direct result, his mother frequently proclaimed, of his unwavering commitment to Torah study. Her message to Lev was clear—Grandpa Levi wouldn't have missed *his* grandfather's yahrzeit. Grandpa Levi would have shrugged off a blizzard and subzero temperatures and walked for hours to honor *his* dead.

Okay, Lev told himself, I'll go home and maybe I'll get frostbite or pneumonia, or maybe I'll get both, and won't they feel great about that!

And he thought: if it had been a conversation between Angela and her parents, there is no doubt that she would have gotten what she wanted. Or even if they insisted that she come home, she wouldn't go. She would stay out all night and when they confronted her, she would concoct some absurd story that would be so implausible that no one with any sense would believe it; but Angela would assert it with such unimpeachable conviction that ultimately, they would just retreat and let the whole thing be.

But Angela was strong and he was weak.

Lev quietly opened the door of the bathroom and peeked out, hoping that Angela was still dozing and hadn't heard his end of the conversation. But she had turned on her side and was watching the doorway. Lev thought she was going to tear into him for not insisting that he stay with her in Red Hook.

"Grandpa Levi's yahrzeit," she said softly. "That's important. You should be home for his yahrzeit." She pronounced yahrzeit as if it were spelled *yacht-sight*.

For the first time, Lev felt a twinge of gratitude to Rabbi Dr. Erwon Arkadi, Angela's rabbi. Angela lifted up the blanket and nodded for him to come over and slip in next to her naked body. As he climbed into bed, she whispered her plan.

"First we're going to get you as warm as a person can get. And we'll take our time, because you want to make them worry; make them get a little hysterical when you don't show up for a few hours; make them think that you're lying under a snowdrift somewhere. And when you get home, don't say a word. Just go into the kitchen and turn on the stove and pull a chair up to it and pretend that you're too cold to even talk. Which is probably what you will be. Just sit there and stare off into space like you've been in a trauma or something and won't never get over it. Because," she said, stroking his face, "we need to start training them, your parents. I'm going to help you train them, just like I trained my parents. Because it's time for us to start getting them to be more afraid of us than we are of them."

Then she smiled a sweet smile, reached down under the covers and began unfastening his pants.

44.

The snow and ice dumped on the city by the sudden storm disappeared almost as quickly as it had come. A few days later, the streets were running with streams of melting snow. Angela and Lev returned to their schedule of liaisons every few days in Red Hook.

"Why don't you ever ask me about Christianity anymore?" Angela asked him. They were in bed, sipping a Diet Dr. Pepper.

"I do ask you. All the time."

"Maybe once or twice, when we first started out. But you haven't asked me about it in months. I ask you about Judaism all the time."

"I don't ask you to ask me about Judaism. I'm quite happy with you not asking me about Judaism at all."

"But I'm curious about what Judaism means to you. Aren't you curious about what Catholicism means to me?"

"I didn't think it meant that much to you. Okay, so what does it mean to you?"

She raised her head off the pillow and took another swig of the Diet Dr. Pepper. She handed Lev the can and sat up. She turned away from him and hugged her knees as she thought about what Catholicism meant to her. Lev could see the subtle ripples of her vertebrae arching down the curve of her naked back. He reached out and lightly traced the arc of her spine with his index finger, pausing at each delicate ridge.

"Stop it!" she snapped. "I'm trying to think."

After a few minutes, she lay back down on the pillow and turned to him. "You're right," she admitted. "Catholicism doesn't mean that much to me. But Jesus does."

"Yes, I know. You told me that a long time ago."

"So how come you don't ask me about Jesus?"

"I told you that I took a course about religion when I was a freshman and I learned a lot about Jesus."

"But aren't you curious to learn more?"

"No, not really. Unless it has to do with what he means to you."

"Do you want to come to church? To see a Mass?"

"No."

"I went to synagogue. By myself—you certainly didn't invite me."

"I'm not interested in going to Mass."

"Is this another veal parmigiana moment?" she asked. "Where you come up with some secret reason that has existed for thousands of years of why you can't go to church?"

"Maybe a little, but it's certainly no secret. Christianity, and the Catholic Church in particular, hasn't been very nice to the Jews, in case you haven't noticed. It's been two thousand years of persecution. Just sixty years ago, the Pope ignored the fact that the Nazis were rounding up and murdering Jews. And now you people are thinking of making him a saint. So my going to Mass is not just dropping in on another religion to see how weird it is, which is why you visited that synagogue. It means something, I mean something symbolic, for me to go to a church."

"Wow!" she exclaimed, "I didn't know you had so much baggage!"

"It's not 'baggage' in the sense that I'm lugging it around unnecessarily. It comes with the territory."

"Is this just your hang-up or your family's hang-up, or is this the official position of the Jewish people?"

"There are no official positions of the Jewish people."

"So this is just you and your fanatical family talking."

"Angela, it's not just me or my family talking. And by the way, they are not fanatics, in case you don't know. You need to understand the history."

And this is what Lev told Angela.

In the spring of 1096, bands of armed Christians began to assemble and move east across Europe toward Byzantium, which they intended to cross in order to conquer Jerusalem from the Saracens. These Crusader armies had been whipped into a religious frenzy by clerics devoted to the idea of regaining control of the Holy Land from Islam. As they made their way across Europe, they turned their zealotry against the Jews. In the Rhine Valley, the Crusaders cornered the Jewish community of Worms, which had taken refuge in the bishop's fortress. The Crusaders gave an ultimatum to the Jews trapped in the fortress: convert to Christianity and leave unharmed, or face death. Rather than convert, the Jewish fathers—and in many cases the mothers—took knives and killed their children and then took their own lives. When the Crusaders breached the walls, they found eight hundred corpses. In Mainz, another Crusader army surrounded the bishop's citadel where more than a thousand Jews had taken refuge; again, the Jews chose to kill themselves rather than convert. Similar fates awaited other communities of France and Germany as the Crusaders made their way eastward.

Lev finished his lecture and turned his head to look at Angela curled up against him. Her forehead was creased with what he took to be skepticism. "Angela, these are just a few examples. There are more—many, many more. So it's not just me taking some fanatic position about not wanting to spend time in a church."

Angela was silent as she absorbed what he had told her. Finally, she asked: "Would your father do that? Would he kill all of you so you wouldn't have to convert to Christianity?"

"No, I don't think so. I don't think he feels that killing your family and taking your own life to avoid forced conversion is consistent with Jewish law. And even if he did, he couldn't bring himself to do that."

"Your mother?"

Lev didn't answer her right away. He thought about his mother and her grim determination about everything; her conviction that the world at large was only there to lure upright Jews to perversion; that desecration and pollution lurked just outside the door or around the corner. And he knew exactly what his mother would do if his family found themselves in a citadel, surrounded by a Christian mob demanding either their souls or their lives. But if he told Angela the truth, she would know immediately how hopeless was their future together, how unattainable.

Angela must have sensed his uncertainty because she said: "I'm looking straight at you and I'm reminding you, Lev, that I can always tell when you're fibbing or covering up something. So don't even think about it."

"My mother," Lev told Angela, "would line us up, youngest to oldest, and she would slit each of our throats, starting with Moti's and ending with mine. And then she would offer the knife to my father. If he didn't take it, she would finish him and then herself."

Angela stared at Lev, her eyes growing larger as she absorbed what he had said. Her face softened in sadness, but then her brow furrowed and her eyes narrowed. Lev thought: Here it comes, here's where she realizes how futile our being together is; here's where she shouts at me that Nino was right when he told her I was a dead-end.

Angela slowly shook her head back and forth. "Gee. Your mother . . . what a woman." Then she looked at Lev, her mouth set in a determined line. "I am looking forward to meeting her someday."

45.

One evening a couple of weeks later, as they lazed together, Angela turned to Lev and asked: "Did you know that a convert to Judaism, it's like she was just like a newborn baby? You know, like her past life wasn't real; like nothing that ever happened to her matters anymore. But still, she's supposed to honor her mother and her father even though they remain Christians?"

"Yes," he answered her.

"And did you know," Angela continued, "that when her Christian mother or father dies, she can say *Kaddish* in their memory? She doesn't have to, but she can if she wants?"

"Are these teachings of the learned Rabbi Dr. Erwon Arkadi?"

"He mentions it, but actually I've been doing some other reading about Judaism."

Lev felt a wave of unease wash over him. "What kind of other reading?" he asked.

"Introduction type of stuff," she said. "You know, the usual stuff by guys like Max Dimont and Herman Wouk. And also some books by Rabbi Joseph Telushkin, guys like that."

Lev was lying on his back studying the tin ceiling and he turned to look at her. "Sounds like you've been doing some heavy lifting."

"You sound concerned," she said.

"Not concerned. Curious, maybe. What's going on?"

"I'm looking at other options. I'm not happy with the Catholic Church right now."

"Oh, no!" he said in exasperation. "Does this have to do with the ravings of Rabbi Dr. Erwon Arkadi?"

Angela meandered her index finger in a random path across his bare chest for a few moments. Then she said, "It has more to do with you than with him."

"With me? Angela, I don't want to be the cause of your leaving the Church."

Her eyes grew wide with incredulity and then dismay. Lev realized—too late—that this was an unwise thing to say, a bad thing to say.

"You must think I'm stupid," she said. "What have we been talking about all these months? This hasn't been Comparative Religions 101, has it?"

"No, of course not."

"Well, Lev," she said, "is it my imagination, or haven't you been telling me all these months one way or another that you can't marry a Catholic? That you couldn't live with the fallout? Hasn't that been the point of all these discussions?"

"No," Lev protested, "I haven't been saying that."

"You haven't? Didn't you tell me that your mother would slit your throat and the throats of your entire family if you brought home a Catholic girl to marry?"

"You asked me a theoretical question and I gave you a theoretical answer! I never said she would literally slit our throats."

"Oh, so sorry that I'm not smart enough to understand what you're saying. So sorry. Then it's fine that I remain a Catholic? We could get married someday—no problems, no complications?"

"Who said anything about getting married?"

Angela looked as if he had reached across the sheets and slapped her face. She leapt from the bed and started pulling on her clothes, not saying a word.

"Angela," Lev pleaded, "don't be like that. Where are you going? Stay here; talk to me!"

She turned on him, her shirt in her hands. "Talk to you about what?" she shouted. "About how you don't really love me!"

Then she burst into tears and just stood there bawling, crumpling her shirt into her face to staunch her tears. Lev recalled what Angela had told him at Christmas—that she didn't cry when things were painful—she only cried when things were over, finished, no longer possible. He reached across the bed, seized her arm and pulled her back onto the mattress. He held her close.

"Don't cry," he begged her. "Angela, don't cry. I do love you. I do. But to leave the Church . . . it's too much to ask."

"You didn't ask me," she said, between sobs. "I volunteered."

"It's too much to ask . . . to become a Jew. It's too hard . . . too terrible to bear all of those obligations when you aren't forced to."

"If you really loved me, you wouldn't say that."

She stopped sobbing, pulled the shirt from her face, turned and looked at him. Her makeup had smeared and smudged around her eyes and for a moment, she looked to Lev as if she had two black eyes, like she was a victim of domestic violence.

"Lev," she said, "I'm not asking you whether you want me to convert. And I'm not asking you to convert—that would be ridiculous." Angela paused for a moment and dabbed the corner of the sheet against her brimming eyes. She took a deep breath and continued. "All I'm asking you is whether you want to be with me. Whether you want to marry me. Not this second, but someday. So you need to tell me the truth. Right now. And you need to mean it."

At that moment, Lev tried to think about how he really felt about Angela, whether he loved her—of course he loved her!—whether he loved her enough to marry her, whether he loved her enough to drag her and himself to the derech, out onto the narrow bridge without railings, out across the perilous chasm and into the thick swirling fog. But all he could think about was when he first shook Angela's hand and it was so delicate that he was afraid that if he held it too tightly, he would crush it, but he was also worried that if he didn't hold it firmly enough, it would flutter away from him.

"Yes," Lev said. "I want to marry you."

Angela's face erupted into a smile and she began weeping again. She slumped against Lev, her tears dripping down her cheeks and onto his shoulder. "Do you mean it?" she muttered, "do you really mean it?"

"Yes," he said. "I really mean it."

She stopped crying and her breathing slowed. Lev lay still as a stone—he thought that if he moved, he might set her off again. Finally, he turned his head and looked at Angela nestled against him. She had fallen asleep. It was as if she had passed out, fainted dead away. Lev held her as she slept and gazed at her face, now marred by tracks of her smudged mascara.

A half-hour later, Angela awoke. As soon as her eyes opened, she jumped out of bed, headed into the bathroom and closed the door. She washed her face, put on fresh makeup and came back to bed. She lay on her side, put her arms around his neck and pulled him toward her as they gazed into each other's faces.

"Lev," she said seriously. "I love you. I love you with all my heart, with all my soul and with all my might." And then she kissed him, a long, lingering, tender kiss.

So the declaration had finally arrived. Lev had told himself that it really didn't matter to him, but of course it did matter, and as soon as she said it, he knew that he had been waiting impatiently a long time to hear it. And Lev thought: How perfect it was! That she had planned it so carefully; that she had obviously taken that phrase *with all my heart, with all my soul and with all my might* from the *Shema*, the paragraph that Jews venerate for its eloquent depiction of the adoration that God expects from His people; she had come across it in one of those books she was reading—maybe even Rabbi Dr. Erwon Arkadi's book—and memorized it just for this occasion. He thought back to the night of the storm, when he had howled his love for Angela into the frigid wind while so enraged at her; and she had thought it was so perfect because it was genuine, without artifice. And Lev asked himself: This statement of love by Angela was certainly comparable to that, wasn't it? I should be just as happy with what Angela said to me as she was happy with what I had said to her, shouldn't I?

But Lev wasn't happy. It had set him on edge, her words, as soon as he heard them, and he immediately knew why, even though he struggled not to acknowledge the reason, to put it out of his mind. But he couldn't. And here is what Lev could not rid himself of: that Angela, despite all of their discussions, all of her reading and study; despite her apparent willingness to consider becoming a Jew for him; didn't appreciate that the kind of love that she declared for him was reserved only for God. Jews knew that you don't say those words to flesh and blood. You declared them when the skin was being torn from your body with iron combs, as Rebbe Akiva had said them two thousand years ago when he was being tortured to death by the Romans; you said them as the Crusader mob stormed up the ramparts of the citadel and you stood with a knife in your hand and your family before you; you uttered them in the stifling freight cars as they rumbled to oblivion in the east.

But you did not say them to each other. Even uneducated Jews knew that. Every Jew in the world knew that. Every Jew.

But not Angela.

46.

From that night on, Lev was consumed by imagined scenarios about how he would tell his parents that he was going to marry Angela Pizatto, a Catholic girl. It wouldn't happen immediately. They would probably wait a couple of years until they had both graduated from Brooklyn College. And, yes, Angela would convert to Judaism, although Lev did not think that would make much of a difference to his parents' reaction. It was true what Angela had learned from Rabbi Dr. Erwon Arkadi: Judaism valued converts; it was acknowledged that those who voluntarily embraced Judaism were as meritorious—or more meritorious—than those who inherited it; and acceptance of converts without reservation was indeed the aspiration. Yet Lev also appreciated that his parents had set in their own minds a host of possible marital options for him, and no one in the family had contemplated his marrying a shiksa, even one who converted. Moreover, his parents, particularly his mother, had never demonstrated that they embraced the more universalistic aspects of the Jewish faith. Hadn't Bubbie Malke emerged from the cocoon of her senility to give him just this warning? So Lev was gloomy—actually terrified—about how his parents would react.

In the meantime, Angela's appetite for Jewish learning was insatiable. She continued to devour huge chunks of *How Strange the Jews!*, but she also began to read every other book about Judaism that she could get her hands on. She peppered Lev with countless questions about Jewish practice. Between these learning sessions, the couple continued to meet in Red Hook to make love. In fact, the more Judaism Angela devoured, the more wanton she seemed to become.

Angela decided she was tired of conducting their love affair in secret, and she said she wanted it to become public knowledge, even though their marriage was still a couple of years in the future. She decided she wanted to meet Lev's family on Pesach, which was only six weeks away; she wanted to attend the family Seder.

"I don't know, Angela, probably not a good time. You understand—too many guests, too many weird relatives at the Seder table. Imagine what it would be like if you brought me home to meet your family for Christmas dinner. With everyone there. Without giving them a chance to get used to the idea first."

Angela brushed off his explanation; she raised her chin and tensed her shoulders the way she usually signaled her intention to engage in combat with Lev. But suddenly, she seemed to think better of the idea. "Okay, so when?" she asked in a low voice.

Lev snapped his fingers and pointed at Angela. "How about after Pesach, but before Shavuos."

Angela studied Lev as if assessing his sincerity. Then she smiled. "Good. I can hardly wait. When do you want to meet my family?"

"I dunno. Let's take it one step at a time."

"You could come to Easter Dinner."

"Oh, yeah, a great time to introduce your Jewish boyfriend, on the day that Jesus was resurrected after the Jews supposedly killed him."

"You might have a point," she conceded.

Lev pictured the introductory meal with his family. His brothers would be spellbound, watching Angela as she chatted everyone up. Their mouths would be open in wonder; but they would be silent, trying to appreciate this new knowledge—that women as enticing as Angela actually existed and were accessible to humble men like the Livitski brothers. They would look at her and then back at Lev and then back at her, their little heads tilted in wonder. And Elya—what would be going through his mind, his heart?

His father would sit back and be charmed by her, submit to her spell. She would talk to him about budgets, about the thrill of puzzling over every line item, of speculating about every contingency that could cause the budget to veer off course, and then about correcting your assumptions to prevent that from happening. Because a budget not only had to have elegance, it also had to have integrity; an inner consistency that resisted the vicissitudes of life, of the world. And once the budget was up and running and had demonstrated its rigor—once it was a living creation—it could be used to mold reality to itself. You could change the assumptions and the program that housed it would alter all the outcomes. You could manipulate the future—indeed, you could actually change it! And perhaps you could even change the present, pretend that things that had previously seemed unalterable, constant, immutable, were actually just projections of your will. You could pretend that you could change the present; you could just punch in a couple of numbers and everything that seemed so predestined, all those things, would change too. And if the present could change, then the future had no choice but to adapt itself to what you made happen in the present.

But Lev's mother would say nothing. She would just sit there with a half-smile on her face and observe her future daughter-in-law. She would exchange pleasantries, but other than, "Hi, how are you, nice to meet you," she would remain silent. Inside her head, however, she would be saying to Angela: "Sure, if you have it, flaunt it, because ultimately, men are all alike, even my son, my *bachor*, my firstborn. So he likes the makeup, the short skirt, the high heels; the blouse that costs more than my best suit. He likes those breasts of yours too: they can't possibly be all real; you must be wearing one of those bras that hold them up like you were holding them in your two hands and pointing them up to the sky. And those underpanties, too, the ones that don't even have bottoms—you must be wearing those too, the ones that your kind wear halfway up their tuches. So that's what my firstborn son likes? He's so bright but so stupid. And look at the rest of them, sitting here, panting after you; even my husband, because you talk about budgets with him like they aren't the most boring thing in the world, which they are."

"Mrs. Livitski," Angela would say, "your roast chicken is so delicious. Lev talks about it all the time. I would love to have the recipe."

His mother would force a tepid smile and offer the platter to Angela for seconds.

And Angela would say: "The kugel is also delicious," but she would mispronounce it just enough to make it grating on his mother's ears—*kookel* she would say.

And his mother would lift her glass of water and think to herself, "I know what the rabbis say about welcoming the convert, how we need to accord honor and respect to the convert. I know all about that. But this girl, this shiksa, is not interested in becoming a Jew. She's just interested in taking my son away from me, of taking him off the derech. And why not? He'll be a good provider; he'll be faithful to her; he won't come home drunk and beat her; he'll be a lot better husband than any of those mafia types that she would end up with if she hadn't put her claws into Lev. But this girl isn't serious. She has no idea what it will take to become Jewish.

"There are so many Jewish girls who are appropriate—beautiful, intelligent, who observe the mitzvos—*chaynedik* girls; every one of them would jump at the chance to be with Lev; they would jump at the chance to be his wife. But instead, Lev brings home this whore. A piece of trayf. She has no idea how hard I will fight to keep my Lev from her. Over my dead body, Angela Pizatto—or over yours."

That's what his mother would be thinking while she took a sip of water and smiled genially at Angela.

But Angela wouldn't be fooled. "Your mother doesn't like me," she would say after the dinner.

"Nonsense," Lev would tell her, "she likes you fine."

"No she doesn't. She hates me. She doesn't want me to have you; she's not going to let me have you."

"That's ridiculous," he would insist.

"No," Angela would say, "she wants me dead. Believe me; I know when someone wants me dead."

47.

Even while Lev compulsively revisited these grim speculations, the two lovers continued meeting in Red Hook as often as they could. The weather warmed and sometimes they even ventured outside and explored the neighborhood. If they walked west for a mile or so, Lev and Angela could gaze across the strait at Governor's Island and further out into New York Harbor at the Statue of Liberty; the skyline of the southern tip of Manhattan gleamed to the north. It was good to get out of the stuffy apartment and begin to enjoy the world again. Lev felt like they were some species of forest mammal who had been hibernating together in the snug cave of the apartment throughout the inhospitable winter. The spring breezes awakened them both, summoning them into a world that was about to be reborn.

They moved deeper into March and soon it was time to celebrate Purim. The holiday fell on a Sunday night, so Angela and Lev planned to meet earlier than usual that Sunday so they wouldn't have to rush with one another.

When Angela arrived in the early afternoon, the first thing she asked Lev was whether he was hungry.

"Nope, I bought a tuna sandwich and ate it around an hour ago."

Angela gave him a dark look. "You're not fasting?"

"No, I'm not fasting."

"But it's the Fast of Esther!" she exclaimed. And she launched into a disquisition based on what she had learned from *How Strange the Jews!* "On the day preceding the evening celebration of the holiday of Purim, the Jews refrain from eating and drinking until after the scroll of Esther is read publicly that evening. The fast is a reenactment of the behavior of the Jewish community of Persia, which, on the instructions of Queen Esther, fasted for three days in order to invoke God's intervention in rescuing them from a plot to exterminate them. Queen Esther herself engaged in this fast before launching her

259

counter-insurgency to defeat the wicked anti-Semite, Haman." Angela declared this information authoritatively, with her hands on her hips. She recited this history almost as if she were reading directly from Arkadi's book, and Lev wondered whether Angela had attained the same facility to recall sections of *How Strange the Jews!* as Lev had to recapture pages of the Talmud. Was *How Strange the Jews!* Angela's Talmud? Had Rabbi Dr. Erwon Arkadi become her Sage?

"So why aren't you fasting?" she asked.

"I fasted until noon and that's enough."

"Until noon? You probably slept until 11:30 a.m."

"I was at morning services at eight."

"Still, fasting until noon on a Sunday—big deal!"

"What's this all about, Angela?"

She sat down next to him on the bed where he had been reading his American history textbook. "This is serious stuff, Lev," Angela explained. "Queen Esther was some amazing chick—she was gorgeous and she knew how to handle all of them: the king, Haman, even her uncle. They didn't know what hit them and then she rescued all the Jews of Persia."

Of course Angela likes Queen Esther, Lev thought. Queen Esther was, after all, the winner of a beauty pageant that established her as the most desirable woman in all 127 provinces of the ancient Persian empire, a winner who knew how to use her sexuality to manipulate everyone.

"Angela," he said, "tonight I am going to hear the story of Queen Esther read. And then again tomorrow morning. And we're going to drink and feast and exchange gifts and give charity to poor people. So I'm going to spend almost twenty-four hours showing my respect to Queen Esther. I think that's enough, don't you? I don't see why I have to also fast a full day. This whole thing happened a long time ago, over two thousand years ago!"

"I can't believe you're saying this! Rabbi Dr. Erwon Arkadi says that Purim is one of the most important things in Jewish history."

"Well, I'm not so sure I agree. Some people say Purim is just the Jewish version of Halloween."

Angela was aghast. "What a load of crap! You don't really believe that, do you?"

"No, but look . . . sure, it was a great rescue, but it didn't change anything for the Jewish people after all. There were plenty of other threats when the Jewish people prayed and fasted and God didn't do anything to help. So we got away with it once. What's the big deal?"

"You're the one who's always complaining about how the Jews get shafted all the time in history, so when you finally get to a holiday where they don't get shafted, it's a bit weird that you don't want to celebrate it."

"I *will* celebrate it. I'm just not fasting the entire day."

Angela didn't say anything, but Lev could see her gears turning as she stared at him. Then she asked: "Did you fast on this day last year?"

"Yes."

"And the year before?"

"Probably."

"Well, then, what possible reason do you have for not fasting this year?"

Lev thought: What the hell is going on here? Why is she harassing me about Jewish observance? I didn't fall off the derech in order to be admonished by some ignorant Catholic girl! Who does she think she is—my mother?

But all he said was: "I've come to realize that these fast days don't mean anything to me."

"Does that mean you won't be fasting on the other days of the year, the days when your Temples were destroyed?"

"I doubt I will."

"Why, all of a sudden?"

"I've seen the light."

"Not a good reason."

Enough—I don't want to discuss this any longer, Lev thought. I want to change the channel. I'll distract her with sex. She uses sex all the time to distract me, to get me to bend to her will. Two can play that game. So he reached over and pulled her to him. He plucked one of her trademark chopsticks from her uplifted hair and it unwound around her shoulders. The other stick fell out onto the floor.

"C'mon," he said into her hair, "why are you on my case about this?"

"I'm not on your case. I just want to understand it."

He began unbuttoning her shirt as she continued. "I mean I don't think these things lose their meaning from year to year. If it meant something last year, it should mean something this year."

He peeled her shirt from off her shoulders and reached behind her and began to fumble with her bra. "Who said it meant something last year?"

"But you did it last year, didn't you?"

"Who can remember?" He cast her bra on the floor.

"And I bet the year before and the year before that," she said. Lev pushed her down on the bed and knelt in front of her, pulling off her boots. He slipped her skirt down and tossed it on the floor. Angela didn't seem to notice what was going on at all—she just kept talking. "So you've been doing all this stuff for a long time, fasting and stuff like that, and now, all of a sudden you find it doesn't have any meaning?"

By this time, Lev had peeled off Angela's pantyhose and she was lying on the sheet with only her panties on. Lev quickly shed his shirt and pants, lay down next to Angela and began caressing her breasts.

"Lev!" she shouted, "I am trying to have a conversation here about something important!"

Lev raised his head from her breast and looked at her. She was glaring at him. "Let's make love and afterward we can talk all day and all night about how strange the Jews are."

She looked at him with fury in her eyes, but she let her head drop back onto the bed. He continued to fondle and kiss her in the ways she loved. He closed his eyes and lost himself in a fog of desire.

Suddenly, Lev realized that her body was not responding; she was lying inert as if she were in a coma. No motion, no noises, no reaction whatsoever. He opened his eyes and glanced at her face. Her eyes were clamped shut and her mouth was curled in a grimace as if she were undergoing some unpleasant medical procedure that she didn't want but knew she had to endure.

Lev looked at her as she lay on her back, inanimate beside him. He didn't want to give up, so he slid his hand down Angela's stomach and under the elastic waistband of her underwear to her crotch. As soon as he touched her there, Angela's eyes snapped open. She swung her arm and slapped Lev hard on the face as he bent over her.

Lev was stunned, not by the force of the blow, but by the anger it conveyed. His first instinct—which he managed to suppress—was to slap her back, the way he would slug the shoulder of one of his brothers in retaliation. Lev realized that he had never before been struck in anger—never. He had been punched numerous times by his brothers and friends when horsing around, sometimes in irritation or because he intentionally provoked a blow. But he had never been struck by another person because what he was doing to that person was so terrible that it couldn't be borne anymore; it couldn't be endured for even one more second.

He felt such shame. No, beyond shame; he felt like a *vessel filled with disgrace and humiliation*—that was the way the Yom Kippur liturgy described sinners. He had forced himself on Angela; he had ignored her pleas to stop making love to her; he had touched her private parts when she didn't want him to. Once again, Lev asked himself how he had come to this moment, a moment when he was trying to force himself on his girlfriend in order to avoid talking about why he was repudiating his religious obligations. How had this happened to him?

An image of a fist came to him, a fist clenched in wrath at what he had done, the fist of Rabbi Berkowitz admonishing him for not following the path to righteousness, for succumbing to his Evil Inclination.

"I'm sorry, Angela," Lev whispered to her. "I shouldn't have insisted. I should have heard what you were saying. Please forgive me." He wanted to finish the sentence by listing all the things he was sorry for, but there were too many shameful things.

After her slap, Angela lay on her back, staring up at the ceiling, her eyes open and unblinking, as if she were no longer alive. Her hands lay at her side, palms open and facing up—hands that, at any other time, were always in motion. Lev remembered those inert hands from the aftermath of their disastrous first date. *This is the way Angela plays dead*, he reminded himself.

"Please, Angela . . . please forgive me."

"I forgive you," she said quietly.

"No, I mean really forgive me. Like just not say it, but really forgive me."

She didn't reply.

"I promise I will never ever touch you without you saying so. I promise."

Angela turned her head toward him but otherwise lay in her corpse-like pose. "I forgive you for that. I believe you. I'm not upset about that anymore."

"But you still look upset."

"I'm upset that you didn't fast."

Despite his remorse, he felt a surge of anger well up in the back of his throat. He almost shouted at her to let it go, to stop meddling in his business. Instead, he made assurances: "I'll fast the rest of the day! I won't eat or drink a thing!"

She turned her gaze from him and looked at the ceiling.

"I'll fast for a whole day later this week to make up for it!"

Angela flung her arms across her face and started sobbing.

"Angela!" Lev exclaimed. "What is it?" He wanted to take her in his arms to comfort her, but after what he had done, he didn't know whether he had permission to touch her anymore.

"Don't blame yourself," she muttered in between her sobs. "It's not your fault! It's not your fault. It's my fault! I'm the one who's ruining you. All of these years you fasted because some Persian guys tried to murder you. And you fasted on the days the others came to wreck your Temples. But now you don't care anymore. You don't care about that stuff anymore. I'm the reason you don't care. I've ruined you; I've made you into someone who doesn't care anymore."

"That's so wrong, Angela. You're not ruining me. You're saving me. You're bringing me into another world, into a new world that I was shut out of."

Lev's comment only made Angela sob harder. She tried to say something, but he couldn't make out her words. He sat beside her on the bed and waited. After a few minutes, she let her arms fall to her sides on the bed and turned her face to Lev.

"A new world?" she sniffled. "You think this apartment and what we do here is some sort of world? You're so naïve! This isn't a world! This is a way out of the world that you think is so great. You think people live like we do—in bed, fucking all the time? They don't live like this. They do all sorts of other stuff that I don't want to do anymore— they watch television and go to movies, go to clubs and drink until they fall down. That's the world you think is so special."

"That can't be right, Angela. This is the real world."

"This world isn't worth nothing. It's a stupid world. A selfish world. It's got nothing to offer a person like you. You can have sex anytime, but you only have one day each year to remember and feel good about Queen Esther, just one day to show her some respect, to not eat anything just like she said."

"That's crazy talk, Angela. There are plenty of days to fast. There are a bunch of fast days each year to remind us that our Temple was destroyed. But Angela, I don't want to remember the destruction of the Temple anymore. It doesn't mean anything to remember random acts of violence and cruelty that make up Jewish history. It means more to find someone to love and share love with."

Angela smiled at him for just an instant. "That's sweet for you to say that," she said, "but you don't get it. You don't get how nothing means anything because you always lived a life where you can find something that means something, where there is more than . . . than . . ." Angela groped to capture the turn of phrase to convey what she wanted. "More than just what's in front of your eyes or just what's in your hands. And now you have forgotten how important that is. And maybe that's my fault." She turned away and looked back at the ceiling, her eyes wide open, unblinking, like she was a cadaver. "I just hope it's not too late," she murmured.

"Too late for what?" Lev asked.

Angela turned away from Lev onto her side and curled up until she was hugging her knees. The discussion was over.

He wanted to lie down next to her and cradle her in his arms, but again he doubted that he was still welcome to do so. So he lay down on his back next to her. And then his cursed memory, that obsessive urge to recall the thousands, the tens of thousands of utterances he had learned during his voyages through the sea of the Talmud, dredged up a Mishna from *Pirkei Avos*, the Sayings of the Fathers: *Any love that is dependent on something—when that thing perishes, the love perishes. But a love that is not dependent on something, will never perish.* The Talmud speaks so infrequently about love that Lev had pondered that statement many, many times, but never could fathom what it meant.

But now he thought he knew what it meant—Angela's love for him was dependent on a *thing*—on Judaism, on his remaining a devout Jew. It wasn't a love that was pure, that was dependent only on him.

And, therefore, if his connection to being Jewish withered, her love for him would wither.

That was his first thought as he lay on his back, his arms extended beside his body on the bed, with his eyes clamped shut, while Angela lay breathing soundlessly next to him.

And then Lev had an even more terrible thought: maybe the Mishna wasn't talking about Angela at all. Maybe it was talking about him. Maybe it was *his* love of Angela that was dependent on a *thing*—on her remaining Catholic, remaining *other*. Maybe it was *his* love that was impure, defective, and that it was his love that would perish. And as he considered this possibility, Lev opened his eyes wide, unblinking. He unclenched his fists and he asked himself: Who's playing dead now?

VIII

Rebbe Yose of Yukras had a beautiful daughter. One day he saw a certain man making a hole in the fence and looking at her. Rebbe Yose said to him: 'What is the meaning of this?'

The man answered him: 'My master, if I have not merited to marry her, may I at least merit to catch a glimpse of her?'

Rebbe Yose turned to her and said: 'My daughter, because of your beauty, you are causing anguish to people; return to your state of dust and let mankind not sin on account of you.'

And so she died.

- Babylonian Talmud, Tractate Taanis 24A -

48.

In their disastrous pre-Purim encounter, Angela had declared her hope that she wasn't too late, but she did not reveal what she feared she might be too late for. Lev interpreted her statement as implying that she was going to take action to ensure she was not, in fact, too late, but even as Lev nervously awaited some emphatic follow-up proclamation, Angela seemed to have forgotten the drama. As the crocuses poked through the scattered remnants of snow on the flowerbeds abutting Ocean Parkway, she seemed to relax. Lev and Angela ventured out of the apartment more often and continued to explore the limited opportunities of Red Hook. They even began planning to embark on other adventures in faraway quarters of Brooklyn and Manhattan as they had done when they first began seeing each other. Angela's enthusiasms, her contagious passion for experience, began to return and infect Lev again, too.

On a particularly bright day in late March, Lev came into the apartment to find Angela buzzing with excitement. He hadn't even taken off his coat when she exclaimed: "Look what I got! On sale! You're going to love these!"

She handed him three packages wrapped in plastic. He quickly glanced at each. "Sheets and pillowcases?" he asked.

"Oh, men!" Angela replied. "They're not just sheets—they're *satin* sheets!"

Lev looked at her blankly.

She shook her head as she tore the plastic off. "These sheets can cost as much as forty dollars a set, but I got them all for fifteen. They're seconds. That means they aren't perfect, but they're good enough for this bed."

"Why do we need new sheets?" he asked.

"We don't *need* new sheets," she explained, "although the ones we use are pretty cruddy. But satin sheets are supposed to be an unbelievable sexy experience. And look at the colors: this bottom sheet

269

is silver and the top sheet is gold, and look—the pillowcases are gold also!" She held each package out to Lev as she regarded them with obvious appreciation.

"C'mon, we're going to make the bed." She began pulling the old bedding off and stuffing it into one of the fraying pillowcases. Angela enlisted Lev in tucking in the silver contour sheet. She flicked the gold-colored top sheet into the air over the bed, and as it floated to the surface, something nagged at Lev as he registered the colors: silver topped by gold. Something was skulking at the edge of his consciousness, something unsavory. And then, suddenly, he was in Tractate *Menachos*, at the top of a slender pasture of Aramaic. He was reliving a story that the Rabbis of the Talmud had felt worthy of inclusion in the tradition. It was the most prurient story in the Talmud that Lev had ever come across. It leapt back into his consciousness when he saw the colors of the satin sheets. And once it had intruded, he could not exorcise it without first revisiting it to learn what it had to teach him.

Lev didn't know how much time elapsed while his brain explored Tractate Menachos, but he abruptly came back to this world when he heard Angela shouting at him: "Lev! Earth to Lev!"

He shook his head to clear it and looked at her.

"Where the hell were you?" she asked sharply. "I know that look— you were in Babylonia! That look—that's the one where you leave this world for the other one, to visit one of your weird tourist attractions in Talmud land. Where were you, Lev? This time I want to know!"

Lev saw that the bed had been made, the silver and gold satin bedding neatly tucked in, ready to accept their naked bodies. A great weariness swept through him, exhaustion so acute that he thought he was going to faint. He sat down heavily on the bed. He felt overwhelmed by the burden of lying to everyone—to his family so he could protect his illicit affair with Angela; to Angela so he could protect her from the overwhelming forces just over the horizon marshaling to overthrow them; to himself about how there had to be a way forward for them that didn't require him to betray the people he loved most.

It had been there all the time, his knowledge of this Talmudic story. Lev had learned it once and had repressed it deep inside his mind where no light could find it and bring it into his consciousness.

It had lain there slumbering while he carried on with Angela. Lev understood that he had bottled it up there only so he could indulge his passion for her. He had on some level always known about it—this story was the reason Lev had refused Angela's relentless pursuit to examine his tzitzis. It had been uncharacteristic of him to resist so steadfastly. He now realized that he had hidden the fringes away from her sight only so they would not bear witness against him, as they had in this story from the Talmud. Lev now knew that he had hidden them from her because he had recognized that the tzitzis were dangerous to Angela and him, and were toxic in some way that could poison their relationship.

The satin sheets were glossy, almost slippery. Lev slid slowly off them to the floor, his back against the side of the bed, his knees up and his head in his hands. Angela sensed that something unique was happening to him, so she didn't choose her normal approach—aggression, relentless probing for the truth. She sat down next to Lev on the floor, put her arm around his neck and nuzzled him, whispering: "Lev, what is it? What is it, Lev?"

And Lev thought to himself: I can't lie to everyone about everything anymore. Now and then I have to tell the truth—no matter what. And even as he told this to himself, he knew he was lying.

"There's a story in the Talmud. I just remembered it. It's not nice."

"Is it about us?" she asked.

"I don't know. It could be."

Lev thought Angela was going to be Angela and say something like: "Don't tell me any stories that aren't nice. There are 5,400 city-states in Babylonia and you know a whole lot of them, so look a little harder and find a story about us that's a good story." But she didn't say that. She looked grim but nodded her head for Lev to continue. She was turned toward Lev as she sat on the floor, with one of her hands resting on the satin sheets, which she unconsciously caressed with her fingers. Lev knew that this story was the last thing Angela wanted to hear. What she really wanted to do was take off her clothes and slide in between the satin sheets and wait for him to crawl on top of her.

But he told her what he had found in Tractate Menachos:

Come and learn about the commandment of tzitzis from an incident concerning a student who was meticulous about this

271

commandment. *The student had heard of a harlot who lived in the cities by the sea and this harlot was so beautiful that she charged four hundred golden dinars as her fee. The student sent her four hundred golden dinars and scheduled a time to visit her. When his appointed time came, he arrived and sat by the doorway of her brothel until the harlot's maidservant bid him enter. . . . The harlot prepared seven beds for him, and on the first six beds, she put sheets of silver, and on the seventh bed, she put sheets of gold. Between each bed she placed a silver ladder, but to reach the seventh, uppermost bed, she placed a ladder of gold. She ascended the ladders and she sat naked upon the uppermost bed. The student began to climb the ladders with the intent to sit naked opposite her. But as he climbed, his tzitzis—each of the four fringes from the four corners of his garment—began to pelt him on his face!*

In shock, he slipped down the ladders and sat on the ground . . .

The harlot said to him, 'By the Master of Rome, I will not leave you until you tell me what flaw you saw in me.'

He replied, 'By the Divine Sacrificial Service, I swear that I have never seen a woman as beautiful as you are. But there is one commandment that the Lord our God has commanded us and tzitzis is its name, and regarding that commandment it is written twice in the Torah, "I am the Lord your God." The first time is to tell us that in the future, God will exact punishment on the corrupt and the second time is to tell us that in the future, God will reward the righteous. At the moment that I was climbing the ladders to consort with you, my tzitzis appeared as witnesses in order to bear witness against me.'

The harlot said to the student, 'I will not leave you until you tell me your name, the name of your city, the name of your teacher and the name of the academy where you study Torah.'

The student wrote the answers to her four questions on a note and put it in her hand.

Lev stopped and stared at the floor in front of him in silence. "It *is* about us," Angela whispered. "How does it end?"

"That's how it ends," he said.

"No, it isn't," she said. "You wrote out the note and left it with me." Angela didn't understand the story as being about a student and a courtesan who lived almost two thousand years ago in Babylonia. She had grasped immediately that the story was really about them—about Lev Livitski and Angela Pizatto. She didn't object that she played the role of an idol-worshipping courtesan. She knew that her role in the story was to play a pagan harlot. "Why would the story tell us that you wrote out the note and left it with me if there wasn't something else that happens?"

"There's nothing else."

"But . . . but I'm holding onto the note . . . so the note . . . it must mean *something*."

Lev didn't answer her. He knew that she was right. He knew that the story didn't just end with the note in the harlot's hand. Although he could not recollect precisely where the story led, he had a premonition that its final destination was at the end of a serpentine road that he didn't want to travel. Lev didn't want to remind himself of what lurked at the end of that twisted path. But Angela was insistent.

"Go back, Lev!" she said fiercely. "Go back to Babylonia and find out what happens to us."

"I'm afraid," he said.

"Go back!"

So Lev traveled back. And this is what he found:

After the student left, the harlot rose and sold all her possessions except for the silver and gold bed sheets. She traveled to Rebbe Chiya's House of Study. She said to Rebbe Chiya, 'Rabbi, please give instructions that they should make me a convert.'

He asked her, 'My daughter, perhaps you are not in earnest to convert for the sake of Heaven? Perhaps you have set your eyes on one of my students to marry him?'

The harlot took the note on which the student had written his information and handed it to Rebbe Chiya.

After she converted, Rebbe Chiya said to her, 'Go and collect your acquisition.'

She married the student and the silver and gold bed sheets that she had originally prepared for them to use in sin, she now arranged for them to use in holiness.

It was a happy ending! Their story had a happy ending! And Lev could turn to Angela with a smile on his face, take her into his arms and whisper the happy ending to her. And they would know that they could be together, sanctified forever. He could return to the derech with his bride—the most beautiful harlot in the known world, a woman so alluring that it was worth four hundred golden dinars to share her bed. And she would be his.

Except Lev wasn't ready. He wasn't ready to return to the derech. Sometime in the last few weeks he had realized that Angela had become ready to ascend with him to the derech. But not Lev. He was not yet ready to return.

Wasn't he supposed to have learned something during these months off the derech? Wasn't that the whole reason he had jumped off it—yes, Lev finally admitted to himself that he had not fallen off; had not been blown off; had not been forced off; Lev had jumped off, of his own volition. But hadn't he jumped off it because he was supposed to learn something? He was supposed to learn something about the non-derech world, the other world that would equip him to crawl back onto the derech at some point and continue. Lev was supposed to learn something about himself while he wandered in the other world.

But what was it that he needed to learn? He had thought there was something in that world that would change him so that when he returned to his world, he would be able to proceed with the assurance that everything he was doing as a Jew was worth doing. Could it be that Lev wanted to recapture that moment when he was eight years old and he had known that what Shloime Strudler had done when he stomped on a lit cigarette butt on Simchas Torah was wrong, just plain wrong?

Or maybe he was supposed to learn how to love? To fall in love, maybe that was it. Did Lev love Angela? Yes, he loved her. He loved her but apparently not enough, not enough to return with her to the derech. He didn't love her with all his heart, with all his soul, with all his might. You don't have that type of love for human beings. You dare not. Maybe the problem, Lev thought, was that we Jews can't serve two masters. We can't love a human being with everything we've got and leave enough love to satisfy God. Because our God is a jealous God—He makes no bones about that; He says it many times, over and over in His Torah. And He makes us choose, no matter how painful that might be. And if we refuse to choose, then He turns His Face from us, He hides Himself from us and we wander aimlessly, lost in the gloom beneath the derech.

So all these months off the derech had taught him nothing. The only thing he had learned was how to sin—his limitless capacity to sin—to sin and to pick up the hem of his robe and sprint after still more sin. Not just more sin, but worse sin. First sex, then deceit in order to continue having sex and finally, betrayal. That was the only thing Lev had learned.

So how could he go back? How could he go back, even with his four-hundred-dinar harlot? Not now. Maybe later, but not now. Soon, he told himself. Just not now.

"There's nothing else," Lev told Angela. "The courtesan in the story is left holding the note. That's all there is."

Angela looked at Lev with such sadness in her eyes that it was as if she were weeping without tears. She wouldn't let herself cry. If she had let herself cry, both of them would know that it would have been over. And they weren't ready for that. So she just sat there and held it in.

And Lev told himself: I'll tell her the rest of the story at the right time. When I've made my peace with everything and I'm ready to return. I don't want her to be unhappy. I'll get straightened out about everything soon and then I'll tell her the rest of the story.

After a while, they got up off the floor, put on their coats and went home. They didn't use the satin sheets that night. The next time Lev met Angela in Red Hook, she had already stripped the satin sheets from the bed, replaced with the rough, stained, old ones. Lev never saw the satin sheets again. And he never asked about them either.

49.

After the story about the student and the harlot, Lev convinced himself that he would have time to work things out, to get accustomed
to the fact that Angela would convert and they would return to the
derech together. As time went on, it didn't seem so inconceivable. He
began thinking of practical things: how long it would take for Angela
to convert; where they would live after they were married; how he
would make a living.

The one thing he couldn't picture was the rest of it: how they would
live religiously; how they would relate to his family; how he could
coexist in the narrowness of Orthodoxy with someone as tempestuous
and willful as Angela; how she would react once she experienced the
real weight and restraint of the yoke of the commandments on her
shoulders. It wasn't what she thought it was, Lev told himself. It's not
just a collection of weird practices that her teacher, Rabbi Dr. Erwon
Arkadi, pretended it was.

But as long as other things occupied his attention, Lev could put
the bigger questions out of his mind. Brooklyn continued to inch its
way toward springtime. The dark waters in the harbor off Red Hook
began to shimmer blue in the early April sunlight. Angela and Lev
began to fantasize about summer—they would go to Coney Island on
Sundays and bring a picnic.

"Wait until you see my bikini," Angela said. "You won't be able to
control yourself."

50.

And then catastrophe.

Lev came home late one night from Red Hook to find his mother waiting for him. She was sitting in the forbidden zone—the living room. The rest of the apartment was draped in the sounds of sleep.

"Come sit beside me," she ordered as soon as Lev closed the front door behind him.

This directive alone was cause for panic. When Lev's mother scowled, wine turned to vinegar in an instant. And once Lev had left childhood for adolescence, she never indicated an inclination for him to sit near her, never mind beside her.

He eased into the room, aware of the cloud of Angela's aroma that he brought with him: her perfume, her skin cream, her secretions.

"Let me get to the point," his mother said as he took his seat on the sofa. "Who have you been carrying on with?"

Lev felt like he had been thrown off the roof of a building and he was spending the last few seconds of his life thinking about something stupid before splattering on the pavement below.

She continued, raising her voice. "Did you think we wouldn't find out? Do you think Brooklyn is a big city where you can disappear from your family and your community and that we wouldn't learn what you were up to?"

Actually, Lev had thought precisely that.

"Brooklyn is not a big city. Brooklyn is a *shtetl*. There are no secrets in Brooklyn!"

She continued her rant. "What makes you think you're so special that you can ignore the rules, that you don't have to live by the rules? What makes you think that it will work out for you? It never works out! People who match up like you're thinking of doing always regret it!"

Before Lev could even attempt to answer, she continued. "You're facing a lifetime of shame, of living in the shadows. You'll always be regarded as a half-breed. You'll never get any respect from anyone. A second-rate life is what you're choosing, without *kavod*." She used the Hebrew word for honor.

Finally, she stopped berating him and sat fuming in silence.

His heart was racing and he felt like he was going to suffocate. "Imma," Lev said to her, "I want you to meet her. She's a wonderful person. I'm sure you'll—"

She cut him off. "Of course, she's a wonderful person. Beautiful, too, I bet. Do you think I'm talking about her? I'm talking about her family, her people. They're the ones who will make your life a living hell."

"That's not fair—"

"Don't tell me about the Syrians," she said. "I know the Syrians. We've talked about this before—I bet your friend Andy from Avenue U introduced you—some good friend he is! Listen, I've lived in Brooklyn my whole life and I know those people. Those Jews will never accept you. You will get no respect from them ever. You'll be lucky to get an *aliyah*—" she used the Hebrew word for being called to bless the Torah—"even at your own *auf ruf*." Now she had lapsed into the Yiddish word for when a bridegroom is called to the Torah on the Sabbath before his wedding day.

Lev was dumbfounded. Someone must have told his mother that they had seen him with a Mediterranean-looking girl, stylishly dressed, and his mother had concluded that Angela must be a Syrian Jew, a member of the clannish and insular Orthodox Jewish community that congregated in southern Brooklyn.

"Imma," Lev said, "it's not what you think."

She cut him off again. "Don't tell me what I think!" she shouted. "The Syrians have nothing but contempt for us Ashkenazim and we won't be treated that way! I would rather you marry a convert than a Syrian Jew!"

And there it was—rescue! Lev imagined for an instant that this must be the way miners who are trapped by a collapse deep within the earth must feel when they first hear the whirr of drills grinding deep into the bedrock on their way to save them. This was the sign that he and Angela could in fact find a way out; they could pick their way carefully through the rubble they had created and make their way up through the darkness into the light of day. Lev could not have hoped for a better opening. It would only take a few artful sentences to set the stage for a future with Angela.

He groped for the right approach. Lev knew he was smarter than his mother; if he wanted to, he could outwit her. He could use all that cleverness and what she had just said to him to maneuver her into having no choice but to accept his marriage to Angela. But at that moment, a feeling of terror welled up inside him, threatening to overwhelm him. Instead of spinning out his argument based on her surprise endorsement of converts, Lev heard himself blurt out: "Imma, you can't be serious! Better to marry a convert than a Syrian Jew? You must be joking!"

"I'm not joking," she said, nodding her head with determination. "The way the rabbis make converts jump through hoops these days, the years of boring classes, the humiliation they are subject to—I'll tell you something: converts who make it to the finish line have got to be pretty serious about becoming Jewish. I'll bet that most converts make far better Jews than real Jews." And then, completely out of character for her, his mother began to wax philosophical. "Not all of them make good Jews, but in my opinion, the Catholics are the best candidates. Not the boys so much, because they're generally a bunch of lowlifes. But the girls make good Jews. Catholic girls make good Jews because they know what it is to submit."

Lev sat in bewildered silence, trying to make sense of what his mother had said, upending all his assumptions about her and her attitudes. And trying to come to terms with what he had said in response and what a sense of dread he had felt the moment it became clear to him that there was in fact a path for Angela and him into a shared future, a Jewish future.

His mother assumed that his silence was acquiescence. "So," she said with finality, "you'll say goodbye to this Syrian girl, correct? In her heart she'll know it's the right thing. Not just for you, but for her, too."

"Yes," Lev replied.

"Good," she said. She looked intensely at him and added, as if she were making an offhand observation, "And you won't be spending so much time anymore at meetings defending the State of Israel?"

"No," he said.

She placed her hands on her knees and pushed herself up from the couch. She forced a perfunctory smile. "I'm glad we had this little talk and cleared things up. By the way," she added, "your father doesn't know about these shenanigans. And now he doesn't need to know."

"Of course," Lev replied.

51.

The next night, Lev arranged to see Angela at their love hotel in Red Hook. When he arrived, she was already there. She had undressed and was waiting for him in bed, under the covers. As soon as he walked in, she saw disaster on his face.

She sat up abruptly. "What happened?"

"My mother . . . she found out about us. She's threatening to hang herself—"

"Let the bitch hang herself!" Angela exclaimed.

"Angela, you know that's not the way it works."

"It works fine that way with me."

"Well, I'm not you," he said. "We just need to cool down for a while. We just need to give it some time."

"Did you tell her you loved me?"

"Of course I did. She wouldn't listen. She went mental on me!"

"What about your father? What did he say?"

"My father?"

"Yeah, what did he say?"

"I . . . we . . . we didn't talk to my father."

"You didn't talk to your father? We need to cool down for a while because you talked to your mother, but you didn't talk to your father?"

"We didn't want to . . . to involve him . . . I mean, get him involved if we didn't have to."

"You didn't have to? You talked to the mother you're afraid of, the mother with the knife in her hand all bloody after she slit all your throats—you talked to your mother? But you didn't talk to your father, your father, the one you're not afraid of, the father with the sweet soul?"

"You know . . . I didn't want to upset him, to make him . . . to make him be upset—"

"I was going to convert!" Angela screamed before Lev could go

281

further. "I was going to convert and you couldn't even be bothered to talk to your father about us? I went to church and explained to Jesus that I had to leave and convert so I could be with you!"

"Angela," Lev said, taking her two hands in his, "converting would only make you unhappy. You don't really want to leave Jesus, do you?"

She glared at him. "Don't patronize me, you arrogant bastard! The truth is you never wanted me to convert. As long as I'm a Catholic, you have an excuse not to marry me!"

"Angela, you don't understand what it's like to be Jewish, to have to meet all the expectations of your parents and your family and your whole community. You're romanticizing it. It's exotic to you now, but once you're immersed in it, you would see how tough it is, how demanding it is. It's always been hard, but now it's even harder than ever, what with the Holocaust and everything . . ."

"Oh my God!" she shouted. "You're not going to blame the Holocaust for this, are you? Have you no shame?" She burst into tears and pulled away from him. She threw herself down onto the bed and wept into the pillow.

Lev tried to comfort her. He sat beside her and rubbed her shoulder. "Angela," he whispered. "Angela, we can continue seeing each other. Nothing has to end. We can still be together. This marriage thing—we don't need to be in such a hurry. Give my parents some time to get used to the idea."

She picked up her head from the pillow. "You don't understand at all, do you?" she said. "You just want to keep fucking me, is all you want. You don't want to be with me in a real way, in a sanctified way. You just want to keep fucking me is all you want!"

"That's not true," Lev protested. "I love you. I want to be with you. But to think about converting and getting married at this point—there's just too many barriers, too many hurdles."

"How dare you say that to me! I decided because of that story you told me. I finished writing that fucking story from Babylonia that your fucking rabbis didn't have the balls to finish! You left me holding the note, but I figured out that the note has instructions on how to go to you, on how to convert. You told me that story to get me to convert! That's the only reason you would tell me such a fucking sad, hopeless, horrible story that didn't have any ending!"

Lev understood that the worst thing was that her accusations didn't even come close to what he had really done in not finishing the story. That was the worst thing.

Suddenly, Angela stopped thrashing around and covered her face with her crossed arms, struggling to control herself, to stop her lungs from heaving. And gradually, she calmed down and stopped sobbing.

She sat up on the bed, crossed-legged. She pulled Lev closer to her and he sat opposite her, looking at her, taking in everything that he knew and loved about her; from her vast eyes glistening with the remnants of her tears to the indentations of her collar bones, her breasts, her ribcage, the slope of her hips that he could stroke and cause her to shudder, her frail wrists and delicate fingers. She brought her face closer to his and she gazed up to the top of his face, at his hairline. Then she slowly examined his face, right to left, left to right, with her eyes lingering on each of his features as she moved her eyes row by row down his face, back and forth, back and forth, as if she were a lens scanning a portrait or photograph. On her face was a trace of a smile as she conducted her survey.

Lev thought: this is what she did so many years ago when she was a little girl and she had perched on her knees on the subway seat and examined the NYC Subway map as her family followed their long odyssey from Bensonhurst to the Bronx, when she had fixed forever in her memory the entire NYC subway system.

When she had finished, her eyes lingering on his lips and then his chin, she raised both of her hands toward his face. The inside of her wrists were lightly touching each other as she parted her hands like a flower opening to the sun. Lev thought she was going to place them on his face, on his cheeks, and gently pull him toward her for a kiss. He closed his eyes in anticipation.

But instead of drawing him nearer, Angela shoved his chest so violently that he went flying, splaying backwards, his torso hanging off the side of the bed. Lev would have fallen out of bed had he not flung his hand out and onto the floor to break his fall.

While Lev struggled to right himself, Angela heaved herself off the bed and charged into the bathroom, slamming the door and turning the lock. He heard her banging her balled fists against the inside of the door as she sobbed. Suddenly, she let out a howl—a horrid scream of anguish. He rushed to the bathroom door and tried to open it. "Open up, Angela!" Lev shouted, as he jiggled the handle and threw his weight against the door. Then he heard her puking into the toilet, deep and long retching that sounded as if she were vomiting her heart out of her body through her mouth.

When she was finished, there was a brief moment of silence, and then: "You've ruined me!" she shrieked. "You've destroyed me. You led me on, pretending to love me. You made me your slave, until I was willing to . . . to dump everything that I had in life—my family, my Jesus! And you just sat there and watched it happen. I agreed to do the hard thing, the one thing that could bring us together, and you didn't even have the courage to force your parents to accept me." She started wailing again. "You've ruined me!"

"I didn't mean to hurt you, Angela. You can go back to everything you cared about," Lev shouted through the door. "No one knows about us."

"I'm not talking about what other people think," she hollered back. "I'm talking about me, what I think, what I know I've done . . . what I was prepared to do. You don't even know what I'm talking about because I don't mean anything to you. You never loved me. I love you, but you don't love me. You haven't even come close to loving me—I can see that now."

Lev resumed trying to open the bathroom door. "Open up, Angela! C'mon!"

Silence. He had his ear up against the bathroom door, trying to hear her breathing. "Angela," he whispered, "unlock the door. Please. Come out and talk to me. Angela."

Lev placed his back against the door and slid down to the floor. He lost track of time—ten minutes passed? An hour? Suddenly, he stood up and tried the door again, jiggling the doorknob, begging Angela to open it.

"I won't come in," he pleaded. "We can open it just a crack. We can talk to each other through the crack!"

Silence. He began pacing around the apartment, back and forth around the bed in the little space available. He saw Rabbi Dr. Erwon Arkadi's book on the floor where Angela had left it earlier. He kicked it viciously and it flew against the wall with a thud, and then fell open on the floor. That damn book! That goddamn book! That was the source of their problems; Arkadi's distortion of Judaism; his compulsion to explain its weirdness, to invite strangers into the four cubits of its peculiarities. Arkadi had seduced Angela into thinking that Judaism's freakishness possessed more profundity than it actually did.

He kicked the book sharply again, and a few of the pages dislodged and fluttered into the air. Then he was on it, his knees on one side of the open book as if he were subduing it, his two hands tearing out chunks of pages flinging them into the air like confetti.

It was taking too long, Lev decided; he would slash the damn book to ribbons. He jumped to his feet and turned to the squalid kitchen where Angela kept the paring knife she used to slit pages from the book. But it wasn't in the one drawer where he knew she stored it. He looked in the sink: empty. He dropped to his knees and scurried about on the floor, looking for the knife. Nothing.

Where was the knife? Where was the nasty little paring knife, sharp enough to gut twenty or thirty pages out of a book with one swipe?

What had happened to the knife?

Lev turned and hurled himself against the door to the bathroom again. "Where's the knife, Angela?" he bellowed. "Where's the god-damn knife?"

He was greeted with silence. He calmed himself and mustered all his willpower to ask softly, reasonably, as if he were having a serious discussion with a child: "Angela, I'm trying to find the paring knife. Do you know what happened to it?"

He was standing before the bathroom door, his forehead pressed against the wood. "I just want to borrow it," he said. "I'll give it back to you when I'm done with it. You don't even have to open the door. Just slide it under the door. That's all. Just to borrow it."

"Ha, ha," he heard Angela mutter to herself. "He can't find the knife. He thinks I have the knife. Ha, ha."

Lev pounded his fist on the door again and commanded Angela, "Open up! Open up right now!"

Lev suddenly decided he needed to call the police. If Angela were locked in the bathroom with the knife, then he should call the police. He clutched at his pockets, looking for his cell phone, but his phone was on the bed. He tore through the sheets looking for it, then saw Angela's purse on the floor beside the head of the bed. He grabbed it and dumped its contents. Mounds of clutter tumbled out: eyeliner, three or four lipsticks, powder compacts, mascara, two hairbrushes, her cell phone. He gave one final shake to the upended bag and the paring knife, wrapped in a jury-rigged scabbard of cardboard and masking tape, flopped onto the pile of junk.

What was the knife doing in the bottom of her bag? Lev had always thought that the paring knife had come with the apartment, that it had been there before they had ever begun meeting in Red Hook, tossed carelessly into the one drawer of the counter beneath the hot plate. But now he suspected the knife had arrived with Angela—that it had always been part of the burden she lugged around in her oversized purse. What did she need to carry a wicked blade like that for? To cut up other books? Enemies? Lovers?

His frenzy ebbed. He returned to the bathroom door and again placed his forehead against its wood. "This isn't it," he murmured. "It doesn't end here, like this. That's not the way it ends for us, Angela."

He thought he could hear her smother a sob, so he continued. "We're not finished with each other yet, Angela. We're not done."

A whimper escaped from the depths of the bathroom. "Just go. I can't be seen anymore. I can't be seen. Go."

"Angela, I can't leave you like this. Come out. Talk to me."

But she just groaned and kept repeating the same mantra over and over again: "Just go. I can't be seen anymore. I can't be seen. Go."

Another hour or two—or three—passed. Lev sat on the edge of the bed and waited. Occasionally, he would try to cajole Angela to unlock the door, but she would not respond. He heard her muttering behind the closed door, but he could not decipher what she was saying. At some point, Lev collected himself, put on his coat and left the apartment. He left her there in Red Hook, locked in the bathroom, with, he imagined, her hands covering her face, her eyes, repeating over and over like an incantation: "Just go. I can't be seen anymore. I can't be seen. Go."

He took the paring knife with him. On the subway platform at Atlantic Avenue, he pulled it from its makeshift scabbard and gazed at its keen edge in the dull platform light, a curved arc flashing like the wake of a meteor plunging through Earth's atmosphere. Then he walked to the end of the platform where the tunnel's mouth gaped and hurled the knife as far as he could into the blackness, into the depths where the hobos would find it as they blundered about in the darkness of their underground cities.

52.

When he got home, Lev pulled off his clothes and climbed up to his bed as quietly as possible. He looked over at Elya and saw the thin beam of light from the streetlight reflected in his open eyes.

"It's over," he whispered to Elya. "Ended."

"I'm sorry to hear that, Lev. You're upset, aren't you?"

"Yes. I don't think I behaved well. I think that I hurt this girl very badly. I didn't think it through. I should never have become involved with her. It was all a big mistake. Big mistake. Poor judgment. If I'd known it would end this way, I never would have started up with her."

"If you didn't intend to hurt her, that's important. You can't beat yourself up for mistakes you made that you didn't intend."

Lev thought: What the hell, Elya, haven't you learned anything all these years? What about Tractate *Chagigah*, fifth page, first side of the page, near the beginning of a long peninsula of text that extends out into an ocean of commentaries, where it is reported that Rebbe Yochanan would weep when he concluded that God, as Master, weighs His slaves' unintentional sins as if they were intentional transgressions? But all he said in reply to his brother was: "Really? C'mon, Elya. We're Jews, after all. We beat ourselves up all the time for mistakes that we didn't intend."

Elya didn't respond. He just lay there watching Lev.

"Can you tell me now why it was so inappropriate? Why it had to be kept secret?"

"She's Syrian. They don't want us as husbands. If you marry a Syrian Jew, you live like a second-class citizen."

"Now I understand." Elya seemed relieved that this was the disqualifying factor. And then he said something that was like a knife in Lev's heart: "You're such a good person. I can see that you yourself are in pain, but all you're doing is thinking about *her* suffering. You are such a good person."

"I need to sleep now, Elya," Lev said. And he turned to the wall so he didn't have to listen to his brother's bullshit any longer.

IX

Why was Elisha ben Abuya called Aher—Other?

After Elisha ben Abuya descended from the Celestial Orchard, he cut down the saplings . . . and questioned the Oneness of God. . . .

A Voice from Heaven rang out: 'Repent wayward sons!—all but Aher! . . .'

Aher said to himself: 'If I have been banished from the World-to-Come, let me go out and indulge in the pleasures of this world. . . .'

He went out, found a harlot and asked her for her services. She said to him: 'But aren't you Elisha ben Abuya?'

In reply, he intentionally violated the Law by uprooting a radish from the garden on Shabbat.

The harlot said: 'This man is clearly not Elisha ben Abuya, but someone else.'

Thus, he was called Aher—'Other.'

- Babylonian Talmud, Tractate Chagigah 15A -

53.

Lev could not stop thinking about that moment when he was idling on the couch in the living room and he said to his mother: "You know, I just don't feel like going today. I think I'll sit this one out." He couldn't stop wondering what would have happened if his mother had said: "Why don't you stay home with me and relax a little? Your father will understand. Let me make you some tea."

Lev speculated that had his mother said that, or something like that, his crisis of faith would never have happened. He was convinced that he would have continued on the path for which he was intended. He would not have glanced over at Angela in class and been transfixed by her. He would not have "ruined her." And Lev would have gone on to meet his parents' expectations of him, to live, as it had been proclaimed when he was only eight days old at his circumcision ceremony, *a life of Torah, marriage and good deeds.*

But his mother hadn't understood then—had never understood—that she held his fate in the palm of her hand. She believed in the clenched-fist theory of life: never relent; never back down; never meet them halfway; never forgive those who wrong you; be vigilant in defending your family and your people from contagion by foreign pathogens. She couldn't understand that if you clutch your children too tightly in your fist, they begin to suffocate, and they will either struggle to escape or they will die.

Isn't that the way this world has always worked, Lev wondered? We honor our parents, but we get no reward for it. A father sends his son up to the roof to retrieve some baby birds, to perform a divine commandment; the son falls from a great height and is killed. More than two thousand years later, a young man is told by his mother to get off his ass and go to synagogue. And he goes, in fulfillment of the commandment to honor his parents. But he, too, falls from a great height and some part of him—some essential, human part—is obliterated on the pavement below.

293

Even though it was Lev who gave up Angela, he could not forgive his parents for his perfidy. Lev resolved that he had to get out of that apartment and his life in Flatbush as soon as possible, and so he devised a foolproof strategy. The quickest way out was success—extravagant, beyond-reasonable-expectations success. Lev had been a desultory student until then, but it wasn't too late to turn that around. He dug in and clawed his way to the top of his class. He finished Brooklyn College Phi Beta Kappa, then aced the law boards and got himself admitted to Columbia Law School.

He didn't tell his parents that he was applying to law school until after he had been admitted to Columbia. When he told his father, his father's hand immediately went to the top of his head, to his skullcap, and he began moving it around in that nervous tic that his sons had observed all those years. At the same time, his father was smiling, proud of Lev's achievement. Lev knew his father was worrying about how to pay the tuition.

"Don't worry, Abba," Lev told him. "I'm going to pay for it myself. I'll take out loans." His father looked relieved and worried at the same time because he couldn't understand how Lev could pull that off. But his father was burdened with so many other obligations he did not protest.

A few days later, his mother confronted Lev in the hallway outside the bathroom and demanded to know why he hadn't told her and his father that he was applying to law school. Lev glared at her and said: "Why? Do you intend to forbid me that as well?"

A look of hurt blazed across her stolid face, as if Lev had splashed her with acid. It was such a look of misery that he immediately repented for having made the remark. But he didn't take it back. He just turned and stalked away from her. And in the days afterward, Lev thought: Angela was right after all—it's better to scream into one another's faces all the time rather than harbor these resentments, these ugly, hurtful thoughts that erupt with such bitterness and cause such pain.

After Lev had walked out on Angela, he had looked for her at Brooklyn College, but he never saw her there again. He spied on the Italian kids as they congregated in the cafeteria, hoping to catch a glimpse. But she simply disappeared from that world. No one seemed to notice except him. The guys that leered at her or put their hands on her ass seemed to have forgotten she had ever existed. None of them mourned her. Only Lev.

A couple of months after the breakup, Lev ran into Marie coming out of a classroom. She looked at him as if he didn't exist, registering no recognition whatsoever. Her utter indifference made Lev feel as if his history with Angela had been expunged, had never occurred.

Once he started Columbia Law School, Lev moved to Morningside Heights. He hung around halfheartedly with the Orthodox crowd. He began dating other women. He tried Jewish women—not from his Orthodox group, but the other kind, the assimilated ones. But even though he had given up wearing his kippah, these Jewish women could tell where he had come from and they weren't interested. Lev decided that he would not date gentiles and he held the line. After a while, he gave up entirely and stopped trying to meet anyone.

After he earned his law degree, Lev dove into the elite law firm world. He started his legal career at a midtown law firm, living in a luxury high-rise on the Upper West Side and making more money than his parents had ever dreamt of.

How could his parents complain about such unbridled success? They couldn't and they didn't. But they suffered nevertheless in the suspicion that Lev was no longer an observant Jew. He didn't rub it in their faces. On the surface, he remained a deferential and obedient son. He showed up for holidays, birthdays and other family events. But Lev let them see nothing of his inner life. When they tried to fix him up with eligible Orthodox women, he would offer a perfunctory thank you, but then he would conspicuously crumple the paper with the name and phone number scrawled on it into a wad, which he put in his pocket. Lev never mentioned whether he was dating anyone; never brought anyone around to meet them. He tortured them by keeping his private life entirely hidden. And because they could only suspect that he had wandered from the derech, they could never confront him about any of it.

Lev supposed that he would eventually meet a woman whom he would be willing to marry, and she wouldn't be a shiksa who was willing to convert. Because Lev didn't want to be married to someone who was a better Jew than he was. He wanted to find a Jewish woman who wore her Judaism so casually that they could live their lives together without poking at it, scratching it, endlessly picking at it. *Jewish* would just be something he and his wife were—not the first thing nor the last thing—but just something they were, the way people think of themselves as college graduates, or Democrats, or vegetarians.

54.

And what of Angela Pizatto?

Six years after leaving her moaning in that locked bathroom in Red Hook, Lev was attending a wedding of an old friend from his yeshiva high school at a catering hall in Williamsburg when he felt a light tap on his shoulder. Before he could turn around, he heard an unmistakable voice.

"Levinski?"

Lev had imagined this day many times, the day when he would bump into Angela. And suddenly, in the last place he would have expected, here she was. As soon as he heard her voice, he stopped breathing. He felt like he was being pulled from a deep coma into consciousness, that he was being jolted back to life by electrodes that doctors place on your chest to shock your heart into beating again, pulling you back from the threshold of death. But he still knew what was expected of him, and Lev played his part.

"Livitski!" he exclaimed and then he turned around.

"Whatever," she said.

Lev was stunned by what he saw. It was certainly Angela Pizatto, but in disguise. She was dressed like a religious woman from the *haredim*, the ultra-Orthodox world. She was wearing a black woolen outfit with no color other than a thin white stripe around the hem of her skirt, which extended a good six inches below her knees. Long sleeves reached to her wrists. Her legs were hidden in thick, gray, cotton stockings that bunched about her knees and ankles. Lev knew immediately that she was married because she was wearing a sheitel, a lackluster wig of hair worn by married women for modesty. And because that was not modest enough, she also wore a hat on top of the wig—a round pill-box type of hat outstanding for its lack of flair. But most disconcerting of all, she wore no makeup. Lev realized he had never seen Angela without makeup in all the time they had spent together. He peered into her face and it was as if he was looking at a black-and-white lithograph of Angela, rather than the flesh-and-blood woman he had known.

Lev could still see in her face traces of the beauty that had so captivated him, but in her religious garb, she was no longer the irresistible, chiseled stunner that she was when they were together. Now she looked less formidable. Now she looked chayn.

Chayn, yes, but still he wanted her, just as she looked right then and there, just as she stood before him; Lev wanted her with the desire that came from that deeper secret place, as it had so many years ago. And again, his Talmudic recall rose up to ridicule him, to torment him, because he thought of the concept of *butel b'shishim*, "nullified in sixty," the idea that if a non-kosher, impure element is thrown into a kosher pot, it renders the entire pot non-kosher if the tainted element constitutes more than one-sixtieth of the whole. And Lev thought: If she feels even one-sixtieth of the desire for me that I feel for her, her marriage is over.

While these thoughts were coursing through his brain, he stood there gaping at her.

"Don't be so surprised," Angela said. "Did you think I was kidding when I said I wanted to convert?"

Lev finally managed to speak. "Angela, I . . ."

"Not Angela," she corrected him. "Sarah."

"Sarah, how did this happen?"

She looked up at the ceiling as she mused on how to answer. He saw her hands begin to move toward her hips, her elbows rising in anticipation of planting the heel of each hand on the delicate slope of her hips, the incline that used to so tantalize Lev. That was Angela's stance that Lev had known so intimately, the one that used to signal to him that Angela's mind was on the prowl and wasn't going to rest until it had been satisfied. But she quickly returned to her new self and simply dropped her arms limply to her side.

"Well, it took quite a while for me to get over you," she said off-handedly, "as you might imagine. And after that, I started seeing guys again, mostly Italian guys, the same crowd I was hanging out with before we took up together. But they just didn't seem very interesting to me anymore. And I stopped enjoying church and all that stuff as well. And I kept thinking about our conversations about Judaism and how different it was. So I went online and hooked up with a class that introduced unaffiliated Jews and potential converts to Jewish learning. And there I met my husband."

"Is he a convert also?"

She laughed. "No," she said, shaking her head. "He was the rabbi teaching the class."

"You're a *rebbetzin*?" he exclaimed.

"Yes," she said, and the whisper of a smile could not hide her pride in admitting it. "We do *kiruv*. You'd be amazed at how many unaffiliated Jews there are who want to reconnect with Judaism. We have two children, a boy and a girl. So far, anyway. The boy is named Yaakov and the baby girl is Esther. She's named after my sister, Estelle. You remember Estelle, don't you Lev? She died a few months after I left home."

Of a broken heart, he said to himself. "I'm sorry to hear that."

Lev thought of Angela sharing the trundle bed in her room with her kid sister, whispering to her the secrets of their time together in Red Hook, and he visualized Estelle smiling at her happiness without really understanding. Angela had lost her best friend, her only friend.

"And the rest of your family?" Lev asked.

"Initially, of course, they weren't happy with my marriage. And of course, not happy with the conversion. But Akiva—my husband—is so polite to them that gradually, they have reconciled themselves to the match." Here, her face lit with a smile of bewilderment. "In fact, my father and my brothers—even my crazy uncles—seem to like him a lot more than they like me. They insisted on watching the World Cup with him last year. They went to Boro Park to buy Akiva kosher snacks for that. Even my mother has calmed down a bit. And they're all crazy about our children, too." She shot Lev a glance and then looked down in embarrassment: "I guess my family may have been a lot nicer than I gave them credit for," she confessed.

So she has married Rabbi Akiva! Lev thought. And he wondered: When her future husband had looked out over the students assembled for that first class introducing them to Jewish practice and saw Angela and her avid, radiant face, did he spit, then laugh, then cry, as the Talmud had reported?

"The whole thing is incredible!" Lev said.

"You know, I've come to the conclusion that my parents really wanted only one thing from me and that thing was the one thing I always refused to give them."

"What was that?"

"Respect," she said, shaking her head and frowning. "Not so much obedience even—just a little, tiny bit of respect. Anyway, I think they worry about my being damned and my kids being damned along with me. But from where they're coming from, why shouldn't they?" She shrugged. Then she recited in Hebrew a verse from one of the psalms that are recited daily during morning prayers: *You have raised my soul from the lower world; You have preserved me from descent into the pit*. Her Hebrew was precise, impeccable, but she spoke with a distinct Ashkenazi accent as if she had grown up in Eastern Europe speaking Yiddish. There was that chameleon thing again, Angela's talent—or perhaps compulsion—for blending in by adapting her speech to her environment.

Lev answered her: "Don't you think, Angela—"

"Sarah!"

"Whatever . . . Don't you think you're being a little dramatic? '*From the lower world . . . from the pit?*'"

"That was another thing you never fully appreciated about me, Lev, how miserable I was, how totally lacking in meaning my life used to be. You were always dismissive of that, as if I didn't really have an inner life—maybe that I didn't even deserve to have an inner life."

"Well," Lev said, "I guess you're no longer held back by my lack of imagination. Your husband obviously is a lot more supportive."

Angela quoted the Hebrew verse from another psalm recited on each major Jewish festival as part of a special service in praise of God, again in her perfect Eastern European accent: *For you have delivered my soul from death, my eyes from tears, my feet from stumbling. I shall walk before God in the lands of the living.*

Lev observed that she was drawn to verses that contended for her soul, that ruminated on the lower world and the pit, and he thought to himself, how very Christian of you, Angela Pizatto, despite everything. And he realized that all these years, this was not the way he imagined they would meet again. No, he had harbored another fantasy—the fantasy that he would bump into her on the street or at a party, and that they'd take up exactly where they left off; that they would fall into bed with each other and the passion would be rekindled, except by that time she would have been cured of her Jewish fixation, and that she would look back at her earlier infatuation with it as merely the distraction of a young adult, a brush with a cult-like way of thinking that had almost come close to swallowing her. But now Lev knew for certain that was not going to happen. He had lost her forever.

Lev wanted to say to her: Angela, do you remember the last time we were at a wedding together? You needed to taste the wild man in me.

Angela, I'm still a wild man. Not for anyone else. Only for you.

Sarah, I'm still your wild man.

But instead, he asked her: "Did you ever become an accountant?"

She waved her hand dismissively. "That was just my one-way ticket out."

"You seem to have found another one-way ticket out."

Again she waved her hand. "Don't try to cheapen my journey, Lev."

"I wasn't," Lev said.

"You were."

Ah, the old Angela, she's still in there somewhere, he thought.

"But what about you, Lev?" she asked. "What have you been up to?"

He told her about his path since they had last seen each other. He made it short—*while standing on one foot* as the Sages would say.

"Anyone special in your life?" she asked.

"No," he replied, and he felt his insides recoil in shame. "I have to tell you, Angela . . . sorry . . . *Sarah*, I still haven't gotten over it."

"You haven't gotten over *it*, but you have gotten over *me*, correct?"

She was smiling a gentle smile, so he lied to her. "Yes," he said. "You're correct."

Her smile faded and her face darkened. Maybe it was the answer she had expected; maybe it was the answer she had dreaded. "You know, Lev, you broke me. You shattered me into little pieces. That's what you did."

"I'm sorry."

"You told me so many lies, hundreds and hundreds of lies. But the worst lie you ever told me was that there was no ending to the story about the student and the harlot. That the note meant nothing. In the history of lying, there could be no greater lie than that."

"I'm sorry."

"I forgive you," she said casually. Then she added: "I forgive you, you deceitful prick."

The slur ran through him with a jolt, not because it was so profane, so incompatible with her adopted ultra-Orthodox persona, but because she said the last three words with that street-fighting tone of guttural aggressiveness that the old Angela used to employ so effectively.

"I'm happy now," she continued calmly, but she wasn't smiling. "I suppose I wouldn't have been able to come over to this world, to the Jewish world, if you hadn't broken me up so badly."

"I'm sorry, Sarah."

"I told you—I forgive you. If I didn't forgive you, you know as well as anyone, Lev—because this is actually what Rambam says—that you would not be able to achieve real repentance, complete *tshuva*."

Lev thought to himself: Angela Pizatto is quoting Maimonides to me! What has become of Rabbi Dr. Erwon Arkadi?

She continued: "I forgive you. But you also know that you can't achieve full repentance unless you have changed. If you found yourself in the same situation, would you do it again? If you can say, 'No, I wouldn't, I wouldn't do it again,' then you've repented. Can you say that, Lev? Can you say you wouldn't do it again?"

He didn't know precisely what she meant. Would I fuck her again? he asked himself. Yes. Would I fall in love with her again? The answer was also yes. Would I lie to her and then betray her? Even knowing from the very outset that ultimately she would break into little pieces, would I start down that path again just so I could pull her close to me in that bed in Red Hook for those few months?

Yes. If that were the only way for me to be with her, then yes, I would do it all over again.

"No, Sarah," he told her. "I wouldn't do it again."

And then Lev thought: How could you, Angela? How could you do this? How could you become Jewish without me? How could you climb onto the derech and leave me here—here under the overpass, with the hobos, the ones who can only warm their hands over trash fires burning in abandoned oil drums? How could you leave me here while everyone I've ever loved continues to make their way—against the headwinds, against the torrential rains, illuminated only by the lightning—to make their way forward forever on the derech that stretches above my underground city, the derech on which we have trudged for more than three thousand years, since Sinai, since God held the mountain above our heads and said: *Either you accept the Covenant or let this be your grave.* How could you?

Angela, you were supposed to be my way back and now I am lost forever.

And then Lev realized that his real fantasy, the one deep inside him—so deep that he had not appreciated it until that very moment—was not the one that he had invoked just moments before, but an opposite fantasy, a delusion that had been lurking in the hidden gateways of his heart: that after he left Angela, she had returned to her shadow-world in Bensonhurst and waited for him. That she was waiting until he finally was ready to find his way back onto the derech. Then and only then, would they meet by accident, and they would take up from where he had ended it. And she would become a Jew and together they would return to the path. And everyone—his mother, his father, his four brothers—would welcome her; they would praise her and say, "Angela was the one who brought Lev back onto the derech. She was the one who saved him."

Yes, he thought, we could have had this life together—she would have converted; we could have become more *frum* than even my parents. And we would be together someplace in Brooklyn with two kids and more on the way. And underneath all of that armor that Sarah had encased herself in—the dowdy clothes, the wig, the ridiculous hat, the filmy gray stockings—that armor would be taken off every night and underneath it would be Angela: the wild Angela who knew every inch of the subways; the fearless girl who stood up to pushy Jewish guys, sulky waitresses and thuggish ex-boyfriends; the passionate Angela, the one who guided his hand to her breast in the diner, who stood naked before him for ten Mississippis; the woman whose eyes rolled back in her head when he touched her thigh and hip bone in just the right way.

And then she broke through his reflections, his sorrow, by asking, "Do you remember when you first told me that you were obligated to remember that you were a slave in Egypt and I made fun of you and I told you how ridiculous that was? Well, who would ever have thought it then, but now . . . now I can say that I *do* remember being a slave in Egypt. I remember it vividly. I remember it in all its details—the terrible images, the whistling of the whips of the Egyptians, the agony of the blows, the exhaustion of pushing the great stones, the stench, the fear, the suffering . . ."

She spoke with a tone of wonder in her voice and Lev didn't know whether she was speaking figuratively or literally. Indeed, he couldn't tell whether she was just sharing with him her hallucinations, or whether Angela had risen to a new plane of spiritual connection and was telling him what God had really meant when He commanded the Jews to remember that they were once slaves in Egypt.

Then she abruptly dropped back to Earth and asked, with a tone of concern, "Are you still *shomer mitzvos*?" She wanted to know whether he was observant or had left it all behind.

"No, Sarah, I'm not."

"Does that have to do with what happened with us?"

"No, it was going to happen anyway. Our affair was just the first symptom. I hate to characterize it like that because I did really care for you, but I feel we should be honest about it. I'm sorry."

"No apologies required," she said with a smile. "I would character-ize it from my perspective in the same way. I was discontented with my world and I started moving to another one. I was already on my way before I met you. Fortunately, you pointed out my destination. I could have wasted a lot of time looking were it not for you."

They stood in silence until it became clear that there was nothing left to say.

"Would you like to meet my husband?" she asked.

Lev thought that perhaps she was suggesting he meet Akiva be-cause she wanted him to see what a great guy she had married, the guy who, unlike Lev, had delivered her soul from death and her heart from sorrow. Then it occurred to him that maybe she wanted her hus-band to see the wretched man Angela had left behind when she had abandoned her earlier, unfulfilling life, the man who had shattered her into pieces.

"No thanks," Lev said. "Perhaps another time."

She persisted. "He's really quite remarkable," she said. "He's got a university education, but he is also a *talmid chucham*." She used the Hebrew term for one who has mastered Jewish textual study. "He has lived in both worlds and I think you would both have a lot to talk about."

Lev suddenly understood that she wanted him to meet her husband Akiva for neither of the reasons Lev had speculated about. Angela regarded Lev now as a target of opportunity—a Jew who had wandered from the path and was in need of *kiruv*—of being brought back to the commandments and to the community.

These kiruv people are all alike, Lev thought to himself. They view you not for who you are but for whom they can make you into. And he also thought: If he's such a talmid chucham, let's have a contest. Go and ask him in what tractate, on what page, on what side of the page and in what line on the page does the Talmud discuss the concept of whether you are responsible for taking an action that leads to an inevitable result; whether you can cut off the head of a chicken and expect that it won't die? Ask him that. And if he can picture that country and that city in that country and that street in that city, then maybe, maybe, I will acknowledge him as a talmid chucham. And Lev said to himself: Let me say that—why shouldn't I say exactly that?

But he held his tongue and merely repeated: "Perhaps another time."

Lev extended his hand the way he had when he had first introduced himself to Angela after the lecture at Brooklyn College. He had momentarily forgotten that in her world, it was completely inappropriate to touch the hand of a member of the opposite sex, even just for a casual handshake. Lev watched her face as she stared at his hand, how it evolved from curiosity to surprise, to judgment and ultimately, to scorn. She looked up from his hand and into his eyes and she didn't even need to shake her head.

He asked himself: Who is this Angela Pizatto to judge *me*? Nothing but an Italian Catholic chick who loved baby Jesus because he was so adorable; who let anyone from the old neighborhood fondle her ass whenever they wanted to. And now she is a Jew who has learned all the worst instincts of our people—the smugness, the absolute certainty that they are right and everyone else is wrong. Hadn't Marie warned Angela about this so many years ago, the way the Jews were always judging everyone, looking down on everyone? Angela is mocking me! She's mocking me, making a fool of me! She refused to shake my hand—a woman who paraded before me naked, who offered herself to me in every conceivable way without hesitation, without my even asking. She knows I'm a fallen Jew; she knows I've tumbled off the derech and that I'm groping in the darkness searching for a way back, scrounging for redemption, for even one tiny morsel of redemption. And here she is humiliating me by denying me even the touch of her hand, just the slightest warmth of her flesh for an instant; not the soft flesh of her breast or the silken surface of her thigh, but just the rough tissue of the palm of her hand.

Angela, you cunt, you, Lev thought to himself.

Sarah, you cunt.

Instead of withdrawing his hand, which was still outstretched in anticipation of a handshake, Lev raised it until it was level with Angela's eyes. He extended his index finger and he pictured to himself Angela lying on her side on the bed naked, facing him. He moved his finger on the trajectory that it used to follow as he glided it over her naked hip. His finger traced from right to left in the empty air the slight rise to the top of her hip, the inch or two of flatness before it plummeted down the ski-slope of her pelvis as it flowed to her waist, and then his finger drifted on the imagined straightaway that was her rib-cage to her breast. As soon as he finished, he pantomimed the entire erotic excursion again.

Angela stood stock still, seemingly hypnotized by his dancing finger. Then her eyes grew wide as understanding began to dawn on her. A blush surged up her face like an explosion and her mouth shifted from a round expression of surprise to clenched teeth of rage. Her right hand flew up and slapped his hand away, and she turned and strode away.

While this was happening, all Lev could think was: Angela has learned to blush! The rabbis have taught Angela to blush! Good for them! Good for them!

And just when he could have stopped, just when he could have pulled back from completing the process of his total degradation, just then, when he had his final opportunity to preserve one last atom of decency, Lev heard himself call after her: "Shalom, *Angela*," pronouncing her name the way he had heard her Italian friends pronounce it—the same way he had heard Cecile say it—with the emphasis on the first syllable. *Annn-jill-uh.*

She did not turn around and gradually, Lev lost sight of her in the crowd.

I've gotten my revenge, Lev told himself, and at the same time he knew with certainty that there had been absolutely nothing that Angela had ever done to him that deserved vengeance. And Lev also immediately understood that he would spend the rest of his life searching for some way to atone for everything he had done to this woman and particularly for how he had just behaved and for what he had just said.

But an instant later he found himself sprinting after her, into the thick of the wedding celebrants clustered around the heaping catering tables, shoving aside people as he plunged deeper into the crowd. He finally caught up to her and shouted, "Sarah, Sarah, stop! Please stop!"

She glanced back at him but kept walking deeper into the crowd. Lev pushed near enough to grab her arm, but he didn't dare touch her. Instead, he skipped around her, blocking her path. Angela stopped short and shot him a look of such fury that Lev realized that had she been holding the paring knife she had used to cut pages out of the book *How Strange the Jews!*, she would have raised her hand right then to slash his throat.

"Sarah," he pleaded, "I'm sorry. I'm so sorry."

"If you think I will forgive you again," she hissed, "you're mistaken. You had your chance!" She glared at him, her brow furrowed, her nostrils flaring. This was the same look she had given Lev so many years ago when she had insisted that he give her another chance by going out with her again, as they confronted one another on Ocean Parkway, the traffic streaming beside them toward Manhattan.

"I don't deserve forgiveness and I'm not asking for it," Lev told her. "But you need to know . . . you need to know one thing." He dug his hand into his pocket, pulled it out and extended his closed fist. He slowly opened his fingers. In his palm was the silver dollar she had given him that Chanukah, the "collector's item." It was the talisman he carried with him—everywhere, always—the last thing that Lev removed from his pocket and put on his bedside nightstand each evening; the first thing that he pocketed each morning; the amulet he reached for and stroked numerous times each day when his abject loneliness threatened to overwhelm him.

She looked down at his hand and the anger in her face began to wane. It was replaced by a deep sadness, a weary anguish that crept up from her mouth to those unforgettable eyes, so luminous even now without the makeup that had always framed them. Then she put her hand up to her neck, dipped her index finger under the collar of her modest blouse and extracted a silver chain. At the end of the chain was the subway token pendant Lev had given her that Christmas so long ago.

She raised her eyes to him and whispered: "Why are you showing me the silver dollar? Do you think I will betray my husband and abandon my children? Do you think I'm still Angela? I'm Sarah now. I'm a Jew. I fear God."

"Then why show me the necklace I gave you?"

"To make you suffer. So that you will always remember what could have been." She closed her eyes for a few moments as if she, too, were remembering what could have been. Then she opened them, reached up to her neck, took the subway pendant in her hand and yanked it sharply. The chain broke and she slowly extended her arm towards him, opening her fist to reveal the pendant in her palm, the chain dangling between her fingers.

"Too late, Lev," she murmured. "Too late." Her voice drifted off.

She turned her open fist and let the pendant and chain fall to the floor. "Goodbye, Lev. If you see me again in the future, don't approach me. Don't come near me. I don't want to see you again, ever. It's not good for me. I've got children. I've got a husband. Show me some *chesed.*" She used the word that in Hebrew means *kindness.* "Please, Lev."

Lev tried to respond, but no sound came out. So he just nodded his head.

Sarah turned and walked away and Lev was left alone, floundering, drowning, in a swirling sea of wigs, beards and black hats.

55.

Lev couldn't bear to stay at the wedding any longer, so he slunk away and caught a subway back to Manhattan. As he stood looking out from the fifteenth floor of his high-rise apartment at the city lights below, the dark swath of the Hudson to the west and the faint glow of illumination of New Jersey beyond, Lev asked himself when his moral decay had really started. Was it when he had first glimpsed the nape of Angela's neck and her profile in the lecture hall? Was it when she caught him spying on her and he didn't look away in shame? Was it when Lev had gingerly taken her fragile hand in his? No, it wasn't any of those times, Lev reflected. The sight or the touch of the desirable can ignite the Evil Inclination, but it does not fuel it. The Sages knew this was the case; they knew that you could be ensnared by passion, or lust, or love—whatever you wanted to call it—and still not lose yourself, not surrender everything to your most sordid instincts. So it wasn't Angela's fault that Lev found her so exquisite. Angela was not the daughter of Rebbe Yose of Yukras, the woman who was too beautiful for this world and so was commanded to go to the other.

No, Lev concluded, his decline had begun the afternoon after their ludicrous first date, when he had invoked Rambam to bless his Evil Inclination to consort with the daughter of an idol-worshipper; when Lev refused to take responsibility for the decision he had already made. If he had possessed the courage to acknowledge that it was his choice whether or not to ask Angela, "So if we were to go, where would we go?" then perhaps he would have been able to preserve some residue of righteousness.

But Lev didn't have that courage. He wasn't Rav Amram the Pious, who was enflamed by a glimpse of the countenance of a woman redeemed from captivity; Rav Amram, who had been aroused enough to lift the ladder that ten men could not raise; Rav Amram, who was only half a ladder away from satisfying his desire, but who instead called out, "Fire in the house of Rav Amram!"

And yet, Lev asked himself: if I had called out, "Fire in the house of Lev Livitski!" who would have heard me? Lev was not surrounded by Sages who would drop everything to rush to the side of their comrade accosted by desire. Lev was surrounded only by normal human beings. But maybe the point of the story of Rav Amram the Pious was not that the Sages came running to save him from sin. Maybe the real point of the story was that he called out—that he stopped halfway up the ladder and called out. Maybe calling out is what matters, even if no one comes running to save you; even if there is no one there to hear you.

But Lev hadn't stopped and called out. Instead, he asked Rambam to give him a nod, a wink. And it was at that very moment that he was lost, at that moment when he first decided that he didn't have to take responsibility for veering down the path he had chosen; when he convinced himself that he could distort everything that he had been taught to revere in order to possess Angela. It was then that he had embraced his own inexorable downfall.

Because there is forgiveness for almost everything, Lev reasoned. There is forgiveness for making love to the daughter of an idolater; even for falling hopelessly in love with her. There is forgiveness for everything except for one thing—betrayal. Betrayal is the one thing for which there is no forgiveness.

The one thing.

These thoughts battered Lev as he stood staring into the darkness outside his apartment. He peered at the pinpricks of light across the river and his vision blurred, the lights swirling and then coalescing themselves into another vision—a page of Talmud from Tractate Berachos, its text almost invisible, hidden in a wide swath of Aramaic with no landmarks on the page to guide Lev's recollection. The Talmud seemed to be struggling to explain Lev to himself: *A person is obligated to bless God for the bad just as he blesses God for the good, as it is written: 'And you shall love the Lord your God with all your heart, with all your soul and with all your might . . .' With all your heart: this means with both your inclinations—with the Good Inclination as well as with the Evil Inclination.* And Lev also recalled that the medieval commentators understood the verse to suggest that each person has two hearts: one devoted to the Good Inclination and one to the Evil Inclination—and both hearts had to love God. But Lev, a man named Heart by his parents, didn't know this. He thought he had only one heart and that if he loved Angela with his one heart, it meant that he must hate God; and if he loved God with his one heart, then he must hate Angela. He didn't understand until it was too late that he had two hearts and that he could love Angela and, at the same time, love God.

Lev returned once again to Rebbe Yaakov and his dilemma. There had to be some explanation. The son obeyed his father and went up the ladder to get the fledgling birds and he chased the mother bird away— but perhaps he wasn't concentrating on performing the mitzvos at all. Perhaps he was thinking improper thoughts, filthy thoughts. But Lev recalled that the Talmud asked that exact question a bit further down that page of Tractate Kiddushin, in a canyon of text before it breaks out into a sweeping savanna, and it concluded that God does not strike us dead merely for thinking about sin. For God to wreak His vengeance, we have to do more than just think about sin—we need to indulge in it, to wallow in it, to pollute in sin whatever remnants of goodness we might have left—just as Lev had done earlier that day when he had mistreated Angela.

Or maybe the son wasn't thinking of anything. Not thinking of per- forming the commandments; not thinking of sinning; maybe he was just concentrating on holding the baby birds in his hands, just tight enough so they wouldn't escape, but not so tight as to crush them. And that's where he had made his mistake. That's why he had plummeted from the roof and was killed. Maybe the whole story wasn't about why God permits evil to manifest itself in the world, particularly evil that hurts those who most want to observe His commandments. Perhaps God had nothing to do with it at all.

And then Lev reflected on Elisha ben Abuya. Unlike Rebbe Yaa- kov, Aher couldn't devise justifications for the death of the obedient son, and he lost his faith. What did Aher see when he ascended to the Celestial Orchard? What did he see that cost him his share in the World-to-Come?

Or what was it that he didn't see?

Two holy men confronted with the same insoluble contradiction to their faith, and one walks from shadow into light and the other from shadow into the deepest darkness. Angela Pizatto, whose heart is ravished by the blighted passion of Lev Livitski, comes to appreciate that the answers reside in a world she does not inhabit, and so she embraces that other world.

But for Lev, who once lived in the world Angela is reaching for, there is no other world to go to. So Lev must become something else— *to go out and sin*—to leave his world with no other destination.

The only path for people like me, Lev whispered to himself, is to become Aher—*Other*—a name signifying nothing in itself, a name that conveys no inkling of what the thing it names might really be, other than whatever it once was, it is no longer.

— T H E   E N D —

NOTE ON SOURCES

Because Talmudic texts are often written succinctly, quotations of such texts in the novel are edited to provide context and assist reader comprehension. Omissions from textual quotations for the purpose of brevity are indicated by ellipses.

References to subway lines in the novel are based on NYC MTA subway service circa 2002, the time period in which the events depicted in the novel transpire.

ACKNOWLEDGEMENTS

It may be surprising to learn that this novel was nurtured in an Orthodox synagogue in which I have been deeply involved for more than thirty years, Congregation Ramath Orah, located in the Morningside Heights neighborhood of Manhattan. For much of that time, I have been privileged to sit next to my friend, Rabbi Joseph Telushkin, my most steadfast reader, critic and champion-in-chief. Thank you, Joseph, for your insights and encouragement, and for believing so ardently in this novel and in me. In back of Joseph sat my most astute and insightful editor, Jack Schwartz, z"l, who I wish could join with me in the launch of this novel, which benefitted so much from Jack's and his wife, Nella Shapiro's, literary acuity and incisive commentary. For three decades I've also shared the same bench with my dear friend and Daf Yomi chavruta, Professor Ari Goldman, whose close reading and tireless encouragement have been so important to my writing. A few seats away sits another wonderful friend and chavruta, Eric Fishman, who shared so much of his time and wisdom in commenting on the novel as it progressed. Sprinkled about the shul are many other Ramath Orah friends who read and commented so intelligently on the novel, including Len Brauner and Beth Moritz, Alfred Neugut and Elie Koolyk, Galit Mizrahi, Dimitry Ekshtut, Ellen Rosen Singer, and Mark Silver.

I want to express my deep gratitude to Carolyn Starman Hessel, the doyenne of American Jewish literature, whose early and enduring encouragement and literary acumen were so critical to my having the confidence to complete this novel and bring it to publication.

My heartfelt thanks goes to three consummate professional reviewers and commentators on literature and culture who commented on and encouraged the completion and publication of the novel: Sandee Brawarsky, Judith Shulevitz and Naomi Firestone-Teeter. I am also grateful to two world-class writers for their counsel and efforts to assist in the publication of the novel: Richard Ford and Joshua Henkin. Many thanks, as well, to the literary agents Deborah Harris and George Eltman, whose early enthusiasm for the book was so important to me.

Thank you to Sarah Cypher, whose developmental editing dramatically improved the novel, to John Knight for his superb copy editing, and to Jenefer Shute and Casey Walker, whose suggestions on early drafts were so helpful.

I'm also indebted to the many friends who shared their precious time to read the novel, think about it deeply and share their comments with me: Beryl Abrams, Douglas Altabef, Daniel Beller, Lewis Bernstein, Bonnie and Hilly Besdin, Margy-Ruth Davis, Vivian Farber, Donna Fishman, Jim Garber, Sarah Holloway, Diane Jacobs, Lilian Stern, Kevin O'Connor, Amy Persky and Phil Waldoks, and Jake Zebede.

Special shout-outs go to David Wasser for his penetrating and exhaustive commentary on the novel; to my writing buddy Robin Politan for her discerning analysis and notes, as well as for her enthusiastic support of my writing; and to my remarkably astute band of friends-from-birth, the Worcesterboys (Rabbi Dr. Dennis Shulman, Jeff Davidson, Paul Rubin, Ron Joseph, Bruce Plotkin and Michael Charney).

The novel was also a family affair, and my love and thanks go to my brilliant and perceptive family: to my kids, Jacob Noti-Victor, Rebecca Victor and Kalman Victor; to my son-in-law, Yaran Noti-Victor; to my sister, Carol Rothman, and to my sister-in-law, Hana Fuchs.

Finally, I express my love and gratitude for her crucial support and encouragement to my wife, Ester Fuchs, to whom this novel is dedicated.

ABOUT

Atmosphere Press

Atmosphere Press is an independent, full-service publisher for excellent books in all genres and for all audiences. Learn more about what we do at atmospherepress.com.

We encourage you to check out some of Atmosphere's latest releases, which are available at Amazon.com and via order from your local bookstore.

atmosphere
PRESS / atmospherepress.com

ABOUT THE AUTHOR

Daniel Victor has written three novels, two novellas, and a collection of short fiction. *The Evil Inclination* is his first published novel. He lives in Manhattan with his wife, Ester Fuchs.

CPSIA information can be obtained
at www.ICGtesting.com
Printed in the USA
LVHW041019010423
742778LV00004B/13

9 781639 888443